USA TODAY bes[...] nominated autho[...] romance. She tea[...] in creative writin[...] Extension's presti[...] she finally gets to utilise the MA and PhD in English Literature that she received from the University of York in England. She currently lives in the Pacific Northwest, with her very own hero and too many pets. Visit her at caitlincrews.com.

Rachael Stewart adores conjuring up stories, from heartwarmingly romantic to wildly erotic. She's been writing since she could put pen to paper—as the stacks of scrawled-on pages in her loft will attest to. A Welsh lass at heart, she now lives in Yorkshire, with her very own hero and three awesome kids, and if she's not tapping out a story she's wrapped up in one or enjoying the great outdoors. Reach her on Facebook, Twitter (@rach_b52) or at rachaelstewartauthor.com.

If you liked *Untamed* and *Mr One-Night Stand*
why not try

On His Knees by Cathryn Fox
Decadent by Alexx Andria

Discover more at millsandboon.co.uk.

UNTAMED

CAITLIN CREWS

MR ONE-NIGHT STAND

RACHAEL STEWART

MILLS & BOON

First Published in Great Britain 2019
by Mills & Boon, an imprint of HarperCollins*Publishers*
1 London Bridge Street, London, SE1 9GF

Untamed © 2019 Caitlin Crews

Mr One-Night Stand © 2019 Rachael Stewart

ISBN: 978-0-263-27375-5

MIX
Paper from
responsible sources
FSC C007454

This book is produced from independently certified FSC™ paper
to ensure responsible forest management.
For more information visit www.harpercollins.co.uk/green.

Printed and bound in Spain
by CPI, Barcelona

UNTAMED

CAITLIN CREWS

MILLS & BOON

CHAPTER ONE

FIVE SEPARATE EMISSARIES had already been sent from competing hotel conglomerates to convince the notably impossible Jason Kaoki to develop the unspoiled private island in the Pacific he'd inherited from his late father, international playboy and real estate tycoon Daniel St. George. All five had failed.

Miserably. And quickly.

Lucinda Graves had no intention of making herself the sixth.

It had taken her forty hours of brutal long-haul travel to make it across the planet. Forty miserable hours from the gray bustle of London in what passed for its rainy spring to this tiny, shockingly bright island sunning itself in the middle of the Pacific Ocean. She was thousands of miles from anywhere, surrounded by nothing but salt and sea stretching out toward the horizon in all directions—a state of affairs that might have made her anxious had she possessed the wherewithal to consider it in any depth.

Because she was tired. More than tired. Somewhere over North America, Lucinda had gone past "tired" entirely and had found herself in the realm of a pure, bone-deep exhaustion the likes of which she wasn't certain she'd ever felt before in her twenty-eight years.

But she was not to be deterred.

She would be the one to land this deal. She knew it.

The simple truth was that she would accept no other outcome.

When failure wasn't an option, she liked to tell herself, the only remaining possibility was success.

The tiny little hopper plane, barely large enough to hold the pilot—much less an uneasy passenger who preferred her jets sized to carry hundreds, the better to imagine it wasn't a plane at all—landed rather too bouncily for her taste over what she assumed had to be some kind of lagoon, the water blue and turquoise and gleaming.

She was too bleary-eyed and hollowed out from too many time zones to care.

When she stepped out of the plane onto the little dock that stretched out over the water—a *dock*, of all things, instead of any kind of proper tarmac, or climate-controlled, civilized airport—the humidity walloped her. It was like a fist, wet and hot. It was an instant, relentless assault and it nearly took her to her knees, right there beneath some rattling palm trees and the careless, blinding sunshine.

Lucinda had assumed she was duly prepared. She'd known she was heading to a tropical island, obviously. And she'd been to beaches before, like the last corporate retreat her company had taken to sun-drenched Spain—where she'd been expected to conduct business while sitting beside a pool, brandishing drinks festooned with foliage and pretending to be relaxed and carefree in a bloody sarong. She'd assumed this would be more of the same, if farther away than a quick hop to Spain. A beach was a beach, she'd assured herself as she'd set off what seemed like a lifetime ago.

But it turned out she wasn't prepared for this remote Pacific island that didn't appear on most maps and had no official name. Maybe it was impossible to be prepared for *this much* tropical heat all at once, heavy and intense.

Her hands went to her hair at once. Bright red and embarrassing, its mission in life was to curl dramatically and unprofessionally at the slightest provocation. Lucinda went to great lengths to keep it neat and sleek. She kept it ruthlessly straight and swept back into a severe bun on the back of her head, which kept it under control but couldn't minimize its upsetting color. Lucinda had often considered dying her hair a more appropriate brown, the better to blend in, but the idea of all the upkeep struck her as wasteful. She'd concentrated instead on ridding herself of her native Scottish accent, because the circles in which she aspired to move had no place for impenetrable working-class Glaswegian accents.

And Lucinda succeeded in all she did, because she didn't allow for the possibility of failure. She never had, from her rough beginnings in one of Glasgow's notorious housing estates to her current position as a vice president in her company's London corporate office. Tropical heat on a Pacific island couldn't change that.

Though it complicated things, certainly. It seemed to curl into her, sneaking beneath her clothes like some kind of insinuation.

Lucinda tried to shake it off as she took in her surroundings, frowning at the sweep of untouched white sand and the wild tangle of jungle beyond, climbing up the green, steep sides of the hills.

"Are you certain this is the right place?" she demanded of the pilot, who had climbed down to the dock ahead of her and insisted on grinning widely as if everything she said and did was vastly entertaining.

Lucinda was not entertaining, thank you very much. She was effective. She was capable. And she was used to being treated as exactly what she was and wanted to be. Stern. Uncompromising. *A straight-edged ruler of a woman*, one of her first bosses had called her. He'd meant it as an insult, but Lucinda had taken it as the greatest compliment and had tried her best to live up to it ever since.

"You said you wanted Jason Kaoki," the pilot replied, still grinning. "This is where he lives. I couldn't tell you if that makes it the right place or not."

Lucinda forced a tight smile, wrestled her sensible and compact carry-on bag behind her and marched off the dock.

Onto the pristine, glaring white beach, which she found even less accommodating than the smirking pilot she'd hired in Fiji, since there were no commercial flights to this place, plunked down in the Pacific somewhere between Honolulu and Nadi. The sand was hot and shifted beneath her as she walked, in a manner she found deeply unnerving. She liked the comfort of concrete. The assurance that when she stepped on it, it would remain exactly where it was, rain or shine.

The beach had its own ideas. That and the humidity...got to her, she could admit.

Lucinda had worn sensible flats, of course, but was otherwise hardly dressed for a romp across the sands. Despite the forty hours she'd spent traveling—one long-haul flight after another, with too many overly bright airports in between—she had maintained her usual workplace uniform. She was convinced a coolheaded, professional approach was the key to landing this account.

Though at the moment, trying not to sink knee-deep into blindingly white sand, she wished she hadn't, perhaps, dressed for her conservative London office all those hours ago in her flat. It might have been wiser to choose something more appropriate for islands much warmer and brighter than the United Kingdom.

Lucinda wasn't one to concede without a fight—or at all, generally speaking—but it took only about ten steps before she was forced to admit defeat. It was too hot. She was a natural shade of Scottish pale that she was afraid might burst into flame at any moment in all this tropical sun and heat, and she was so uncomfortable that she'd stopped thinking about her goals and was caught up in thinking about how she *felt*. That was unacceptable. She stopped, sinking deep into the sand, to shrug off her black jacket and kick off her matching flats, and wore nothing but her wrinkle-resistant blouse and sleek pencil skirt as she stormed the rest of her way toward solid ground.

Once there, she paused by another picturesque palm tree to dump the beach out of her shoes and slip them back on. And also to catch her breath, accept the likelihood that she was already breaking out in blisters from the relentless sun beating down on her, and try to get her bearings.

If the map on her phone was any guide, and she'd done enough research to know it was, there was precious little on this island. It was almost entirely undeveloped, save the sprawling house Daniel St. George had built here and a single, ancient hotel that had been thrown together in the 1950s in service to an Australian oilman's fantasies of world domination. The hotel had never opened and now sat as a monument to the perils of too much money with no good sense.

She shoved her inadequate sunglasses higher on her nose as she peered down the length of the beach, frowning until she saw the hotel in question, peeking around a picture-perfect curve dusted with palm trees as it reached out toward the blue horizon. The old hotel squatted there with its midtwentieth-century facade and squat, flat shape, reminding Lucinda far too much of the block of flats she'd lived in as a child. All of which should have been torn down before the dawn of the twenty-first century, as far as Lucinda was concerned.

If she had her way, the sad old hotel wouldn't make it through the summer.

There was a kind of track—she wouldn't call it a road, packed with red dirt and sprouting weeds in the center—that skirted along the edge of the beach and wasn't yet overtaken by the encroaching jungle. Lucinda marched along it, her eyes on the hotel. It didn't get any prettier as she moved. But with every overly warm step, she entertained herself with notions of what could be.

A private island resort, catering only to the wealthiest and most exclusive clientele. The kind of fantasy island retreat most people only dreamed about, made a reality right here. She drew up plans in her head, ignoring the blazing sun. The humidity. The unmistakable knowledge that her makeup, or what was left of it all these hours after she'd last applied it in a restroom in the bowels of LAX, was almost certainly melting off her face.

It was a deceptive ten minutes' walk—when it looked as if it ought to be five—from the dock to the old hotel, and when she drew close the building was even worse than she'd imagined. Lucinda knew it was all the rage in places like Los Angeles to pretend that so-called 1950s "style" was exciting and hip. But all that self-consciously cheerful midcentury modernity was pointedly retro and depressingly functional, to her way of thinking. And had no place in this secluded, remote setting. No, thank you. The point of a private island like this was seduction. Mystery and possibility, not the depressingly plain and boxy building that rose up before her like an Eastern European prison.

The setting cried out for magic. Secluded bungalows and private coves, as if the world beyond no longer existed. Not a squat, ugly horror that was little better than a roadside motel.

Lucinda strode up what might once have been a driveway before the jungle had claimed it and pushed her way into the lobby. It was dark inside, and quiet, and she blinked as she waited for the glare of the sun outside to fade so she could see how bad it really was.

There were potted plants that she thought might be fake, a shame in a place where the hills all around burst with green and bright, fragrant blossoms. Heavy, dark furniture that matched the hotel's dark walls and made her think of men with thick gold chains and too much chest hair—potbellies and ugly Hawaiian shirts to match. Not exactly the sort of luxury and elegance, wrapped up in a tropical package, that a place like this should offer.

When her eyes adjusted to light, she started—

Because she wasn't alone.

There was a man sitting there on one of the old couches, his bare feet propped up on the sad wicker table in front of him and his back to the big, open space that led out toward the beach and let the sea in.

Two things occurred to Lucinda at once.

First, that she hadn't laid eyes on another living soul since she'd stepped off the airplane and left the pilot grinning after her. She hadn't heard a single sound that suggested there were people anywhere nearby. This really, truly was a deserted, private island.

And of all the possibilities Lucinda had gone over in her head approximately nine thousand times, she hadn't really let herself think too much about the meaning of that word—*deserted*—or the fact that she'd gone ahead and marooned herself here with a stranger. A man.

Not just any man. *This* man.

Which led her to number two. The man she'd
come to see was far more devastating in person than
in all the pictures she'd studied of him—and she
was fairly certain she'd scoured the internet and had
found every existing image, because she was nothing if not thorough.

But thorough research had not prepared her for...
this.

The man watching her, still lounging there on the
old sofa, was...too much.

Her breath left her in a confusing rush she couldn't
control, as if the very sight of him was a swift punch
to her gut.

Jason Kaoki lounged there before her, kicked back
in what passed for a seating area in the hotel's sad
lobby as if he was as much a fixture as the shiny,
fake plants. Except nothing about him was the least
bit sad. Lucinda told herself it was the thrill of finally making it here into his presence—after all the
calls and emails he'd ignored for months now—that
shot through her when their eyes locked. Because
what else could it be?

But her mouth was remarkably dry. And there
was a shivering thing trapped there, just beneath her
skin. Because it turned out the most reclusive of the
St. George heirs was a big man.

A very big man, she amended, and more disturbing by far, all of him was...exposed.

Well. Not all of him. Just the entire expanse of his

considerably well-muscled chest, with nary a sign of a potbelly, unfortunate chest hair or clanking gold chains. There was a dusting lower down that narrowed as it snuck beneath the band of the long shorts he wore, but his chest was otherwise astonishingly… smooth. Muscled, flat pectorals and a stunning display of ridged abdominals. And there was no reason Lucinda's gaze should linger there, or lower still, on his clearly powerful thighs in the shorts he wore low on his narrow hips. Or anywhere else on the great and glorious *sprawl* of him, all of it rangy and muscled and accented with beautiful tattoos, like something out of one of those superhero movies Lucinda was far too busy to see.

Dangerous, something in her whispered, insistent and low. *This man is* dangerous *and you're a fool to get this close to him.*

And goose bumps broke out all over her arms and neck in emphatic agreement.

Lucinda studied him intently, hoping he wouldn't notice her intense reaction to him. She already knew his stats by heart. That he was six feet and four inches tall and had always possessed this same intense athleticism whether he was playing organized sports or alluring his legion of fans on social media as he surfed and climbed mountains and leaped out of planes. She'd expected him to be attractive in that sporty, relentlessly American way.

But nothing had prepared her for his sheer, overwhelming magnetism. There was something about him that filled the whole of the shabby lobby like a pulse. A flame. As if he was distinctly and inarguably more *male* than any man she'd ever encountered before.

She felt as if she was breathing him in, and worse, close to choking on it. The mad part was, she wasn't sure she'd mind.

Meanwhile, he was also far more than merely *attractive*. No antiseptic word could describe him. His skin gleamed a nutty brown, as if he'd just this minute wandered in from cavorting about in the surf and wasn't entirely dry. His hair was dark and black and raked back from his face as if he'd used one of his large hands, carelessly. And he had the face of a sinner. Or a very suggestive saint, all arched black brows and knowing dark eyes shot through with a hint of gold.

He looked like a dream lover another sort of woman might conjure straight from the sea in a place like this, made of old volcanoes and deep tropical rain forests. And then spend a lifetime or two trying to please with all that bright fire and heady green.

Lucinda was immediately appalled that she'd descended into such theatrics, even in the privacy of her own mind.

Especially when he smirked, as if he knew exactly where her head had gone.

"Let me guess," he drawled, his voice deep and

rich. Decidedly amused and lazy with it, as if part of him was still stretched out in a bed somewhere— *stop it*, she ordered herself fiercely. "You came all this way to sell me something. Sorry, darlin', but I'm not buying."

"You don't know where I came from," she said, almost by rote. Almost as if she had to prove to herself that she wasn't under some kind of spell. "It could be from the next island over."

"The next island over is hours away on a plane. And no one who lives there is as blindingly white as you."

Lucinda might have wished that she had a little more time. To pull herself together. Or back into shape, anyway. To make sure her hair was under control and that she didn't look as she suspected she did right now—a dripping-wet, likely bright red mess after her walk up from the dock. She could have used time to prepare herself the way she liked to do before big, important meetings.

But she already knew this man would be difficult. She'd expected that. She'd gathered all the information she could from her competitors, all of whom had been delighted to have a drink and assure her that *she* had no hope of succeeding where they had failed. *The man looks for weakness*, one of the previous five failures had brayed at her over his martini. *Like a shark.*

Accordingly, Lucinda didn't stammer or excuse

herself or attempt to ease into small talk. All she did
was smile back at Jason Kaoki in all his astonishing
flesh, there in the abandoned old lobby.

Cool and controlled, as if he didn't get to her at
all. As if it had taken forty seconds to get here to see
him, not forty hours, and she was well rested and perfectly relaxed. And while she was at it, she quickly
reviewed everything she knew about this most maddening and elusive of the St. George heirs—the three
sons and one daughter who had been revealed to be
the old playboy's children by the same will that had
accorded each of them one of his luxury properties.

Jason Kaoki had grown up in Hawaii, bouncing
back and forth between the Big Island and Oahu
with his mother and her extended family. He'd gone
on to play college football on the mainland, had enjoyed a brief stint in the pros afterward, followed
by a run of lucrative endorsement deals that continued to this day. He was rumored to spend most of
his considerable fortune on philanthropic pursuits
all over his beloved Pacific Islands, from schools to
veterans charities, though the precise amount of any
actual donations he made were always kept wink-
ingly anonymous.

The man put on a good show on social media, but
in truth, he liked his privacy. He was hard to find
and even harder to pin down to any kind of meeting. When Daniel St. George's will had been read
and this island had come into play, corporate hotel

consortiums like the one Lucinda had clawed her way into had taken notice. The others had tried their best to convince Jason to develop this island the way his father had clearly planned to do after he'd built a house here, and fold himself into their well-known brands, but he'd denied them all.

He didn't need money. He already had a measure of fame. It was almost impossible to talk to him, her contacts had assured her, much less convince him of anything.

But then again, Lucinda had something none of them had.

She wasn't here representing a tired old brand, for one thing. For another, she was a woman. And better still, she wasn't the least bit afraid to use whatever feminine wiles she possessed to get what she wanted. What was the point of having wiles in the first place if not to use them at will? She'd never understood why so many people clutched at their pearls at the thought. She assumed they were the sort of people who had been born with a great many weapons at their disposal, so could pick and choose between them to decide which to use. Lucinda had never had that luxury.

And she didn't need her research to tell her that Jason Kaoki was an extremely heterosexual male, though it had—in the form of a thousand pictures of him with pouting, female arm candy on three continents. Not to mention his often risqué commentary

on his romantic pursuits for the benefit of the fawn-
ing paparazzi.

She could see it with her own two eyes, right here
on this island in the middle of nowhere. She could
feel it like another presence in the lobby, a raw lick
of flame in her bones. And her flesh. She could see
the flare of interest in his dark eyes and the way
those black, arched brows rose. The way his almost
disturbingly sensual mouth curved as he looked up
at her.

She could use it.

So she smiled her best rendition of something seductive. She smoothed her hands down the sides of
her skirt to emphasize her hips, and was suddenly
glad her blouse edged toward sheer, with the suggestion of her breasts beneath. She had every intention
of using the weapons she had when she sat down on
the couch opposite him to negotiate.

With her entire body, if required. Because Lucinda was here to win.

By any means necessary.

CHAPTER TWO

JASON KAOKI STARED at the woman who'd appeared before him dressed in head-to-toe black like the god-damned Grim Reaper, right here on his island like the ghost of lives he didn't want.

Lives he had outright rejected. Repeatedly.

"Are you going to stare at me all day?" he asked her, with the kind of lazy grin he liked to use on people who came at him in suits. "It's an interesting sales pitch, I'll give you that. Though I'm not sure it's effective."

His grin usually sent them running, alarm stamped all over their faces. Especially when he combined it with that tone.

Because Jason never tried too hard to hide his rougher edges.

But if he expected this newest suit to look stricken, or apologetic, or even faintly nervous like all the rest, he was disappointed. She left her little wheeling bag—also black—near the lobby doors and marched across the tile floor to settle herself against the low-slung couch opposite him. She sat as if she owned the place and him, too, which was definitely a bold approach. Then she crossed one decidedly well-formed leg over the other in that ridiculously tight skirt that belonged in an anonymous corporate office somewhere far to the north of here. She even folded her pale, slender hands in her lap, pious and prissy, and regarded him as if she was the one doing him a favor.

It should have put his teeth on edge, like all the teachers and social workers and coaches who'd tried and failed to civilize him always had. But this one was different from the parade of doughy accountant-types, each more arrogant than the last, who had traipsed out here and thought they could talk down to him.

For one thing, he had the feeling that if he could peel away all those laughably inappropriate black layers and see the woman beneath, she'd be hot. Sweet. A perfect snack for a man with a voracious appetite. She had hair the color of fire, and Jason was an elemental kind of guy. He wanted to take her pretty hair out of that agonizing-looking bun she'd slicked it into and get his hands in it. He wanted to see how all that fire smelled now that the sun and the sea had gotten in there and tugged a few strands free. He wanted to bury his face in its thickness and see how hard that got him.

Just to pull up a few urges at random.

What he couldn't tell from looking at her was if

she knew she was hot or not. And if she did, was she hiding herself in the funeral garb on purpose? Did she think that would work?

It didn't. Her breasts were plump and round and begged for a man's palms through the almost-sheer fabric of the fussy blouse she wore. She was tall for a regular woman—meaning, she was tall, but not one of the models he usually gravitated toward because they had legs that went on forever and that looked good draped over his shoulders while they fucked. And despite the tight-assed expression on her face, there was no disguising the flush on her high, ivory cheeks—currently from the sun, he figured, but he knew he could do better—and the full, soft lips he'd greatly enjoy seeing wrapped around his dick.

Jason was entertained.

And he couldn't recall the last time that had happened in the presence of a suit.

He admired whoever had thought to stop sending all those boring tools and uptight douche bags here to talk at him until he scared them away. He wanted to applaud whoever had finally figured they were better off sending a hot little package like this one instead. Because the only thing better than an obviously hot woman who appeared ready to go and easy to get was one a man got the pleasure of unwrapping himself.

The quiet had stretched out between them, with nothing but the sound of the waves on the beach out-

side to divert attention from the way they were staring at each other.

Jason grinned. A little social discomfort didn't
bother him at all. But he couldn't say the same for
all the mainlanders.

This one broke the way they all did, but she kept
her cool, businessy smile in place.

"It's nice to meet you at last, Mr. Kaoki," she said,
in an English accent with something richer beneath
it. Like an extra kick. He liked the way it moved over
him, then settled in his cock. He wished she'd follow
suit. "I appreciate you seeing me without any kind of
appointment. For the record, I did try to make one."

Her voice was, if possible, even more prim and
proper than she looked, if he overlooked that burr
beneath.

Jason had always liked the wild ones. The feral
creatures who could keep up with him. But the more
he stared at this defiantly pale woman with her gorgeous hair ruthlessly wrestled into submission, the
more he wondered if it was the ones who pretended
to be civilized who were the wildest underneath.

Something in him—and not just his dick—wanted
to rise to that challenge.

"*'Mr. Kaoki?'* Jesus Christ. Who the hell is that?
Sounds like someone who needs his ass kicked. I'm
Jason."

Her polite smile didn't dim, and against his will,
he was impressed. Each and every one of the wussy

little men who'd sweated at him in this very same lobby had looked nauseated and ill at ease by this point. Because douche bags always imagined they could manipulate a big, loud, dumb jock—and they were always surprised and disconcerted to discover that this particular dumb jock was a whole lot more difficult to handle in person.

Not his prissy little redhead, sitting rigid and sure on the old sofa like that painful-looking bun of hers was pulling her spine straight. "I'm Lucinda Graves."

"Why am I not surprised your name is Graves?" When she frowned, Jason shrugged. Expansively. And noted, with interest, the way her gaze followed the play of muscles in his shoulders. "Maybe you're too jet-lagged to notice you're in the South Pacific. Here we dress in pretty flowers and aloha and not a whole lot else. But you came dressed for a funeral."

She rustled up that smile again, twice as polite this time. He figured she considered it a weapon.

He thought that was cute.

"I'm sorry if my professionalism offends you," she said coolly. "I'm only trying to treat you with the courtesy due your position."

"You mean my money, not my position. I don't think you'd give a rat's ass about my position if it wasn't directly in your way. Much less any courtesy."

"On the contrary, Mr. Kaoki. Manners never go amiss. Especially in trying situations."

Was she scolding him? Jason thought she was. And even stranger, he found it just as hot.

Which probably said some shit about him, but he had no intention of analyzing it.

He shifted where he lounged there across from her before his unruly cock announced itself. He rubbed absently at his side, and once again her gaze dropped to follow the movement. All over the tattoo he'd gotten when his football scholarship had come through, so he'd never forget where he came from.

And Jason didn't think she was the type to find ink quite that fascinating.

"I have to be honest, Lucinda." He made her name a meal and discovered that he was actually good and hungry. Bordering on straight-up starving. "I don't really think you know how trying this situation could get. Let me know if you want that to change."

She blinked, but didn't touch that. Smart girl.

"I represent an international hotel concern," she started again, but he thought that smile of hers was more strained than before. He interpreted that as progress. "We specialize in extraordinary properties aimed toward top-tier clientele who expect—and can afford—the best. I'm sure you already know the development potential of this island is astronomical. And I say that as someone not given to exaggeration."

"The development potential of anything is astronomical if the person who owns it keeps saying hell no to slick offers and obsequious dickheads in ugly suits." He studied her for a moment, lingering on the flush across her high cheekbones and the freckles that were coming out over her nose. "I'm pretty sure you already know I don't want to develop shit. You look like the type who would know that kind of thing before you stepped on an airplane to force a meeting. What makes you think you can show up here and convince me when no one else could?"

She blinked again, and her eyes—entirely too blue for his peace of mind—got canny. And Jason might look like a barbarian. He'd cultivated that image, in fact. Wild and loud and nothing but noise, because it suited him to be underestimated. The truth was, he'd always liked women with brains. It made life a hell of a lot more complicated, sure. But complicated was often a whole lot more interesting.

"I'm hoping that I can change your mind." Her gaze was steady on his. "Why don't you tell me what you think that would take."

Jason laughed. It was a big laugh, just like him, and it filled the lobby. One of his more poetic exes had once told him it was like a volcano. As an island boy, born and bred to be respectful of Madame Pele and her works, Jason was more than okay with that comparison.

Especially when it seemed to bother the shit out of the tight-assed corporate creature perched across from him, who stiffened at the sound.

"I'm not going to talk contracts and deals, sweet-heart," he said when his laughter died away. "Fun fact. People don't move to private islands without names in the middle of the Pacific Ocean if they want to be tracked down. And yet you people are like ants, one after the next, rolling up to ruin my picnic."

"I don't want to ruin your picnic," she said, and he was almost impressed that she managed to get that out through her pursed lips and that attempt at the same polite smile. "I just want to make you a rich man."

"I'm already a rich man."

"You can always be richer."

He laughed at that, too. Because she had hair like fire and skin so pale and resolutely sunless she glowed. And she was dressed in those stiff, dark clothes that looked as sad and dreary as whatever dark, rainy place she came from.

"White people always want to get richer," he ob-served. "It's just money, Lucinda."

"Spoken like someone who has too much of it, Jason," she fired back.

And he saw her, then. The real woman tucked away behind the prim and the proper, and *she* was bright. Sharp and wild. All teeth and snarl, and Jason wanted to tangle himself up in her and see if she left marks.

Something in him uncurled, then heated.

"If you don't want money," Lucinda said after a

moment, her tone too precise, as if she was wrestling herself into submission—which Jason wanted to do himself, "what do you want?"

"I don't want anything. And if I did, I'd go get it. I don't need help from corporate assholes."

She looked impatient for a second, but wiped it away in the next. "Everybody wants something, Mr. Kaoki. All you have to do is admit it."

He let the things he wanted settle into him, hot and greedy, and made no particular attempt to hide the burn of it as he regarded her. His reward was a splash of deeper color in her telltale cheeks.

"I don't need to see your tedious fucking blue-prints or pay attention while you yammer at me about secluded coves, lanais for days and forests of tiki torches," he drawled, aware he was landing hits every time her flush deepened. She was an open book and he was almost positive she didn't know it. That only made this more fun. "Building some snooty resort here isn't going to make me happier. So what's the point? Why would I bother? Hawaii is already occupied. Your fancy clients can go ruin it some more whenever they get the hankering to play colonizer."

She didn't miss a beat. Her eyes were a cool, fathomless blue, like the ocean he loved on a tem-pestuous day—and there was something about that comparison that rubbed him the wrong way. Like it was settling into him. He tried to shake it off, concentrating on what she was saying instead.

"Maybe it's not your happiness we should be concerned with. Think about all the good you could do if you brought jobs and investment to the area."

"Baby, I don't know what you read about me, but my happiness is the only thing I'm concerned with."

"You give away more money to local charities than most people in the Pacific Islands will ever make."

"That's a rumor," Jason replied lightly. "An unproven rumor because people like to think the best about other people. The truth makes them itchy."

"People think the best of others? When?" Her laugh made him restless. "I think you'll find they really don't."

"Whatever. I'm a selfish man, darlin'. I amuse myself and that's about it. And nothing about ruining this island with another bullshit resort that pollutes the place strikes me as all that amusing."

"I had no idea you were such an environmentalist."

"I'm not. I'm selfish. I like my beach empty, my jungle wild and my roads clear. The point of a private island is that no one else is on it."

"Right." She seemed to take that on board. Her eyes narrowed as she looked him over, like she was trying to find his weaknesses. He gazed back at her, boneless and unconcerned. "But even selfish men want *something*."

"There's nothing I want I can't get, Lucinda. I don't need to make bargains with strange women. I don't even need to have this conversation, but that's the kind of guy I am. Nice to a fucking fault."

He grinned at her, letting his edges show again, and he wasn't entirely surprised when she didn't look away. She was a lot tougher than the men who'd come here. Or more determined, anyway.

One more thing that shouldn't have appealed to him. But Jason had always been a sucker for a little grit.

"Oh, yes," she murmured. "You're very *nice*. That's the word I'd choose to describe you."

"Feel free to pick a better one."

But she didn't take him up on his invitation. Instead, her body language changed, right there in front of him.

Jason watched, fascinated, because she didn't melt. She didn't go boneless and seductive, or start fiddling with the buttons on that shirt of hers to start flashing him those perfect breasts. The straight edge of her spine didn't curve in the slightest.

And yet there was no doubt that something changed.

He could feel it between them, a thick, humming kind of tension. He told himself he was amused by this latest attempt to get at him, but his cock wasn't laughing. It was fascinated, too.

More than fascinated.

And he was getting hungrier by the moment.

"Are you offering me something?" he asked.

Her gaze had turned speculative. And she was tilting her head to one side in a manner designed to make him rock hard and ready. "My understanding is that in the past, you've kicked everyone who came here off this island within hours."

"Now my buddy just waits at the dock," Jason agreed, genially enough. "So he can take you right back to Fiji. You can go now, if you want."

Her smile was a thing to behold. It wasn't that polite one she'd been bludgeoning him with since she'd walked in, professional and distant. This one took over her whole face. It was like the sun coming out from behind clouds, the sudden shock of heat and brightness making his chest feel tight.

All he could think about was tasting that fire. Drowning himself in it. Making her burn hot until she screamed.

But she thought she was playing him, so Jason didn't move. He waited.

"What I want is for you to let me stay," she told him.

So very prettily.

Jason grinned. He'd been hit on by so many beautiful women he'd lost count before he left for college. And he was Hawaiian—technically half-Hawaiian, but he'd never bothered to recognize the haole douche bag tourist who had seduced his mother and left her high and dry—which meant his standards for beauty were pretty damn high. He rarely bothered with corporate types. Sticks up the ass didn't get him off.

But everything in him was encouraging him to make an exception in Lucinda's case.

"Now, why would I do something like that?" he asked. He let his grin hint at his greed. "What's in it for me?"

And then surprised himself by settling back and waiting for her to convince him.

CHAPTER THREE

LUCINDA DIDN'T KNOW what the hell she was doing.

She had always been about a plan. Making a plan, following a plan and sticking to a plan come hell or high water. She researched, she got herself ready and then she executed said plan without ever straying into too much dangerous spontaneity. That strategy had served her well her whole life—but something about this island made her feel outside herself. Inside out, stretched thin, too hot and too exposed, all at once.

It's the jet lag, she told herself. But there was the distinct possibility it had more to do with the man lounging there across from her, watching her with lethal intent, than the island or what it had taken to get here.

The truth was that while she wasn't averse to using whatever inducements she could throw at Jason Kaoki, she wasn't entirely sure she'd be the one getting what she wanted out of the bargain if she did.

He wasn't like other men.

He wasn't like anyone she'd ever met.

He was *too big*, in every sense of the term. He was built on a grand scale, sure, but there was also his laugh. His wicked, challenging grin. That steady dark gaze of his that told her in no uncertain terms that he truly didn't need or want a damned thing from anyone...

But that he might take it anyway, if it was offered.

There's no reason you can't make him an offer— that *offer—right here and now*, she told herself stoutly, still holding that simmering gaze of his. The notion made a deep shiver wind its way through her, making her hold herself even more still for fear he'd see exactly what she wanted to give him. What she was willing to trade.

She didn't know what she was doing, but she needed to figure it out. And fast.

Because she needed this. She needed to win. She needed to prove herself, once and for all, in a way that no one could claim was theirs or take away from her or dismiss. Lucinda was so tired of fighting for every last scrap. She didn't like to admit it to herself, but she knew it was true. After a lifetime of hustling, *she was tired*. She wanted to be done with the dustups, once and for all. She'd been swinging and scrabbling all her life, and she wanted the big prize this time.

She wanted to rest on her laurels for a change. She

wanted to see what the world looked like when she was sure of her place in it. At last.

And there was no doubt that landing Jason Kaoki and this jewel of an island would do the trick. It would be the making of her. She could leave her firm in a blaze of glory and go out on her own. Maybe stay in one of the exclusive properties she worked so hard to build, for a start.

No one back in London thought she could do it.

"You're wasting your time," her direct superior had told her, sighing loudly to make certain Lucinda knew she was bothering him when she'd dutifully told him her plans. He named the much-celebrated president of a rival boutique hotel corporate body, who had only the week before sneered at Lucinda in a trendy gastropub as he'd assured her the Kaoki property was lost to developers. "If *he* can't make it happen, no one can."

"I can do it," Lucinda had said with tremendous certainty and confidence.

It had only been partially feigned.

Because she'd studied Jason Kaoki. And she hadn't concentrated only on his investment portfolio like everyone else, all those cold numbers and figures. Lucinda had immersed herself in all his social media accounts. She'd watched old interviews and read articles on his early prowess on the football field.

She'd convinced herself she *knew* him.

"If you can, you'll be a legend," her boss had replied, with a laugh. Indicating how unlikely a prospect he thought that was. Because he might like how hard Lucinda worked, but he certainly didn't think she had it in her to become *a legend*.

And it turned out that the scrappy little nobody from that grotty flat in one of Glasgow's most notorious tower blocks wanted to be a legend. Very badly, in fact. She didn't want to work for anyone else. She didn't want to report to her boss, who was decent enough as these things went, but still liked to take credit for her best and brightest ideas like they were owed to him.

Then laughed at her when she showed her belly by clearly indicating she wanted more.

Goddamn it, but she wanted this win.

That was why she'd taken her annual leave and spent her own money to haul herself here to make her own legend, her own way.

Only to discover that not only was Jason Kaoki as difficult as advertised, he was difficult in a completely different way than she'd anticipated. And more worryingly, *she* seemed to be someone else when she was in his presence.

She told herself, once again, that it was the heat. The tropics, bearing down on her relentlessly. The lobby was open to the weather and the breeze that wound its way in one side and out the other did very little to cool her off. Instead, it danced over her, making her feel electric and strange. And *aware* of too many things she'd prefer to ignore altogether.

The press of her thighs against each other. The heat her own body generated. The touch of the breeze itself, soft and warm all over her, like a caress.

"Tell me what it would take," she said now. Again. She focused on Jason. On the task at hand. "Tell me what you want and I'll give it to you."

He looked…sinful and dangerous. Deeply, inarguably dangerous. Alarms went off inside her, one after the next, and she had to fight to repress a shiver of unease. Or whatever that feeling was that nipped at her and made her wonder if a person could spontaneously combust, after all. Right here and now in an ugly, forgotten hotel.

"I appreciate the offer," Jason said, in that drawling, suggestive voice of his that danced all over her like a terrible fire. Far worse than any tropical breeze. "But I don't think you can."

She told herself the sun and the heat were getting to her, that was all. She was Scottish and she lived in London. She was built for gray skies and buckets of rain, not white-sand beaches and glaringly blue skies without a stray cloud in sight. There had been entirely too much sunshine on her walk from the dock to this sad old hotel, and she was much too pale to handle it. She was experiencing some kind of prickly heat reaction to the weather, nothing more.

He happened to be here, but he wasn't the cause of it.

It was crazy to imagine otherwise.

"I don't do business meetings," Jason told her, and that same insanity swept through her again when his mouth curved, prickly and too hot and clearly not the weather at all. "I'm not into presentations in boardrooms. I hate bankers and proposals and sober contract negotiations. Ad men make me want to break things. I don't like suits—" and he nodded at her, indicating that he didn't like hers either "—and I don't trust anyone who would wear one or sign up to sell snake oil in that kind of place in the first place."

There was absolutely no reason Lucinda should feel the sting of that as if he'd slapped her. Who cared what he thought about her outfit or her job? What did overly rich men know about anything besides themselves and their net worth?

She forced a smile, though she was afraid it wasn't nearly as bland as it ought to have been. "This kind of input is helpful. Tell me what kind of meeting you like, where you'd like it to take place and how you'd like everyone involved to dress, and I'll make it happen. No snake oil allowed."

Jason's dark gaze gleamed with a molten gold that was much more dangerous than the breeze or the relentless sun outside. And his grin reminded her of a pirate's, wide and filled with entirely too much dark intent.

She couldn't quite breathe.

"You might not like my suggestions," he pointed out in that lazy way of his, layered with sex and sin.

"I don't have to like your suggestions," Lucinda replied tartly. "This is about you. What I like or don't like is immaterial."

"If you say so."

And Lucinda had always prided herself on being able to read people. It had been a necessary component of her climb out of the hole of her poverty-stricken childhood. She could read people like a book, and she'd always read them at lightning speed, because that was the only way to avoid her drunken father's fist or her perpetually bitter mother's tongue. She'd learned how to avoid the unsavory characters who lurked in the tower blocks, and how to tell the difference between a bored kid and a dangerous criminal when they often looked alike. She'd honed these kinds of skills when she was young and they'd served her well ever after.

The more she could read her superiors and her clients, the better she could anticipate their needs. The more she did that, the more indispensable she made herself, and that was how a girl from nothing made herself a vice president at a multinational corporation when most of the people she'd grown up with had never made it out of the same housing estate where they'd been raised.

Lucinda considered her street smarts an essential tool in her kit.

But she understood it was useless here. With him.

Jason Kaoki was a mystery. A deliberate one, if she didn't miss her guess, but a mystery all the same. Because he was lounging around wearing nothing but those low-slung water shorts of his, showing off acres and acres of brown skin and a selection of artistic tattoos. His dark hair was much too long for conventional sensibilities, he grinned far too wide and often, he laughed uproariously at the slightest provocation, and everything about him gave off the impression that he was wide open. Easy and amiable and approachable.

But the five men he'd already ejected from this island proved that none of that was true. He might laugh loud and long, but it would be a very great fool indeed who imagined he was easy. In any way.

Against her will, Lucinda found herself wondering why a man who had everything—who had been blessed with all that undeniable athleticism to win himself a place outside his own humble beginnings, instead of having to fight for a way out with a mix of cleverness and desperation as she had—needed to hide in plain sight.

But that wasn't her business. The resort she wanted to build here was.

And this wasn't the first time in her life Lucinda had been forced to sit with a smile on her face, fight-

ing to remain calm while other people decided her
future at their whim.

As God was her witness, if she could make this
work, this would be the last.

"Okay," he said, after a lifetime or two. With that
same dark gaze heavy on her, like a foot on her neck.

That was hardly a helpful image, she chided herself. Especially when her body responded to it as if
it was something sexual.

And worse, delicious.

Lucinda eyed him. "Okay?" she echoed.

"Okay," Jason said again. That impossible mouth
of his curved and the gleam in his gaze turned considering. Or challenging. "Get changed. We're going
surfing."

"Surfing?"

"I don't think I stuttered, darlin'."

Lucinda battled to keep her feelings off her face.
Her palms ached, and she had to glance down to see
that she was digging her own nails into her palms.
She uncurled her hands. Painfully.

"You didn't stutter. But I don't surf."

"Then it's time to learn," he told her, all drawl,
heat and challenge and something she was very much
afraid was anticipation all over him. "Because I don't
trust anyone who can't ride a wave. And I certainly
won't negotiate with them."

Obviously, the last thing Lucinda wanted to do
was get in the water.

She hardly swam at all. She'd learned as a matter of course when she was a teenager, because she'd been born on an island and thought it was ridiculous not to know how to swim if the opportunity presented itself. It had been a practical decision. A matter of survival, like most things involving her childhood and her path out.

Surfing was something else entirely. The word itself made her bristle at the image of lanky blond men drooping over California beaches, all abs and lazy accents.

"I didn't come here to swim," she told Jason as crisply as possible. "I'm afraid I brought a very limited wardrobe with me, none of it appropriate for water sports."

Jason was still lounging there on that couch, like some kind of deity surveying his universe in comfort. Lucinda scolded herself for the thought—but scolding herself didn't change the fact that was how he looked.

"No worries." His easy drawl made her think of heat. Light. The thick, sweet seduction of the tropical air—

Settle yourself, madam, she ordered herself, aware the voice in her head sounded a great deal like her mother's.

"I certainly hope you're not suggesting I simply toss off all my clothes and leap into the surf like some kind of demented mermaid," she said tartly.

And instantly regretted the impulse. It was…not wise to talk about taking off clothes in the presence of a man like this. She understood the magnitude of her mistake instantly. She thought the air was already seductive, but suddenly it seemed to burn. As if there was a clenched hand around the both of them and it started to squeeze tight.

Lucinda couldn't breathe. Her eyes felt wet, as if the tension was making her tear up. She felt much too hot to keep lying to herself about prickly heat or sun when she was sitting inside and the only source of heat anywhere around her was Jason.

Something changed on his face, making him look even more wicked and wild than before. And it didn't help that there was so *much* of him. Naked and gleaming and right there—

She was afraid the fire in her was visible. She had to find a way to freeze or she didn't know what would become of her.

"Nudity is always encouraged." Jason's voice was a low drawl, as wicked as his expression. "But no need to make yourself sick about it, darlin'. I got you covered."

He rose then, shifting from that lounging, lazy posture to his feet in a smooth, athletic shift that made something deep in Lucinda's belly turn over. And hum.

She understood something then, in a flash. That this was all an act. That there was nothing about him that was lazy in the least. The lounging, the grinning, the *darlin'* and the drawl—these were all masks he wore. To conceal the truth of him that she should have known already. He was a world-renowned athlete.

A predator, not to put too fine a point on it, in a world of prey, and he apparently liked to hide right there in plain sight.

He was big, entirely too dangerous, and now he was towering over her in the dim hotel lobby.

And Lucinda had never been so aware of her own pulse in her life. It throbbed in her wrists, her neck, her breasts, and seemed to glow to the same rhythm in her pussy.

She stopped pretending there was any possibility that she was going to breathe normally.

His gaze was still on her and she felt…frozen, but not in any kind of ice. If a bright, white-hot flame was immobilizing, that was what caught her. Held her.

Had her tipping up her chin to stare him straight in the eye while her imagination went wild. What if he reached down and pulled her to him with one of those outsized hands? What if he took both of those big, capable hands and put them on her body? What if he—

Jason smirked, that mocking, knowing curve of his wicked mouth that told her she wasn't the only person who could read others easily. Too easily.

He didn't say a word, he simply padded across the hotel lobby. He disappeared behind the scratched, dark wood desk and into what she assumed was some kind of office.

And he took the storm with him, leaving Lucinda gasping for air in his wake.

Without him in the lobby, it was nothing but tired, old midcentury furnishings, questionable corporate art and the sound of waves crashing down on the beach outside.

And she couldn't tell, for long moments, if it was the waves she heard or her own heartbeat.

Lucinda got to her feet, feeling as rickety on her flats as she would have if she was wearing impractical stiletto heels. And she hated that she wasn't sure if her knees would hold her as she made her own way across the lobby floor.

But she pulled herself together—or near enough—by the time Jason emerged from the back office again. And she would die before she would confess such a thing out loud, but there was a part of her that was grateful he stayed on the other side of the desk when he came out. It wasn't much, just that long, ambling counter of once-polished wood, but as far as Lucinda was concerned it might as well have been a fortress separating her from him.

She would take what she could get.

He tossed a scandalously small handful of brightly colored scraps across the desk and Lucinda found herself staring at them as the soft heap slid along the wood and came to a stop in front of her.

It took her longer than she cared to admit to understand that it was a bathing costume.

Part of one, anyway. It was all strings. What wasn't an actual string was pink and bright and not something Lucinda would ever consider wearing in private. Much less while supposedly conducting business.

But when she lifted her gaze to his again, she could tell that this, too, was a challenge.

"It's called a bikini," Jason said, as if he was talking to a child. A very dimwitted child. "You put it on and then go in the water. It's that simple."

Lucinda felt something shake, deep inside her, that she was terribly afraid was fear. Panic, even, when she'd been so sure she'd knocked the panic right out of her years ago.

But there was no sign of any tremor in her hand when she reached out and placed it on the soft, small little pile this man seemed to expect she would put on her body. And then wear right out in the open, in and out of water, where he could see her—

Lucinda's mind cartwheeled away from that.

"How fortunate that you have a selection at hand," she said crisply, and was proud of her tone.

He grinned. "People leave the strangest things behind here. But don't worry. It's clean."

It was an innocuous enough statement, so Lucinda

had no idea why it licked through her as if he'd said something dirty. Very, very dirty.

She forced herself to smile. She hoped it looked cool and controlled, but at this point, she had to focus all her energy on keeping herself from shaking like a leaf. "I appreciate you providing me with some of your castoffs, I do. But I'm afraid that I have a terribly fair complexion. Perhaps you noticed. I came to this island to do a little business, not frolic on the beach. I'm quite certain that if I step outside, I'll be sunburnt within an inch of my life. In minutes. So thank you, but I do think I had better decline this lovely offer."

"Don't worry, Lucinda." Jason's voice was a low rumble. Dark and stirring, and her name in his mouth made her pussy ache. "I have suntan lotion, too. And I'm more than capable of making sure I don't miss a single spot."

CHAPTER FOUR

HE DIDN'T THINK she would do it. He would have bet on it.

Jason found the skimpiest bikini he could in the leftovers from some party his father—not that he liked to think of Daniel St. George that way, or at all—must have thrown here while he was still alive. Jason told himself that he was doing it to force her to turn around and storm off, leaving him in peace, the way all the others had, because that was the only way he could see this going. No way was Lucinda Graves, Queen of the Tight-Assed Corporate Types, stripping off all her layers of stifling funeral clothes and catching a wave.

And he definitely wasn't torturing himself imagining that body of hers, the one that he could barely glimpse there through all her dour swaddling clothes, in a few immodest strings and hopeful triangles.

A few strings and triangles and nothing else.

Just like he definitely wasn't hot and hard and

ready to go at the idea of smearing suntan lotion all over her lush little body.

This was a dare, that was all. To force a conclusion to this little drama so he could go back to his busy schedule of doing absolutely nothing where no one could see him, the better to get his head right. The bikini was a gauntlet, thrown down the hotel desk in bright pink Lycra, and he fully expected her to balk.

But he'd underestimated Lucinda.

A surprising fact that made him only that much harder and more interested in this, he could admit. He'd done little more than roll his eyes when his buddy had called him from Fiji to let him know another suit had booked a flight to his island.

"Another one incoming," he'd said, laughing.

"It's a private island, brother," Jason had growled. "You could say no."

"Where's the fun in that?"

Apparently, part of the fun had been failing to mention that this time, it was a woman instead of the usual smarmy dudes. That had been a nice surprise for Jason when she'd walked into the old hotel, without the usual salesman swagger of the others. He'd taken one look at all that porcelain paleness and had wanted nothing more than to get his hands all over her. And leave some marks.

But then, Jason was well acquainted with his own animalistic urges. Some might say he reveled in them.

He would never be a monk. But he'd taken this time to sit on a pretty island the father he'd always hated had bought and built a pretty house on to ask himself why he always looked for oblivion. In a bottle. Between a pair of sweet thighs. Testing his adrenaline in high-risk adventures. His mother had called him out after the reading of his father's will, and Jason wasn't built to ignore the woman who'd raised him—on her own, because the rich haole who'd literally left her pregnant by the side of the road couldn't be bothered.

"You're so busy making sure you're nothing like him that guess what?" His mother had shaken her head at him, as if Jason had disappointed her. He would rather she'd slapped him upside his head. It felt about the same. Worse, maybe. Then she'd twisted the knife. "So many women everywhere you go. Do you know their names? Or do you like the fact you're carrying on his tradition of anonymous encounters everywhere you go? Seems to me you're just like him, after all."

That had sucked.

Jason had removed himself from all temptation the very next day.

But what was he supposed to do when temptation wandered onto his very own deserted island? With an agenda all its own?

He didn't want to be a piece of shit like his father. But he was only a man.

He watched Lucinda's struggle play out across her perfect oval of a face. Her blue eyes gleamed from temper or emotion, and she looked at him like she was considering taking a strip or two out of his hide—or trying—but her flush mouth pressed into a tight line instead. She had a tough little chin, he noticed when she lifted it, high and belligerent like she was ready to fight.

But she didn't take a swing at him. She didn't try to talk him down. Instead, she did the last thing he'd imagined she would do. She reached out and snatched up the tiny bikini from the front desk.

"You'd best find a bottle of sunscreen, then," she said in her prissy voice that seemed to wind itself around his cock. He told himself it was only because he'd restricted himself from women at present. That it was nothing personal. But he wasn't sure his unruly dick got that message. "I won't be a moment."

Jason watched, fascinated and filled with something a little too much like that adrenaline he was supposed to be taking a break from, as she swept around the corner of the front desk and slammed the office door behind her.

And Jason had been through a lot of shit in his time. He'd been forced to sit and wait for things outside his control to play out when he was younger, and he couldn't say he'd ever enjoyed the experience. Not when he'd been a young hothead determined to prove that he was worth the life his artistic mother had given up when she'd had to clean hotel rooms to support the both of them. Not when he'd been a member of a team, subject to the whims of his teammates and coaches.

Not now, either. In these later years, he had cultivated patience. Or the appearance of it, anyway. He'd learned how to breathe. How to relax. How to focus his aggression and attention when needed, and turn it off when it was nothing more than a hindrance. Or that was what he'd been working on here, in his hideaway from the world and the man he was becoming against his will.

Waiting for a woman to change into a bathing suit shouldn't have registered at all. It shouldn't have gotten his blood pumping. And there was absolutely no reason he should feel like a kid, randy and wild, as one moment stretched out into the next and he couldn't seem to do anything but imagine her... arranging herself into that bikini.

Would it even cover her? Would she try to wear something over it?

And his heartbeat was like a drum as he pondered these questions, pounding out a rhythm that seemed to land heavy in his cock.

Something shifted in him as he waited, making him feel restless and on edge. It took him a minute to figure out that it was a pang of regret.

That he hadn't gone with her into that office to

help her out of those clothes. That he wasn't even now treating himself to that first, lush view of all her pale, sweet skin. That he wasn't the first hit of Pacific sunshine she would get today, his gaze bathing her in light and heat.

Maybe followed by his mouth.

He should have laughed at that, he knew. He was Jason Kaoki, for fuck's sake. He could have any woman he wanted, and had—apparently to such an excess that his mother had felt the need to comment on his life choices.

"Everyone's looking for the next Daniel St. George, son," she'd said, pruning her plants on the lanai of the house he'd bought for her with his first million—though she'd refused to move into it, claiming it was *too haole*, until somewhere around his fifth or sixth million. "I guess you decided to rise to the challenge."

Because Jason's brand-new half siblings didn't make half as much noise as he did in the tabloids. The oldest, Thor Ragnarsson, was some kind of Icelandic Viking. He ran a hotel way up there on the top of the world that catered to sexual pleasures among consenting adults, but he rarely made the covers of magazines. The next oldest, Charlie Teller, kept his past murky and his profile low enough to suggest there was a reason he avoided attention. Their half sister, Angelique Masterson, had gone off and gotten herself involved with an honest-to-God prince, which probably would have made more of a splash if the two of them hadn't spent most of their time off in the prince's kingdom with a far-better-behaved press corps.

That left only Jason and a world fascinated with his exploits whether he liked it or not.

He wanted to change that, sure. He was working on it. But in the meantime there was no reason he should be tied in knots over some prissy accountant-type who'd shown up on a tropical island in a business suit. A dark black business suit. He was taking a break, he wasn't hard up.

It was ridiculous. *She* was ridiculous.

Which was when she threw open the office door and stepped out into the lobby again, and his head went blank.

He could feel every drop of blood in his body surge downward, pooling in his cock so fast and so swiftly it was almost painful.

Jason had received punches to the face and in the gut during his brawling years that hurt less, and had knocked him back less, than the sight of Lucinda standing there in a tiny string bikini he had clearly chosen for no other purpose than to torture himself.

It was possible he swallowed his own tongue.

He expected her to cower. To hunch her shoulders over in an attempt to hide herself from view in such a tiny excuse for a swimsuit.

But not Lucinda.

Instead of any hunching or cowering or other evidence of insecurity, her too-blue eyes clapped to his and held fast.

And if he wasn't mistaken, the look she was leveling at him was a sheer, unmistakable challenge. As if she was taking his dare and making it worse by shoving it straight down his throat.

Because she didn't lurk in the shadows. She didn't try to cover herself. Prissy, prim, uptight Lucinda—because he was sure that was who she'd been when she'd walked into this lobby—sauntered out of the back office like a wet dream.

Her shoulders were back, giving him a perfect view of those plump, round breasts that should have been a little too much for the bikini top. His palms itched to explore the suit's structural integrity, but he kept them to himself.

Barely.

The brightly striped triangles of the top strained over taut nipples he wanted to taste with his own tongue, and below, another triangle covered her pussy. It left nothing but a string between her ass cheeks while it also told him that she likely sported a Brazilian, because the good stuff was so neatly concealed from his view.

Everything else was Lucinda.

God help him.

When he got his brain out of his cock, all he could think was that she looked like a sculpture. Something carved in marble or ivory, by man's loving, tender hands.

He only wished they had been his.

She was so starkly, distinctively pale, in defiance of all the sun and sand and bright blue sky that made this island what it was. And the spate of golden freckles, tossed here and there over her body, only seemed to draw attention to her ethereal, impossible beauty.

She'd left her hair slicked back in that killer bun that gave *him* a headache, but that was an argument for another time.

Because she came to a sultry kind of stop before him like the goddess of a religion he wanted to practice, suddenly, more than he wanted to breathe.

She held his gaze, hard and sure. And if he wasn't mistaken, there was a light of triumph in those sea-colored eyes of hers.

"Are we surfing?" she asked, with a lilt in her voice that he knew was yet another challenge. "Or are we just going to stare?"

Jason knew, beyond the shadow of a doubt, that his monastic retreat from the world was over.

And temptation had won.

Hallelujah.

CHAPTER FIVE

THE ONLY WAY out was through, Lucinda told herself stoutly.

She would brazen it out no matter what, she'd decided when she'd stepped into the office. She'd never yet backed down from a challenge and there was no way she'd come this far to allow *this* to be the first time.

She might have found the bikini distressingly skimpy, but that was all it was: a bathing costume.

It was only as awkward as she allowed it to be.

Sheer force of will kept her moving with her head high. She pretended she couldn't feel the sleek caress of the cool tiles beneath her feet. Or all that thick tropical air, like an intimate caress.

All over her body.

Lucinda's practical, survival-focused swimming lessons had taken place under controlled circumstances, in secure one-piece bathing costumes appropriate to the task at hand. That being learning how not to drown, not showing off her body.

She might as well have been naked in the ridiculous bikini Jason had given her. He'd clearly expected her to refuse to wear it on those grounds, but what the hell. She'd never been ashamed of her body and there was no reason to change that now.

Especially not with the way Jason was staring at her, looking nothing short of gobsmacked.

That would do quite nicely, thank you. A quick strut out of a dusty back office in a questionable string bikini shifted the power balance between them—Lucinda could feel it as easily as she could see it—and that felt a lot like a welcome victory.

If Jason wanted to stare, she was happy to give him something to stare at. It was nothing to her but another bargaining chip.

Though if she thought about it too much, she would feel foolish nonetheless—because her research had showed her the sorts of women this man preferred and none of them had skin the color of a dead fish's underbelly, fetchingly covered in freckles and topped with flaming ginger hair—so she didn't let herself.

She swayed toward him, letting one hand drift to the counter beside her, one hip jutting out.

And watched Jason Kaoki's famously sultry eyes go black with heat.

If the price of this kind of power involved flinging herself into the waves and letting the surf dash her to pieces on the beach, Lucinda decided it was well worth it.

Because the more he stared back at her, fire all over him like a different kind of storm entirely, all she could think to do was burn.

"I need protection," she said, and it wasn't until that gaze of his burned hotter and his expression shifted to something far more male and knowing that it occurred to her that her words could be misinterpreted.

Or maybe she did know. Maybe, after all these years of practical, dependable choices and considered forward momentum, it turned out that really, all Lucinda wanted to do was light matches and play with fire.

It cost her to keep her voice cool, but she did it. "For the sun, Mr. Kaoki. I need SPF 50, at the very least. Don't you think?"

He looked as if it took him a minute to rouse himself from whatever daydream he had drifted off into. And it didn't take a lot on her part to figure out exactly what that daydream entailed, since she could feel the kick of it in her own blood.

And between her legs like a sweet, insistent fire.

She told herself it was the fact that she was nearly naked, with her ass hanging out and all of her bits on display. It was the fact that the breeze could wash over her, touching parts of her body she wasn't sure she'd ever bared outside the privacy of her own shower. That was why she felt so animated. So intensely *alive*.

Outside herself, she told herself, the way anyone might feel after such a long trip.

But she knew that wasn't true.

What was true was that she felt more inside her own body than she ever had before.

Lucinda shoved that odd notion aside. Because Jason was moving again. For a brief, terrified instant she thought he was reaching for her—

And she knew, even as she categorized it that way, that what she felt certainly wasn't *terror*—

But he didn't put his hands on her, and Lucinda had to swallow back a protest. He pulled open a drawer an inch or so away from her. Then another one, rummaging around until he found a bright orange and blue tube it took her entirely too long to understand was the sunscreen she'd requested.

Their eyes met. Held.

"Come on," he said, his voice gruffer than before. "Let's go."

She wanted to demand that he put the lotion on her here and now, but she didn't. Maybe because, for all her bravado, she thought that if they stayed here in this dim, deserted lobby—just the two of them— she would find herself in a whole lot more trouble than she'd bargained for.

She tried to ignore all those clamoring parts of herself that wanted exactly that. And when he started walking out from behind the desk, she followed him. After losing a pitched battle with herself, she stopped pretending she was more high-minded and let herself gaze at the stunning expanse of his muscled, tattooed back as he stalked across the lobby in front of her.

He was beautiful, full stop.

And as they walked out from the lobby area onto what once had been a 1950s version of the sort of flowing, open-space lanai that Lucinda wanted to build, he became only more beautiful. As if he was meant to be outdoors on an island just like this one, a part of the sun, the inviting ocean before him and the gleaming white sand that beckoned. He stopped at the edge of the terrace near an old iron railing, his eyes shadowed as the sun beat down on him. He didn't say a word as he gazed down at Lucinda. He only lifted one of his big hands and motioned for her to turn around with one lazy finger.

Which is not a sexual act, she snapped at herself.

She ordered herself to brazen it out, already, and made herself turn her back to him as if she had all the confidence in the world and he was the one finding it hard to keep his tongue in his mouth.

And as if she wasn't casually exposing the whole of her backside to him, with nothing but one fragile string across her back and another around her hips to break up his view of...all of her.

She was facing the sea. Her eyes hurt, from all

that glare and deep blue, but she didn't shut them. She didn't dare.

That felt too much like surrender.

Her heart kicked at her, anticipation and something else she wasn't sure she could name clattering around inside her and leaving chinks wherever it hit. She heard a click when he opened the tube of lotion. The squeaking sound of the tube as he squeezed it.

Then there was nothing but the breeze dancing up from the sea, smelling of salt and green. The fragrance of all those brightly colored flowers she couldn't name because they didn't bloom in cold, wet Glasgow or gray London. The rattling sounds of the coconuts in the trees, the restless rattling of the palms. She could hear raucous birds in the distance, and the tumble of the surf, but there was nothing else beyond it or beneath it.

No traffic. No sirens. No people.

She felt as if she was standing on the edge of the world, and worse still, a steep and dangerous cliff as beguiling as it was deadly. The devil behind her, the blue sea before her, and her own treacherous body smack in the middle.

This time, when she broke out in goose bumps, she knew he could see them. His low, rich chuckle tumbled over her like a different kind of touch altogether.

Lucinda didn't have time to fight it off, because that was when his hands made contact.

And she stopped breathing.

He started at her neck. He traced the delicate column down, then spread his big, wide palms out to take in her shoulders. His palms were hot, hotter than the sun beating down from above, and spread fire everywhere they touched.

And they touched everything. Every inch.

He traced her shoulder blades, then moved farther down, all along the indentation of her spine. Then he tracked the flare of her hips.

He covered every inch, then moved lower still. He paused to get more lotion, then slicked those hard, intensely masculine hands over the curves of her ass.

Lucinda…fell.

Right off that edge into sheer insanity.

She stopped worrying about trifling concerns like goose bumps. She stopped trying to control her breath. She let go of her threadbare control as she tumbled fast and hard over the side of the cliff she'd imagined in her head, and the world disappeared.

There was nothing but here, now.

There was nothing but Jason Kaoki and his talented, impossibly calloused and tender hands, working their way over every square inch of her overheated skin. He didn't linger anywhere in particular, which made all the places that longed for his attention heat up, as if in protest.

And deep inside her, something turned over, then

began to hum like an engine, low and insistent and wired to the soft heat between her legs.

He smoothed his palms down the backs of her thighs, the hollow of knees that already felt too weak, and then down to her calves.

"Turn around," he ordered her, his voice like gravel.

It didn't occur to Lucinda to disobey.

She turned and instantly everything was worse. Or maybe better. Certainly hotter, because now there was no pretending that she was standing by herself on the edge of the world having erotic daydreams of a man's touch.

A touch she could feel cascading over her, through her, then deep into her. Making her quiver, deep in her pussy. Making her want to shift, run— *something* to release the impossible pressure building inside her—

Because he was right there in front of her, big, brawny and almost indescribably beautiful.

Jason crouched down before her, so tall that he still came up to her chest. And he was so close that when he slicked more lotion on his hands, then looked up, the world shuddered to a halt.

That pulsing pressure between her legs grew. She could feel it in her toes. Her breasts. Her stiff nipples.

His eyes were dark fire. And she could see, so clearly, all the things he wanted. All the images that were chasing each other around and around inside his head, as if they were both watching the same movie that starred the two of them.

But he didn't do anything except reach for her foot, then start making his way up one leg. Then down the next.

Each slick slide of his big hand over her flesh made her…tremble. Each lazy, smooth bit of heat collected in her pussy and made her clench her thighs to keep from surrendering to all that pressure and need and longing.

When he reversed direction and shifted his attention to her belly, he slowed down. Or time did.

Lucinda knew she was breathing too fast. That she was showing too much and surrendering whatever claim to power she'd had inside.

That it was entirely possible her body was about to betray her, right here and now.

But she couldn't seem to stop herself.

And she couldn't seem to care, either. Something she was sure would concern her when this was over. But he was moving higher now, smoothing his way over the slopes of her breasts, and her mind went blank.

Blank…yet full of color and sensation, all of it spiraling down through her body to wind her tighter and tighter. Her clit was so ripe and ready she might simply tip over that edge all on her own the next time she squeezed her thighs together.

But she didn't. Somehow, she didn't.

His hands were wicked and left her shaking, yet he never went too far. He was restrained if not strictly clinical—but that only made the heat and need between her legs worse.

He slicked the lotion, smelling of coconut, over the exposed curves of her breasts and then moved higher, as if he was unmoved either way. Which only made Lucinda feel more exposed. Time ground to a halt as he worked, until there was nothing but the sound of her own breath, the beat of her heart and the rough slide of his fingers over her skin.

She could feel every touch as if those talented fingers were working her clit.

And she shuddered, close. So close—

"Give me your face," he ordered her, his voice gruff, and Lucinda didn't understand why it felt like some kind of surrender when she obediently inclined her head toward him.

Or why she felt like this was another frankly sexual act, the way he smoothed the last of the lotion over her forehead, then her cheeks and jaw. He took extra care with her ears, carefully covering the strip of space behind each one, and even ran his palms over her hair.

And when he was done, he moved his hands back to her cheeks and held her face there.

And everything in Lucinda...throbbed. She could feel it in her breasts, her clit and everything in between. She could feel that shuddering inside her, tipping her toward that edge again, sweeping over her and through her in a trembling rush.

Bright and hot and like some kind of madness, caught up in the light and the breeze and the tumbling waves behind her.

So close— So close—

And she knew full well it wasn't the scenery that made her shiver, it was the man kneeling before her.

Jason studied her, his dark gaze frank and carnal, and the heat of his palms made her ache. Her breasts were too full, her belly quivered uncontrollably, and her pussy was soaking wet with molten heat.

And her clit was a breath away from taking her over.

She wanted him. All of him, so huge and hard and outside her experience in a thousand different ways. Lucinda had no time for seduction. She preferred to throw back a few drinks, then find a likely lad in an upscale bar. Back to his to get off, then out the door.

This felt nothing like any of those half-drunk encounters, with Lucinda always on top and in control, then gone.

This felt like melting. This felt wrong, somehow, but delicious all the same, a part of the bright sun and the palm trees overhead and the insistent caress of the air all around her.

Thousands upon thousands of miles away from everything she knew.

Lucinda felt electric and helpless all at once and told herself she hated the sensation.

But that was another lie.

The truth was that scalding, insistent heat between her legs.

She was *so close*—

But she refused.

She refused to come like this, from suntan lotion and his hands on her skin. She refused to allow herself to lose the game like that, before she'd even begun to play it. She refused to hand over control.

She refused.

Her gaze locked to his, she made herself breathe. She found the rising crest of that tide and somehow, someway, pushed it back.

Before it could sweep her away where she stood.

And for a moment there was nothing but the little bit of space between them and the fact she hadn't come. Because she, by God, was in control of something here. Not the heat. Not what she was wearing. Not whether or not he'd let her build her hotel.

But Lucinda would come when she wanted to come, thank you.

"Let's go, darlin'," Jason said, low and dark, with too much knowing heat in his gaze and in the curve of his beautiful mouth. Especially when she stared back at him in challenge, daring him to call her on what she'd done. "It's time to get you out in the water."

CHAPTER SIX

THE WAVES USUALLY brought him nothing but peace.

No matter what else might have been going on in his life—whether it was football, or simply existing on the mainland that always seemed so far removed from anything he knew—Jason had always found his place in the water. Give him a board and a free hour and he'd find a wave. And with it, a way to get back to what mattered.

But he'd miscalculated with Lucinda.

He kept thinking she would back down. But she didn't.

He never expected her to put on that bikini and come back out of the office. And once she had, and he'd predictably lost his shit, he'd figured she'd draw the line at his putting his hands all over that tight, curvy little body of hers.

Instead, she'd refused to give in to the wild heat that was still blazing between them. And she'd come out of it a little bit flushed with SPF 50 all over her, while he felt like a sixteen-year-old kid with a boner in gym class.

It would have been funny if it was happening to someone else.

"I don't know how to surf," she announced.

He'd hauled two surfboards down to the water's edge, pretending the whole time that he wasn't going out of his way to make himself busy with this most minor form of manual labor just to see if he could calm the fuck down. Newsflash: he wasn't calm.

Jason shot her a glance. She was standing there with the Pacific licking at her toes. There was nothing but a string separating her ass cheeks, and her breasts in the bikini top were valiantly fighting gravity. And still she was talking down to him like she was the queen of fucking England.

"I know how to swim. But I've never surfed." Her blue eyes glinted, a lot like the sunlight on the Pacific all around her, and filled with the same intense challenge. "I've never quite seen the point, if I'm honest."

"You don't look for the point in surfing, you just surf. The point finds you when you're ready."

"That almost sounds philosophical."

"If you need me to write you a poem about the communion between the waves and the rush, the sea and the sky, you're never going to get it. And if you're never going to get it, you might as well get the fuck off my island, Lucinda. Now."

Once again, he expected her to look a little bit

cowed at that. So of course she didn't. "I don't need poetry. But some basic instruction might not go amiss."

He was getting wound up, and that wasn't him. And it wasn't smart, either.

Jason had never let his emotions get the best of him. Emotions were fuel, nothing more, and this was no time to change that. Because this woman might look like a sweet dollop of cream slapped down in the middle of the Pacific for no other purpose than to get him hard—to look him in the eye and refuse to come for him—but that wasn't why she was here. She wasn't a wet dream come to life. She was one more shark dressed up in business clothes, looking to make him a developer dickhead, just like the old man who was nothing to Jason but a sperm donor.

Fuck Daniel St. George, and fuck Lucinda Graves, too.

For some reason, he didn't just up and say that.

"Surfing is like most things in life," he growled instead, scowling at her. "It's as simple or as complicated as you make it. All you have to do is balance on the board, then stand up and keep balancing. Once you do that, you ride the waves. That's it. That's the secret. But how well or how badly you do that entirely depends on you."

That chin of hers, entirely too aggressive for a tiny slip of a woman who was likely only as dangerous as that red hair of hers was real, lifted. Suggesting to him that maybe the hair really was natural.

"I have excellent balance, actually."

He shouldn't have found that at all entertaining. "Do you, now?"

"I come from a long line of ornery Scottish Highlanders, as a matter of fact. What that means is that I can drink wee drams of whiskey all night long and still walk a straight line." She lifted one milky white shoulder, then dropped it. "Balancing on a bit of water should be nothing."

He laughed at her. Loud and long, and he wasn't even performing his laugh the way he often did around people who were interested less in him and more in the things he had—his celebrity, his money, his island. It was genuine this time, and like the hard-on that wouldn't go away, it told him things about this woman and her effect on him that should have scared the crap out of him.

But he was too busy laughing. "I like your confidence."

She smiled at that, which didn't do anything for his self-control. "I would have thought it was pretty clear that any woman willing to travel forty hours to meet a man who was as likely to kick her off his island as say hello didn't lack for confidence."

There was some kind of foreboding kick in him at that, like an alarm. It went off, and there was no pretending otherwise, but Jason didn't heed it.

He heeded a different urge entirely and reached over to smooth his hand over her sleek red hair, hot in the sunshine and still tied back so tightly to the back of her head, like the world would end if it ever tumbled down.

And he knew. One way or another, he was going to get his hands in all that hair and bring it down out of that tight-assed bun. He could picture it so clearly. Lucinda riding him, those perfect breasts right there to get his mouth on, that hair around him like a curtain, and his cock so deep inside her that he was half-blind with it.

He felt half-blind now. And he knew.

It was only a matter of time.

But that time wasn't now. And he was going to have to find a way to cut down on all those complications he didn't want to feel, but did, before they wrecked him. Because he had no intention of letting this woman—or any woman—wreck him.

That line of thought should have been sobering, but he was in it now. He wanted his hands all over her, and the truth was that Jason had grown accustomed to getting what he wanted.

Go big or go home, motherfucker, he told himself.

"Enough talking," he drawled at her.

He nodded at the surfboard at her feet. Then stood there, making no particular attempt to hide his smirk as Lucinda eyed the board as if she expected it to rise from its slumber and turn into some kind of alligator. Jaws and all.

But, of course, she didn't ask for any help. She

didn't argue with him. She set her jaw at a mutinous angle and then she awkwardly dragged the board into the water, hurling herself through the breakers with more ruthless determination than any kind of skill.

He was impressed despite himself, because hard-headed women hit him straight in his sweet spot. Whether he liked it or not.

Jason followed, throwing himself on his board and paddling out into the lagoon, keeping an eye on his redhead as she splashed around, making more noise than headway.

"Do you need me to tow you out?" he asked after watching her flail, his voice just silky enough to make her glare at him.

"Well, I don't know how to answer that, do I?" she retorted, and he was delighted to hear more Scotland in her voice than before.

That told him two things about her, and fast. One, she had the exact simmering, redheaded temper he'd imagined she did, which made him that much more motivated to experiment with all that fire and fury in bed. And two, that just as he had been forced to ease up on his Hawaiian pidgin and so-called "surfer" accent when he'd headed to the mainland—because all those haole fuckers interpreted his way of talking as evidence of stupidity—Lucinda had clearly done something similar with her accent. He didn't have to know the history of the United Kingdom to figure that anyone who could sound like that redheaded Disney princess in the cartoon one minute, then cover it up like she belonged on the BBC the next, had a lot of the same issues he did.

Of course, imagining that their issues matched— or should, if he looked hard enough—told him any number of things about himself he had zero interest in analyzing just then.

"Are you asking me for help, Scotland?" he asked lazily, ignoring the tightening sensation in his chest as he sat up on his board and relaxed into the roll of the waves beneath him. "Or are you just complaining?"

"It's evidently quite important to you that I make a fool out of myself according to your preferred method. I wouldn't wish to let you down."

"I'm out in the water with a nearly naked woman. What letdown are you worried about? The worst thing that's going to happen to you is that you fall off, and if there's a God, lose that bikini. I'm here for it."

She raised two fingers at him, but he somehow didn't believe that she was making that particular V for victory.

And then he sat back and laughed himself silly as his angry, no longer dour or businesslike redhead tried to hurl herself up onto her surfboard.

He lost track of how many times she scrabbled up, then tried to get to her feet, only to lose her balance and have the board shoot out from under her.

She fell over and over, splashing into the waves

and then paddling furiously to the surface, but she always tried again. She kept muttering out filthy curses in that increasingly more obvious accent of hers, one after the next. Sounding more and more Scottish as she went.

Jason sat back on his own surfboard, busting a gut laughing and watching the show. When she fell for approximately the nine millionth time, he reached out and caught the tip of her board with one hand as it shot away from her. And he studied her when she bobbed up to the surface, rising and falling with the swell of the water.

"You about ready to admit defeat?"

She bared her teeth at him. "Death first."

But when she swam over to climb up onto her board again, he reached down and hooked her under one arm. Then hauled her out of the water, up and onto his board. He settled her between his legs, then he reached over and clipped her surfboard to his, countering the jerky little movements she made with his thighs.

"Are you trying to dump us both in the water?" he asked lazily enough, and snaked an arm around her waist, pulling her back against him. "I don't think you understand balance. Maybe in a global sense."

"Let me guess. You're going to teach me. It's my lucky day."

Jason figured it was his lucky day, anyway. She was sleek and wet. The breeze had dried him off, which meant she was cool against his chest, and fit there between his thighs a little too perfectly. He wanted to settle his mouth in that place where her neck joined her shoulder. He wanted to push her forward onto her hands, lift that fine ass of hers and settle into her from behind—and who cared if they drifted all the way out to sea?

But he did none of those things, because he was a goddamn saint.

"Settle down, Scotland." She wiggled a little, then stopped when he pressed his thighs tighter against her, and he liked that a whole lot more than was wise. "You need to stop thinking about all the ways you can conquer the surfboard, and more about the way the water's going to conquer you if you don't respect it a little more."

She scowled over her pale shoulder, gleaming with a new spray of golden freckles. "I thought the entire point of surfing was conquering the bloody water."

"We already covered this. Stop looking for *the point*. Start looking for balance. And because I can tell you're not going to get this, balance isn't about conquering anything. It's about letting yourself become a part of it and taking what you need."

This time, Lucinda sighed. "Nothing in your portfolio suggested you were a new-age hippie."

She sounded appalled.

Jason laughed again, and had the distinct pleasure

of feeling the way she shivered in response, right there against him. He could see the goose bumps that rose on her neck and snaked down her arms. He was fascinated and more than a little hot himself, but somehow kept himself from licking them up with his tongue.

"I'm not a hippie, darlin'. I'm Hawaiian."

He moved then, setting her farther in front of him on the board, liking how easy it was to lift her and move her where he wanted her. Then he jackknifed himself up, bringing his feet out of the water and onto the board, then standing in a single swift movement that he'd practiced so many times it didn't require thought. And before she could comment on it or jerk around on the board, he reached down and picked her up, too.

"What are you *doing*?"

And Jason knew that she had no idea how panicked she sounded, or she would probably have bitten off her own tongue.

He kept hold of her. "Relax."

"Right. Because, first of all, everyone relaxes on command. The best thing to say to someone when they're not relaxed, in fact, is *relax* in exactly that tone. That does the trick, every time."

"Stop talking, Lucinda."

He pulled her close to him again, with one big hand on that soft, sweet belly of hers. And he wanted nothing more than to eat up the way she shuddered, then flushed red. Everywhere.

But he didn't put his mouth on her the way he wanted to do. Instead, he held her there, keeping the board balanced beneath them as they floated.

"You don't fight the waves. Fighting them is a quick way to end up face down in the water. You feel them. Every one of them."

He could feel her tense. Every sweet little curve of that lush body of hers, wound up and ready to fight no matter what he said. But instead of hurling something back at him, she only shuddered again, holding her arms out from her sides.

Like she'd seen surfing on television once.

"Good girl," he murmured approvingly, and then grinned at the little noise she made in response to that. "Balance," he said again. "You're never going to beat a wave into submission. But you can ride it."

And for a while, all they did was stand there like the surfboard was a paddleboard and let the ocean do its thing. One wave after another lifted them up, then brought them down again. Over and over, without end.

It was the rhythm of his life. It was his own heartbeat, there in his chest.

It was what brought him back to himself and it was why he'd come here, where no one was around to snap pictures of him or get in his face about his father or football or both, so he could find that heart-beat again.

But helping Lucinda find that same rhythm charmed him, somehow. And made his actual beat a little faster.

Eventually, Jason let go of her and let her find her feet on her own. Once she got the hang of that, he jumped off the board, leaving her to do it on her own. When she had that down, he unclipped the boards and pulled himself onto the other one so he could watch her.

"Now what?" she demanded, her body in the cor-rect position, if far too rigid. And the frown on her face a clue that she wasn't anywhere close to relaxed or balanced.

But he gave her points for trying.

He pointed at the water. "Now you jump in and climb up on your own."

It took her a few tries to get in the water and pull herself out, then stand up on the board, finding her feet beneath her.

"Good job," he said. "Now you catch a wave."

"'Catch a wave,'" she muttered, as if he'd said *catch a star*, or something. "Right. I'll just *catch one*, shall I?"

But he knew she would, because for all the mut-tering and the scowling, she kept trying. She never flipped out. She simply fell down and got up again. Over and over and over.

It was impossible not to admire her.

Or want to get his hands on her again, with more desperation than he was comfortable admitting, even out here where there no witnesses to his foolishness but the waves and the sky.

"You're going to start paddling," he told her. And realized when he heard the intensity in his own voice that he was entirely too invested in this woman doing the very thing he'd wanted her to fail at before. He wanted her to get up. He wanted her to ride the wave. He wanted her, and he didn't know how to handle that. So he ignored it. "When you feel the wave pick you up, you get up and you ride. Got it?"

"It's that simple, is it?"

Though her voice was skeptical, they had been out in the water too long. No matter how grumpy she sounded, she obeyed him.

Jason liked that a whole lot more than he should have.

"It's that simple," he promised her. Gruffly.

And when the next wave came, he put his hand on the back of her board and threw her into it.

Then watched with an intoxicating mix of pride and greed as his tight-assed little redhead pulled herself up, balanced herself beautifully and rode her first wave all the way into shore.

CHAPTER SEVEN

LUCINDA HAD EXPECTED surfing to be a grim, brutal exercise.

Like anything else she had done to claw her way and her current position, she'd assumed it would be unpleasant and if she was lucky, she could look back on it with a certain smugness born of having survived it. There was always some or other feat to perform, so she could prove herself to whoever it was who held the thing she wanted and thereby convince them to give it to her.

There was always a test. Always a series of hoops to leap through.

She'd expected surfing, of all things, and in a micro-bikini, to be no different.

It had never even crossed her mind that she might enjoy doing something she'd always viewed as remarkably, even laughably, pointless.

But the truth was, it felt like flying.

Better.

And at some point, she would have to think about

Jason's laughter, or the way he touched her. The way he pulled her against his body and the unmistakable proof of his arousal that he'd neither thrust against her nor hidden. Nor, for that matter, apologized for.

As if all that sexual awareness that wound around the two of them was as matter-of-fact as the water. The sky. Just nature, doing its thing.

She would have to think about all of that, certainly. And she'd been firing off speeches in her head, one after the next, each more haughty and self-possessed than the last—

But then she caught that wave.

And everything changed.

Because it felt better than flying.

It felt like joy.

Something in her chest expanded, bigger and brighter than anything she'd ever felt before, until she was sure her ribs had to crack wide open to let it out.

It was that mad hurtle, blue below and blue above, in a rush of exhilaration.

When she made it to shore that first time, she turned right around and headed back out.

And did it again and again.

The truth was, she never wanted it to end.

There were too many things to think about once she came out of the water. Her position at her company. Her ambition. What she had riding on convincing an impossible man to do something he very clearly didn't want to do. The fact she hadn't slept or ate in a very, very long time.

Too many things, none of which seemed to matter or stick to her as she let the waves lift her and hurl her toward the sand as if she was one of them.

It wasn't until Jason caught her by the arm, after her last marvelous ride that was still humming in her and making her giddy, that she came back down to earth with a thud. Or maybe it wasn't earth, exactly, with that big hand wrapped around her upper arm and his dark gaze on hers.

And in her, too.

Reminding her of what had almost happened earlier with an electric jolt.

She'd lost track of how much time she'd spent out on the water. How many times she'd let the waves pick her up and take her on that amazing rush of a journey. But she knew it was enough that she'd completely forgotten to grumble to herself about what a chore it was to have to prove herself to yet another man with power over her.

That should have scared her, but she'd forgotten to let that happen, too.

She'd been aware of Jason, of course. She'd been simply riding the waves as she caught them and proud of herself that she stayed standing, but he was...art.

As if he and that board and the sea were all one,

working together to create a kind of magic. Art and skill and raw beauty blended into one—

But it didn't pay to think too closely about Jason Kaoki, Lucinda reminded herself sharply. It made her aware of the way the sun felt heavy on her eyelids, as if all that shine had weight. Of the greedy thing between her legs that pulsed and hummed, hot and ready, still.

This close, if she would just…

The fist of lust that punched deep into her gut, and didn't let go, seemed heavier than before. But she refused—again—to let it take her down.

"Enough." And his voice was another problem, heavy like the sun and with as much potential to scar her. "The tide's changing. And even if it wasn't, sunscreen doesn't last forever."

She might have argued with him—and she opened her mouth to do just that—but he didn't stick around to debate the matter. He scooped up her board under one arm, his under the other, and sauntered up onto the beach again as if neither one of them weighed more than a twig.

She followed him onto the sand, scowling and annoyed that she had no other option unless she wanted to float about like a hapless jellyfish. It wasn't until her feet sunk into the white sand again that she realized how deeply tired she was. But this time, in a different way than she'd been before, fresh off the plane.

This time it felt wilder. She was exhausted, yes,

but she still felt connected to the ocean all around them. Humming with it, somehow.

For some reason, that made her even more furious.

Jason walked up to the edge of the beach to put his surfboards onto a rack there, beneath a canopy stretched between two palm trees. And Lucinda followed because that was why she was here.

But suddenly, she was *outraged* by that fact. There was something scooped out and hollow beneath her ribs and it was making it hard to breathe.

"Did I pass your test?" she demanded, moving from the sand onto the grass, as he wrestled the boards into their proper places.

Well. He didn't *wrestle*. He was so strong the boards looked like they were made of Styrofoam.

Lucinda had been gearing up to unleash a little of her temper, but she couldn't seem to hold on to whatever had been poking at her as she'd trudged across the sand. Instead, she was caught by the play of muscle, brown skin and dark black tattoos that made up his astonishing back.

She felt her own breath go shallow. And that hollow place inside her chest changed, too. Intensified, maybe, until it was gleaming and wild and intimately connected to that delicious ache in her pussy.

This is a professional interaction, no matter how unorthodox, she lectured herself.

But she was standing there practically naked with some wild current she barely understood streaking through her like lightning, one strike after the next, and words like *professional* didn't seem to have much meaning.

Jason turned back to her at last, raking that dark hair back from his face.

He was so beautiful she thought her knees might give out. She could admit that to herself, but she was made of sterner stuff than that.

She'd already proved it once today, when she'd refused to let herself come simply because he was touching her. She would keep proving it, because collapsing at his feet in a heap of sunburned flesh and legless need wasn't quite the power play she was going for here.

"Well?" She made her voice much sterner than she felt, and told herself feeling anything at all was a betrayal. "Did I acquit myself appropriately? This was a game to you, I assume. Did I win?"

"You got to spend hours surfing at an unspoiled beach pretty much by yourself," he replied, his lazy drawl made of pure fire while his dark eyes glittered. "Some people would call that winning."

"What would you call it?"

"A decent start."

Her heart thumped at that, hard. Because that wasn't a demand that she leave, and now. It wasn't a smirk and a *no*. And anything that wasn't a direct no was just a yes in waiting, her first boss had always said.

Lucinda had taken that to heart. She smiled at him, and reminded herself that she was, in fact, practically naked. Why not use it?

Maybe her smile got a little flirty. Maybe she shifted her weight to her advantage. Whatever worked.

"Does that mean you plan to give me more opportunities to convince you, I hope? Or will I have to fly back to Fiji on a tiny little puddle jumper wearing nothing but this?"

She didn't know why she said that, much less in that tone—not *breathy*, because she was a woman of action who was never breathy, but it was close.

Until his expression changed, that was.

That smile of his turned dangerous and there was something about the way he held that predator's body of his. She couldn't have explained to another person what it was, or how it changed, only that it did.

With almost too much heat to bear. So much heat she was terribly afraid she would melt into a puddle right there at his feet.

Part of her even thought that would be a relief. Then she'd simply evaporate and not have to navigate this electric, sensual line with him.

"The bikini belongs to me, Lucinda," Jason said after a long, hot moment with his gaze all over her like she was already naked and spread out beneath him. "I don't think I'd like it to wander off to Fiji."

She had the insane, likely overly optimistic thought that he wasn't actually talking about a bloody swimsuit.

"Excellent," she said, instead of giving in to all that melting. Even though her eyes felt slicked with it. And her nipples were so tight they hurt. "Shall I pick a room in the hotel, then?" His gaze darkened, which shouldn't have been possible, and she hurried on. "To stay in, of course, while I try to convince you."

"Only if you want to camp out with no electricity or running water."

She shrugged, and wasn't the only one who was entirely too aware of how her breasts swayed with the movement.

"Is that another test?" She tried to make herself sound bored. Or unbothered, at the very least.

"Why would your ability to squat in an abandoned building convince me of anything?"

"Why did you insist we get in the water? That seems even more random, doesn't it?"

She expected a lazy smile. Some throwaway comment. But instead, something flashed across Jason's fallen-angel face that she wished she could understand.

"I learned a lot about you out there. You're tenacious. Stubborn as hell, in fact, but when given new information, you don't insist on clinging to the old. You're adaptable. And you're not afraid to use your body. Or throw yourself face-first into new sensation."

Her heart was acting up again, but she didn't want to follow the sudden urge she had to reach up and cover it with her palm. Because he saw too much already, and he didn't need to know how vulnerable she felt.

She wished she didn't know it.

"All that from a dip in the sea and some paddling about?" It was a fight to keep her voice light. "What's next? Will you tell me all the details of my childhood trauma after you watch me walk along a garden path?"

"Maybe later."

He reached out then, and Lucinda knew with every cell in her body that she should dodge that hand of his. She should do whatever it took to keep him from touching her, because if he did, again, she would…but she didn't dare finish that thought. And she didn't dodge him, either.

Just as she didn't question why she'd raised the issue of childhood trauma in the first place.

Or why that heat in his dark gaze gleamed with something new then that looked far too much like compassion.

She wanted to scream at that until it went away, but she didn't do that either.

"I'm hungry, Lucinda. Are you?"

Even as Jason asked that question, his hand curled around one side of her neck, his thumb moving up and across her jaw to trace her bottom lip.

Once, then again.

Lucinda understood that she had only played with fire before. Sunscreen, his hands and jumping on and off surfboards in a friendly sort of sea the temperature of a bath. All very tame, really.

Because it was nothing next to this.

He was staring down at her, his mouth unsmiling and a blaze in his dark gaze.

As if he was daring her not to burn into ash where she stood.

Some part of her thought it was already too late.

"To clarify," she heard herself ask in her most prissy, posh, put-on British accent, "are you talking about food, then? Or…?"

"Hunger is hunger, Scotland."

"I feel certain there's an argument to be made there. But either way, I like to be prepared."

She had the sense of his laughter, that great, glorious, raucous sound that could scare the birds from the trees, though he didn't make any noise. Still, it was there in his dark eyes. In the way he looked down at her, his wide shoulders blocking out the sky.

"I'm hungry," he told her, his voice as black and rich as the volcanic rock scattered all over the island, looking deceptively soft when it was the opposite. "I want food. And then, like as not, I'm going to want to fuck. But I think you know that already."

His thumb moved lazily over her jaw, as if he was already moving inside her. As if it was a preview of that thick, deep surge she was already imagining.

Obsessively.

And Lucinda's mouth was too dry. She couldn't

seem to find her tongue. She couldn't tell where she ended and he began, not when there was so much blazing tension between them that it felt like some kind of new element. Volcanic like everything else here.

"I take it that you mean me," she said, what felt like a thousand years or so later. In a thin, reedy sort of voice that didn't sound like hers at all. "You want to feed me. And then…"

"Fuck," he supplied without a shred of shame, a hint of a curve in the corner of his mouth. "Yes, Scotland. I want to fuck you. A lot."

"Is this how you negotiate, generally speaking?"

"It hasn't been. But there's something about you that makes me want to make an exception."

She should have been horrified. Outraged and appalled, certainly. She should have screamed *me too* in his face and taken to the internet in a blaze of fury. But once again, she seemed to lack a certain affronted prudishness. A weapon was a weapon, after all.

And she was the one in a string bikini with her ass hanging out. An outfit she had chosen to wear, then frolic about in, when she could so easily have declined his offer and played it from there.

She hadn't wanted to decline. She'd wanted what she'd gotten, which was his full and unwavering attention.

She still wanted it.

But she also wasn't an idiot.

"And what happens if I fuck you?" she asked, and it was her turn to sound a little lazy. "Do I get to build my resort in all this paradise?"

He laughed at that, out loud this time, and sure enough a set of birds pelted themselves out of the nearest tree, squawking all the way. "That would have to be some fuck. Are you sure you can live up to that standard?"

"Are you afraid you can't?"

This time, his laughter was a dark flame all its own.

And she was running out of ways to burn. Lucinda was beginning to worry that the only logical next step was implosion.

"I don't really do tit for tat," Jason drawled, his hand still hot and pressed against her skin. "As tempting as it sounds, I don't use my dick as currency. Which is a good thing for you, darlin', because I don't think you could afford me."

She opened her mouth, but he shifted his thumb and pressed it against her lips, shutting her up.

But she could have stepped back. She could have slapped his hand away. Hell, she could have bit him.

All of those things would require she want him to let go of her, however. And Lucinda...didn't.

"Here's how this is going to go down," Jason said, all rumble and dark promise. "I'm going to take you back to my house, which has food, electricity and a shower. My buddy already flew back to Fiji today.

One way or another, you're spending the night. How you want to spend it, and where, is up to you."

"But the resort—"

He shook his head. "I don't do strings, Lucinda. Or bargains. I'll let you decide if you think getting a piece of that ass will soften me up or not. I can't guarantee it either way."

"What if that's not good enough for me?"

And somehow she wasn't surprised when all Jason did was shrug, then drop his hand. "It wouldn't be the first time I used my hand. I know it won't be the last. I'll live."

And then he turned and left her there as he headed back up toward the empty hotel.

"Am I supposed to follow you?" she called out after him. "Is this yet another test?"

He turned back, though he didn't stop walking, and his smile was enough to make her heart stop, as wide as the arms he stretched out like he was taking over the whole damned world.

Or maybe just her.

The bastard.

"You need to do you, Scotland," he told her, but there was that laughter in his voice again, as if he already knew what she'd choose. As if all of this was inevitable. "I already told you what I want. The question you need to ask yourself is what you want in return."

CHAPTER EIGHT

Before she'd set foot on this island, Lucinda had known exactly what she wanted. It had been a clear path: find Jason Kaoki on his private island, convince him to build the resort of her dreams, ascend to a higher, better level of the life she'd always wanted. And in all those hours of travel, it had never occurred to her that things might go differently—because she was very, very good at getting what she wanted.

That was how she'd risen out of her dreamless, upsetting childhood in the first place.

Now she was running on a combination of fumes and *surfing* and Jason Kaoki's dangerous hands all over her might-as-well-be naked body—and that straight, obvious path seemed a good deal less clear.

She ordered herself to get her head on straight, but after all that time tumbling around and around in the sea, she wasn't sure what direction that was anymore. She followed Jason back up into the dim hotel lobby instead, hanging back as he went into the office and reemerged with a soft pile of dark black that it took her moments to realize were her own clothes.

And surely she should have been embarrassed by the fact that he was now holding her panties and bra in those hands of his... But she was all embarrassed out, it seemed. That was what happened when a person spent hours barely dressed in a string bikini, climbing on and jumping off a surfboard out in the water. She had precious few inhibitions left. Lucinda eyed the clothes in his hands. Then she lifted her gaze to the fire in his and let the flames simmer there between them for another breathless moment that felt a whole lot like forever.

At some point she would have to get used to all this...intensity, wouldn't she?

Or it will kill you, a dour voice inside her chimed in.

Jason didn't say a word. He came back around the counter and thrust her clothes into her arms. Though he didn't explicitly tell her to follow him, Lucinda felt that was his clear intention when he moved toward the doors. She found herself hurrying along behind him, having to work overtime to keep up with his long, deep stride though she'd always considered herself a fast walker. He was just that tall. A saunter on him made her have to think about running.

And there was no reason that innocuous, innocent thought should have made her breath catch again, but it did.

He waited when they reached her bag as she bent down and shoved her armful of clothes into its main compartment. And when she straightened, he swept the bag up in one hand and headed back out into the sun. It struck Lucinda as a kind of thoughtless, matter-of-fact chivalry. As if he hardly knew he was doing it.

And it made her throat ache, because she was used to doing for herself in all matters, great and small. Her father had never carried a thing but his own drink. The many men she'd worked for had never offered any kind of courtesy without strings attached. There were no offhanded displays of chivalric impulses.

Lucinda had to frown ferociously to keep that same ache from flooding her eyes, thank you, sure that this was more evidence that she needed to sleep—and fast—before she became someone else entirely. Someone soft and feminine and fluttery who might actually weep over a man carrying her bag.

The very idea should have made her laugh.

It was surpassingly odd that she didn't.

She followed him instead. Jason didn't have any shoes on, but his bare feet were clearly used to the abuse of the old, cracked concrete outside, because he didn't slow down when he hit it. And by the time Lucinda picked her careful way after him on her soft, complaining toes, he had already gone around the side of the building. He disappeared beneath an overhang she hadn't noticed on her way in and drove back out again moments later in an open-topped Jeep.

He pulled up beside her, then looked at her like a cautionary tale brought to vivid life. He might as well have been waving a sign that read BEWARE STRANGE MAN IN CAR WHO WILL TURN YOU INSIDE OUT WITHOUT TRYING.

Lucinda assured herself it was no more than another Pacific breeze that trickled down the entire length of her back then, making her want to stiffen against it, then run for her life.

She did neither one of those things. Because she was on a deserted tropical island far, far away from anything and there was nowhere to run, for one thing. And because her feet were burning and walking around without any shoes on was surprisingly uncomfortable, for another.

She ignored the sensation flooding her, from the soles of her feet to her traitorously soft pussy and, higher still, to the heart that was going wild in her chest. At least none of these things showed, or she hoped they didn't, as she pulled open the passenger door—which took her a moment to locate, as it was on the wrong side of the vehicle—and climbed up beside him.

Very much as if she had her own sign, and it read something like ABSOLUTE IDIOT.

She was then deeply grateful that Jason drove a Jeep, because it was wide open to the island around them. And that meant that when he put it into gear and started driving, it was noisy. Too noisy for any more pointed, barbed conversation with all that fire between each syllable.

Lucinda didn't have to pretend to be cool, unbothered and aggressively at her ease. There was no conversation at all, so she wasn't required to watch her tone and mind her words. There was only the wind in her ears, tugging at her hair so that wet strands pulled free and blew all around her. She had seen this coveted spit of land from the air, a stunning little jewel in the middle of all that deep blue water, and she'd seen the pristine beaches all around.

But settled back in the passenger seat of Jason's Jeep that he navigated with one lazy arm looped over the steering wheel, she finally looked around and saw the island itself. There had once been an active volcano here, leaving the hills steep and covered in green all these years later. The jungle was everywhere, in the thick scent of growing things, the exultant plants and glorious flowers that Lucinda had never seen back home. They were too big here. Too bright, in too many colors.

The road, such as it was, hugged the beaches. Jason drove away from the old hotel, bumping his way over dirt and grass on the rutted track before rounding a point that stretched out into the water, made of the same dark, volcanic rock that burst out from beneath the green everywhere Lucinda looked.

When the road ended a while later, he turned up toward the hills. He wound his way around the side of another steep, green incline, climbing until they were far above the same rocky point they'd passed below.

The jungle opened up over a grassy bluff and the house that sat there, surrounded by gleaming green lawns that edged up against the thick jungle on all sides and nothing else in any direction but the brooding blue sea.

Lucinda caught her breath. It was the most beautiful house she'd ever seen in her life. It was all polished dark wood and windows, somehow looking as if it was meant to be here on the top of this mountain with a view of eternity. As if it had been crafted here, the same as the steep hills around it or the shore below.

The main house sprawled out in an easy sort of U shape, claiming the flattest part of the bluff. But Jason didn't drive up to the front door. He skirted the side of one wing, then drove a bit farther up the hill to one of several tidy, smaller houses that nestled half in and half out of the jungle.

"Shower, change, whatever," Jason told her after he'd leaped from the Jeep, carried her bag to the front door of the nearest cottage and swung it open for her. Lucinda trailed after him, feeling more than a little loopy, and telling herself it was the jet lag.

But as he towered there over her, blocking the door to the cutest little cottage she'd ever seen with those wide, sculpted shoulders of his, she acknowl-

edged that maybe the loopiness had nothing to do
with air travel or time zones at all.

That maybe, just maybe, it was him.

"Whatever," she said. Echoing him.

Or possibly, making a choice.

"There's a fully stocked bar." His dark eyes gleamed.
"Feel free to choose your poison. When you get hungry, come find me."

She turned because that was easier than holding
his gaze. She blinked at the great house that was now
below her, and the unbroken expanse of the Pacific
in the distance.

"Is it a game of hide-and-seek, then? Will you be
tucked away in a closet somewhere?"

"I'm not one for staying in the closet." He let out
a belt of that laughter of his that did things to her
defenses that she was afraid to look at too closely.
For fear that there would be nothing left but rubble
where they'd once stood. "I'm pretty much upright
and out loud about everything I do, Lucinda. That I
can promise you."

"If you don't hear from me for a week, you can
assume that I got lost in the west wing of your man-
sion and likely require medical assistance," Lucinda
replied crisply, because it was that or start wondering what sorts of things he was so up-front about.
So *out loud.* "Or am moldering away in the attic like
the family ghost."

"You won't have any trouble finding me. If you

could make it to the island, I figure you can make it through the house, too." His mouth curved. "And I don't believe in ghosts, either. If you want to haunt me, you can do it to my face."

"That's not really a haunting, then, is it?"

"Depends on how you do it," he said, all drawl and heat.

And Lucinda expected some kind of grand exit. Something suitably dramatic while she was still wearing so little, as a fitting end to this wild rush of a day. A fierce kiss, perhaps, to underscore his power—

Or your own longing, something inside her chimed in, much too knowingly.

But all he did was wheel around, then jump back into his Jeep with another display of that mouth-watering, athletic grace that she suspected she'd be replaying in her head for some time to come.

And he drove off, leaving Lucinda to stand there on the threshold of the lovely little cottage, vibrating with need and hunger and all kinds of things she had no intention of doing anything about. Ever. And certainly not with him.

No matter how much she wanted to.

Inside, the cottage had high ceilings with fans to move the air around and was done up in light colors to make it all seem that much breezier. She gave herself a stern talking-to as she wheeled her bag in, then set up in the master bedroom with its high bed and floating canopy, and a view from the windows that made her sigh.

She lectured herself into the bath, where she took a shower to get the salt out and combed her fingers through her hair at last, despairing of the state it would be in when she got out. Then she sat down for a soak in the tub, filling it with lovely potions that turned to bubbles, smelling of coconuts and fruity drinks.

And kept right on making speeches to herself.

Yes, she'd put on that bikini and pranced around, and she'd definitely encouraged his attention. Not to mention his hands on her.

It had been important to stay in control earlier. To keep herself from coming to prove that she could— and to further prove that he was only as in charge as she wanted him to be. She wasn't sure she believed that, entirely, but she'd wanted to prove it and she had. But now it was time for the next step. She had no qualm whatsoever with sleeping her way into the resort she wanted. She'd been accused of doing it a thousand times already, because she was a woman who'd risen through the ranks, and so many people imagined that could happen only one way.

It hadn't.

"Certainly not," she said out loud as she climbed out of the bath and wrapped herself in a big, fluffy towel, so soft it nearly made her eyes prick with those lurking tears. The very thought of sleeping with her selection of bosses was deeply, deeply unappealing—just as it had always been. "The suggestion was more than enough, thank you."

Lucinda had always held herself as perfectly willing to use her body to get what she wanted. She'd believed she would, given the right set of circumstances, because why not? It was her body to do with as she pleased.

She simply hadn't found the right circumstances.

Here in this cozy cottage tucked away in paradise, she worked a comb through the heavy, sodden mass of her hair and wondered if she'd finally found those circumstances. But unlike every other time she'd asked herself if she was ready to cross that line, she couldn't help but wonder if the fact she was leaning toward a no was about her sudden desire to be as professional as possible with a man who had no interest in rules, or—and something pinged in her when she got there—fear.

Because Jason was nothing like the men who had flirted with her before at all different levels of business. Jason bore no resemblance whatsoever to middle managers or overly familiar VPs.

Lucinda had never been afraid to use whatever weapon she had on hand, which had so far meant there had been no need to pull out the biggest guns. Not when it was so easy to smooth her way into a deal with a suggestive smile, or a bit of banter that Human Resources would likely frown upon.

Jason was different. He was significantly more frank and direct than any of the men she'd known. And she suspected that such frankness would translate into the way he touched her, too.

Hell, she already knew it would. She'd had actual sex with men that was less erotic and carnal than the way Jason had put smoothed sunscreen on her skin. He'd had her trembling on the edge of an orgasm without even touching her nipples or her clit.

Lucinda blew out a breath, aware that was shaky and insubstantial. It made her laugh at herself and all this...*tottering* she was doing here. As if the sand and the sea had taken her knees out from under her, or he had, and she couldn't find her way back to solid ground. But she had to, so she would.

Of course she would.

She left her hair in its natural state of despair, curling this way and that down past her shoulders, as she helped herself to one of the decadent robes hanging there in the bathroom suite. She slipped it on, then padded back out to the bedroom, sighing a little—again—as the view captured her. She didn't dare test out that bed, because she knew she wouldn't get up again if she lay down, so she moved to the big, French-style windows that made up the length of the cottage's outside wall, and pushed them open.

Once the windows were thrown wide, the bedroom sprawled out onto its own private lanai, with a trellis on one side covered in flowering vines and that glorious view everywhere else. She moved over to the chaise that had been set at the perfect angle to watch the sea and the sky and sat down for just a moment, pulling her legs up beneath her.

She meant to sit for only a second, to inhale that incredible view and maybe settle herself a bit while she did.

But when she opened her eyes again it was dark.

It was *dark*. There were more stars than she could make sense of up above her. And all her limbs were heavy, suggesting she'd been asleep for a long while.

Lucinda was confused, but she swung her feet around and got them on the floor again, realizing only as it bounced around her shoulders that her hair had dried on its own. She didn't have to look in a mirror, she knew what a horror she'd visited upon herself. It would be impossible curls for days, spiraling around all over the place and making her look like a banshee.

And nobody was looking to open a luxury resort with a banshee.

She felt stiff and far older than her twenty-eight years as she rose to her feet. She yawned so hard her jaw cracked and then her heart kicked at her, because she didn't know what day it was. Or what time it was.

Or if she'd missed her chance with Jason because she'd tumbled off into an unexpected sleep of the dead.

Talk about a rookie move.

Lucinda scrubbed her palms over her face, then staggered back into the bedroom. She swept up her watch from the nightstand where she'd left it, holding it as she kept going so she could peer out the front windows of the cottage. The main house sat there before her, lit up against the night. Better still, there were the perfect tiki torches of her dreams lighting up the path that led down to it.

A glance at her watch told her it was half past nine, coming up on ten.

She had slept for more than eight hours.

Straight. And possibly without moving.

She hurried back into the bedroom, flipping on the lights as she went. Then she stared at herself critically in the big mirror that was propped against the interior wall of the bedroom, no doubt to reflect the sea and the sky back to whoever stood there, the better to feel lost in all that blue.

But tonight she was more focused on the banshee before her and what she could do—and quickly—to sort out her appearance. Her hair would take hours to blow-dry and then straight-iron into submission. And Jason had made his derision about her professional clothes perfectly clear back at the hotel.

She didn't have to go through her bag to know that what she'd brought with her was little better. Lucinda had an office uniform she preferred and she wore it exclusively. She hadn't cared that everyone else had stripped down when the company had gone to Spain. She'd maintained her usual look. But for some reason, it all seemed wrong now she was here.

Or she did, now that she'd woken up in all this tropical splendor, with the night air soft and thick against her as she moved. The idea of trying to strap herself into a pencil skirt made her want to cry.

Which was obviously the hunger talking, she told herself sternly. Because despite evidence to the contrary on this island, Lucinda was no crier.

She went over to the closet in the bedroom and wasn't particularly surprised to find lengths of fabric hanging there when she opened the doors. Because of course every possible detail had been thought of here. This was exactly what she wanted a resort to feel like to its guests. Home, but better.

The fabric before her was as soft as it was appealing. Different sarongs, if she wasn't mistaken, in bright colors, featuring glorious printed flowers and vaguely tribal patterns. She chose something in blue, wrapping it around her breasts to make a sundress and tying it off with a knot. Her hair was more of a challenge, but she managed to scoop it all up. Then she fashioned a far messier sort of bun than she would ever have been caught dead in elsewhere, piled up high on top of her head.

And found herself breathless yet again, as she stared at the creature before her in that mirror.

She looked bohemian. Wild. She wasn't sunburned as she'd expected she would be—as she usually was

after any exposure—but her skin was no longer its
usual shade of shocking white. She almost…glowed.
And her freckles had come out, everywhere, making her look near enough to golden. If she squinted.

She hardly looked like herself, really.

And what was scariest about that was that the notion didn't terrify her the way she knew it would have
back in London. She had worked so terribly hard to
make herself the very particular, very sternly moni-
tored version of Lucinda Graves that she'd been for
years now—all work and very controlled play.

But she was in Jason's world now. And it didn't
matter whether or not she adhered to her own strict
standards. What mattered was that she found a way
to work her way into his.

This was nothing more than a costume.

"The proper uniform to get the job done," she told
herself staunchly.

But she was far too aware of the whisper of her
thighs against each other as she walked out of the
cottage and headed down the path into the sweet,
inviting night. She was aware of the movement of
her hair on her head, when she preferred to keep it
slicked down so tight and so hard that she never felt
it at all. She was aware of the air against her skin,
the breeze from the sea, carrying salt and green and
flowers to swirl all around her. Even the light seemed
different here, dancing on the end of the torches as
they lit her way. More mysterious. More seductive.

More dangerous, she snapped at herself.

When she made it to the house, it was wide open. What she'd taken to be windows from a distance were simply open spaces that let the night in. Living areas blended one into the next, rolling from one seating area to another, with nothing but high, arched ceilings above, ceiling fans everywhere, and the sense that she wasn't indoors at all. That this was just another part of the jungle.

Jason had said that it would be easy to find him, so she paused inside the first great room, then followed the only sound that she could hear over the kick of her heart. It was faint, metallic and musical. She made her way through a well-stocked library, a game room and then out onto another terrace arranged around a fire pit that felt as if it had been hewn from the mountain itself.

That was where she found him.

For a moment she could only stare, dimly aware that she'd come to a complete and sudden stop.

Jason looked as if he had been dreamed up by the island, by the jungle and the sea as one. He looked like a raw and elemental part of the same tropical wildness, out there against the night.

He had put on a pair of battered jeans that rode low on his hips, filled with holes and tatters, but nothing else. He held an electric guitar on his lap, but it wasn't plugged into anything. And he was playing it, picking out a tune as he sat before the lick of the fire, his bare feet propped up on the lip of the wall that surrounded the fire pit.

As if he'd been conjured from the flames.

His hair was down, too long and yet perfect for him. And if Lucinda had thought that he was beautiful with all that sunlight bathing him in brightness before, she had no words to describe what the night did. How the firelight moved all over him, making him look made of poured honey, all male and beautiful.

God help her, he was so absurdly, impossibly beautiful it hurt.

Just like this island.

She drifted closer because she couldn't seem to help herself, and she didn't have it in her to interrogate all the ways that should've sent her running for the hills. Maybe she'd slept it off. All she knew was that he called to her and he didn't have to say a word to do it.

"I had no idea you were musical," she said when she was close to him. Because that hadn't been in the extensive portfolio she'd compiled.

"I'm not. I just like to mess around."

He stopped playing, though he still held the guitar across his lap, and he turned that dark gaze to her.

Lucinda had no idea why she submitted herself to his scrutiny. Why she stood there before him and did absolutely nothing while his gaze...had its way with her. He took his time, looking her over from head to toe then back again, as if she was his.

As if she had never been anything but his, and never would.

And when his eyes met hers again, he was smiling.

She expected him to say something off-color. Something suggestive or unnervingly direct.

But instead, he nodded toward a table off to the side. "You look hungry."

It turned out she was ravenous. So starved, in fact, that she could hardly bother herself to see what he was doing as she went over to table laden high with more food than anyone could possibly have eaten at once, and dug in. She didn't ask how the hot things were hot and the cold things were cold. This was obviously the sort of place that was actually filled with staff, who were all the more impressive for remaining unseen. Unless…

"Did you cook all this?"

That laugh of his was her answer, and she shivered slightly as it scraped open the night.

"I'm good at a lot of things," Jason said, his dark, rich tone encouraging her to wonder exactly which things he meant. "But cooking is not one of them."

Lucinda was so hungry that she left that alone. She ate until she was full, and then she sat back, sighing in delight, and feeling more like herself than she had since she'd woken up in the dark, thick with confusion.

She rose again and picked her way back over to

the fire so she could drop down beside him on the low couch where he sat.

"I didn't mean to fall asleep," she said as he set his guitar aside. "I apologize. You shouldn't have had to wait around for me."

"I didn't." His dark gaze touched the side of her face, then returned to the fire. "I do live here."

And her belly was full. She was dressed like a stranger. There was no backtracking, so she might as well dive ahead.

"And why is that, exactly?" she asked, shifting so she could treat him to her own version of frank directness. "As far as I can tell you have no sentimental attachment to anything that was your father's."

"I hate that motherfucker," Jason agreed. Almost cheerfully, but the fire was full on his face and she could see the way his eyes narrowed. "The only reason I wish he was still alive is so I could tell him that to his face."

"You would actually tell him you hated him?" She considered. "Before or after you knew he planned to leave you something in his will?"

"I didn't want any part of that will and I still don't." Jason shrugged. "He made my mama cry. That's not something a man forgives."

"Did you know him at all when he was alive?"

Jason's expression grew impatient. "I'm pretty sure that any research on my life at all would give you the answer to that question. But no. I never met him. That was his thing. Get a woman pregnant, disappear and then leave the kid he made some money and a hotel in the will. And if I know anything about rich assholes, he thought that made up for his lack of parenting."

"Then I don't understand." Lucinda kept her voice quiet and her gaze steady. "If you have no sentimental attachment to this island, why not make it into a resort? And why come stay here?"

"This was the last place he built before he died." Again, that low growl of a voice tumbled over her, making her want to shiver. But she didn't. "It was suggested to me that whether I liked it or not, I was turning out more like the old man than I was comfortable with. I thought I'd come here, marinate in all things Daniel St. George and see if that was true."

"Did he spend a lot of time at his various properties alone?"

This time, Jason's laugh had an edge. "He wasn't much for alone time when there were so many women eager to keep him company."

"Let me make sure I'm following this. You hated your father. You hated everything he stood for, and everything he was."

"Dear old dad," Jason drawled in agreement. "The dick."

"So you're hiding out here, ten thousand miles away from anywhere, to make yourself feel bad. This entire island is a beach-laden hair shirt bristling with palm trees to you."

"I barely wear a shirt as it is. Certainly not a hair shirt."

"You must know that hotels were the only thing that Daniel St. George was any good at. And he was very, very good at hotels. Why shouldn't you reap the benefits of that?" Lucinda kept her gaze trained on him, pretending she didn't notice the temper that lurked there. The warning that she had already gone too far. "Especially when it's not as if you're saving this place as a tender, emotional monument to anything."

"Lucinda." And the way he said her name was its own shudder running through her, lighting her up. Reminding her that whatever else this man was, he wasn't entirely tame. And a smart woman would do well to remember that. "Why the fuck does this mean so much to you?"

CHAPTER NINE

"I'M SO GLAD you asked," Lucinda replied in the same slick way she'd said everything since she'd eaten, when Jason preferred her ruffled. Messy. Real. "You're a man who enjoys elite status. You must know that distinctive properties such as this one cater to—"

"No."

She stopped talking, blinking. Jason shook his head at her, ordering himself to calm down. Now.

It didn't matter that she'd wandered out here dressed for the islands at last, instead of some stuffy boardroom. Her flowing sarong reminded him how sweet her curves were, and how they felt beneath his hands, so lush and feminine. And her hair. He could see all the curl in it, a bright riot on top of her head, and he was this close to just putting his hands in it here and now the way he'd wanted to from the start.

She looked wild and delicious and he liked everything from the freckles all over her shoulders to the dazed way she'd looked at him when she'd walked out on this terrace. It all seemed to hum in him, then settle in his cock like a fist.

But none of it mattered if she was going to mouth all the same bullshit.

"I don't want a sales pitch," he said when he was reasonably sure that he was going to keep his hands to himself. For the moment. "I could get that any-where, and believe me, I have. You hauled your ass all the way here, and you stayed. You surfed. That's more than all the rest of them can say."

"I bet they didn't look as cute in that bikini."

Jason filed away the fact that when her hair wasn't scraped back into a headache, Lucinda was funny. But he didn't laugh. He waited. And when she cleared her throat, he pressed his advantage.

"Tell me why you care," he said again, with even more intensity. "You're talking about building a hotel, not a refuge for some endangered species. There's an old hotel falling down on this island al-ready. Why build something new? Why pretend it matters so much?"

"Because it does matter."

Maybe she surprised herself with that, because she instantly sat up that little bit straighter. Her blue eyes were guarded, but she kept them trained on his. He expected her to back right off. To say something else to defuse the tension, or try to shove them back toward something professional.

Good luck with that. He'd never felt less professional in his life.

When she stood up in a rush, he thought she was going to take it even further and just walk away. It was possible he'd read her wrong, and she was truly nothing more than shiny brochures and boardroom presentations.

But she didn't run. Instead, she clasped her hands in front of her and faced him.

"I grew up in a housing estate in Glasgow," she said, and her accent changed again, blurring the vowels and shading the consonants. He liked it. "I think you call them projects in the States, but it's all the same. Depressed and often desperate people crammed into small spaces together."

"I'm familiar with the phenomenon."

Lucinda inclined her head. "The tower block of flats where my family lived is notorious to this day. Filled with crime, poverty and every other social ill you care to mention, we had it in spades. They've knocked those towers down now, and good riddance. But that was my home. I was born there, raised there and had every expectation of living out my life there."

She looked away and unclenched her hands, as if she'd been holding them so tightly that she'd hurt herself. Which made Jason want to do things that didn't make sense to him, like simply…hold her. Until she felt better.

He shook that off. And she was talking again, staring into the fire.

"I can't express to you how grim it all was. What it was like to grow up in all that gray concrete, never knowing that there was so much better out there. Shows on television didn't seem real, not when we lived in such a prison. It was just the telly, beaming in something someone made up so we'd forget where we were. But when I was seven, I happened upon a travel magazine at school one day. I think one of the teachers must have left it behind. And oh, wasn't that something?"

She shook her head, but Jason was caught by the way her eyes lit up. They reminded him of his beloved sea, out here in the dark. They were that fathomless. That beautiful and changeable, all at once.

"The places in the magazine were real. Not something made up for a television show. They were real and they were beautiful, and that changed the way I thought about everything. When I was a little older, I sneaked down to the grand old railway hotel in Glasgow to see if a hotel could make me feel the way the travel magazines did. And this was before it got a face-lift, but I was in awe just the same."

Jason felt a little too close to awe himself as he watched the fire move over that wistful expression on her face.

"And from that point on, I knew that hotels were

the only kind of fairy tales that mattered," Lucinda said, turning back to him, her eyes grave. "Because people could live in them. They could come from whatever life they had, whether it was a stately home somewhere or a grotty little bedsit, and they could live a different life for a time."

"If they could afford it," Jason said, with maybe too much derision in his voice. Because he wasn't sure if he was determined to slap reality on her—or himself, for getting caught up in the story she was telling.

"I can't think of many things I'd rather spend my money on than a dream come true," she replied softly. "That's what a hotel is. The better the hotel, the better the happily-ever-after. It should be made clear in every small detail. The softness of the sheets. The beauty of the view. The excellence of the staff. Each and every part of the fairy tale builds the story as a whole."

She waved a hand toward the house, the last Daniel St. George property. The one his sycophants claimed meant the most to him. Why did that notion make Jason want to burn it to the ground?

"I look at a place like this and I think this is the kind of paradise that normal people want to remember for the rest of their lives. And wanting memories like this becomes the kind of dreams that make normal life worth living. I would happily scrimp and save for a week in a dream come true. I have. Would you?"

Jason felt as if he'd been waiting years for her. All the hours she'd been asleep, for sure, leaving him prowling around this place with all his rough edges driving him crazy. His mouth was dry. He was practically beside himself, if he was honest, but he could still control that. Or pretend well enough.

What he couldn't seem to wrestle into submission was the sensation blowing up his chest, making him want nothing more than to take every dream this woman had ever had and make it come true. Right here, right now.

And that made him feel ripped in half. Dumb and blindly stupid with all these *feelings* he didn't like and didn't want.

But he wanted her more.

"I never would've pegged you for starry-eyed optimist," he managed to say without betraying his own distinct lack of chill.

Her mouth curved slightly, and the light in those blue eyes didn't dim. "That's funny. I'd call myself a realist."

"A realist who arranged her life around happily-ever-afters and dreams coming true. Because that's real practical."

"I know you know what it's like to grow up with nothing," she said softly. "Lucky to find shoes to put on your feet. Much less ones that fit."

"That's the cool thing about growing up in Hawaii. Shoes are optional."

"Everything you have, Jason, you built for yourself. With your brain. With your body. With every shrewd decision and every stellar athletic performance. I didn't play football. But I did educate myself into a university degree. Just as I've performed my way into every position I've held. No matter how I got it."

His heart was doing weird flips. He rubbed at it, like that could shut it up.

"I hope that means you have flexible morals and no compunction whatsoever about sleeping your way around." Jason grinned, wide and maybe a little desperate. He hoped she couldn't see that part. "Just like me."

"I use whatever tools I have at my disposal," she replied, a faint line appearing between her brows. "And that's all I'm asking you to do in return."

"Fuck a lot?" He leaned back in his seat, despite all the roaring insanity inside him, like he could lounge there forever. Like he was on the verge of terminal boredom. "I can do that."

Lucinda started pacing then, back and forth in front of the fire pit. Jason should have found her agitating. Instead, the only word that seemed to dance around inside him was *adorable*.

As far as he could tell, it was one more way to make sure he knew he was boned.

"I'm talking about this island," she said. "The opportunity to create something truly special."

"But again, only for the kind of people who can afford it. And I'm betting every single one of them will remind me a little too much of the giant douche who built this place. Why would I want that?"

She shot a look at him with *Why are you here?* written all over it.

But that wasn't what she said. "When you create destination fantasies, you might be surprised to discover what sort of people think it's in their best interests to get there. One way or another."

He told himself all that carrying on in his chest was irritation. Not even temper. "Oh yeah? How many luxury properties do you stay at every year?"

"As it happens, I'm not great at taking all my allotted holiday time. I'm sure you've experienced that kind of pressure before. The people I work with are obsessed with status. Which means I have to be, too."

She kept making connections between them and Jason didn't want any part of that. There was only one part of him that liked connecting, and his dick didn't talk.

"But you're not into that, of course. You're above that kind of thing. Like every other woman who's chased after me since I got that football scholarship."

She did another lap.

"What interests me about high-status properties are what can be done with them," she said, as if he was having a serious conversation with her. Instead of acting like a sulky teenager. "And how much of an immersive experience they provide. Because the sad truth about many high-status operations is that they rest on their laurels and don't offer the paying clients much of anything besides the bill. I prefer experiences. I want clients to forget about the outside world entirely. I want leaving one of my properties to feel like leaving home, and I want it to haunt them once they're gone."

"I told you my position on ghosts."

Her gaze met his again, and he was sure she could feel the sizzle. So sure, in fact, that he found himself paying more attention to the way she was walking back and forth in front of him. More quickly each time. And her breath getting more and more shallow with each pass.

Making it clear to him that he wasn't the only one feeling crushed in the grip of the tension between them.

What did it make him that he was actually relieved? When he couldn't actually recall the last time the faintest sexual urge he'd had wasn't heartily and enthusiastically requited?

"I know that you're a man who likes to do good, Jason."

"That's nothing but a nasty rumor."

"I know it's not only a rumor. The truth is that the kind of conscious luxury experience that I'm talking about will preserve this island. And allow all kinds of people to experience what makes all the Pacific Islands so special in the first place. Of course, tourism can cause its own problems. I don't deny that. But how can people realize what they ought to help save if they can't experience it in as close to an unspoiled state as possible?"

Her face changed when she was truly animated. When she wasn't buttoning herself up in funeral clothes or beating her hair into submission. She was flushed with this passion of hers, her eyes bright and her voice intent, and he wanted to be inside her with such ferocity that it might have scared him.

If he wasn't so sure that it was only a matter of time.

"I might not be a natural beach person," she said, sounding fully Scottish and wholly *alive* as she wedged herself farther beneath his skin with every word. "I might personally prefer the shade of a tree to the glaring heat of white sand midday, I grant you. But this place is seductive. It's magical. It's not only that people will never want to leave here. It will make them happy to stay here. I don't know much about your father, or not much more than anyone else, but it doesn't take a rocket scientist to figure out that whatever else he was, he certainly wasn't a happy man. And it seems to me that creating a space for happiness in a place he built to be more of the same empty life he already led is the greatest revenge you could possibly have on him."

That caught at him.

Lucinda warmed to her topic, and her hands got into the act as she started talking about all those blueprints and building codes he'd already told her didn't interest him. And it was true. He didn't care. But he couldn't seem to take his eyes off her.

And the fact she'd unerringly narrowed in on the one thing he wanted that he couldn't have.

Revenge.

"Maybe we can dig him up, animate him and kill him all over again," his half sister, Angelique Masterson, had suggested a few hours ago on one of the weekly calls the heirs of Daniel St. George—Jason's half siblings—were obligated to have.

Angelique had been sitting somewhere in one of the beautiful rooms of the hotel she ran in the desert kingdom of Sadat, where she'd charmed a prince and met all the extra terms Daniel St. George had thrown in her path, simply because she was a girl. She'd been toying with the choker necklace she wore all the time now, its elegance somehow working with her full sleeves of tattoos. Only Angelique.

Revenge on their late and unlamented father was a topic they returned to often, as it happened.

"That makes me feel warm all over," his half brother Charlie Teller had said from Italy, kicked back on a terrace with pastel houses falling down the cliff behind him and the sound of a woman's voice in the background—his wife, presumably, doing her lawyer thing just out of range. Charlie had smirked. "Almost like we're a real family, after all."

"My understanding is that this is the way of all families," the oldest of the half brothers had said. Thor Ragnarsson looked every inch the modern Viking he was, standing near a window in one of those suits he loved, and Iceland's endless snow swirling around behind him. And no sign of his forbiddingly smart, purple-haired professor. "Endless grudges, revenge fantasies and petty squabbling. I suspect that makes us real already."

"That sounds a whole lot like white people problems," Jason had rumbled, letting out one of his trademark belly laughs. Mostly because he knew his half siblings found him both baffling and confronting. "In Hawaii we call it *ohana*. It's a way of life, motherfuckers. We don't squabble like little bitches. We eat. It's hard to get fired up about some petty bullshit when your belly's nice and full of a good kalua pork and there's nothing to do but sit around talking story."

But for all his protestations to his half siblings, who had all gotten a hell of a lot happier since they'd first started these online meetings thanks to finding themselves some steady loving in one place or another, that wasn't quite how he felt about Daniel St. George. Or himself.

Or about the things his mother had said to him when she'd called him out.

Or, hell, even this island.

He hadn't put it in the stark terms Lucinda had. But now he couldn't think of it in any other way.

Was he finding himself here? Or was he squatting in this house, deliberately not using the island the way his father would have? Like that could somehow stick it to the old man beyond the grave?

He focused back in on Lucinda, who was still pacing around in front of him, warming to whatever point she was making.

The importance of fragrance to help create the feeling of effortless hospitality, if he wasn't mistaken.

And just like that, Jason was done.

The next time she paced too close, he reached out and snagged her. She made a satisfying, high-pitched sort of squeaking sound as he hauled her into his lap, and he was just animal enough to delight in it.

Then she was right there. Right where he wanted her, her chest heaving and her eyes so wide he was sure he could see forever in them.

"Scotland," he growled. "Shut up."

And then, fucking finally, he got his mouth on hers.

CHAPTER TEN

THE ENTIRE WORLD burst into flame, as if the long-dormant volcano that had made this island roared back to life and took Lucinda first.

There was no easing in. No getting her bearings. Jason picked her up and threw her into a wall of a wave the way he had out on the water, head over heels in a mad hurtle that tasted like whiskey and aroused, impossible male, and she had no choice but to swim or drown.

Lucinda chose to swim.

She wrapped her arms around his neck, held on to all that brawn and muscle like he was hers, and opened her mouth beneath his.

And the way he licked into her mouth was better than plain old fire or his clever hands slicked with lotion. It was deeper, hotter and indescribably dirty.

Lucinda got the distinct impression that he wasn't playing around.

He had her in his lap, and within moments his hand was streaking up her leg beneath the soft fabric she'd wrapped around her. And the only thing she could think to do with all that sensation and heat was shift herself so he had better access. So she did. And he took it.

She knew his touch already and she thrilled to it, making a greedy sound in the back of her throat that should have humiliated her as he found his way between her thighs. But there was no room in her for humiliation. Not when he finally found his way beneath her panties and into the slick heat of her pussy.

At last, she thought fiercely, with a deep, full greed. *At last.*

If she thought that he would toy with her a little now, play with her and drag this out because he could, she was mistaken.

He kept his mouth on hers, kissing her deep and hard and so intensely it made her feel hollow with longing. Then he shifted her on his lap until she was kneeling astride him, her pussy against his cock with only his jeans and the scrap of her panties keeping her from taking him deep inside her.

It was like falling. Flying. Tumbling end over end, and Lucinda couldn't tell if she wanted to go on forever or she thought it might kill her. But she knew that really, she didn't care which. Or what happened to her.

Just so long as it never ended.

Jason reached between them. His rough fingers yanked at her panties until they gave way, and she knew she should care that he'd ripped them off her. And she did, but only because it somehow made his tongue in her mouth taste that much wilder.

He pulled his jeans open, making a dirty, gritty kind of sound as he dragged out that hard, heavy cock of his that had been haunting her for what already felt like her whole life.

She felt the blunt head of it, tracing over her pussy and hitting her clit, then moving through all that molten heat while she saw stars. Once, then again, like he wanted her to get a feel of him.

Or wanted her to get dizzy.

And this time she had no intention of holding herself back, she thought as he pulled out a condom and sheathed himself. She wasn't sure she could have if she tried.

His hands gripped her ass, hoisting her up and into position, so he could start working all of that thick, heavy length inside her.

Lucinda was shuddering now, trying to push herself deeper onto him than he would allow her to go because she needed all of him, now. But he maintained his grip and kept her to a mere inch, then a retreat, then another even slower inch.

"I hate you," she managed to say, there against his mouth.

She could feel that laughter of his rumble in his big chest. Though at first she thought it was yet another earthquake tearing her up from the inside out.

"I can tell."

He worked her lower, then lower still, until she was sure she was spread-eagled over him. Pinned wide and waiting for him to fill her completely. It was enough to make her pant and sweat, but it still wasn't enough.

He still wasn't there.

He worked her farther down his massive shaft. He hitched his hips to back up again, grinning when she made a sound of protest.

And then he surged that last little bit inside her, dragging the base of his cock over her clit as he sheathed himself to the hilt.

It walloped her.

She went spinning straight over an edge she hadn't seen coming with such a wild, intense punch that she found herself crying out right there against his mouth.

All Jason did was laugh, then lick it up, too.

And then, when she was shaking out her wild, incandescent release—only dimly aware that the sarong had come unknotted to pool around her hips, leaving nothing between them at all—he began to move.

Her.

He wrapped his big hands around her waist and moved her up, then down, as if she was weightless. As if she was a toy, and he was using her to pleasure himself as he chose—

A notion that nearly made her come all over again when she'd hardly finished the first round.

He made a sound, something low and deep that she knew was a command, and there was no reason she should have understood him.

But she did.

She did—as if they were connected in more ways than simply the huge cock that filled her too wide and thrilled her too intensely in turn.

Lucinda arched against him, moving to take even more of him with each deliriously slick, hot slide. And giving him what he wanted, which was her breasts right there at his lips.

He sucked in one nipple, then played with it. He rolled it inside the wet heat of his mouth before releasing it, with a distinctly dirty popping sound, and then moving to the other.

And Lucinda lost herself in that sharp tug. In the insanity of his beautiful cock inside her. In all the ropes and chains of fire and need that stormed through her, connecting her nipples to her pussy and all of her to his mouth, his cock, the heat and the glory.

Everything was that fire that had raged between them from the start. Sensation and sheer madness, tighter and tighter with every thrust. His cock was too big and just right, and he worked it inside her over and over again.

Until she thought she might die from all this pleasure. Until she was so wet she was sure she might drown them both. And still he played with her breasts, letting his hands slide down lower on her ass so he could hold her in a way that struck her as even more filthy than before.

Especially when he found the rest of her with his thumb.

And he wasn't the least bit shy about toying with what he'd found.

She made a helpless, glorious keening sound. Jason's mouth dropped to her neck, and she felt the very instant that his control finally snapped to match hers. When he stopped moving her the way he wanted and simply fucked his way into her like his life depended on it, too.

And that was when she got to ride him as she liked, hard and deep and wild.

Her hair had fallen down, somehow, and for once she didn't care that it danced all around them.

She let it flow as it liked, too, as she arched into him, moving her hips in an intense rhythm until she was too full, too close to bursting—

All fire and too good—

The world aflame and *too much*—

And when he let out a shout, pumping himself into her, she went with him.

Shattering into pieces all over again. Pieces Lucinda thought would never fit together the way they had. Not ever again.

But as she cracked open and lost herself in it, she couldn't say she cared.

Neither one of them moved for what felt like a forever or two.

There was nothing but the sounds of their breathing, harsh and loud and meshed together the way their bodies still were.

There was the crackle of the fire somewhere in the distance. The breeze, scented with the sea.

Ages later, Lucinda finally remembered her name.

Long years after that, she managed to lift up her head, helped considerably when Jason reached out to smooth back her hair with one hand.

She felt as if there were worlds bubbling up inside her, so many things she needed to say that she didn't know how to fit into the necessary syllables and sounds. All of which made her chest ache as they sat there, unsaid.

She felt…changed.

As if this hadn't been sex at all, that brisk release she knew so well and often courted back home, but something much darker. Deeper. Intense and unknowable.

"Jason…" she whispered, and he was still inside her. Still an impressive length, but the sound of his name made him thicken.

And then he smiled, wicked through and through.

She felt it like a new sun, beating down on her from a new high noon.

And everywhere it touched her, she blazed.

"I like a good appetizer, darlin'," he drawled, threat and promise in that voice of his. In that gleam of gold in his dark eyes. In his cock lodged deep inside her and hardening, already making her shudder all over again. "And that was more than good. But now? I'm really fucking hungry for a meal."

When Jason led her into his bedroom, to the great, wide bed that took up most of the space, Lucinda decided that this was her turn to shine. What happened by the fire pit wasn't her usual style. It had come on like a storm.

Maybe he's a storm, something in her said.

Lucinda wanted no part of storms, or fire pits, for that matter. But she was good at bedrooms. She knew exactly how to play here.

It was strange to have her hair down and curly, but she didn't let that get to her. She didn't let it throw her off. And as they got near the bed, she turned to Jason and slid her hands upon his chest, still mouth-wateringly bare and just as hard and muscled as he looked. He gazed down at her, his dark eyes intense and shot through with that intoxicating gold that made her breath catch.

But she didn't want to catch her breath and let his gaze go to her head. She wanted to take what happened between them and steady it, somehow, inside her. It was only sex, after all. There was no need for her to feel as if it was eating at her bones, changing her, turning her into something else—

That's enough, then.

She was coming over all angsty when that wasn't her way. Lucinda concentrated on Jason's impossible beauty instead.

He looked down at her hands on the sculpted ridges of his abdomen and smiled. Then he took a moment to shuck off his jeans and toss them aside before he came back to stand before her, naked at last. His confidence and sheer maleness was nearly overwhelming. She wanted to…breathe him in. She wanted to bury her face against him, close her eyes and feel his hard, corded arms wrap around her and hold her.

She wanted him to make her feel safe.

And that set off just about every alarm she had inside her.

Lucinda blinked, hoping against hope that nothing showed on her face. She directed her attention away from odd urges inside her and toward the things that actually mattered here, standing next to a bed with a beautiful man. And at Jason's cock, already mouthwateringly hard again, and with a fresh new condom besides. She wrapped her hand around him, smiling when he was finally the one to let out a jagged sort of breath.

As long as it wasn't only her.

She felt herself get wetter. Hotter. She was already imagining that thick, hard length inside her again—

Get on with it, she ordered herself, before she started building up fantasies of his keeping her safe again, when she knew better than that. Lucinda was the only person who could keep herself safe, and even if that wasn't true, a night with a man she'd only just met was no place to explore her poor, broken heart, for fuck's sake.

She let go of his cock and slid her hands up the wall of his chest again. He was standing between her and the bed, so she thought she'd cut to the chase. She smiled up at him, hoping she conveyed all the seduction and heat necessary, and then she pushed him. She put her weight behind it.

Usually, they fell right over in a willing and lazy sprawl, but Jason didn't move an inch. She might as well have shoved a mountain.

"If you want something, Lucinda, ask."

Already that was different. It wasn't part of the usual script. Lucinda scowled at him—also not normal—and pushed at him again. "Lie down."

He still didn't so much as sway. His gaze left hers, tracking over her curls instead, and something about the way his expression changed made a different sort of heat wash over her. It felt connected to that same urge she'd had before, to...*cuddle*, God help her.

Lucinda thought she would rather die.

And everything was already out of control. The fact she'd fallen asleep the way she had earlier instead of charging ahead with her grand plan to win

this man over. The fact they'd had sex like that, outside, hot and wild—and decidedly not the way she
generally had sex.

Not the way she wanted to have sex, she amended
inside her head.

But she wanted that damned resort more than she
wanted to hold on tight to her own control issues.

"Lie down," she said again. "Please?"

"Okay," Jason said, too easily. And after what
seemed like far too long.

He smiled at Lucinda in a way she thought was
mocking, but she didn't allow herself to react. And
only when she was sure he was going to continue
doing it forever did he move back, clearly because
he'd decided to move and not because she wanted
him to move, and stretched back on the bed.

She didn't like the fact that he'd wrested control
from even that. It made the whole thing feel…fraught
with peril, somehow.

But she ignored it, because bigger things were at
stake here. She pasted her smile on her face again
and then she moved toward him, climbing up on
the bed and crawling her way up the length of his
big, rangy body until she could seat herself astride
him again.

The choreography to this was simple, no matter
that Jason was by far the most intense man she'd ever
met. Lucinda had worked out the kinks years ago.
It didn't matter how big the man was, or how their

bodies fit together otherwise. Push him down on his back, climb on board, and she could make her own fun. Then leave.

It was easy gratification. And better still, the men in question always enjoyed the show she put on as she did all the work, so there were never any complaints.

Lucinda chose not to analyze exactly why it was so important to her that she put this situation with Jason back on that kind of footing. The only kind of footing she understood.

She reached down between them again, still smiling as she went to wrap her fingers around him so she could hurry this up and get all those strange *feelings* out of her—

But he wasn't waiting in breathless anticipation to see what she would do, the way he should have been. Instead, his big hands came up and speared into her curls until he was holding her fast above him.

Making a mockery of her sense of control.

"I don't know why you put your hair up at all." His voice was a low, intense rumble that made goose bumps rise all over her skin. "You should keep it down. Always."

Lucinda opened her mouth to tell him two things. One, that her hair wasn't professional like this, and two, to stop talking so she could get to work.

But instead, he tugged her down and set his mouth to hers.

And the things he did to her mouth defied such a sweet, adorable little word as *kiss*.

By the time he was finished, she was shaking, everywhere. And more confusingly, she was on her back with Jason above her, pressing her down into the mattress.

"Wait," she managed to pant out. "This isn't how this is supposed to go!"

"Seems right to me," Jason murmured, his mouth at her neck, and then his cock was right where she wanted it, working its way inside her. Then sliding home.

And she was arching in sheer delight, unable to help herself. She was desperate to rub her breasts against the steel of his chest all over again. Wild to shift her hips so she could take all of him. More of him. *Everything.*

"I want to be in control," she threw out there, a shot against the seductive dark *greed* for him that was pulling her under.

And this time when he let out that laugh of his, dark and deep, she could feel it as if it was a part of her. From his cock so deep inside her to her own hard nipples pressed there against his chest. As if she was part of the laughter, made of it, and humbled by it, too.

It made her pussy clench.

"Yeah, no," he growled, laughter and something a lot more intense in his voice. "That's not how I roll."

And then he proceeded to take her apart.

He used his fingers against her clit to make her come in a rush, sobbing.

Then he flipped her over and took her from behind, forcing her to make fists in the sheets as he slammed into her, over and over, until she was begging him.

To stop. To never stop. To take her with him.

To go on forever.

And when she was limp from yet another impossible rush of an orgasm, like a tornado ripping through her, he gathered her to him yet again. He lifted her hands above her head and pinned them there against the mattress with one of his palms.

And then, astonishingly, he slowed down.

"You might as well come," she whispered at him, because that was her version of shouting at this point. "I'm done. There's nothing more in me."

"Don't sell yourself short, Scotland. You can always come again."

"I can't."

"You can't or you don't think you can?"

"*I can't.* And I would know, since I'm the only person here who knows my body."

"That sounds a lot like a challenge."

And he took his sweet time answering that challenge.

Jason set his mouth to one breast, licking and sucking until she couldn't help the moans that burst free from the back of her throat. And when he stopped, it was only to shift over to the other breast, then start all over again. Then he let go of her hands as he slowly, slowly made his way down her body as if he had all the time in the world.

As if there was nothing he ever had to do again but taste her. Everywhere.

He settled himself between her legs, pushing her thighs wide to accommodate his shoulders, and the very *vastness* of him made Lucinda feel shaky all over again.

"Don't waste your time," she told him as he bent his head toward her pussy. She shook her head. "That doesn't do a lot for me."

"Too bad," he replied, with that lick of laughter and too much heat in his dark eyes "Because it does a whole hell of a lot for me."

And in case she hadn't already gotten the message, when he leaned forward and licked into her, Lucinda discovered that she didn't know her own body at all.

She'd always found oral sex boring and vaguely embarrassing besides. It was so…clinical yet messy. Men were always so chuffed with themselves that they bothered. They always seemed to want prizes, applause, even more attention for the performance. When most of the time, Lucinda used the time to go over her to-do list. Or contemplate her shopping list.

Perhaps wonder if she'd switched off the gas when she'd last cooked a meal.

But when Jason set his mouth to her pussy, it was like a lightning strike.

She felt it like a bolt, so intense that for a second she couldn't tell if it was pleasure or pain that seared straight through to every last part of her body. Her toes sang as loudly as her clit, and that was before he started using his tongue.

There was nothing decorous about the way he ate at her, raw and wild, as if this was the meal he had been talking about all along. As if he truly was starving, she was what he wanted for dinner and he by God was going to eat his fill.

She started coming, bucking her hips into his face, but he didn't stop. He kept going, using some insanely hot combination of teeth and tongue and even his chin. And as if that wasn't enough, he kept making that dark, growling sound, humming sensation into her.

And she came. And came again.

As if he was magic. As if she'd never actually met herself and he was the expert. And as if, given the opportunity, she could come forever.

And only when her eyes had spilled over, her throat was scraped raw and she'd lost track entirely of where she was and who she was and what plan she'd had for this encounter did he crawl back up the length of her body, dropping kisses wherever he went like he was staking his claim on her flesh.

Lucinda wasn't sure she minded if he did.

Only then did he thrust inside her again, raw and savage and finally as out of control as she was.

And she was coming again, or she was still coming, and then he was coming with her, and it was like flying.

Like a wave that never ended, rolling and hurtling a blue and beautiful rush, straight on to the horizon.

It felt like forever.

Which was how Lucinda knew, beyond a shadow of a doubt, that she'd made a critical error of judgment where Jason Kaoki was concerned—and a terrible mistake.

CHAPTER ELEVEN

LUCINDA WOKE UP the way she always did, in a sudden, panicked rush. As if, should she be expected to fight in the next instant, she would be ready—

Except she'd already fought and lost.

That unpleasant truth slapped at her, making her usual panic rise high and hard inside her.

She sat up straight in Jason's wide bed, blinking around the mess of it—sheets strewn about, the pillows thrown here and there—and tried her best not to recall every last smoking-hot second that had led to each damning bit of evidence. Each pointing to exactly where and when and how she'd lost control of herself and this situation completely.

Jason was stretched out beside her, commanding even as he slept. And it took her a distressingly long moment to understand that the silvery light playing over all those perfect, brown muscles and powerful limbs came from the moon up above, pouring in through a skylight she hadn't realized was there.

Because all she'd seen was him.

It was time to leave. *Now*, something in her urged her, *before it's too late*.

Lucinda didn't want to know what *too late* meant, not when her body didn't feel like hers anymore. Not when her hair bounced all around her in a horrifying red tangle and she could still feel Jason as if he'd left fingerprints all over her. Worse, there was a not-insignificant part of her that hoped he had.

And none of this was how Lucinda usually behaved. She knew how to handle herself in business and in bedrooms with equal focus and reserve. She'd never been tested, really. She moved forward, eyes forever on the prize. The next hotel. The next orgasm.

And she never, ever looked back.

Lucinda didn't know how to handle the part of her that wanted nothing more than to lie back down and snuggle up against Jason's sculpted side. The part that wanted to breathe in his scent a little longer. Maybe feel the weight of his heavy arm again.

And best of all, be there when he woke up.

But that was something Lucinda never, ever did. Not even on a private island across the planet from everything she knew and all the rules she'd made to survive that cold, gray life. She didn't do morning-afters. She didn't do cozy wake-ups or cuddles or lazy breakfasts, much less the kind of sex that went along with those things, so syrupy and intimate and *no bloody way*.

Of all the things Jason had done to her, from that bikini to surfing to his deliciously dirty imagination in bed, she thought this was the worst. The most unacceptable and unforgivable.

He had made her into just another dreamy-eyed idiot, like all the rest. All the women who came and went from her company because they lost their focus. All the girls who had let boyfriends turn their heads at university. Not to mention her own mother, who had complained endlessly about Lucinda's father but had never dreamed of leaving him and his drunken rampages.

That Lucinda had managed to claw her way out had been treated like a betrayal. It had taken only a few disastrous trips back home from university for Lucinda to understand that her mother would have preferred her only child died rather than better herself in any way—because that was much too confronting.

So for all intents and purposes, Lucinda had gone ahead and died. The hapless, bullied Lucinda who had lived with her always-rowing parents might as well have been dead, because the Lucinda who had taken her place was nothing like her.

She wasn't soft. She wasn't malleable. She was a creature of goals and focus who allowed herself only brief, strictly controlled releases in the form of sex she controlled and the orgasms she produced with very little assistance.

Jason had ruined everything. Or would, if she didn't take back what little control she could.

She rolled out of the bed, her heart kicking at her as if she was running a race. Or as if she'd found a terrible truth about herself in the wide bed with its carved koa headboard—one that was moments away from being shared with the world. It was that panicky, laced through with shame.

But there was nothing she could do but what she was doing. She retraced the steps she'd taken in what seemed like a different life, all those hours ago. Out of the master bedroom without a backward glance, straight out onto the terrace, letting the moon dance all over her body as she moved through the soft night. She didn't like it. It felt too much like another trespass. The seduction of the air itself that had made her far too susceptible to the man.

And she could still feel him. *Still.* She was afraid to look down at her own flesh in the moonlight, because she was more certain with every step that he hadn't left handprints or mouth prints. Those would fade. She was far more afraid that he'd tattooed himself deep into her. That he'd marked her permanently.

You are changed forever, something intoned inside her, as if from on high.

Her pussy liked that idea entirely too much, blooming with a new heat even as Lucinda made it back to the fire pit and found the sarong she'd discarded there hours ago. When Jason had hooked an arm around her and hauled her over his lap and altered the shape of things.

You are changed, that voice said again, and she scowled, because she didn't want any changes, thank you. She liked herself just as she was: ambitious, determined and immune to the emotional highs and lows other people seemed to feel with such alarming regularity. Lucinda had experienced enough emotional turmoil as a child to last her a lifetime.

She wanted her life smooth and tailored. She wanted her hair and her clothes the same way. The current state of her hair, with her curls an exuberant disaster all around, appalled her. As did her state of undress.

When she picked up the sarong from the ground and wrapped it around her torso, her fingers felt clumsy and shaky. It took her several tries to knot it into place, each one a separate indictment of this pit she'd fallen into. And yet, when she was as dressed as she was going to get and ready to march herself back to her cottage and sort herself out, she just stood there.

As if the moonlight was a confessional.

Everything that had happened since she'd woken up from that unexpected and highly unprofessional eight-hour nap flooded through her then. She hardly knew which thing to take out and examine first when they all crashed over her together. The fact that she had actually told Jason Kaoki—a property owner she wanted to bring on board, not her bloody therapist—the reason why she did what she did? A secret so deeply lodged inside her that she had never said it out loud to another living soul? He didn't need to know why she liked hotels. No one needed to know that.

How was she supposed to go on trying to get him to develop this island now? What was she supposed to do now that she'd exposed herself so completely?

And that was all before they'd had sex.

Though maybe she needed a new word to describe what had happened between them. Because she understood the mechanics, and she'd thought she'd understood her own body's reactions, but she had never experienced anything like what had transpired between her and Jason tonight.

It had about as much to do with what she thought sex was as a unicorn did with a tiny plastic toy shaped like one.

Lucinda shuddered, standing there in the dangerous tropical moonlight with only the embers of the fire that had blazed in that pit remaining. Glowing at her like the sparks of all the things she'd done with Jason, daring her to pretend it had all been bog standard. Easily dismissed.

And not the most overwhelming, raw and intimate experience of her life.

She squeezed her eyes shut, curling her hands into

fists and blowing out a long breath. But that didn't change the fact that inside, she felt as if she'd survived an earthquake. Or lived through one, anyway. All that remained of her was rubble and ash, crushed down into smithereens.

With aftershocks racing through her when she least expected it, since every time she thought about the things they had done, her pussy throbbed. With greed.

And she didn't need to walk back over to the master bedroom and peer inside again, because the sight of Jason sprawled out across the bed with moonlight all over him would be burned in her head forever.

Even asleep, he commanded attention.

Hell, even asleep and nowhere near her, he was all she could think about.

Lucinda had no choice but to accept what she'd already known—what she'd thought distinctly after the first time Jason had turned her inside out on that bed. Which hadn't even been the first time he'd turned her inside out.

She had made a mistake. A big one.

Lucinda had assumed that she could come here and convince Jason to build her the resort she'd always wanted. She'd dismissed the men who'd assured her that Jason Kaoki was impossible to persuade. She'd hand-waved away all the lectures she'd received on the topic, because she'd been sure she could do things all those men couldn't. She'd been prepared to use all her usual weapons of persuasion. Even her body, if necessary.

Looking at all the pictures of him splashed all over the internet, she hadn't imagined she'd mind the sacrifice.

But it had never crossed her mind that he could actually touch her in any way. That he could somehow disarm her, sneak in through her heavily armored defenses and turn what she'd thought were her weapons into weaknesses.

Because now Lucinda was hungry, too. She felt desperate. Vulnerable and bruised with longing. There were tears pricking at the back of her eyes and that scraped-up sensation in the back of her throat.

She *felt*.

And that was unacceptable.

Lucinda could accept defeat. Or she thought she could, in theory—having never had that much exposure to it before. But there was no way in hell that she could function like *this*. Cracked wide open, a stranger to herself, quaked by all that intimacy.

Worst of all, exposed.

Because every crack in what she'd assumed was her unassailable foundation proved that she was no different from her mother after all.

She didn't look back when she finally wheeled around and headed for her cottage. She walked fast, her gaze steady and ahead of her, already calculating how to get the hell off this island and away from the man who, it turned out, was the most dangerous opponent she'd ever faced.

A war she hadn't seen coming and had lost without firing a single shot.

Lucinda was gone when Jason woke up.

Sunlight streamed into his room from all the windows that doubled as sliding doors, just the way he liked it. Light danced over him while the breeze washed him awake, trailing over his skin until he remembered where he was and who had been there when he'd finally exhausted the first, bright wave of his lust for Lucinda, who wasn't quite the stuffy suit when she wasn't wearing one.

He reached out to find her before he opened his eyes, but the bed was empty. And more telling by far, cool to the touch.

As if she hadn't been there in a long while.

He didn't like that. It was downright disturbing how much he didn't like that. His heart was doing those weird flips again, his ribs felt tight and the sensation that he was well and truly boned pressed down on him. Everywhere.

Jason had no choice but to laugh at himself.

Since when had he been possessive? And when had he ever woken up alone and been pissed about it because he wanted more, instead of being grateful that the woman had cleared out without having to go through a tedious scene?

He jackknifed up to sit where he could see the view. Palm trees dancing in the breeze and the blue sky indistinguishable from the sea where they met. A sweep of pure, untouched glory that some men might kill for.

And all he could see was Lucinda and the way she flushed red when she came.

He laughed at himself again, then took himself off to a very hot shower that did absolutely nothing to set him straight. It was like Lucinda was imprinted on him, and what was really freaking him out was that, when he stopped wondering how she'd managed to sneak up and sucker punch him, he didn't hate it.

And not only because the fact that a woman *could* get to him meant he wasn't Daniel St. George.

When he finally made his way out of his bedroom, he was clean, but definitely not okay with the fact she'd run off while he was sleeping. And he was still laughing at that as he made his way through the open, graceful rooms of this house he'd never wanted. This house his father had built but never lived in, as if he'd imagined that one day he might actually turn into the sort of person who would *want* the things this house offered. The view and the privacy, sure—but also the quiet contemplation that went with it.

Jason had never met the man, but that didn't sound like Daniel St. George's style.

He made his way to the lanai off the kitchen where

he usually sank into his morning routine of a whole lot of excellent Hawaiian coffee and his laptop before his workout—except today, Lucinda was sitting there.

Right there on the white sofa with the unimpeded view of the mountainside sloping off into the surf.

And the wild-haired woman wearing nothing but a sarong, pretty much every wet dream he'd ever had, was gone.

In her place was the woman who had first appeared in the old hotel lobby yesterday. It was the hair he noticed first and with the biggest kick to the gut, slick and straight and hauled back from her face so hard it made his temples ache. Like she was daring it to attempt to curl. And as if that wasn't enough, she wore a blouse of black silk, another severe skirt and an impassive expression on her pretty face that almost blanked out those gorgeous freckles.

"Another funeral?" he asked, sounding all kinds of lazy when he wanted to fight something. Her, for example. "So soon?"

CHAPTER TWELVE

LUCINDA'S BLUE EYES were frigid when they met his. A lot like the smile she aimed at him, which he knew she would probably tell him was *professional*.

When all Jason wanted was to taste her on his tongue again.

"I came here to talk to you about a resort, Mr. Kaoki," she said, with no trace of Scotland in her voice. It was all BBC vowels and that excruciating politeness, as if he didn't know how she begged for more. "Yesterday got off track, and I apologize. I shouldn't have allowed you to bait me."

"Is *bait* a fancy British word for *fuck*, Scotland?"

He could feel the temper and heat kicking around in him, and he was pretty sure they were obvious in his voice. Maybe all over his face, too. But she only smiled, winter straight through.

"Today instead of cavorting about in and out of the surf, I thought we could revisit the key points of my proposal."

Something kicked at him with that, another unpleasant gut punch if ever there was one. He told himself to ignore it, but the sensation of the kick lingered, making him…edgy. "I told you already. I don't give a shit about proposals."

"If what you want is sex, I regret to inform you that's not why I came here. I understand if yesterday blurred the lines. Nevertheless, I think we really must get ourselves back on the right path."

"Are you sure?" Because he knew how to make her scream. And he wanted to peel her out of all that unrelenting black and make her bright red again. All over him. "It seems to me like you were more than happy to use your body if it got you where you wanted to go. What if that's the only path I know?"

But he didn't want to be the guy who loomed over a woman while he said something like that, so he settled himself in the chair at an angle to hers and made a quiet little show out of lounging there, bonelessly, like he was *this close* to falling back asleep.

Rather than hot and hard and ready. Which, right at this moment, he didn't feel she deserved to know.

"Where I want to go is a luxury resort with worldclass amenities and personal butler service," she told him, sounding faintly apologetic. He knew perfectly well it was a tactic. A strategy. There wasn't a shred of apology anywhere on her. "Not another tour of your bedroom."

Jason was prepared to manfully let that go, because his possessiveness was his problem and she certainly didn't owe him anything and blah, blah, blah, but she smirked. She didn't even pretend to hide it.

As if this was her letting him down easy. *Him.* As if he was some puppy who didn't know the difference between a run-of-the-mill one-nighter and what had exploded between them last night. Over and over again.

"You said you wanted a dream come true, Lucinda. And your dream came true in my bedroom easily enough. Repeatedly, in fact."

She rose to her feet, a fluid, elegant movement that made him regret that he'd thrown her childhood dream in her face. And he didn't understand how he could legitimately regret that while also wanting nothing more than to mess her up all over again, with his hands and his mouth. He didn't like her so prim. So cold. Not now that he knew exactly how hot she ran and how loud she screamed when she got what she wanted—

And it was astonishing to him that he could care this much. About anything, when until now, he'd thought the only thing he was capable of feeling was the exhilaration and fear of doing stupid shit like jumping out of planes, climbing very big rocks with no ropes and living too large and too fast like he didn't care if it imploded around him. He'd been so sure he'd burned right through all those feelings other people seemed to have. He'd been so sure he was safe and numb.

But he couldn't seem to stop. Not here, with Lucinda.

"This is my fault," she said quietly. No trace of apology, but something else on her face that made him feel pretty much anything but lazy. "I underestimated the effect that kind of long-haul travel would have on me. To say nothing of the jet lag. Add to that the tropical heat and all this sunshine and I'm afraid I gave you nothing but mixed messages." She inclined her head. "I have no one to blame for that but myself."

Jason recognized that tone, though it took him a moment to place it. And then he did.

"Are you letting me down easy?" He let out a deep bark of laughter that should have razed the house, and had very little humor in it besides. "You have got to be fucking kidding me."

"If you truly don't want to develop this island, ever, then we have nothing more to discuss." The worst part was, the smile Lucinda aimed at him wasn't even brittle. It was pitying. "I'll wish you well, call for my return flight and be on my way. It will be as if I was never here at all."

And he watched, temper kicking at him, as she waited there with that same faintly pitying look on her face. For him to say something, he assumed, that didn't have anything to do with his dick or how wet he knew she was, right now.

Nothing came to mind.

Or nothing that wouldn't lead to high volume and his hands in her pussy, anyway.

When he only stared back at her, fully aware that he was looking at her like this was a boxing ring and the bell was about to ring, she nodded. As if he was merely confirming all her suspicions. Then she turned smartly on one heel—because she was actually wearing fussy mainland shoes in this island house, which Jason felt like yet another insult—and started away from him.

Like that was that.

And Jason, always a little too in touch with his animal side for his own good and other people's peace of mind, was surprised to look down at his own, tense body and discover he hadn't in fact sprouted fangs and fur. Because that was exactly how wild he felt. Like he was four seconds away from some full-on wolf shit.

"This isn't a power move, Lucinda," he growled out after her, taking maybe too much satisfaction when she stopped walking as if he'd yelled. When he'd wanted to yell his head off, but hadn't, because he could be a fucking gentleman when he felt like it. "You can tell yourself it is, if you want. I bet you are. But you know and I know that what you're doing is running away. Scared out of your mind."

She made a sigh into an opera with the suggestion of eyes rolled up into the back of her head, though she didn't actually roll them at him. Or not where he could see it, anyway. She turned back around to face him while she did it, and this time, there was a razor's edge to that smile of hers.

At least it was more real.

"I don't generally find business scary, Jason. I don't generally find business emotional at all." She cocked her head to one side, a move that no one had ever managed without aggression behind it. He was sure she knew it. "Do you? Maybe that's an American thing?"

He didn't know he meant to move. One minute he was sitting where she'd tried to leave him, there on his own lanai without even a cup of coffee. And the next he was towering over her—taking particular notice of the way her pulse betrayed her, there in the hollow of her throat, while she stared up at him. Silently daring him to comment.

He was happy to oblige.

"That's a load of crap. And you might be happy to lie to yourself, Scotland. But don't try lying to me."

"I'm not lying."

"You are. You're so full of shit I can practically taste it from here."

Her smile was bland, though her blue eyes blazed. "I'm sorry if you find reality confronting. But that doesn't change it, I'm afraid. Reality is reality, no matter what you think about it, and no matter if you're used to bellowing and blustering and blowing it all down."

"Here's a little reality for you."

He hooked one hand around the back of her head and hauled her to him. He took her mouth with no holds barred, like he was trying to imprint himself on her. Forever, with this one insane kiss.

Because he knew she could feel the kick of it. The sucker punch. All that fire. All that need.

And he didn't have to worry about what the hell he was feeling, did he, when she was so busy denying it.

"That's what you're afraid of, darlin'," he said, through his teeth and against her lips, the taste of her flooding him. Making him want to beat his chest or something, roaring out that she was his. The way he felt, that could easily be his next move. "You think I can't tell?"

She shoved him, hard and a little unhinged, and when he let her go—when he fucking felt like it— her blue eyes had gone stormy. Telling him all kinds of truths he figured she didn't want to face.

Well, join the club, baby, he thought.

"I'm truly sorry if you're the sort of person who confuses sex with emotion," she bit out, because of course Lucinda would dare to say something like that to him. Him, of all people, a man who was known as such a hound dog that his own mother had suggested he go off somewhere and deal with himself. *Him.* And she was still going. "I can't help you with that, because I'm not. I'm sorry if you thought there was more going on here. I don't ordinarily mix business and pleasure, and this is why. The potential for confusion is too high, I'm afraid."

"I'm not confused."

That smile again, sharp with pity this time, and it didn't matter that he knew it was all for show. It still stung.

"I'm not trying to insult you, Jason. I know you're famous and used to a certain standard of treatment. You're obviously very attractive. And yes, of course, you're talented and exciting in bed."

"I'll be sure to put all that on my fucking résumé."

Lucinda spread her hands wide, a gesture that was possibly meant to look soothing, but all he saw was the lie beneath it. And all over her face. "But none of this means anything to me. No matter how much you want it to be different, sex is just a bit of sport to me."

He wanted to break something.

Instead, he laughed at her.

Because he knew this routine. Hell, until now he'd thought he'd invented it. He literally couldn't count the number of women he'd had to speak to the same way she was speaking to him now.

"Karma is a bitch," he said. "You could argue that I've earned this." But he shook his head, and he settled his hand on the nape of her neck again. He was pretty sure she wanted him to. Wanted him to touch her but didn't dare ask him to, because that would undercut this whole show she was putting on. And

she didn't bat at his arm, so he knew he was right.
"But not from you."

"I don't know what you're talking about. What
I do know is that none of this, or any other emotional reaction you might be having, has anything
to do with my purpose for being here. So if you'll
excuse me—"

"Here's your problem, Scotland," he drawled, almost enjoying himself again. Almost. "I've given
that speech so many times myself that I know you're
full of shit. Because I was there last night. I know
exactly how I turned you out. And now I know way
too much about how your body works to believe a
single thing you're saying to me."

This time she rolled her eyes where he could see
it.

"I sense this is going to come as a big shock to
you, but despite what you might have been taught
your whole life, women are just as able to compart-
mentalize as men. And I know this may well be a
surprise, but an orgasm isn't the same as an emotion. *Even for girls.*"

Jason didn't need lessons on orgasms from a
woman he'd given so many to, but he only grinned
at that. Maybe a little dangerously.

"We're not talking about *girls*, plural. We're talking about you. Maybe you're used to orgasms that
aren't emotional, but that's not what happened. Not
with me."

And the admittedly very small part of him that might have wondered if he was wrong about that eased when he saw that storm darken her eyes again.

"I can see it's important for you to believe that, but that doesn't make it true."

"You cried, Lucinda. Sobbed, I think is the term. Over and over again."

"I'm going to chalk that up to jet lag."

"Exhaustion is a killer. But you'd just had an eight-hour nap."

She shoved at his arm, and he let her dislodge him again. Then he watched her step back, every part of her bristling, yet under control.

He had a perfect memory of when she'd tried to shove him down backward on the bed, then take over. And somehow he knew that had been the moment when everything had changed for her. Where she'd surrendered to something he wasn't sure she understood, but clearly had to do with the same control she was exerting now.

The overly tamed hair, no hint of curl.

He hated the sleekness of it. The artificial smoothness. He felt it like an assault.

"My plane should be here in an hour or so," she said, her voice clipped and cool, no matter what he could see in her eyes. "I'd appreciate it if you could drive me back down to the water."

"You'd appreciate it." Jason shook his head. "What you think running away is going to solve?"

"I don't have a problem that needs solving," Lucinda retorted. Then shook her head sadly, as if she felt sorry for him. "But I'm beginning to think that you do."

He wasn't going to argue that. He wasn't going to *argue*, at all.

Jason wheeled around and stalked back to his bedroom. He threw his jeans on over the boxer briefs he'd been wearing on their own, found the keys to his Jeep where he'd left them and headed back out to the main part of the house. As if she'd anticipated his every move—something he couldn't say he liked, at all—she was waiting for him, her little roller bag beside her and a certain smug look on her face.

Jason told himself to breathe. Let it go, no matter how tight his chest felt or the insane things that kept running through his head.

Because maybe he'd had this coming, after all. Maybe she really hadn't felt the whole damned world move the way he had, and maybe that was something he was just going to have to deal with.

Maybe his mama had been right and he'd become his father, and this was his wake-up call.

"It's all right if you need to sulk," Lucinda told him as she climbed into the Jeep, her voice as sharp and smooth as her hair in that hateful bun. "I won't think less of you for it."

"I'm not sulking," Jason told her, and he kept his hands to himself. No one ever had to know it almost killed him. "I'm grateful."

And he let her stew on that as he drove her back down to the beach. He waited with her on the dock, in a brooding kind of silence that seemed unstable and flammable, until his buddy flew in.

Then he loaded her up onto the little hopper plane, watched it fly away and told himself *good riddance.*

Over and over again, in the hope it might stick.

CHAPTER THIRTEEN

JASON SET ABOUT living his best life, the way he'd been doing since he'd arrived on this island.

Today was no different. What did it matter that the night had ruined him and there were now blue eyes he couldn't seem to banish from his head?

Maybe he deserved to be ruined.

"A man isn't made by the things he collects," his mother had told him after the will had been read and all the bequests made, as if a hotel mattered from a man who could have been a father but hadn't bothered to try. Right after she'd compared Jason to Daniel, to really stick that knife in and twist it as only she could. "But by the content of his heart and what he carries there."

"I don't know what that means," he'd replied grumpily, though he'd tried to keep the temper out of his voice because it was his mama talking and she deserved his respect.

"I know you don't."

"I don't have a single thing in common with that—"

"Jason." That was all it took. Just his name. He'd cut himself off and his mother had shrugged, her dark eyes on his like he was still a kid. Maybe he always would be, as far as she was concerned. *"Pa'a ka waha."*

He knew the phrase, Hawaiian for *observe, be silent and learn.* "If words are exiting your mouth, wisdom cannot come in," the saying went.

Sometimes it also just meant: shut your mouth.

He'd taken it on board then, and he did now, too. He surfed like it was his job. When he'd done his best to exhaust himself he came in, dried off and drove himself back up to the silent house, where he put in another few, vicious hours in his gym.

Until he sweated the mean out of him. Or tried his best.

And when his phone rang, indicating another one of those damned video calls he'd used to have to suffer through only with his PR people and now had to deal with at least once a week, and with his shiny new family to boot, he took it.

Even though it wasn't the right time or place for their strained family discussions, mandated by their father's will and trust.

"I think this is the first time I've ever seen you without palm trees in the background and a shit-eating grin on your face," his half brother Charlie drawled, all his usual Texas in his voice and a sunny balcony behind him with a different sea entirely in the distance. "I don't how to process that, brother."

Jason wiped his face with the nearest T-shirt and produced a grin. "Aloha, dick."

"Oh, good. There's that island charm I hear so much about."

"I'm thinking about burning this house down," Jason said, conversationally. "The lawyer said Dear Old Dad spent years building it. Almost like he planned to live in it one day, though I know that can't be true. He wasn't one to settle down, and particularly not this far out of the limelight. How would he get all that attention he was always jonesing for?"

Charlie's head tilted slightly to one side, the blue eyes everyone but Jason had shared with Daniel St. George going canny. "I was calling to tell you some deeply boring shit about the hotel industry that Angelique passed on because Thor's on a plane and I'm nothing if not obedient. But if you're burning down houses, I'm suddenly way more interested."

Charlie wasn't obedient. Fun fact, none of the children Daniel St. George had left littered around in his wake were particularly obedient. Hell, if they'd met under different circumstances, Jason might have considered them friends. Or decent drinking buddies, anyway.

"He left you fuckers hotels," Jason pointed out now, warming to the topic he'd been turning over in his head while he tried to exhaust himself. "He left me a whole island. Why should I turn it into a hotel? Why should there even be a house here? Maybe the greatest kindness I could do is give this whole place to the jungle again, like the old man never existed in the first place."

He had the strangest sensation he wasn't really talking about the island, but he didn't care to explore that notion. He found himself rubbing at his chest as if his heart hurt again, but he didn't like that very much, either.

Lucinda was on a plane somewhere. She'd claimed she felt nothing.

He should have felt nothing himself.

"I don't really get the drama," Charlie said after a moment. "You don't have to run the hotel. You don't have to do anything. You don't have to stay there if you don't want. You can just own it and go about your business."

"That's a great idea. And then I can be him in every possible way."

"Or not." Charlie shrugged. "Don't get me wrong. I'm not a fan of the guy. But I'm also not exactly crying a river over my circumstances these days. And I wouldn't have any of the things I do if it wasn't for the old man's will."

"You're not the one in danger of turning into Daniel St. George."

Charlie's grin was razor-sharp, reminding Jason that this particular half brother had spent most of his life playing outlaw games in the wilds of Texas, surrounded by far more dangerous men than Jason had ever been.

"If you don't want to turn into the old man, brother," Charlie said quietly, "it's real simple. Don't."

Jason listened to the business-related part of the call then, but after they hung up, he wandered outside and found himself brooding out at the view. The sky, the sea. And all the impenetrable jungle in between, with chattering birds in the trees and the dance of trade winds over his face.

All this tropical beauty that didn't go along with all he thought he knew about the man who'd made him. It was too remote here. Too unspoiled. Too perfect.

But then again, the real truth was that he didn't know Daniel St. George at all. He'd never met the man while he was alive. He'd had to read all the same articles and watch the same videos online that the rest of the word had if he wanted to know anything about the guy. The only thing Jason really knew about his father was how he felt about the man's absence. The stories he'd told himself as a kid to explain that absence. And the understanding he'd come to over time of what that brief affair had done to his mother.

And yeah, maybe he'd spent a little too much time and energy pushing himself to be the best he could be in everything he was even remotely good at, just to prove something.

Not to his mama, who had adored him since the

day he was born. Not to his actual *ohana*, his mother's people spread out over the Hawaiian Islands, who had actually been there for him while his mama worked her butt off and tried to keep him fed and clothed and happy.

In his football heyday, interviewers had always asked Jason where he'd gotten the drive to pursue the game the way he had. And he'd always told them some bullshit cobbled together from the kinds of things he thought he ought to feel, always bringing it back to his mother's sacrifices.

But he knew the truth. And here on this deserted island, with only the pieces of himself Lucinda had left behind, he let himself face it at last.

He'd spent his entire life trying to get his father to notice him.

He'd figured if he got a little famous, if he made a little noise, sooner or later his birth father would show up. Tell him how the desertion had been a mistake, or in Jason's best interest, or something. Maybe even hit him up for money. One way or another, Jason had figured he'd smoke the asshole out.

But Daniel had never shown up. If he'd been proud of Jason at all, he kept to himself.

The only thing Jason had of his father was his silence.

And if his mother was correct, the dedication to losing himself in disposable pussy because that was a hell of a lot easier than connecting with other people.

In case he had any doubts about that, Lucinda had given him a crash course in what it looked like to experience some crazy, life-altering intimacy and then fall all over herself to pretend it hadn't been that at all.

Had that been part of it, too? Had he been afraid that if he stopped roaming around the planet, sleeping with everything that moved, he'd lose the only link he had to a father he was pretty sure he wouldn't even like?

That had the ring of unfortunate, uncomfortable truth inside him.

But the other thing he knew was that when push came to shove, he was far more his mother's child than his father's.

And Leilani Kaoki had suffered exactly one fool, one time. Never before and never since. Daniel St. George had been her one mistake, and she'd spent every day since making sure she raised up a son who knew how to see the truth of everyone he encountered—even himself. Eventually.

And Jason knew a little something about excuses, sure. And the way a person could hide right there in his own mirror, if there were enough excuses at hand. How that could go on and on for years, but sooner or later, there was only a reflection in that mirror and too much truth to bear.

Why wouldn't *you build a resort here?* Lucinda had asked.

And Jason grinned now, while the breeze teased

his face and the sea sighed its way onto the rocks far below.

Because that was an excellent question.

And he knew just how he was going to answer her.

Lucinda rejoiced in her welcome home to England, four miserable travel days later. She'd had to wait longer than she'd liked in Fiji to get on a plane to Los Angeles, there in the sweltering heat. And had been forced to wait in too-sunny California for a seat on a plane back to London, too, for what had seemed like another eternity.

But when she'd finally made it onto a red-eye headed for the UK, Heathrow hunched there when they'd finally landed, gray and wet and green, like a song of homecoming.

She smiled as she surrendered herself to the tender mercies of the Tube that whisked her along beneath the London streets. She told herself she was merry and bright, despite another round of serious exhaustion hanging on her like a cloak, as she walked from the Tube stop back to her flat. She was happy every time she heard a horn, or screeching tires, or the rest of the clattering noise and dismal tumult of London.

Lucinda was sure she'd never been so happy in her life as she was to let herself into her flat, then find her way to the rain-streaked window in her lounge that looked out over a dingy rooftop and a few brick walls.

No assaulting sunshine. No complicated blue sky and sea, stretching on toward forever.

No half-naked man, all temptation and wickedness.

Just London, doing its thing. It made her imagine that all she needed was a good sleep and she'd feel like herself again. How hard could it be to forget about her too-brief time on a fairy-tale island? After a good sleep it would feel like nothing more than a dream, she was certain.

Lucinda staggered off to bed, slept for hours and woke up to treat herself to tea and toast. No platters of dramatic fruit, everything garnished with coconut and soft breezes. Just a proper breakfast on a rainy Thursday morning, like any other.

She thought about taking another day to settle herself but decided against it. Her endless hours of travel had allowed her to play her time on that island over and over again in her head. She'd relived every touch. Every sound she'd made, on the surfboard or in Jason's bed. What would lying about her flat do but make it worse?

She needed to put all of that behind her. Now.

Lucinda took a certain grim pleasure in her usual routine. The attention to her hair, her makeup. The heels she wore because practicality had its place, but sleek, stylish, wearable weapons were a woman's best friend.

And then, telling herself that she was *perfectly*

fine and suffered no ill effects or emotional residue *at all*, she headed back into work.

She was so busy congratulating herself on her escape from paradise and the terrifying lure of the most astoundingly beautiful man she'd ever met that it took her entirely too long to notice the way everyone in the office was staring at her.

"Is there something on my face?" she asked her harried assistant after she'd run the gauntlet of the executive floor. A little more sharply than necessary, perhaps.

"You're quite tanned, actually. That's surprising." Her usually reliable and practical assistant shook herself, as if she hadn't meant to say that. "But you're a legend, Lucinda. That's the main thing. You did it. You really did it."

Lucinda blinked. "What did I do?"

"You know." Pandora shook her head, admiringly, as if Lucinda was being coy. And then made it all worse by nudging her with her shoulder, as if they were friends. "They should have known better, shouldn't they? Lucinda Graves always gets what she wants."

Lucinda had the faintest inkling then—but surely not. Surely there was no way. Still, she was too taken back by the possibility to lecture her assistant on proper office decorum.

Especially when the phone rang and her presence was requested in the executive boardroom. Immediately.

"Congratulations," Pandora whispered after she put the phone down.

Lucinda turned and headed for the boardroom, done in achingly posh wood with gold accents and featuring a priceless view over London. She'd always loved that view. She liked to walk the long way through the office so she could look at it, always visible behind the clear glass walls that invited everyone in the office to see what it looked like when important meetings happened. Who attended and who dominated.

She had studied that room, and she'd vowed that one day, she would look out to see London at her feet and all of upper management gazing at her as if she was the star.

And she could see it happening as she walked toward the room. She saw all the men in their suits turn to watch her approach. She lengthened her stride, aware that she looked bulletproof and flawless, just the way she liked it.

She might not understand this moment, but it was hers, and she'd take it.

But then the sea of business suits parted, and everything changed.

Because Jason was here.

In London. In her office.

His back to that glorious view of London as if she was the only thing worth looking at.

And worse, he wasn't standing in the middle of

the executive boardroom with his miraculous chest out and all those acres and acres of brown skin and perfect tattoos on display. Lucinda felt that keenly, like one more betrayal.

Because Jason was wearing a black, obviously bespoke suit that hugged that big, athletic form of his in a way that made her blood turn molten in her veins. He'd scraped his hair back and fastened it, and that was terrible, too. It made him look like some kind of elegant marauder, and she couldn't bear the heat of it.

Much less the way his gaze caught hers through the glass.

As if he knew all the things she wanted so badly to hide. The anticipation in her belly that was easing its way lower still and changing into fire. The catch in her breath. That damnable weakness in her knees, just because he was near.

Every single lie she'd told herself over the past few days about how happy she was to get away from him.

She wanted to run, screaming. She wanted to keep on going, past the boardroom and back out into the gray morning. She wanted to pretend none of this was happening.

But that was the coward's way out. And Lucinda was no coward, no matter how much she wished otherwise this morning.

She lifted her chin to a properly belligerent angle. Then she shoved open the glass door and stepped inside.

Instantly, it was like the two of them were alone. As if there weren't all those other faceless executives in between them, judging them. Jason's gaze slammed into her the way his cock had, over and over, and she knew that he could see an answering heat all over her face.

She knew that he could see everything.

Especially all the lies she'd told herself—and him—to get her away from that island in the first place.

Someone said something, but she didn't know what. Or care.

Because even on a dreary, wet Thursday, surrounded by suits and wearing one himself—to blend in—there was nothing but wildness in the man who stood at that window and dared her to come at him. Sheer, untamed wildness, and what was wrong with her that every single thing in her thrilled to it?

As if she'd been carrying the same kind of wild around inside her, all this time.

And he knew that, too.

She could see that he did. She could *feel* it.

"Good morning, Lucinda," Jason said, those dark eyes glinting at her. Challenge and temper and what she very much feared was retribution. "Congratulations. You convinced me to build a resort on my island after all."

CHAPTER FOURTEEN

"You should look happier, Scotland," Jason drawled after he cleared the room. He was standing by the windows in this stuffy, confining office, his dark gaze fastened to Lucinda's like he could see straight through her. It almost frightened him how much he wanted to believe he could. "You won. You get what you wanted all along. Surely that calls for, if not a celebration, a smile?"

And her familiar scowl made his heart beat a little faster.

"This isn't about winning. This is a highhanded bit of strategy. The best defense is a good offense or whatever you Americans are always ranting on about." She stood straighter, as if she was seconds away from taking a swing at him. Which he would have welcomed, because he knew how it would end. "When you and I both knew you flew all the way to England because you didn't like the fact that I left you without your express permission."

After the executives had swarmed around Lucinda like ants on a picnic lunch, offering her all kinds of congratulations that didn't make it to the envy in their eyes, Jason had demanded some privacy. Not that there was much of it in this glass box of a room that might as well have been a fishbowl. The men in their suits all filed out, baring their teeth and murmuring their grudging appreciation Lucinda's way as they went. Some tried to glad-hand Jason, too, but he stared at them until they slunk away.

Now it was only the two of them and too much glass. And all he wanted to do was strip those dour clothes right off her. All that relentless, ruthless black. The angrily slicked-back red hair when his mouth watered for her glorious curls. He could see that the shoes she'd worn on the island had been a concession because here, the shoes she wore were skyscraper high, with red on their soles and killer points as heels. She looked mean and sharp, and he loved every inch of it.

He ached, everywhere, that he didn't have his hands on her already.

Especially when she was glaring at him as if his presence here was some kind of betrayal.

But Jason was holding on to the advice Charlie had given him. Hard. If he didn't want to be like their father, he didn't have to be. It was that simple and that complicated.

Their father would never have chased a woman

across the world. Their father had barely managed to remember a woman's name the next morning, or the location of the children he'd littered about the planet.

Step number one of not being Daniel St. George was the fact Jason had gotten on that plane. He'd decided that in the final tally, he didn't really care what happened on that island he'd never wanted and didn't know what to do with himself. He wasn't attached to it. He didn't have any dreams about it one way or another.

But he wasn't sure he wanted to go on living the same old life he'd already been living. Not without Lucinda.

Wasn't that a kick? She was the one night he never wanted to forget. If he had to chase her down on the other side of the planet, well, he was prepared to do that and more. He was more than happy to hunt her down. Lure her in with the resort she wanted. Keep her close with the one thing he knew she couldn't resist. Not without removing herself entirely.

Him.

"You don't want to build any kind of resort on that island," Lucinda was saying, her pale red brows pulled tight. Jason could see the sun on her face in the form of all those cute freckles, but her skin looked pale even so. Her blue eyes were too big, too wide, and her mouth might have been painted in a bright color he very much wanted to taste, but she pressed her lips flat. "You want to keep it as some kind of sulky tantrum. A monument to a man you're terrified you've already become. I understand that."

"Yeah. You sound real understanding."

"I'm not going to pretend this is professional, because I think we ripped through that boundary a long time ago."

"It was never professional, darlin'."

Lucinda's chin lifted higher, which should have been impossible. "Do you really believe that you're the only person in the world who has a shit father, Jason? I don't know how to break this to you, but that doesn't make you special. It makes you alive, that's all. You should count yourself lucky that your shit father was considerate enough to ignore you for your entire life. Mine was far less accommodating."

She laughed, though there was precious little humor in the sound. "And mine didn't leave me a luxurious private island, complete with a stately home for my personal use, plonked down in the middle of the sparkling Pacific Ocean as an apology. Last I heard, in fact, my father has drunk his way through several stints in prison, at least as many bouts of liver disease and more lost jobs than you can count. And he's still going strong, no doubt beating up my mother and terrifying neighbor children just the way he used to do me. So you will forgive me, I hope, if my sympathy for your plight is somewhat dim."

"Good rant, Lucinda," Jason drawled. "Have you been stewing on that one ever since you left Fiji?"

She looked past him and blinked. Then squared her shoulders as if she'd forgotten that they had an entire audience clustered there on the other side of the glass, pretending that they were going about their business. When she looked back at him, her hands were curled into fists at her side, and Jason knew her well enough now to understand that that storm in her gaze was turmoil. Emotion.

Not that she'd admit it. Not his stubborn redhead.

His heart kicked at him again.

"As a matter of fact, I did not spend a series of unpleasant long-haul flights having fights with people who weren't there. I do try to avoid that whenever possible." Lucinda sighed, as if her pissy, prissy voice irritated her, too. "If your goal was to disconcert me, I'm afraid you've come all this way for nothing. I don't know why you suddenly want to develop the island, but if you're under the impression that I'm going to come over all noble and refuse to do it because you're so clearly using it as a bargaining chip in whatever psychodrama you have going on in your head, I'm afraid you're going to be quite disappointed."

"I don't give a shit about the island, darlin'," Jason said quietly. "If I wake up one morning filled with regret that I developed this one, guess what? I can buy myself another one. As you pointed out, the place itself has no sentimental value to me. But it does to you."

"Wrong again." She quirked her lips into that frozen, polite smile that she probably didn't realize just made him hard. "I'm not a sentimental person. It's not in my nature."

"Maybe not in the past. But you didn't know me then."

This time her laugh was straight-up patronizing. "This conversation is becoming deeply embarrassing."

She didn't say, *for you*. She didn't have to say it.

"I don't embarrass easily," Jason replied. He smoothed his hand down the front of his monkey suit, amused when her gaze tracked the movement. And even more entertained when her eyes snapped back to his, her cheeks flushing when she saw he was watching her do it. "You can have my island. And develop it anyway you want, tiki torches and private coves out the ass for all I care. We can sign all these contracts and all the lawyers can wet themselves with this clause and that clause. Whatever. But you and I are going to come to different kind of agreement."

She regarded him coolly. "I'm listening."

So stuffy. So clipped, like she was the Queen talking down to a dirty peasant. But she should know better. Because she and Jason weren't that different, underneath it all. He knew all about her now. And he knew that trash like the two of them loved it when they were underestimated. Hell, it gave them life.

"You already gave me your body once," he said,

low and lazy, like this was a bar instead of a board-room. "All I want is more."

Color stained her cheeks, but Lucinda didn't flinch. Her cool expression didn't change at all. "De-fine 'more.'"

"You," he said, very distinctly and directly. So there could be no mistake. "In my bed. As long as it takes."

"As long as it takes to have sex? I think we both know that's no time at all. Did you really fly all the way here to ask for a quick shag?"

"For as long as it takes to build your resort," he said, patient now as he waited for that to sink in.

The color all over her cheeks deepened. Her eyes narrowed. And at her sides, those adorable little fists grew so tight her knuckles whitened.

"You understand, of course, that you're not talk-ing about another night. Or even a week. It will take years."

"I understand."

Her throat worked. "You can't possibly want that. You don't."

"I'm pretty sure I asked for it. Explicitly and di-rectly."

"Right. You mean you want me in one of your beds. When and if you have the urge. Like your own, personal call girl. Is that it?"

Jason laughed. "If that's what you want to call yourself, I'm all for it. I like a little role play."

She shuddered, then clearly tried to hide it. "So whenever I'm in the vicinity—"

"You're going to spend a lot of time in the vicinity," Jason interrupted her smoothly. Because this was the key point. "It's a remote island, Scotland. You're going to spend so much time there, making it what you want it to be, that really, it doesn't make sense for you to do anything but move in."

Her lovely, lush mouth dropped open. Her blue eyes clouded over with confusion.

And everything in Jason pulled tight.

"Move in," she echoed faintly. "With you."

"I can't think of a better way to get you in my bed every night, can you? Much as I love flying around the planet, it's kind of a long commute from my island to London."

"This is ridiculous. You're just…taking the piss."

He loved it when her accent slipped. When her eyes flashed. When she used expressions he was quite certain weren't considered strictly appropriate in a business setting. Something she was normally so concerned with.

Jason was perfectly happy to be the reason she lost her cool.

"I told you what I want, Lucinda. It's the only way for you to get your hands on my island. So really, the choice is yours."

"What kind of choice is that?" As if she heard her own voice echoing back at her from the glass wall, she cleared her throat. And he watched her pull herself together. He watched her pull that smooth, cool mask into place again. "I imagine you think this is something else I'm likely to balk at. Well, guess again. I can't say my ambitions have ever extended to becoming some man's live-in fuck toy, but if that's what it takes." She lifted her shoulder, then dropped it, her gaze defiant on his. "I'll do it."

"Then it sounds like we have a deal."

"That cottage would be a perfect place to make my base of operations," Lucinda said, musingly. "When you feel the need to go fishing around in the international model pool, as you tend to do so often, that's fine. There will be beds aplenty and no need to overlap in any of them. And I'm sure there are hotel bars aplenty in all those resorts on Fiji should I need to scratch an itch."

Jason opted not to think too hard on how she'd go about scratching that itch, because if he did he was likely to shatter all that glass that hemmed them in. He considered shattering it anyway, but restrained himself.

Barely.

And who knew he had all that greedy possessiveness in him?

"That's not how this is going to work, baby," Jason said instead, his gaze so intent on her that he was surprised she didn't bow beneath the pressure. "I'm not going to share. Neither are you."

Lucinda stared back at him for what felt like a small eternity. Maybe two. He watched that pulse in her throat go nuts. He watched those knuckles get even whiter.

"Jason. You do realize that what you're suggesting sounds an awful lot like…"

She didn't finish.

"A relationship?" He laughed. "It does sound like that, doesn't it? But don't worry, Lucinda. You don't have to call it that if it scares you."

He expected her to jump on that word and insist that nothing scared her, but she didn't. Her gaze wheeled around the room and yet he knew, somehow, that she wasn't seeing a thing.

"I can't possibly imagine why you would want such a thing," she said, sounding something like panicked. "I don't believe you do."

"Believe it."

Her mouth actually fell open again, her eyes coming back to his and fixing there in confusion. She started to say something but stopped, almost as if the words weren't forming the way she wanted them to.

And all of these were victories, Jason knew. But not the one he wanted.

"But…" She shook her head. "You don't do relationships. Ever."

"And look where that got me. I might as well be following the Daniel St. George playbook, step by asshole step. It all led to the same place. That's not the life I want."

"If what you want is a relationship, I'm quite sure you can find any number of women to oblige you. All you need do is swan out into the street and stand still a moment. You don't need me to facilitate any of it."

"I want you."

Lucinda blew out a breath, and suddenly she didn't look like a fighter. She looked shaky and uncertain, and that made his chest hurt even more. "No. You can't. It doesn't make any sense."

Jason moved toward her then. And he considered himself a martyr of the highest order when he didn't simply put his hands on her and throw her on the table that took up most of the space in this fishbowl. He stopped when he was close—close enough to cause a little comment out there on the other side of the glass, maybe.

Let them stare, he thought.

"It's like this, Scotland," he rumbled at her, trying to keep his hold on himself intact. Trying to ignore the hundreds of ways he could feel it fraying. "I know why you ran off the way you did. Feelings are messy. That's why I spent my whole life avoiding them, but guess what? They caught up to me anyway when you sauntered into my crumbling-ass hotel. And I could have come here, and made pretty speeches, but that's not the way to your heart."

"My heart?" she echoed, looking appalled. She looked around as if she wanted to back up, but the table was behind her. She frowned at him. "This is about business, Jason. It's all very unorthodox, I grant you, but still business."

"Call it business if you want," he said, easily enough. "I don't really care. If an island is what it takes to buy some time with you? I'm going to call it cheap. Because I think what really scares you is that you can't maintain this business bullshit. You could do it after one night, sure. You could crawl out of my bed, run away in the dark and put your armor back on. But you won't be able to do that month after month. Year after year. Then what?"

Her lips trembled. "You're insane."

"That's not the word I'd use. But the one that fits would freak you out, so sure, I'm insane. The question is, are you willing to put yourself on the line or are you too afraid? It's a simple choice, Lucinda."

"There's nothing simple about this!"

"You know that I can make you come," Jason said, calmly. "Over and over again. So what's the harm? You get to live in a beautiful house, come so hard it makes you cry regularly, and work on building the resort of your dreams. It seems to me the only reason you wouldn't jump at the chance is if, deep down, you know that the reason you left in the first place is that you can't have that kind of sex, with me, without getting your heart involved after all."

And he reached over and pressed two fingers over her heart, as punctuation.

This time, she flinched. She swatted at his hand, but ended up hooking his fingers with her palm.

And he was almost surprised that she didn't take a swing at him, the way she was looking up at him then, like she wanted to kill him with her own hands. But he could see that there was something almost desolate behind the flash of fury.

If he could, he'd let her kill him if that would take the desolation away.

"The joke's on you, Jason," she threw at him, fury and despair in her voice and all over her face, and he got it then. She'd already killed him. The man he'd been before she showed up on his island was good and dead, and here he was instead. Ready and willing to do whatever it took to make her happy instead of…whatever this was. "Because I don't have a heart. And I could live with you for the rest of my life, and that's not going to change."

He wanted to grab her up in his arms and kiss her until that darkness lifted. But he knew his way around armor, so he grinned instead.

"Great," he said, and even shrugged lazily. "Then you have nothing to lose."

CHAPTER FIFTEEN

LUCINDA DIDN'T KNOW how many earthquakes and volcanic eruptions could go off inside her and leave her still in one piece. She was surprised that her bones hadn't shaken their way out of her limbs, so deeply did she feel that trembling. She felt ripped open. Hunted.

And the damned man was grinning at her. *Grinning.*

"You don't want this," she said, possibly not for the first time. "You only think you do because I didn't let you do the leaving."

And abruptly, Jason stopped grinning. Reminding her—in a way that made her head spin—that he was no lazier than she was. That he could put it on the way she did a good business suit.

"I do want this," he told her, and that light in his gaze looked like temper then. Something that made her shiver for a completely different reason, because she could practically still taste the last time he'd lost control, so deep inside her. She couldn't breathe. "I want to get to know you in every possible way, Lucinda. I want to taste you on my mouth. I want to feel you, deep beneath my skin. I want long, lazy mornings, and impossibly dangerous nights. Another and another and another. Don't tell me what I have an appetite for, because that only makes me hungrier."

"The only reason you think you want me is because you can't have me."

"I've already had you and it wasn't enough." His gaze was narrow, black and setting off explosions inside her. "Do you think I chase around after every woman I touch who sneaks out before dawn? Here's a newsflash. I don't."

"You don't like the fact I walked away from you." She'd grabbed on to that and she was going to run with it. Because Jason was a very particular kind of man. All rangy and predatory and practically bursting with confidence and this is what they were like. "That's all this is. And I don't see why I should have to uproot my life for some adolescent fantasy—"

"Baby. I can assure you, not one of my fantasies is adolescent."

And Lucinda felt that like a new fire, all over her body. Inside. Outside. In and out of all the earthquakes and eruptions until she was lit up like Guy Fawkes Day or New Year's Eve.

Until she didn't know what part of her was fireworks and blinding light, and what was left of her, safe and quiet.

"They'll all say I slept my way to the top," she said, switching tactics.

But he laughed at that, too, lifting his chin toward the rest of the office. The office Lucinda had completely forgotten about. "Like they don't already."

She frowned at him, not sure what shook her more. That he could shrug off something like that. Or that she clearly could, too, since she hadn't given a thought to what her superiors might be thinking about her or this situation since she'd walked in the room and locked eyes with Jason. And besides, she knew he was right.

What was happening to her?

And she hated that this was so easy for him. That everything was so easy for him. He could inherit an island from a father he'd never had to hide from and live on it as some kind of stunt. He could buy himself a new island if the first one didn't suit. He could beat her back to England, just to march into her office— her sanctuary—to make a point.

To make demands.

And worst of all, he could offer her things she was afraid to dream. Because she knew better.

If she lived with him, slept with him and woke with him, melded her life with his— Touched him and tasted him and settled into him, even if she knew that it had an end date and that it wasn't reality—

Lucinda simply couldn't risk it.

She had spent all of this time doing her very best

to make sure no one ever got a look beneath her icy exterior. Not so much as a glimpse. She'd never abandoned her armor, ever. Not in all the years she'd fought to rise to her current position.

Not until she'd found herself on a tropical island with Jason Kaoki.

And now she was terribly afraid that deep down inside her she wasn't even remotely as hard as she pretended to be.

She forced herself to concentrate on the latest outrageous thing that Jason had said instead. *Because it's easier*, something in her whispered.

"They do not think I've slept my way to the top and they won't. You have no idea how hard I've fought for every single thing I have." She hurled the words at him, aware as she did that she meant them. That this wasn't as simple as a new tactic. The words...hurt. "You have no idea the hills I've climbed or what it's cost me."

"You're wrong." His voice was as intense as hers. His gaze was fierce. "I know every single inch of those hills, baby. And believe me, I know the price."

"Don't make me laugh." But she did, and that hurt, too. "Some of us weren't blessed with athletic prowess and matinee idol good looks. Some of us can't smile our way into a better future, we have to claw for it. One broken fingernail at a time."

And she had never seen that expression on his face before. No grinning, no glinting gold in his dark eyes. His beautiful face was like stone, and something inside her turned over.

As if this, at last, was the true Jason Kaoki.

No mask. No bullshit.

And something foreboding shivered to life inside her again. Or maybe it was yearning, thick and deep.

If she didn't stop him, she could never go back. Lucinda understood that deep into her bones.

If she didn't keep him from taking this conversation where it was headed now, she would never be the same person who'd walked into this office. Never.

She knew that as well as she knew her own name.

But the truth of the matter was, she hadn't come back to England the same Lucinda who'd left. She'd already changed. The woman who'd set foot on that island wasn't the one who'd run away from it.

And she remembered something he'd said during those perfect, endlessly sweet hours on the water. That there was no beating a wave into submission. There was no making it jump through hoops or do her bidding.

There was only enjoying the ride.

Let go, something in her whispered. *All you need to do is let go.*

But Lucinda didn't know how.

"There's not one thing you can tell me about fighting your way out of nothing that I didn't live through myself," Jason told her then, a kind of ferocity making him simultaneously more lethal and more beautiful. And making her skin feel so tight she thought she might crack wide open. "I'm not crazy, Lucinda. I know we only had one night together. But what a fucking night. I'm willing to put everything I have on the line to see if what I think is there is really there."

"Everything you have." She made a scoffing noise, but the fact her voice was shaking rather took away from the effect. "An island you don't give a toss about, that's all."

"My heart, Scotland." His dark eyes blazed down at her. "I'm talking about my *heart*. I've loved one woman in my entire life, and she's the one who told me to get my shit together and stop acting like a man who broke her heart and mine before I was even born. You think I'm not scared? You think I expected you to come wandering onto my island? Here's a fun fact, Lucinda. You don't go and hide out there on the edge of the end of the world if you're expecting company."

Her mouth was dry and her eyes were suspiciously damp. "You don't know what you're asking."

"I know exactly what I'm asking," he threw at her, and his voice was harder then. Bigger, like it was leaving marks on him, too. "I know all the things you had to swallow down to survive. All the times you had to smile when you wanted to rip someone's throat out. All those soft, pampered little rich kids who didn't know how good they had it, telling you how to live. Believe me, I know. You want to fight everything you see because it's the only thing you know how to do. The only thing you're any good at. My God, baby, you have to know that I'm right there with you."

"Then why are you fighting?" And Lucinda felt an odd weightlessness, a shuddering, and understood on some dim level that she'd lost control. Of this interaction, certainly. But worse, of herself. She'd lost any sense of where they were or who might be watching. Worse, she didn't care. And all the while her heart kicked at her, so hard she was sure it was already in pieces. "If you know, why are you saying all these crazy, impossible things?"

"Because I don't believe we're broken," he roared, or maybe it was only Lucinda who shook. Not the glass walls. Not London. "I don't believe that all the things we had to shove aside to get where we wanted to go are lost forever. I believe they're right here." And he slammed one big hand on his chest then. "Right fucking here."

She thought she said something, but her head was making too much noise. Her heart was like thunder.

"You humbled me, Lucinda," Jason said, and she could hear him perfectly. As if he was inside her, inside that thunder. "You made me feel like a god and you made me want to cry like a child, and the only way I could think to convince you to give this a shot was to make it one more fucking transaction, because that's what you understand best."

"It's who I am," she whispered.

"I don't believe that all you are is ambition." Jason's growl dared her to defy him. "Just like I don't believe the only thing I'll ever be good at is throwing a football. I think there's more. I want more. And Lucinda, I want you to want more with me."

There was no reason that she should be crying. Fat, wet tears tracking down her cheeks and wrecking her. There was no reason that she should be shaking as if she was cold, her teeth chattering, one more earthquake working its way out from inside her.

There was no reason that sex with this man should have felt like a sacrament, or that leaving him should have felt like chopping off a limb, and how was she supposed to go on with all these feelings bursting out of her?

"I decided a long time ago that I had to make a choice," she told him, her lips nearly numb with the effort it took to keep from screaming. "Other girls had the luxury of their emotions, but not me. I made a plan, then I executed it. I didn't waste time worrying about others people's feelings, and I had no time at all for mine. There was only the plan. And my life was absolutely fine. It *is* absolutely fine. I don't need...this."

You.

"But what if you don't have to hide?" he threw right back at her. "What if you don't have to build your dream for other people to live in it? What if you can live your own?"

"Shut up," she tried to shout at him, but it was barely a whisper.

"What if," Jason said, very quietly, though each word felt etched in stone, "you didn't have to work so hard to make other people happy? What if you got to just…be happy?"

She didn't know when his hands had come up to grip her upper arms. She didn't know when he'd dropped his face to hers, so close that she was sure she could taste him already.

And she was aware that her whole company was right there on the other side of that glass, no doubt staring at this display—but for once in her life, Lucinda didn't care what anyone else thought of her.

What if…?

Two little words with too much weight, careening around inside her.

"Some people don't get to be happy," she managed to say, though her voice caught. "The best they can hope for is to be focused. Driven. And if you achieve what you want, in the end, it feels like the same thing."

"Bullshit, baby," Jason retorted, dark and sure. "I don't know what 'driven' tastes like. But I have a pretty good idea that happiness tastes like this."

His lips touched hers, and it wasn't the mad passion of the island. It wasn't that drugging, intoxicating jolt of electricity.

Or it was that, but it was so much more, too.

He tasted like promises. Like dreams come true.

Like happily-ever-afters and a whole wide world of *yes*.

She found her hands on the lapels of that beautiful suit and she pushed herself back from him, her eyes too full with feelings she didn't have the slightest clue how to name.

"Jason." And his voice was hardly a prayer, though it felt like one. "Don't you understand? The only thing I know how to do, the only thing I *can* do, is fight."

"Then fight," he dared her, a light she couldn't let herself believe in shining there in his eyes. "Fight like hell, Scotland. I can handle your fight. Are you kidding? It turns me on."

"Everything turns you on." But she shook her head, afraid to give in to that odd urge to laugh her way through this. "I just don't think—"

"Don't." His hands moved to cup her face, brushing the dampness aside with his thumbs. "Don't think. Fight. But Lucinda, stop fighting me. Fight for me. Fight with me. And who knows? Maybe we'll build a whole lot more than a resort."

And she thought about surfing. About climbing up on that board and finding her balance on the shifting waves beneath her. No plan in the world had helped her then. There had only been learning to lean, to balance, to shift her weight and find her way.

And once she had, she'd flown. She'd catapulted into all that blue, fast and free.

Kind of how she felt right now, with Jason's hands on her face and his dark gaze on hers, all that expectation and hope and that swelling thing, that ache, that joy, she was too scared to name.

But she didn't have to name it. All she had to do was stand up, find her feet and commit herself to the ride—knowing that Jason was right there beside her, all the way from here to forever, if she'd let him.

If she'd just let him.

She stopped shuddering. She took a deep breath.

She tipped back her head, she let a smile crack her whole face open, and for the first time in her life, Lucinda Graves…let go.

CHAPTER SIXTEEN

A LITTLE MORE than two years later, Lucinda woke in the middle of the night. She knew it was the middle of the night because the clock on her bedside table told her so, but the insistent light outside the windows told different tale.

Because this far north in an Icelandic summer, there was nothing but daylight no matter what time of day it was.

Lucinda had been here two days so far and she wasn't sure she could ever get used to it the way the locals seemed to.

She swung out of the huge, imposing bed and padded over to the window. Outside and far below, the surging sea hurled itself against a spit of volcanic rock that jutted out from the rocky coast. She thought, not for the first time, that it looked as if it could belong to the island she now thought of as hers—well, hers and Jason's—though it was much, much colder here. Even though it was supposedly summer.

She wasn't surprised when she felt Jason come up behind her. She hadn't heard him move, but she was used to that now—the fact that such a big man could move so quietly. And she could feel him these days, as if they were connected.

He pulled her back against his chest, so she could feel all that sweet, drugging heat of his. He was like her own personal furnace.

"Come back to bed," he rumbled in her ear.

"Maybe I don't want to come back to bed," she said, though she was smiling. It had taken her a long time to get used to smiling so much. Her cheeks had ached so much the first few months that she'd secretly worried there was something wrong with her. When she'd finally confessed her fears to Jason, he'd roared with laughter. And then made her ache in a whole different way. "Isn't this supposed to be a famous sex hotel? Maybe I want to check out the dungeon."

His response was instant and unmistakable. "Just say the word, baby."

Lucinda's body shivered into instant, red-hot awareness, the way it always did. It didn't matter how recently she'd had him—in this case, in a glorious, screaming rush on the very bed that waited for them across the room—she always wanted more.

More, and then more still.

The past two years had been one dream coming true after the next. Lucinda had built her resort

with painstaking care. And had quit her company—
and their snide remarks about her relationship with
Jason—the moment it was done, the better to branch
out on her own. Pandora had come with her, and together they'd gone even further than Lucinda could
have imagined on her own. She'd gotten everything
she'd ever wanted, and so much more, and she'd
gotten Jason, too—the thing she hadn't known she
wanted. The thing that made all the rest of it matter.

Which wasn't to say it had always been smooth
or easy.

The funny thing about armor was that prying it
off proved just as hard as putting it on in the first
place had been. Meaning, one painful moment after
the next. Together and apart. Neither one of them was
good at backing down, and sometimes they fought
because that was what they knew how to do.

But Jason demanded intimacy. And Lucinda
found that the more she gave, the deeper it went,
and the more it turned out she had to give, after all.
Which made her crave the very intimacy she feared.

It was a circle, maybe. But at the center of the circle, there was Jason, and he was worth it.

God, was he worth it.

"Come to bed," Jason said again, with more of an
order in his voice this time. "Maybe you forgot we
have a fancy wedding in the morning."

"A fancy commitment ceremony, I think you
mean. Isn't that what it said on the invitation?"

"I don't know." Jason was tired of waiting, clearly, because he leaned down and hauled Lucinda up, tossing her over his shoulder as he turned back to the bed. "Blah, blah, blah, the professor likes her lectures. I don't really care what they call it as long as they're happy."

"You're a romantic caveman," Lucinda said, laughing. And enjoying the view of her man's perfect ass as he walked. "That's what I love about you the most."

He tossed her down on the high mattress, coming down after her. And he wasted no time pressing her down against it with every inch of that hard, sculpted body.

They fit together like puzzle pieces. Flush and true.

"Say that again," he rumbled at her.

Because it had taken her a long time. A very long time, and then a little bit longer still.

I love you, she had said, purely by accident one day. The resort had been well under way and entering its final phase. All Jason had done was appear on the worksite with a special cup of coffee he'd made just for her. She looked up, accepted the cup and lost her mind.

I love you, she had said, and it was as if the sun rose all over again. That was the look he'd given her.

Right before he showed her exactly how he felt

about those words, without even locking the door to the construction trailer she'd used as an office.

She still wasn't over it.

"I love you," she said now, hushed and awed, the way she always was.

Because he wasn't simply beautiful outside—though he was that all right, in spades.

Jason was the kind of beautiful that left marks. That encouraged her to better herself, particularly when she least wanted to do it.

He'd taught her to let go. And in return, she loved him the way his father hadn't, or couldn't. With every single part of herself. Every dream, every wish.

Everything she had, she gave to him. And he gave it right back.

She felt the thick head of his cock against her entrance, and she was already—always—hot and wet and ready for him. White night, tropical storms and everything in between. All she really needed was this. Him.

"I love you," she said again, like a vow.

"Damn right you do," Jason growled.

Then thrust his way inside her, bringing them both home.

The wedding—or ceremony, or whatever it was—was surprisingly sweet, Jason thought the next day.

Thor and his professor, Margot, exchanged vows, though not the kind of traditional vows that Jason was used to. Very little honoring and possessing, and a whole lot of promising and hoping.

Jason realized, as he stood in the small group before the altar they'd made out there on the rocks with the sea as fierce witness behind them, that he'd never seen Thor smile like that before. Not once in all those video calls.

It made him smile, too.

"Is the Viking actually a marshmallow?" Angelique murmured from beside him, one hand toying idly with the choker at her throat. "Can a Viking *be* a marshmallow?"

"A Viking perhaps," her prince, Zain, said from her other side, a faint smile on his mouth. "But not, I think, a prince."

The two of them exchanged a heated look, and Jason smiled a little wider.

On Zain's other side, Charlie was shaking his head.

"Nobody wants to be a marshmallow," he drawled, all kinds of Texas in his voice. "Especially a Viking."

But Jason saw the way Charlie gazed at his wife, Maya, who jiggled their toddler on her hip, murmuring something to him as the little boy's lower lip trembled. And his smile got even bigger.

"I don't need a marshmallow, thank you," his own woman said from beside him, prim and faintly disapproving. "I like a little fight."

And Jason turned the full force of his smile on

Lucinda, because he knew that a knockdown, drag-out firefight always led to the hottest makeup sex. But he also knew that when he got sweet, she cried.

So she could pretend she didn't like a little marsh-mallow goodness if it made her feel tough. He knew better.

Up on the stone altar, Thor and his woman made their union, whatever they called it, real. They kissed, their friends and family applauded, and Jason decided that he might not know his brothers and sister as well as some people knew their siblings, but he liked them all the same.

And as the crowd moved to the tent set out on a bluff next to the hotel, up above the sea, Thor and his brand-new wife came to stand with this little knot of people whom Daniel St. George had brought together.

Hell, Jason thought. Maybe the old man wasn't much of a father in his lifetime. But he'd done all right after his death.

"To weddings that aren't weddings," Charlie's wife, Maya, said, grinning at Margot in her pale red dress.

"Because there's so much more to marriage than the ceremony that starts it," Margot replied, but she was grinning so wide it made all her blue and purple hair bounce a little.

"To *ohana*," Jason said, grinning at them all. "To

all of you, my brothers and sister. And to our dearly departed father, who made all of this happen."

"Fuck that guy," Charlie said lazily.

They all laughed and lifted their glasses, and Jason felt a different kind of peace settle in on him then. When he looked down, it was Lucinda, with her arm around him and her curls everywhere, just the way he liked it. She was pressed up close to his side, her arm around his waist, because she knew.

That his feelings about his father were layered. And he could laugh about it sometimes, but other times it ate at him. He'd shown her all of him, the ugly and the sweet, and she'd smiled at him and asked for more.

And he thought that there would probably be no more perfect moment in his life. Than this. Real *ohana*. His siblings who were more like friends every day.

And the love of his life, freckles across her nose and her hair like fire.

"I'm going to marry you," he told Lucinda then. "And soon, Scotland. So you might want to get your head around it now."

Everyone around them laughed, but his gaze was on his woman. There was a time she would have turned bright red. When talking about private things in public would have made her want to keel over where she stood.

But they weren't the same people they'd been

when they'd met for the first time in that falling-down hotel.

They'd knocked the old building down, and with it, all those outdated and unnecessary parts of themselves they'd been forced to build into this fortress or that weapon to scrape their way through this life in the first place.

But now they had each other. They didn't need all those walls and sharp edges.

Though they'd kept a chunk of that building, to remind them. It sat like a sculpture in one of their gardens.

Lucinda smiled at him now, big and bright on this strange, cold island, while the rest of his family cheered.

"I'll marry you," she threw back at him, her voice rich and Scottish all the way through. "But you'll bloody well *ask*."

He heard his brothers roar with laughter. He could hear his sister do the same.

And his woman's eyes were blue like his ocean, his sky.

His everything.

Jason was not a man of small gestures. He sank down to his knees, opened his arms wide and did absolutely nothing to quiet himself as he laughed, too.

And he knew that everyone was staring at them. He reveled in it.

He reached into the pocket of his fancy jacket

and pulled out a small box. He cracked it open so she could see the ring that nestled there. Two perfect sapphires, one for each sea they'd crossed to find each other. The Pacific and the Atlantic in turn. And in the center, a brilliant, fiery diamond, which couldn't come close to the fire he felt every time he looked at her.

But it was a start.

"Lucinda," he belted out, like he was his own goddamn church bell. "I love you. Are you going to marry me?"

"You're damned right I am," she replied fiercely, and then catapulted herself straight into his arms.

And that night, on the top of the world on another volcanic island not his own, Jason celebrated his family.

The father he'd never known, who'd lost out, as far as he was concerned. The brothers he enjoyed more every time he saw them, and their fascinating wives. The sister he liked more every time he met her, and her prince.

The woman who had made him whole. And bright.

And so happy that sometimes, he was positive he was the one who was dreaming, after all.

He thought about family, and he thought about love, and there in that bed in the hotel that Thor ran, he and Lucinda started working on their own.

Three months later, she married him. She wore flowers and a sarong, his brothers and sister and their spouses looked on, his mother cried, and when it was done Jason threw the best damn luau the Pacific Islands had ever seen.

Six months after that, Lucinda gave birth to their first child. A baby boy.

They named him Daniel, for second chances.

Because they were living theirs, every beautiful day for the rest of their lives.

* * * * *

MR ONE-NIGHT
STAND

RACHAEL STEWART

MILLS & BOON

My first Mills & Boon has to go to my mum and dad, for instilling in me their passion for books from a very young age.

To my mother, for her wild ways, which certainly shaped my ability to produce work that tends towards the heated end of the spectrum, and to my father, for always believing in me.

My only regret is that my mother didn't live long enough to see me welcomed into the world of Harlequin Mills & Boon—so, Dad, you need to celebrate enough for the two of you now, okay?

Love you both always. Thank you for making me, me.
xxx

CHAPTER ONE

PATIENCE—HE WASN'T known for it. Why should he be when he'd worked his entire life to ensure he got everything he wanted, when he wanted it?

Flicking his wrist, he checked the time. Eight twenty-five.

Where the hell were they?

If being late was a last-ditch attempt at angling for more money, then Tony Andrews was an even bigger fool than Marcus had had him pegged for.

He waved away the approaching waitress who was eyeing his empty glass. He'd already indulged in a whisky and filled his one-drink-while-on-business quota. He wasn't fool enough to indulge in more. Although the girl's perfect parting pout made clear that it wasn't just a drink being offered.

Not tonight. He smiled back.

He might be considered an arrogant ass by many, but no one could accuse him of lacking in manners. Even his questionable childhood hadn't beaten those out of him—much as his father might have tried.

It was hardly her fault he wasn't up for it. She had appeal aplenty, if surgically enhanced assets and peroxide hair were your thing.

But tonight was about work.

And work was work.

Sex was sex.

Never should the two be mixed. Not if you wanted to stay focused and come out on top.

He watched as she weaved her way back through the intimate arrangement of tables, breaking his gaze to scan again the people occupying the circular floor space of the exclusive rooftop venue. Andrews had chosen it for convenience, it being located only two blocks down from his London HQ.

Very convenient for Andrews—*not so sodding convenient for him*. He rolled his shoulders and re-checked his watch.

What the hell was he doing?

He should've left ten minutes after the hour, not sat there like some obedient monkey.

But then, he wasn't there simply to catch up with the man he was in the process of buying out. He was there to be introduced to Andrews' business partner— soon-to-be *his* partner—Jennifer Hayes, before they signed on the dotted line.

Not that the introduction would make any difference; the deal was as good as done. But professional courtesy made him stay. That and the fact he was curious to meet her—the exec who'd turned a business into the largest successful start-up the industry had seen in years.

He was convinced Andrews hadn't been responsible for it. It was a wonder the man could still see straight, with his mounting gambling debts and outside work attentions. And then there was the drink problem. No one had confirmed it, but Marcus was sure he had one. He knew the signs well enough, thanks to dear old Dad.

So, yes, he doubted Andrews had done a full day's work in years—and that meant one thing: Miss Hayes was the one carrying the company; she was the one he was effectively buying into.

He'd read her profile, noticeably devoid of any pictures, and figured her to be late thirties, early forties. A woman with shrewd business acumen, a bearing that bordered on cold, and a definite force in the boardroom—all of which he'd respect her for. So long as they were on the same page.

It intrigued him that he hadn't come across any pictures. Not even a professionally enhanced shot used to support all those public accolades. Maybe she didn't go in for that kind of vanity. Or maybe Andrews did all that for her. He was certainly everywhere. Even the *Forbes* article he'd thrust into his hands at a charity auction last month, when he'd put forward his proposition, had highlighted the success of the business but featured Andrews alone, his greased back hair and cocky grin filling half the page.

The memory of that expression goaded Marcus further now as he waited and waited, fingers drumming on the tabletop, his patience hitting breaking point.

Seriously—enough was enough. The papers would be taken care of in less than twenty-four hours regardless. He might as well meet her then.

Tugging at the cuffs of his shirt, he made to stand up just as the cables of the glass elevator started to shift. *New arrivals?*

He settled back and waited for them to come into view.

It wasn't Andrews. That was immediately obvious. The small, balding lift attendant was being dwarfed by a statuesque redhead who made even the impressive lift look small. He wasn't the only one noticing either. Her hair was pulling every eye in the room. Its cascading waves ran down her back, glinting in the ambient light, impossible to ignore.

Its dramatic colour was a striking contrast to the black dress that clung to her curves before halting modestly at the knee. His gaze dropped lower still, to her exposed calves, to the subtle shimmer that teased with the possibility of stockings. And then came her shoes, her severe black stilettos…

Heat assaulted his groin.

Fuck me.

He wasn't going anywhere. Not just yet. Andrews could have the extra time for free…

Jennifer glanced at her watch and cursed under her breath. Eight-thirty. She was late. She hated being late.

But then, what did Tony expect, calling her at the eleventh hour and asking that she meet him for drinks? The blasted guy should know better than most what kind of workload she had.

Hell, who was she kidding? He couldn't give a shit what her to-do list looked like. Truth was, *he* was the cause of most of it. His increasing absence these last couple of weeks was pushing her to the brink and sending her stress levels through the roof. And yet here it came, that little voice in her head…

He has so much going on...he needs you...his family needs you...

But, hell, *her* family needed her too—her mother and her sister. Not just financially, but physically, and he was stretching her so thin.

But you owe him. He doesn't owe you. There's the difference.

She let go of a slow breath, easing the tension out with it, and gave the lift attendant a polite smile of gratitude. He returned it to her chest and she sighed anew. *Seriously?*

Stepping past him, she adjusted the deep V in her wrap-around dress and cast her eyes over the softly lit room. *Where are you, Tony?*

His gregarious personality was enough to project a homing beacon, and the room was decidedly absent of it. Most people were split into couples or foursomes—all save for one man. Her breath caught, a peculiar awareness taking hold.

He sat at a table beside the glass wall. A great seat from which to enjoy the far-reaching cityscape below, although his eyes showed no interest in the vista. No, they were well and truly pinned on *her*, projecting an intensity that had her skin prickling with such thrill.

Hell, she wanted to stride straight over—the urge was almost making her do just that—but sense prevailed. Tony wanted to see her. Hopefully he could explain away his crazy behaviour, and put her mind at rest over the future.

Giving a small sigh, she headed for the bar. A drink—that was what she needed. Anything to take the edge off.

Slipping onto a bar stool, she crossed her legs and replaced her clutch with the leather-clad drinks menu.

'Good evening, Miss Hayes, what can I get you?'

She looked up to find Darren, the head bartender, approaching with a smile, his hands busy drying off a glass. She returned his smile easily and scanned the list, honing in on a vodka martini and figuring that had to be strong enough.

He cocked an eyebrow when she made her request. 'Shaken, not stirred, *madame*?'

His Scottish-accented Bond impression had her laughing, and the sound was alien to her ears. It had to be weeks—months, even—since she'd had a proper giggle. Maybe *she* was the one in need of a good shake, never mind the drink.

'However you recommend it.'

'You sure?' He raised both brows. 'It's pretty strong.'

He knew her too well. She didn't do spirits. A spritzer was her usual drink of choice. But a spritzer just wasn't going to cut it. Not tonight. It wasn't just Tony, it was her increasing concern over her mother too. She was getting worse and there was nothing Jennifer could do to stop it.

Her heart fluttered painfully and she pushed the thought aside. *Not now.*

'Sounds perfect,' she said, flipping open her clutch and retrieving her mobile to check if Tony had at least messaged. But she'd not even lit the screen before her eyes sidled away, drawn to the brooding silhouette not twelve feet away.

He was tall—she could tell that even with his body folded into the deep bucket seat. The ankle of one leg casually rested atop the knee of the other. The designer cut of his dark suit and tan leather shoes spoke of money, although whether he had any was an entirely different matter. She'd learned that quickly enough in the city. People only had to dress to impress and it attracted wealth like bees to honey.

But there was something in the broad set of his shoulders, accentuated as they were by his tailored jacket, and the confident air in his relaxed poise that had her certain he wasn't all about the front.

And what a front...

Her eyes drifted upwards. The crisp white shirt sat smoothly over his torso, no hint of spread. Then they drifted higher, to the last fastened button of his open collar and the hint of dark hair curling there.

Her pulse skipped, her mouth watered and her eyes snapped back to her phone. *Not now!*

Seriously, what was *wrong* with her? Was she that desperate to get laid? That fed up with her trusty vibrator that her body was putting up a fight? Truth was, there was no time in her life for that complication. Mr Dildo didn't talk back, didn't require care and affection. He didn't require time that she didn't have.

Between her office and dashing back and forth between London and Yorkshire each weekend to be with her family she was all out of that.

But one night, though. Think of the possibilities...

Heat simmered low in her belly as she activated her phone screen. *No notifications.* She fired off a brief Where are you? message and placed the device back on the bar, her heightened awareness picking up on movement from the man's direction. She watched him crook his finger to the blonde waitress hovering nearby and an inexplicable pull ripped through her.

Christ, he was reeling her in too.

She nibbled the inside of her lip, drinking in his rakishly long dark hair, the chiselled set to his jaw that softened delectably with his easy grin. And then there were his eyes—so compelling. She couldn't make out the colour, but there was something about them, something deliciously sinful...

Her tummy contracted with a barrage of heat, and in that second she knew she wanted to leave with him. That she wanted one night of crazy. No names, no real talk, just wild, no-holds-barred sex.

Could she do it? Hell, would he?

It wasn't in her nature, it wasn't like her, but being 'like her' was hard fucking work and she needed this...needed him.

Mentally, she undressed him, button by button, stroke by stroke, her thighs clenching tight in their folded position.

'One vodka martini.'

'Huh?' Her eyes snapped to the bar, to Darren placing a mat and glass before her.

'Your drink.' He smiled teasingly. 'Distracted, much?'

'Quite.' *And that was an understatement.*

Warmth fed her cheeks as she took hold of the olive stick propped inside her glass and began to stir with it, her focus on the mini-whirlpool she created while she set her thoughts to chill.

Get the meeting with Tony out of the way first.

Raising her drink, she sampled it, a small hum of appreciation escaping her as the chilly temperature contrasted with the burn of alcohol in a strangely pleasing way. She took another sip and felt her shoulders start to ease, her posture soften.

Ah, Tony, maybe you've done me a favour, dragging me out.

She rolled her head on her shoulders, her eyes seeking him once more— *Fuck.* Their gazes collided, the invitation in his sending lust tearing through her.

To hell with Tony, and to hell with doing what was right all the time!

Just give him twenty minutes...

Gah—She forced her attention to her phone and issued him a text that said as much.

Five minutes later, fizzing over with the prolonged wait, she caved and beckoned Darren over.

There was no harm in putting things in motion.

'You're not ready for another?'

She grinned, high on the thrill. 'Please...'

He chuckled. 'Okay.'

Placing a fancy tray of bar snacks in front of her, he set about making her drink.

She eyed the food, her tummy growling. She'd missed dinner again. Taking up a few snacks, she savoured one before asking, 'Do you know what Mr Distraction is drinking?'

He sent her a knowing look. 'You wanting to send him one?'

'Maybe...' Playfully, she popped in another snack, chewing over it and relishing the instant hit of salt. 'So, come on—do you know?'

He smiled as he worked, his eyes flicking briefly to the man in question. 'He's a J&B man.'

She licked her lips clean, her eyes flitting to Smok-

ing Hot Guy, and then to his bottle of choice on the
shelf. Hot Wealthy Guy… J&B… An image of the
hottie in *American Psycho* flashed before her eyes
and she swallowed, hard.

*Okay, Okay…yes, you want a night of crazy, but
maybe you should know something about him first.*

'What's got you looking so serious?' Darren asked,
picking up on her shift in mood.

'I was just wondering…' Her voice trailed off as
she considered the talented bartender. Darren knew
everyone that came and went. 'What do you know
of him?'

'Can't tell you much.' He strained the liquid into a
fresh glass. 'I've not seen him before, but there were
some guys at the bar talking about him earlier. Rec-
ognised him from some article or other.'

Her ears pricked up. 'An article?'

'Yeah, you know the sort—one of those professional mags, I reckon.' He popped an olive in the
glass and placed it before her. 'He's a CEO in the
technology field.'

She sucked on the inside of her lip, suppressing
the surge of excitement. *No CEO was going to turn
out to be a nutcase.*

'Well, fancy that…'

'You sure do.'

She grinned and plucked the olive from the glass,
popping it between her lips as her eyes hit Smoking
Hot Guy's.

Damn sure I do!

CHAPTER TWO

IF HE HAD to watch her pop another olive in her mouth, her eyes alive with wicked suggestion… He circled the rim of his glass with his index finger, the move rhythmically in line with the heat coiling through him.

He really should've left when he'd got the bail-out text from Andrews. Instead he'd sent a brief acknowledgement wrapped up in a warning.

Be at the solicitor's nine a.m. prompt for contract exchange or else.

And then he'd settled back.

He really should've been more annoyed too, but it was fascinating what the sight of a blazing-eyed redhead enjoying her fill at the bar could do. And he wasn't just referring to the olives—there were the bar snacks too. Whatever they were, they had her licking her lips and her fingers with such teasing that between that and the olive-sucking his lower body couldn't get a let-up.

And, Christ, those eyes—they pierced him from across the room. The warm lighting of the bar glinted off their depraved depths as they came back to him again and again, demanding his attention, drawing him in, giving him hope that she wasn't waiting for someone else to appear.

She was chatting to the barman now, her perfectly poised body leaning in as they exchanged words, their easy flow of conversation suggesting she was probably a regular. The guy nodded to her and moved away, freeing her once more, and he sensed her attention returning to him. His breath halting, his hand paused over his glass. And then her mobile lit up and her eyes dropped to it. She gave a flicker of annoyance and then a smile. She tapped at it and placed it back on the bar.

Now her eyes came to him and, *fuck*, were they calling.

His gut clenched, his jaw tightened and the room disappeared. *Something had changed.*

'For you, sir.'

Not now. Grudgingly, he looked to the voice and found the blonde waitress hovering, a tray with a lone drink resting upon her palm.

'J&B.' She took hold of the glass and bent to place it on the table. 'From the lady at the bar.'

His gaze dropped to the glass and he smiled.

Hell, Andrews, you've actually done me a favour.

From her elevated vantage point upon the bar stool she watched him straighten and plant his feet, the move sending her heart into her throat.

Oh, yes, come for me...

He lifted his glass off the table and started towards her, his tall, imposing frame filling her vision, his eyes lighting up every nerve-ending in their path as they raked appreciatively over her.

She turned on her stool to face him, sipping at her drink as she waited until he was within earshot, and then she smiled. 'It's lovely of you to join me.'

He tilted his glass. 'I wanted to thank you for the drink.'

Wow, that voice. She drew a breath as her body flared. It was deep, husky, rough…the perfect mix for a body that exuded power. And that accent—she couldn't place it, but it was there, teasing her.

'And I wanted to thank *you* for improving my out-look this evening.'

He rewarded her with that easy grin, his eyes sparking and pulling her in. They were the colour of chocolate, the dark and rich kind, and they were on fire, burning into her as he said, 'You and me both.'

'Is that so?'

'You *know* so.'

'I know no such thing.'

He gave a small chuckle and reached past her, plac-ing his glass on the bar. She twisted into his arm on impulse, felt his scent invading her, the heady mas-culine cologne sending lust slamming into her core.

'Perhaps I can convince you over another drink?' He leant back against the bar-edge. 'What can I get you?'

What could he get her?

She wanted to laugh as the word *you* rode on the tip of her tongue but instead she looked to Darren, 'I'm already being taken care of.'

He followed her gaze. 'Is that another vodka martini?'

'It is.' She smiled, her fingers toying with the empty stick still floating in her glass. 'I think I've found a new favourite drink.'

His eyes travelled from her to the stick. 'It's quickly becoming one of mine too.'

She could take a guess at why. She would have said as much if he hadn't spoken first.

'So, what brings you here?' He angled himself towards her, his forearm resting on the bar-top, his fingers coming to hover just above her knee. 'Beautiful woman, no companion—it just doesn't fit.'

Beautiful? She loved how that sounded coming from him, loved how close his fingertips were reaching. If she just uncrossed her legs they would brush against her, those long, capable fingers that were sure to possess such skill...

'Business or pleasure?' he probed.

Her eyes shot back to his, her thighs clenching anew. The way he said it—*pleasure*—it rolled off his tongue like a physical caress.

'I was meeting someone...' She was barely aware of the words coming out of her mouth.

'Was?'

'They cancelled.' She lifted her empty stick and nibbled at its end, needing to do something—anything to keep herself busy. 'What about you?'

He eyed the stick, a pulse working steadily in his jaw as he took up his drink once more. 'Business.'

She could hear it then, in that one simple word, an edge to his voice. A barely contained need that matched her own.

Her attack on the stick ceased, and her breath was

shallow as she struggled to say, 'Are you finished for the evening?'

'Never even started,' he said, that same husky edge to his voice teasing beneath her panties. 'Lucky for me, they cancelled too.'

'Lucky?'

He nodded, his lips quirking over his drink as he took a sip.

'And why's that?' she said, dropping the stick to caress away the strain building in her throat.

'Isn't it obvious?'

'Maybe—but I'd like to hear you say it.'

He placed his drink on the bar, his eyes coming back to her, ever closer. 'Do you always get your way?'

'Most of the time.'

'Why is it I can believe that?'

He reached up to brush her hair behind her ear, his delicate touch sending an excited ripple through her, and then he trailed it down, the ripples multiplying exponentially.

'What makes you say that?' she asked, barely audible.

He studied her, his eyes dropping to her lips, their depths flashing darkly as she swept her tongue out to ease their sudden dryness.

'I get the impression you can be quite persuasive.'

She knew what she wanted to say, knew it was brash, knew it was out of character, but… 'Does that mean I can persuade you into an evening of pleasure?'

His brow flickered, the only show of surprise at her proposition, and then he grinned: a slow, heart-stopping smile that unveiled a dimple in his right

cheek, the boyish feature at odds with the virile mas-
culinity emanating from the rest of him.

'Is that what you're offering me?'

'Would you accept if it was?'

He leant closer still, his breath teasing at the delicate channel of her ear. 'Why don't you try me?'

Heat flooded her breasts, her belly, her blood, and
the world around her evaporated as she twisted into
him, her lips instinctively seeking his…

'Your drink.'

What?

Her disorientated gaze swept to the bar, to Darren
sliding her drink before her.

Oh, God!

'Thank you,' she blurted, hurrying to mask the
swamping disappointment. But he spotted it anyway,
his smile apologetic as he picked up her empty glass
and moved away.

'How about we take this conversation to my table?'
came the appealing proposition from alongside her.

She brushed her fingertips across her lips, now
thrumming with their near encounter, and flicked
her eyes back to his. 'I'd love to.'

He'd had to work hard to stop himself from saying
place instead of *table*. And still he wondered—would
she have said *I'd love to* in that soft, balmy tone if
he had?

She gazed up at him with those green come-to-bed
eyes and he wished he'd found out.

'After you,' he said, gesturing to her.

He made to pick up their drinks and then stilled,

his concentration broken by the sight of her slipping from the stool.

Between the uncrossing of those seriously long legs and the cleavage he was working hard not to drown in he found himself rooted. Her height impressed him once again as she met his eyeline, her scent wafting up to him.

Not that he had any idea what herb or flower was involved in the making of it. But he liked it. *A lot.*

'Don't forget the drinks,' she threw over her shoulder with a provocative smile, her eyes sparkling with mischief, desire, amusement... He hadn't a clue.

It was taking his all to keep the conversation flowing and his own desire in check. Trying to read every fleeting expression that crossed her face and not jump to the conclusion that she was on the same desire-driven wave as he was nigh on impossible.

Grabbing the drinks, he followed her to the table, his eyes fixed on the sway of her hips, the fall of her hair as it brushed along the gentle flare of her bum.

What it would be like to have that same hair flung across his bedspread? Or wrapped around his fist as he drove himself into her—? *Fuck, he was getting hard just thinking about it.*

And there she went again, staring up at him as if he was seconds away from being devoured.

Now, perched on the end of the low-slung seat that had remained vacant at his table, her head came cock-high and heat rushed to his groin in greeting.

Adding to his pain, she crossed her legs, the action forcing her dress to ride high and reveal the top of a stocking, he was sure, before she righted it.

Too late. The damage was done. And she knew it.

She'd watched the entire thing play out in his face.
And, hell, he wasn't even convinced the low lighting
was enough to conceal the bulge down there.

He held out her drink. 'For you.'

'Thank you,' she said, her delicate feline fingers
slipping over his own to take it from him.

The contact was soft and brief, but total dynamite
to his over-active imagination as the image of her
taking hold of something else ransacked his mind.

He watched as she lifted the glass to her glossy
full mouth and tilted it, the clear liquid flowing into
her as the olive bobbed at the base of the drink. And
then she closed her lips and swallowed, her tongue
emerging subtly to take away the remnants. The sight
was sweet perfection to behold, utter torture to his
straining cock.

'Are you going to sit?' she said up to him, her
raised expression making it clear she had caught him
staring, good and proper.

Did he care?

Did he fuck!

'Apologies,' he said, dipping his head in mock regret, his grin telling her he wasn't sorry at all. 'I confess to getting lost in the sight of you.'

It was corny, it was overly smooth, but again he
didn't care. It was the truth.

He placed his drink on the table and took his own
seat, feeling her eyes upon him the whole time. The
nature of her thoughts penetrated the air.

'A penny for them?'

Her smile widened. 'Something tells me a man like
you should know well enough that you never ask a
woman that question.'

He gave an easy laugh, staving off the heat raging below his waist. 'What if I said there's something about you that makes me want to ask that question regardless?'

She set her glass down and pressed her elbow into the arm of her chair, leaning in towards him.

'Then I would tell you…' she began, her voice low and husky, each word spun out as her fingers took up a slow caress over the exposed valley of her chest. 'In that case I would divulge *exactly* what I'm thinking.'

He would have—could have—dragged her away from the bar that very second. The way her eyes beckoned him, the way her wandering hands lured him, the blood surging to his cock—it was all getting too much and he hadn't so much as touched her.

And, fuck, did he want to.

The need ravaged him. He wanted to taste every last bit of her, stroke her until she begged for him to complete her, fill her body until she could do nothing but scream his name.

And yet she couldn't. They had shared a lot in a few electrifying glances, but they hadn't so much as covered the basics of *My name is…*

They should at least get that covered. 'Perhaps we should start with introductions?'

She laughed. 'Introductions?'

'Yes,' he said, surprised at her reaction. 'You know—me Tarzan, you Jane, before we get carried away with this—' he waved a hand between them '—undercurrent.'

'Undercurrent?' she repeated, her eyes dancing over the word, her fingers still doing their crazy damn tour of her body. 'You know, I think you've summed it up perfectly.'

His eyes followed her fingers, his control teetering as he succumbed to the pull of her caress.

'So?' he pressed, his brain only half on the attempted introduction.

'So...?' she mimicked teasingly, the action both maddening and arousing. And then she dropped her hand to take hold of the stick floating in her drink and all thought of conversation disintegrated, obliterated by the sight of the inoffensive little green ball slowly being stirred around.

It was coming—he knew it—and the power of that sight, up close and with every alluring detail to feast upon, had his knuckles turning white.

'Who needs names in this day and age?' She lifted the olive out of her drink and tapped the stick against the rim of the glass to rid it of excess vodka. 'Don't you think there's something to be said for leaving a little mystery?'

She looked at him on the last word, the stick pausing to rest against the glass edge. 'It's not like I'm here looking for a meaningful relationship.'

He wanted to say something smooth, but she had him stoked to silence. The perfect package was at his disposal—sexy sophistication brandishing a *fuck-and-leave* policy. He didn't do relationships—they were for the weak and the needy. And, hell, if you weren't weak at the off, you soon would be when it fell apart or, in the case of his dad, got ripped away. Then it would ruin you.

He lifted his glass and took a careful sip, swallowing down the unwelcome memories and throwing his focus onto the attractive bundle before him. 'You and me both.'

'Well, then, wouldn't you rather…' she leaned across the table and brought the olive to her lower lip, her cleavage forming an alluring backdrop '…we just got the hell out of here and had some fun?'

She parted her luscious pink mouth and popped the olive inside, her lips closing around the stick as her eyes held his with deliberate tease. Then slowly, painfully slowly, she pulled it out, her lips rolling outwards as they held the olive inside, stripping the stick bare.

'I make that three olives now.' His voice rasped, his mouth drying up at the inviting slickness of her lips.

She considered him, her throat moving captivatingly as she devoured the green ball. 'Three—really?' She smiled playfully, dropping the stick into her glass with a ting. 'You're very observant.'

'When something's worth observing I'd say I am.'

'Is that what I am? Worth observing?'

'You with that drink—*definitely*.' His voice was tight with the effort of holding back, and his lack of control was so alien he knew he was in trouble. But right now he didn't care. 'In fact, if I was a religious man, I'd say the devil invented drinks such as those.'

'The devil?' Her brow furrowed and she nibbled thoughtfully at her lip, the innocent gesture smashing the last of his restraint. 'Because of the corrupting alco—?'

'No,' he interjected, pushing himself out of his seat and striding to stand before her.

She looked up at him questioningly, her throat bobbing as she swallowed. He knew he'd surprised her but, he couldn't wait any longer. To hell with where they were.

Reaching for her hand, he took hold of it and tugged her to her feet, the force sending her unresisting body right up against his own, her eyes flashing as they lighted on his mouth so close to her own.

'Because they make me forget all decency and do this…' He cupped her chin and roughly took her mouth in his, his tongue taking no prisoners in its desperation to sink inside.

An explosion of sensations went off at once. She tasted like heaven, like the olive, the vodka, the traces of gloss across her lips… And then she sighed, the soft, feminine sound escaping her lips as she gave way to his invasion and he lost himself in her. Her hands snaked through his hair, her tongue seeking out his own, twisting and flicking, tasting and probing…

His surroundings disappeared as every sense focused on her: her kiss, her smell, the feel of her breasts pushed up against him, the little sounds she was making, the desperate buck of his cock as it pressed into her lower belly.

There was a movement behind him, the brush of a chair and a muttered 'Excuse me.' It filtered through his brain, through the haze.

'Get a room,' a voice said.

His internal voice or a real person? He didn't know. He didn't care.

But he should care…

He should!

Reality came crashing down—he needed them out of there. *Now.*

Forcing himself to slow down, he tried to part their

mouths, their faces. He was rewarded with her teeth nipping at his bottom lip. A playful protest that felt anything but…

'Spoilsport,' she complained, and her pout was to die for.

He took a steadying breath. 'You're cheeky, sweet-heart.'

One hand still cupping her face, he freed his other hand to rub it across his own, trying to get himself composed. He should be more unnerved by his lack of self-control—but fuck did he want to run with it regardless. Something told him that letting go would be worth it. That *she* would be worth it.

He scanned the bar. No one seemed to be look-ing their way. But that wasn't to say they hadn't been seconds before. That voice had sounded real enough.

'We were having fun,' she said, drawing him back, her eyes wide and alluring.

'We *were* having fun.' He repeated her words. 'But I think we could have more fun elsewhere. I can have my driver here in five?'

Her eyes flittered and his chest tightened. *Was she going to refuse him?*

'Driver, you say?'

'Yes.' He moulded his free hand into her back, pressing her against him, against the hard swell of his cock. *Don't deny me.* 'I promise he will see you home safely…after…'

He continued to caress her lip with the pad of his thumb, loving how her tongue would dart out sporadi-cally to moisten the path for his touch.

'In that case you'd best call him,' she said softly, her hand coming up to take hold of his fingers and pressing a chaste kiss to their tips. 'I'll go and settle up.'

And just like that she was on it, stepping out of his hold and taking up her bag from the table, heading for the bar. He watched her go, his eyes hooked on the sweet sway of her body, he blindly retrieved his phone from his jacket pocket. He dropped his gaze just long enough to dial his driver and, efficient as ever, he answered in two rings.

'I need you outside in five,' he said into the phone.

'Sure thing, Mr Wright. Where we heading?'

'Home.'

He cut the call and thrust his hand through his hair. He didn't take women home. He went to a hotel, or their place. That way he could leave when he was good and ready. Certainly before morning. But the thought of sharing this woman with an audience a second more, or navigating the whole reservation thing.... He didn't have the patience. Or the inclination.

But to take her home—what the hell was he playing at?

CHAPTER THREE

JENNIFER TOOK HER time heading to the bar, sensing his heated gaze upon her and wanting to give him a worthy show. Her posture was smooth and assured, her hips moving with teasing provocation, her hair swinging subtly with each step.

On the outside she screamed control, but on the inside… She was on fire for him. The blood pumping through her system was heated beyond comprehension.

She wanted them alone. *Now*. But racing to the bar was hardly going to scream sex appeal and the very idea brought a laugh to her lips.

'Good night?' Darren said, not missing her little eruption.

'The best,' she said, placing her clutch on the bar and sliding onto a stool.

'Glad to hear it.' He gave her a knowing grin but left it there, his professionalism overriding as he asked, 'So what can I get you?'

'Both bills, please.'

'Sure.' He raised a cocktail shaker to the side of his head and started rattling it with gusto. 'Give me one min.'

'No problem.'

She propped her elbows on the bar, her head resting on her hands as she watched him work. She likened herself to the contents of the metal contraption being so expertly worked in his hands—shaken and about to be devoured. She smiled blissfully, the idea suiting her just fine.

It amused her that he'd wanted her name. It was a sweet gesture—*too sweet*. She didn't want sweet. Sweet only led to complications—the kind that brought feelings, even relationships. And there was no place in her life for any of that. Her career came first. Her career and her family. She had no time for more. Not yet.

No matter how hot, how sexy, how interesting...

She twirled her hair around one finger. No, she needed him to be all about the sex—definitely just the sex. Someone like him would be too dangerous, too much of a distraction, to have around for long.

But as for the here and now... A little shiver ran through her as she conjured up those eyes, that smile, the dimple.

She glanced over her shoulder. He was on his phone but he was watching her, just as she'd known he would be, the carnal blaze of his eyes heating her from across the room.

'Here you go.'

Darren's voice pulled her back to the bar and his outstretched hand, containing a silver tray with two bills. She slipped her card on top, trusting him implicitly to have it right. 'Just pop it on there.'

'No problem.'

His eyes flicked behind her as he moved to the till

and she realised her impromptu date had moved. She could sense his approach radiating down her back, her fine hairs prickling in anticipation beneath the delicate fabric of her dress, and she strung the sensation out, waiting for Darren to return her card and wish her goodnight before she turned.

'I hope you don't mind…' she said, looking up, and her words went the way of her brain, combusting on the pull of his eyes, that smile, that dimple…

He raised a bemused brow. 'Mind…?'

She smiled through the desire. 'I settled your tab too.'

He looked surprised. 'You did?'

'I did.' His reaction amused her. 'Do you always look this surprised when a woman pays her own way?'

'I can't say I'm used to it.'

She rolled her eyes. 'Well, welcome to the modern world.'

He laughed, the sound husky and amplifying her already spiking libido.

'Point made,' he said, placing his hand in the small of her back and stirring up a truckload of nerves. 'Shall we go?'

She grinned up at him. 'Unless you want this modern woman to throw you over her shoulder and carry you out, I suggest we do just that.'

His laugh deepened and the desire to kiss him, to feel that excited resonance against her mouth had her on fire.

Soon, Jennifer!

She forced her legs to work and they headed to the lift, noticing that this time the attendant chose to avoid looking at her all together. What a nice change.

Even nicer still, the hand on her back started to wander, his fingers moving to caress rather than hold, his heat penetrating the thin veil of her dress and making her tremble.

He bent his head, his mouth hovering close to her ear, 'Are you cold?'

She fixed her gaze straight ahead, fear that she would set upon him and give the attendant an eyeful making the glass doors suddenly riveting. 'No.'

But two can play at that game, she told herself, sidestepping in front of him, just enough so that she could conceal her hand as it made contact with the front of his thigh.

He gave a sharp intake of breath, his thigh tensing beneath her splayed fingers and making her smile in satisfaction. *Payback!*

He was a delight to explore. The strong rigidity of muscle flexed as she stroked upwards, circling from his outer thigh to the inner—

His hand shot to her arm, his fingers gently gripping her in what she assumed to be a silent message to behave.

No chance.

As the lift descended she teased and coaxed until his hold eased enough for her to reach her target—his very tip. Lightly she brushed up and over. He hissed against her ear and her belly coiled with exquisite heat.

She traced around him, revelling in his growing reaction, coveting his size, his girth, his length…

She filled her hand and squeezed. He bucked within her palm, a cough erupting from his throat, and her smile grew as the lift came to a gentle stop.

Before them the doors opened, and she released him with a playful tap, stepping forward to exit with the attendant. He followed close behind.

The private hallway was deserted. Sounds of the busy city reached them from outside, but the window-less entranceway blocked it all from view.

'Have a good evening,' the attendant said, stepping back inside the lift and pressing the button.

She watched the doors close and the lift start its ascent, waiting for the attendant's eyes to be out of sight so she could—

Whoa!

Startled, she found herself being spun into him, her eyes and mind barely registering his hold before he was propelling her back against the cold marble wall, his lips coming down to crush her own. He pinned one hand to the wall above her head; his other running up and down her side in brutal exploration.

Heat exploded within her, the ache between her legs flaring with such force she wanted to cry out as she kissed him back, her hands thrusting through his hair, her tongue delving into him, fighting with his own as she desperately sought more.

But he tore his mouth away, pressing his forehead against hers, his ragged breaths sweeping down her front. '*You* are a tease.'

'You started it.'

She yanked him back to her. He obeyed for a split second, his tongue flicking teasingly into her mouth, and then he was breaking away to travel down her neck, his teeth nipping and grazing with dizzying effect.

'*God, yes!*' she cried, head arching back, hands invading his jacket as she strove to feel every bit of him. The hard muscles of his chest twitched and flexed as she explored—smoothing, clawing, pulling at his shirt.

The hand at her side reached the hem of her dress and he shoved it upwards, his fingers gripping the underside of her thigh as he lifted it, forcing her to wrap her leg around him.

He raised his head to gaze down at her, his hand tracing the band of her stocking, tension working in his jaw. 'You're dangerous.'

'You like?' she said, trying to focus through the haze.

'Love.'

He twanged the suspender and she gave a heated shrug, shoving a hand through his hair. 'It's a power thing.'

He growled, the sound animalistic, lighter fuel to her raging heat as his mouth reclaimed hers and both hands took hold of her thighs to lift her entirely against him. The cool air swept over her damp panties, followed sharply by his rock-hard cock, its trouser-clad presence driving against her. She bucked with delight, her mouth breaking free to let go a frenzied moan.

'I'm losing my mind,' he said into her collarbone, feasting on her skin as he thrust her upwards, bringing the valley of her chest to his face, his hot breath and slick tongue creating an insane combination that had her breasts pleading for him.

But suddenly he froze.

'Shit.'

She looked down at him, her body writhing, her

lungs struggling for air. And then she felt it—the phone in his jacket vibrating into her thigh.

'It'll be my driver,' he said, his voice gravel-like and rumbling through her.

'Of course,' she breathed, fighting for control over the insane rush and thriving off it all the same.

Shaky, she lowered her legs and he helped her, waiting until she was safely on her feet before shrugging his jacket into place and fishing out his mobile.

He stepped back, tapping at the screen and raising it to his ear, his other hand trying to put some order back into his hair. The sight made her smile. *She'd* done that to him. He'd let her. They'd both lost all control and the realisation was exhilarating.

She worked to straighten out her clothing, her hair, her racing body. All the while telling herself she should be grateful for the interruption, that indecent exposure wouldn't go down well for either of them.

But the thrill of it. Of him. In public—here and now… It appealed *too much*.

'On our way.' He spoke into his phone and then cut it off, slipping it back into his pocket and turning that sexy, *fuck-me-now* smile on her as he offered his arm. 'You good to go?'

She nodded and hooked her arm in his. 'Let's be quick about it.'

He gave a laugh and together they strode down the hallway and out of the building.

Directly outside, on the congested street, squeezed into a parking space she could scarcely believe it fitted into, sat a pristine black limo, its driver waiting at its rear. He straightened as he set eyes on them, and she knew for certain that this was the driver he had spoken to.

If any doubt had remained over what Darren had told her then it would've been wiped out now. Yes, he was definitely CEO material. A very successful CEO at that. She was considered successful herself, but even she didn't possess the wealth that brought with it this kind of service. Or maybe she did…she just didn't get to see any of it…

'Evening, Mr Wright,' the driver said as they approached, his eyes dropping briefly to her as he gave a respectful dip of his head.

Wright?

She smiled up at him. The name fitted him well— he certainly felt like *her* Mr Right.

But then he could be called Mr Tickle and she'd probably think it just fine right about now.

'Colin,' her Mr Wright said, 'this is Miss…' He faltered and looked down at her.

She realised he was at a loss, thanks to her enforced air of mystery, and gave a laugh. It all seemed rather ridiculous now. As if they needed any mystery to add to the fire already searing between them!

'Miss Hayes,' she said, beaming at his driver. 'But, honestly, you can just call me Jennifer.'

His arm froze in hers and his eyes narrowed, a look she couldn't identify sweeping across his face. Something about it panicked her. But then it was gone, his eyes were calming, and he looked back to his driver.

Had she imagined it?

It was dark…the street lighting wasn't great…

'This is Miss Hayes,' he said.

Hadn't she just told him that?

'And she needs a lift home.'

What the fuck?

'Home?' She couldn't keep the surprise out of her voice.

Just then the heavens opened—great big dollops of water raining down on them just as she would have said more. They hunched forward against the onslaught as the driver swung open the rear door and told them to get in. He would get the address from them when they were safely inside.

Pulling her with him, he forced her to fold into the back seat of the car. Her brain was rambling, trying to come up with a reason—any reason that didn't imply an end to the evening's affairs.

He wouldn't have the audacity to lead her on and then... No, it wasn't possible. He must be suggesting they both go to her place. But that wasn't happening. That was *her* domain.

She waited for him to close the door before she sidled up to him, her fingers toying with the top button of his shirt as she hooked her head beneath his chin.

'It's a nice idea to go to mine, but if it's all the same I'd much rather go to yours.'

He didn't say anything and she gazed up at him. He was staring at a point over her head, and the taut lines of his face sent the hairs prickling at the back of her neck.

'Is something wrong?'

His eyes flicked to her and away again. 'I'm not sure this is a good idea.'

'You can't be serious,' she said, her hand stilling, her eyes falling to his mouth and the grim line now forming there.

She hadn't imagined his need. It had mirrored her own. If he was having a last-minute change of heart out of respect for her feelings, and all that sentimental crap, then she would see to it that he forgot it.

She let her hand trace down his front and felt his body turn rigid.

Outside, traffic sped past, delaying the driver's attempt to round the vehicle and get inside. She had time...

Lifting her head, she used her nose to brush the hair from behind his ear. The scent of his dampened hair product was fresh and masculine, tantalising her as she pressed a kiss to his skin, her tongue flicking out to taste. His jaw clenched and his arm at her back tightened, neither gripping her to him nor moving away.

'I want you,' she whispered into his ear, and his breath hitched.

His waning resolve urged her on. She nuzzled him as her hand slid down his front, over his torso, the buckle of his belt, his zipper, to his left thigh, where she knew the length of his cock lay. She felt it swell obediently into her palm as a curse ripped from his throat.

Victorious, she used her teeth on his lobe. 'See... you want this too.'

She gripped him hard and he inhaled sharply, a hiss forming through his teeth.

She traced the edge of his ear with her tongue as her hand started to move over him, around him. 'Just tell me you don't and I'll stop.'

Jennifer...' He groaned her name as he pressed

back into his seat, his lower body riding upwards to increase the pressure of her hand.

'That's it, baby,' she cooed. 'Feels good, doesn't it?'

'Fuck, yeah,' he rasped, and she felt her carnal prowess take a bow, the power going straight to her head, liquid heat pooling between her legs.

The front door yanked open—*shit!*

They both sat bolt upright, like a pair of teenagers caught in the act, faces flushed, eyes wide.

The driver clambered in and glanced over his shoulder, his expression one of pure professionalism, as though they hadn't a hair out of place...or several—

'Where to, sir?'

'Home.'

The driver's brows lifted. '*Your* home, sir?'

'That's what I said.'

Then he hit a button that had the privacy glass sliding up.

Was that stuff really private?

She was about to ask when he took hold of her hips and swung her over his lap, the speed of the move sending a surprised gasp from her lips that swiftly turned to a moan as she found herself over the very hardness of him, her knees straddling him, her dress thrust up to her hips. He raked a hand through her hair and yanked her mouth down to his own, his tongue pillaging, his hands rough upon her thigh and her hair.

Hooking her hands around his neck, she clung to him, desperate to keep their mouths connected while her body started to ride his clothed hardness in mindless abandon.

Vaguely she was aware of his hands shifting, his

fingers hooking beneath the dress at her shoulders and shoving it down, imprisoning her arms to her sides.

He broke away, forcing her back so that he could look at her.

Her breasts bloomed under his burning gaze, her nipples straining beneath the light padding of her bra. He brought his hands up to her shoulders, his touch now gentle and prolonged as he slid them beneath the straps, taking them down to meet the ruched fabric of her dress before returning to smooth over her shoulders and down her front.

She bit back a whimper of anticipation as he met with her bra and then he slipped his hands inside, his heated palms brushing fleetingly against her taut and swollen peaks before they dipped to cup her, the brief contact an erotic torture as they begged for more.

'So beautiful…' he said softly, his hands weighing her in his palms as his thumbs stroked upwards, their pads meeting with her pleading buds and rolling over them.

Pleasure shot through her, and she threw her head back as a moan tore from her throat.

'You like that?'

'Yes!' she cried. The heavenly combination of his hands on her body and his hardness at her clit had her rocking wildly, and she could feel the tell-tale tension mounting.

'I need to see you.'

With those gruff words he took hold of the band of her bra and tugged hard, forcing her breasts to spill out. He groaned, his head coming forward as he closed his mouth around one stiff peak, sucking it back into the cavern of his mouth, teasing it and then releasing it to let his teeth nip, his tongue lap. He did the same with the other, one hand coming up to join in the attention, his fingers pinching and rolling, his palm groping.

Outside, a car horn sounded as another torrential wave of rain pounded at the roof. The worldly sounds were a reminder of where they were, but it only served to take her higher, every bit of her becoming a tense powerhouse about to crack.

'I'm gonna come...' she moaned. 'I can't take... I can't...'

His answer was to nip harder, to drive her hips against him, to encourage her further, higher than she could ever remember being with any man. And then she was crying out. Her body was going into spasm as wave after wave consumed her. She heard him groan as he buried his head in her chest, holding her against him, taking each rock of her body until she was spent.

With cheeks flushed, she made herself straighten, conscious of time passing. 'How long do we have?'

'About twenty minutes.'

He traced a hand down her back and she shuddered at his lustful gaze. 'Perfect.'

'Is that so...?'

She made an affirmative noise as she bowed to press a kiss to the bridge of his nose, his lips, across his jawbone... Reaching his neck, she flicked her tongue out and revelled in the salty essence of him, knowing he was overheating at her hands.

'And why would that be?'

His voice cracked on the last word as she cupped him, her fingers testing the rigid length of him. She was desperate to expose him to her hands, her gaze, her mouth…

'It's time enough for me to return the favour,' she said, placing her hands on his thighs and slipping from his lap, coming to nestle on her knees between his feet on the floor.

The car took a bend and she steadied herself using his legs, her fingers biting into his flesh.

'Easy,' he said, taking hold of her arm and using his free hand to gain purchase on the trim of the car.

She smiled up at him. *Christ, he was so hot.*

She wanted to imprint the sight of him in her mind, all dishevelled and feverish. The feeling of excitement at having him at her mercy, the heat of his grip on her bare arm, the cool air of the car keeping her exposed nipples pert and alert. Her clit had barely recovered and the throb was back with a vengeance.

She dropped her eyes to his belt, to his zipper, the fastening taut as his hardness pressed against it. Her mouth salivated as she smoothed her hands along his thighs until they reached the object of her fascination.

'You are truly beautiful,' he said, the hand at her arm dropping to cup her breast, his fingers and thumb caressing her sensitised skin.

The knowledge that he was enjoying the sight of her semi-nakedness was just as thrilling as his touch. She bit her lip against the resurging tension. *It was his turn.*

Forcing herself to concentrate, she fed the leather of his belt through the loops. The metal from its buckle jangled as she parted it, the sound oddly thrilling, making her fingers quiver as she undid his button. Then, taking hold of his zip tab, she paused to look at him from beneath her lashes.

'You can tell me to stop, if you want?'

She was purposely teasing him, needing to have the memory of his earlier hesitation forgotten, obliterated by his total surrender.

And she had it.

He looked to her with almost pained ferocity, his expression dark and erotically charged as he thrust one hand into her hair. *'Fuck, no.'*

She gave him a wicked grin, his impassioned response going to her head as she slid the zipper down. 'That's better.'

CHAPTER FOUR

BETTER—IT WAS fucking better.

But then…

It could hardly get any worse.

Marcus threw his head back, his hands flying to the edge of his seat, eyes squeezing shut as he tried to push out the moral judgement threatening.

He shouldn't be letting her do this. They shouldn't be doing this. *When she realises who I am…when we have to work tog—*

Her fingers slipped around his cock, killing off all thought as his eyes shot back to her.

Fuck, she was beautiful!

Her green eyes, vibrant and captivating as they flicked between his own eyes and his crotch, seared him, blinding him to the reality of the situation and the gravity of it.

She pulled him out and gave a small gasp, her eyes widening as she took in his entirety. Her open appreciation was like rocket fuel to his swelling erection. Then she moved her hand over him, her gaze wrapped up in the sight of him, and the heat surged forcibly to the head of his dick, his thighs trembling beneath him. He gripped the side of the car tight, his teeth gritted tighter.

He was going to shoot his load over her any moment.

'*Jennifer...*' The effort of forming her name made him sound pained.

But she didn't even break focus. Her hold tightened and her dainty pink tongue flicked out to moisten her lips. The move was so carnal and electrifying he bucked within her fingers and she shot him a look, cheeks flushed, eyes hungry.

A groan tore through his throat. Beautiful didn't even cut it!

She was still half naked, her arms restricted by her dress, her tits propped upon it and pressed together while she explored him, their darkened peaks luring him, the valley between tight and evocative. How he'd love to thrust himself inside that channel, watch as he jacked all over...

Fuck! She's going to be your business partner! She has no idea who you are!

Salacious heat spread through him. He was damned. No matter that he knew it was wrong. The idea had now brought an erotic twist which swamped all else and had pre-cum escaping his swollen head. He looked down to catch her brushing across it with her thumb, its pad spreading it teasingly down the underside of his cock, her eyes marvelling like he was the best thing she'd ever seen. And then she met his eye, bowed her head.

Fuck, fuck, fuck!

His nails bit into the car's upholstery, his eyes fixed on hers, pre-cum seeping anew, and blindly she dipped to taste him, flicking out her delicate tongue and cleaning him like a fucking ice lolly.

His glutes clenched. 'Jennifer…' he breathed.

He was so close.

She answered his plea with a smile that screamed smut and slid her mouth over him, surrounding him with her inviting wetness. The head of his cock collided with the back of her throat, blood rushing to feed it, and his mind turned dizzy with the heat streaking through his body.

She undulated, circling her tongue the length of him as she sucked him back, her free hand slipping down between her legs to work herself at the same time.

Fuck yeah!

The sight had his cock ramming into the back of her throat and she gagged, the sound obliterating all remnants of his control.

Releasing his hold on the car seat, he shoved his fingers through her hair. 'Take it!'

She moaned in response, the sound guttural, vibrating around his plundering cock. He heard her take a breath through her nose and then she sank, burying him in deep. He'd never felt anything so intense, seen anything so goddamn erotic. This redhead, on her knees, with his hands rammed in her hair, her cheeks hollowed out as she worked the whole of him throat-deep, her hungry eyes glittering as she watched him, her arm shifting frantically as she got herself off.

He pulled her head up, the suction making his balls contract, and her eyes looked to him in lustful surrender, telling him to dictate, to drive…

'Fuck, sweetheart.' He drove her down over him, setting her to his rhythm, his depth.

The cabin was filled with the smacking sound of her cheeks. In and out. In and out.

He wrapped her hair around his fist, his other hand gripping at the seat-edge as he lost total sight of where they were, who they were. All he could see now were those lustful green eyes and that perfect mouth, his cock slick with her saliva...

He wanted to warn her, but his orgasm ripped through him, its force blowing his mind as he held her head still, watching himself explode into her, her eyes sparking as she drank him in.

She took his all like a heavenly drink, her mouth moving over him as her moans filled the cabin, her body rocking between his legs as her own orgasm claimed her.

He didn't want to blink, didn't want to miss a second. He softened his hold in her hair, his fingers starting to caress rather than hold, his eyes absorbing the vision that she was.

When she eventually shifted to straighten her clothing he helped her. She smiled at him, her hands slipping her breasts back into her bra.

The brief sight was enough to make him wish he could go again. And he would go again—no doubt about it. Very soon.

He knew that tomorrow would bring with it a hell of its own, but for tonight their fates were sealed, and he wasn't letting her go until he had her in his bed and was buried inside her.

'Thank you,' she said, wiping her fingers across her swollen lips.

Now, *that* made him laugh. She had him doing that a lot. 'I think I should be thanking you.'

'My two to your one—I owe you,' she said matter-of-factly, pulling her dress into place and climbing back into the seat.

'You *owe* me?' *Hell, he liked the sound of that.* 'In that case, thank away. I'll be calling it in shortly.'

'Thank you,' she said again, softly, her eyes dancing as she leant in and pressed a brief kiss to his lips.

His mind exploded with the image of her naked and sprawled across his bed. He was supposed to be righting his own clothing, and yet the desire to pin her back in his car burned through him.

Christ, none of this boded well for the future.

He zipped up his trousers in self-disdain. He didn't do sexual distraction. Not on this level. And definitely not at work. But that was exactly what the future held.

He was going to have to function alongside her for however long it took until he was sure the business was working towards the strategy he wanted. Until *she* was working towards the vision he depicted. It might be a fifty-fifty business partnership, but experience dictated that things went a whole lot more smoothly the quicker people came around to his line of thinking.

Would she be any different?

Fuck knew.

Especially now that he had screwed her. Had let his dick get in the way of all good sense. All good business sense.

Ah, hell, get over it!

They'd had sex—simple as. He hadn't known

who she was at the outset. He'd tried to stop it. She'd pushed.

She'd wanted nothing serious. And he had delivered.

It would be fine.

His gut twisted. It wasn't fine. He'd let his libido get in the way of business. *Hell, he was still doing it.* He *never* let that happen. The moment he'd known he should have shut it down. *Hell, he should be shutting it down now.* And yet…

Alongside him she wriggled in, and instinctively he wrapped his arm around her, pulling her up close. *What the hell was he doing?*

She gave a tired sigh. 'This feels nice.'

Nice? Jesus, his lips actually twitched with a smile. She thought this was *nice*?

He shifted back in his seat, testing his head against the curve of plush leather and finding it surprisingly inviting. *Okay, so he could see the appeal…*

Had he really never done this before? Lain back in his chauffeur-driven car and relaxed. He scanned the roof of the vehicle, the soft fabric and the lights designed to soothe, and realised the answer was a definite no.

He shouldn't really be doing it now either. Not when he could be catching up on emails, phone calls, the latest press releases in the technology field, or pondering the potential shit storm about to hit between himself and his new business partner…

She gave a small sound, the comforting noise at odds with his inner wrangling, and he quit, pushing everything away but the feel of her body curling into his own.

He would deal with it all when the time came, but for now...

'Sir, sir... Mr Wright!'

The noise was incessant, as was the shaking pressure on his shoulder. *What the fuck?*

His head shot up, his eyes flying open in disbelief. *He'd fallen asleep!*

He pushed through the brain fog, registering the heavy warmth of his companion on one side and the chill attacking the other through the open car door. He looked to the hand on his shoulder and then to its owner, leaning in from outside—Colin.

The driver met his gaze and promptly straightened, his hand falling away. 'Sorry, sir.' He cleared his throat. 'When you didn't respond on the intercom I gave you an extra twenty minutes. When I tapped on the glass and you still didn't respond...' He gave an awkward shrug.

'It's okay, Colin.' Marcus spoke softly. He wasn't ready to disturb her. She was so peaceful, curled up almost childlike against him, her breathing deep and even. She was out of it.

How tired can she be?

A foreign emotion curled around his gut, the force of which had his eyes snapping away. He was being a fool—they couldn't very well stay there.

He looked to his driver. 'I'll rouse Miss Hayes and then you can get off for the evening.'

'It's fine, sir. I'll wait and take her home when you're ready.'

'No,' he said on impulse. 'She can stay with me for the night.'

If Colin was surprised he knew better than to say anything. Hell, Marcus was surprised enough for the two of them. None of this was *normal*.

But then, *she* was far from normal. She was *the* Jennifer Hayes. His head spun anew. How could he have pegged her so wrong? He'd deemed her older, colder, nothing like the intoxicating bundle now hauled up against him.

She had achieved so much, and yet there was no way she was even his side of thirty. He tightened his arm around her, admiration going to his head even while anxiety crept in.

No, he definitely couldn't let her go without explaining who he was, what he would be to her from nine a.m. tomorrow, clearing the air and dealing with the fallout.

Goddamn you, Andrews!

If he'd only turned up and done what he was supposed to then none of this would have… *Ah, hell!* He didn't want that either. He wouldn't wish away their evening—not if his life depended on it.

But there was no denying it was a bloody mess.

Next to him, Jennifer stirred.

'Hey…' He bowed his head to hers. 'We're here.'

She mumbled and snuggled down further, teasing out a smile from him despite his creeping unease. A gust of cold air swept through the car and she wrapped her arms tighter around her chest but made no attempt to rouse herself.

He looked to Colin. 'Get the doorman to escort us. I'm going to carry her up.'

'Of course, sir.'

He disappeared off and Marcus turned his attention back to Jennifer. Settling her down on the back seat, he slid out of the car and reached back inside, his arms hooking under her. She folded into him naturally, her head dropping into the crook of his shoulder, and he was straightening up by the time Colin returned with the doorman.

'Bring her bag, please,' he said to him, and then to Colin, 'I'll see you at eight.'

Keen to get her out of the cold, Marcus headed into the building. The doorman, complete with bag, beat him to the waiting elevator and swiped the card for the penthouse.

As they ascended Jennifer rubbed her face against him, her delighted little noises doing weird things to his chest. He knew the doorman was doing his damnedest to stay professional, working hard to conceal his bemusement at the situation. Marcus couldn't blame him. It was weird for him too.

What the hell was he doing?

He should have woken her up, got her address and had Colin take her home. But even as he acknowledged the thought, he dismissed it. This way he had a chance to keep control of the situation, tell her who he was and get it dealt with.

The lift came to a stop, the doors opening onto his private foyer, and he stepped out. He gave directions for the doorman to leave the bag and bade him goodnight. Now he was standing in his vast suite, his creature comforts surrounding him, and there was a woman he barely knew curled up in his arms.

For the first time in his adult life he had no idea what to do and, boy, did it grate on him.

If she'd been awake it would have been different. There were plenty of options that sprang to mind. Like an honest conversation, for one. As well as the not so virtuous options which, despite his recent release, still got too much of his vote.

And for that reason alone he didn't dare wake her.

Not yet.

He needed his control firmly in place before she set those evocative eyes on him again. Bizarre, really, as his control was the one thing he had always been able to depend upon. But it had fallen by the wayside tonight.

It had to be the illicitness of it all. Surely once the cat was out of the bag it would all become entirely manageable. *She* would be manageable.

He looked to the various doors. There were two bedrooms. He could put her in the guest room. It was nice, cosy enough. His body immediately rejected the idea, and his mind came quickly to its aid—*You can't leave her to wake up without you. She'll have no idea where she is.*

It was a good enough reason for him.

Striding purposefully towards the master suite, he told himself he was doing right by her and kicked open the door. Reaching his bed, he pulled the covers back one-handed and set her down.

She turned into the mattress on contact, her body relaxing as he pulled the quilt to her chin, her long, lithe form folding into the charcoal-grey as if she belonged.

A warmth spread through him, irking him to turn away and head for the door.

Since when did the sight of a woman in his bed appeal?

The truth was *never*.

Because he'd never let it happen before.

Behind him, she gave a soft moan, the sound lulling his resistant gaze back. She shifted, her hands hooking into the pillow beneath her head and drawing it closer. His throat closed, his body heated, and he had to force his legs to work, to stride from the room straight down through the foyer and into the living area, where his glass drinks cabinet beckoned.

He debated how much he'd consumed already. Not quite two J&Bs. He could stand another. Just one.

Pouring himself a careful measure, he went to take it up when his phone buzzed with the arrival of a text message.

He pulled it out and checked the screen, his hand clenching around it as his stomach turned over.

I've been calling you for a week. Since no police have rung I assume you are still alive and just being ignorant. Call me back. Gran x

A bittersweet smile pulled at his mouth—*she was never one to mince her words*—and guilt swamped his unease. Yes, he should have rung, but no matter how he played it, how he tried to talk himself out of it, his grandparents, for all their devotion, brought with them the past.

And the past could go fuck itself.

Still, he owed them a call.

Hell, he owed them many.

Fingers moving deftly over the screen, he promised them he'd be in touch and then placed it on the side. Taking up his glass instead, he glanced down into the swirling amber liquid and felt his stomach turn anew.

Fuck.

He swiftly put it down, the harsh twang of glass hitting glass barely registering as the memories flooded him, his hands falling into fists at his side as he tried to push them out. The painful reminders of where pain and booze could take someone, of the many beatings he'd endured with the stench of drink permeating the air, of his father, so broken and twisted—

Let it go. You're not him. You never will be.

He strode to the glass wall, his sights fixed on the glittering city lights, and took a breath, trying to empty his mind and finding it impossible.

And then he thought of her—the distracting bundle curled up in his bed—and, no matter the trouble that was coming, he felt something inside him ease.

CHAPTER FIVE

IT WAS THE scent that hit her first—the hint of male cologne, all warm and woody and decidedly comforting to Jennifer's sleep-addled brain. She wrinkled her nose into the plushness cushioning her head, revelling in its luxurious feel. So soft. So nice. Much nicer than the feeling coming off the rest of her.

She stretched out and froze. She was still fully clothed. The jagged edges of her underwear bit into her skin, the brush of the quilt against her stockinged legs and the pinch of her stilettos was alarmingly peculiar.

And then came a faint noise, the unmistakable sound of snoring.

Jennifer slept alone. *Always* alone.

And now she was awake, cocooned in the scent of male and definitely not alone!

She shot up, her hands fisting into the sheets around her, her eyes blinking rapidly as she adjusted to the darkness of the room. It was huge. The bed she was in was huge, the floor-to-ceiling glass walls taking up half of the room were huge.

And then she saw him—her Mr Wright—his sleep-slackened body reclining in an armchair at the oppo-

site side of the room, his silhouette outlined by a view
of the moonlit Thames.

This had to be a dream.

But if it was a dream surely she would remember
going home? Surely her every sense wouldn't be on
high alert?

Then it all came flooding back. The bar, the elevator, the car ride to his place. Everything. In all its
flaming hot glory. And in spite of her clothed discomfort she felt her body heat; her breasts flushed
and her clit came alive.

He was exquisite. Even in the dusky light she could
sense his power, feel his appeal...

His jacket lay across the arm of the chair, his forearm resting upon it. His other arm was folded, his
hand curving over his inner thigh, his trouser-clad
legs relaxed and spread. Open and vulnerable. The
sight did things to her, things with a potency that
almost scared her, and she flexed her fists into the
bunched-up fabric of the sheets.

How could one man have this much effect? She
should have been sated and at ease now. Ready to
throw her all back into normality and sneak away.
No need for goodbyes. They'd both got what they
wanted. But...

Her eyes travelled up the length of him, pausing
over the open collar of his shirt where the top four
buttons lay undone. Her throat dried at the exposed
hint of chest, the arousing arch to his neck as he fell
back against the curve of the chair, his chest falling
rhythmically with his gentle snores.

Fascinated, she folded back the bed covers and
planted her feet to the floor, inwardly wincing as

her imprisoned toes made painful contact with the ground.

She dipped to remove one shoe and then the other, her toes curling blissfully into the plush fabric of the bedside rug as she smiled.

Had he thought it too intimate to remove them while she slept? Did he not care that her heels had likely damaged his expensive bed linen?

Pushing off the bed, she padded towards him, not really knowing what she was about and half expecting him to awake at any second and pin her with that desire-provoking gaze.

But he didn't move. His breathing remained heavy and even, each raspy intonation teasing at her senses.

As she came to a halt above him her gaze fell to the side table. His mobile, an unfinished glass of what looked to be whisky and her clutch resided there. She glanced at her watch—it was three-thirty in the morning. It was time she left. But even as she thought it her body balked. The idea of leaving without enjoying him one last time, of resisting the desire already burning, was too much.

Beads of perspiration pricked between her breasts and across the back of her neck. Her skin was clammy and her dress made her feel claustrophobic from sleeping in it. The need to be out of it had her hands taking up the hem and pulling it over her head.

The cool air swept across her skin, over her exposed nape as her hair was lifted away, and a delightful shiver ran down her spine.

She couldn't leave.

Not yet...

Letting the dress slip from her fingers, she stepped

forward, her knees coming up against the chair-edge between his legs. She leaned forward, placing one hand on the chair-arm while the other brushed away the hair that had fallen across his forehead, her eyes scanning his beautiful face.

Stunning even when in slumber, this man could ruin all her best laid plans if she gave him the chance, she was sure of it.

But a last goodbye… *Where was the harm?*

Lowering her mouth to his, she brushed her lips against him, tasting the whisky on his breath and repeating the move. His lips gave way beneath her coaxing pressure and she dipped her tongue inside. He was yummy—all warm, whiskyed up and tantalising to her senses.

His eyes fluttered, his hand twitched and then his eyes opened, wide and surprised. 'Jennifer?'

'Shh…' she said, pressing her index finger to his mouth and loving the heated firmness beneath her touch. She dropped her head to flick her tongue out, let it probe alongside her finger, tasting him, teasing him.

He tried to move beneath her, his hands coming up to take hold of her waist, his touch searing through her skin, but she wasn't ready for him to take control.

'Stay,' she commanded, raising her head to gaze down at him, her hands pressing into his shoulders as she pinned him back in the chair.

He looked up at her, his eyes dark and glittering in the low light, his entire body rigid as he succumbed to her will, freed her so she could focus on the fastened buttons of his shirt. One by one she undid them, all the while her eyes fixed on his.

And he watched her, his gaze burning into her eyes, her lips, the valley of her chest, then moving down to the V of her legs as she stood before him, his hands shifting to caress the lace band of her stockings with mesmerising intent.

She tugged the shirt out of his trousers, releasing the last of his buttons and parting the fabric for her hungry eyes. Her mouth like sandpaper, she took in each exposed inch, stroking the shirt off his shoulders, feeling the heat of his skin burning through her fingertips, his muscles rippling beneath her caress. The only sound in the room was their elevated breathing, and her ears were attuned to every hitch in his as she traced her fingers over him, toying with the smattering of hair across his pecs, her thumbs circling each puckered nipple before travelling lower.

He sucked in a breath, his anticipation clear, and she smiled, her fingers closing over his trouser fastening. No belt this time. One less hurdle. Popping the button free, she worked the zip, her hands brushing his hardness with their movement and sending her clit on a frenzied dance.

Pinning one hand on his hot, naked shoulder, she slipped her other inside his briefs, felt her own breath catching as he bucked into her palm. He was so big, so hard and ready.

She flicked her tongue out to moisten her lips, a whimper leaving her throat as she looked at where she held him, drawing him out, her hand sliding over him.

'*Fuck!*' He gripped her thighs, fingers biting. '*I want you.*'

Her eyes met with his own. 'I want you too.'

Straightening, she reached for her clutch as the

hands over her thighs slid inwards, his fingers seeking her out. She flicked open her bag.

He slipped beneath her thong, one finger gently brushing against the swollen nub of nerve-endings and sending her bucking against him. He did it again and she moaned, her head gliding back, her attention on the bag momentarily forgotten. He rolled her clit, working her to fever-pitch with his perfect rhythm, perfect pressure, perfect everything.

She rocked against him, biting into her lower lip as she tried to stave off the spread of tension long enough to locate the little foil packet tucked inside her bag.

Pulling it out, she tossed the clutch to the floor and used her teeth to break it open. He groaned beneath her, the fingers of his free hand coming up to probe at her opening, teasing, plundering, teasing some more.

She was on the verge, her mind screaming *Not yet* as she forced herself to step back, to break his touch.

He slumped in the chair and she dropped to her knees, reaching out to take hold of his rigid length and offer him up to her mouth. She flicked her tongue across his tip and he hissed, his hands flying to her hair, his eyes burning down into her as she smiled her pleasure.

Bringing the condom to his head, she held his eyes and rolled it down, securing it to his base before standing and closing the distance once more.

'Take off your bra,' he commanded suddenly.

She bit into her lip again, the tightness in his voice making her body overheat as she dutifully did as he asked, undoing the clasp and letting it fall away.

He cursed under his breath, his eyes burning into her chest as her breasts fell free, their sensual weight goading her clit, their tightened nipples singing in the exposure.

'Turn around.'

Again, she did as he asked. She could feel her wetness slick between her thighs as she moved, the skimpiness of her thong offering no protection from her readiness for him.

'I want you to sit on me,' he said, his hands coming up to take hold of her hips.

An erotic shudder broke through her and slowly she lowered herself, one hand slipping her thong to the side, the other coming down to take hold of his length and position him at her entrance.

His very tip teased its way in. A delicious heat engulfed her and she sank herself down, crying out and clenching him tight as he filled her so completely, so perfectly.

He gave way to a ragged breath. *'Fuck me, baby...'*

His reaction went straight to her head, to her clit, to her core, and then his grip on her hips squeezed as he lifted her up and over him, again and again. Slow at first. Savouring. And then more rapid, more desperate.

His chest came up to press against her back, his hands thrusting up to her breasts, his palms groping, his fingers toying, their attentions ferocious with his own need and driving her own.

'You're so fucking hot.'

She moaned her response, her hands biting into his thighs as she propelled herself over him.

'Here.' He took hold of her hand, brought it to her breast and squeezed her palm over her own flesh, showing her what he wanted. *'Christ, yes!'*

Her other hand flew up, mimicking the mindless caress at her other breast, freeing his hands to take control of her hips once more, giving her the rhythm she craved.

'Yes, yes, yes…' she cried, her head rolling back as she gave herself up to the tension spreading through her like wildfire.

He caught at her thong, pulling it taut over her clit, and the pleasure-pain was intoxicating as he continued to thrust her over him, pushing her to the brink.

And then she exploded, the sensation shattering through her, her muscles clenching wildly around his cock and taking him with her. The tremors of his body mixed with her own as he encased her in his arms and gripped her to him, taking them both back against the chair.

He rested his chin on her shoulder, his uneven breaths tickling at her flushed skin. It was blissful and bittersweet. For a goodbye, it had to go down as the best she'd ever had.

'We should talk,' he said suddenly, his chin jutting into her flesh as he spoke.

His words had the effect of an ice shower on her overheated body but she didn't tense up, didn't want him to sense her unease.

'Later—or rather, in the morning,' she said calmly, turning her head into his and pressing a kiss to his temple. 'First you need to get some proper sleep. What possessed you to take the chair?'

He shrugged, his grin warming her anew. 'What can I say? I'm nothing if not a gentleman.'

'You call what we've shared this evening gentlemanly?'

'Point taken, yet again,' he said, manoeuvring her so that she sat across his lap, his sated cock slipping out to rest beneath her behind. 'Not complaining, are you?'

She gave a laugh. 'What would you do if I was?'

'You don't want to know.'

It was how he said it, rather than what he said, that had her body heating with mutinous anticipation. She wanted to press, wanted to coax the words out of him but didn't dare. He played to her carnal desires so effortlessly, so perfectly...

'Is that so?' she said simply, it was a question, but it didn't ask for a response, and to ensure he got the message she snuggled down into his shoulder, her mouth clamped shut as her disgruntled body tried to force out a moan, her mind conjuring up a variety of reactions to her potential complaint.

'Not tonight, though, hey?' he said, pressing a kiss to her head and standing effortlessly with her in his arms.

He strode to the bed, his legs taking a wide stance as he kept his trousers in place. In spite of her emotional turmoil she laughed, his gallant candour leaving her momentarily on cloud nine. And then he deposited her on the bed, breaking their contact.

'I'll be right back,' he said, straightening and heading for a doorway that she assumed led to the bathroom.

'Don't be long,' she called after him, turning into the quilt and preparing her *I'm fast asleep* pose.

She didn't want to risk delaying her departure with conversation. She just needed to leave—and she would once he was asleep. A sudden heaviness hit her, deep in the belly, and she wrapped her arms tight around her middle, fending it off.

She'd had her one night of crazy; she'd had her fun. It was time to get back to reality—a reality without Mr Distraction in it. It was for the best.

It really was.

CHAPTER SIX

SHIT. SHIT. SHIT.

The words had been echoing through his brain for the last two hours, ever since he'd woken to find her gone. The only evidence she'd ever existed was a hurried *Thank you x* on a scrap of paper placed on the pillow.

Thank you. He had been worth that, at least.

But gratitude was the last thing she'd be feeling shortly. In just over an hour, when he turned up at her office and told her who he was, he was certain he could say farewell to a thank-you or a repeat.

A repeat.

He wanted to shake himself. *Was he mad?*

Sex was sex. He could get it anywhere.

What he couldn't get was another business partner like Jennifer Hayes.

He could hear his body laughing at the idea even as he shot the thought down.

Work had to come first. He would tire of her eventually, as he had every other woman. She wouldn't be any different—he wouldn't allow it.

And he wasn't about to put it to the test.

He needed to get the situation under control, and

swiftly. He just had to hope he hadn't screwed their working relationship along with her.

But she was a professional and he was banking on that to save him from too much of a scene in the office. It wasn't the ideal location for delivering the news, but what choice did he have? A phone call wouldn't cut it—not when she could simply hang up. And he wasn't about to risk her getting wind via anyone else.

He was also banking on her sound business acumen making her realise that ultimately his presence in the company could only be a good thing.

Plus, they'd both had fun. That had to count for something—*right?*

He combed his hand through his hair and wiggled the knot of his tie. Stress really wasn't in his make-up...

Across the table Tony Andrews sat in discussion with his solicitor. Documents were being passed to and fro, and the scratch of pen on paper broke the air as each one was signed. But the buzz that usually accompanied such a sound was non-existent, drowned out by the very real possibility that he was heading into World War III.

His own solicitor, to his right, leaned towards him. 'It's not too late, you know...'

It wasn't the first time he'd said that this morning. He was astute. He knew Marcus. Had worked with him for a decade. He knew something wasn't right and assumed it was the deal.

'No, it's all good, Roger,' he said, his gaze resting on Andrews as the man looked to him questioningly. He saw the flash of relief in his eyes before he looked back to the paperwork and wondered yet again at the man's situation.

He was clean-shaven, smartly turned out, his blond hair greased back as per usual, but it was his eyes and the dark circles beneath that told of the stresses beneath the slick exterior.

There was also a tell-tale scent that one might mistake for an overly strong cologne if one wasn't as attuned to it as Marcus. It didn't matter that he'd spent two decades free of it, of *him*, it still affected him as if it was yesterday. As if he was still that little boy hiding away as his father rolled in night after night, intent on taking out his demons on the one person unable to evade him.

His nails bit painfully into his palms and slowly he unfurled his fists, forcing himself to relax, throwing his focus into Tony Andrews instead.

He would feel sorry for the man if not for the fact that he'd brought it on himself. Or the fact that Jennifer was suffering as a direct result. She was clearly hitting the point of exhaustion if her tiredness last night had been any indication. If Andrews had been a decent business partner who pulled his weight she wouldn't have been in such bad shape.

Jennifer… He gritted his teeth. He never should have believed her when she'd suggested they talk in the morning. He should have known it was bull.

Christ, how many times had he done that himself? Escaping before morning, before all the questions and the hopes for a future…

His ego took the hit even as he respected her for the move.

And what did it matter? Soon she wouldn't be able

to walk away from him. He felt the buzz then—the spark of excitement in his gut.

'Mr Wright, if you could do the honours?'

Andrews' solicitor beckoned him, twisting the pages of the contract so they were facing his way and sliding them across the polished wooden surface of the table.

'Of course,' he said, taking up his pen and signing as Roger directed.

With each scrawl of his name the passion thrived, the excitement, the buzz… Only it definitely wasn't this acquisition that was doing it. It was *her*—Jennifer—being tied to working under the same roof as him.

The confusing realisation should have bothered him—*but did it?*

He couldn't see past the buzz to care.

Jennifer was having the morning from hell.

Tony letting her down last night was one thing. Tony not turning up to the morning's company-wide briefing was something else altogether. How could the employees trust their direction if he hadn't even turned up to deliver his part?

She gave way to a groan and collapsed back into her chair.

'Hey, don't stress—you did a great job.'

She looked to Anna, her optimistic, ever-cheery personal assistant, and smiled. 'I could've walked in there wearing a pink tutu, reading a fairy tale, and you would still tell me I'd done a great job.'

Anna set a fresh coffee down on her desk, her face lighting up. 'Ooh, now there's a thought—one for the next briefing, hey?'

In spite of herself, Jennifer laughed and took up
the drink. 'I'll make a note.'

'Great,' she said. 'And while you're doing that I'll
go and see if I can track down our elusive Mr Andrews.'

'Thanks, Anna.'

Anna turned on her heel and headed for the door,
pausing on the threshold just long enough to say, 'You
know, maybe you should take a leaf out of his book
some time and take a break. Leave him to pick up the
pieces for a change.'

Jennifer gave a non-committal snort. Anna meant
well, but seriously, there was no way in hell she would
leave the company in *his* hands. Not now.

She looked out to the buzzing office on the other
side of the glass wall, to the employees she had a duty
to protect, and decided she had to push for his signa-
ture on the Shareholders' Agreement. She didn't like
to force it, but it was time.

Her solicitor would certainly be relieved. He'd
made no bones about how stupid he thought she'd
been to continue operating without one. But, hell,
she'd been naïve and young, thinking some great gift
had come her way when Tony had offered up the joint
venture. She hadn't thought for a second that he would
change so much, that he would destroy her trust so
spectacularly.

Her mind decided, she wiggled her mouse to wake
up her computer screen and Marcus Wright stared
right back at her, filling it up.

*Yes, she'd looked him up. Yes, it had been the first
thing she'd done when she'd hit the office at seven a.m.*

It hadn't taken her long to find out enough. It was

surprising she hadn't come across him, considering they worked in the same industry. But then she didn't focus on the people, rather on the companies and what they were churning out. And she knew of his company plenty well enough.

As for him—he was big news. Well-regarded, highly esteemed—not only in the business world but for his charity work too. His name came with accolade after accolade. The perfect chocolate box mix. And now she'd sampled him how was she supposed to move on?

She groaned again. Her head landed on her palm as she sulked into his photo.

'Why couldn't you come along in ten years' time?' she muttered, twirling the mouse pointer over his delectable mouth. He was perfect. Both sexually and on paper. Her absolute Mr Right. Only she wasn't ready.

Her eyes slid to the family photo on her desk— Mum, Dad, her sister, her—all so happy. Especially her. She'd been leaving for university that day, buzzing with excitement over the future. No one could have known that twenty-four hours later her dad would no longer be with them. Taken too soon by a heart attack brought on by his determination to be everything to everyone.

And she'd made a promise—to herself and to him—that she would be the success he had dreamed of her being. That she would secure the future he had wanted for them all.

But she wouldn't make the same mistake and pursue it all at once—a successful career *and* a family of her own.

She wanted both, but a relationship, her own family—that could wait. She was only twenty-eight. She had time to wait for her financial circumstances and the company structure to be such that she could strike the right balance.

At least that was what she'd thought before her mum had got sick. Now she wasn't so sure of anything. Her tummy twisted painfully and she pressed her palms into the desk.

Get back to work...you're safe with work.

She looked at the computer screen and promptly closed down Mr Distraction. It was for the best. Losing herself in spreadsheets would help and she had work to do: financing the new product stream, sorting out resources...

Her thoughts trailed away, her eyes trailing with them, and the sight of someone exiting the lift across the office caught her eye.

It wasn't... It couldn't... What the fuck?

She catapulted out of her seat, knocking over her coffee in the process. The steaming liquid seeped across her desk, but she couldn't move, couldn't care. Her entire being was set on the man striding with absolute confidence towards her office—*Marcus!*

Excitement surged, her pulse tripped, and alarm bells resounded through her head as her best-laid plans sensed jeopardy. But he'd tracked her down, sought her out, and her heart swelled even as her stance hardened.

You can't have him.

The shrill ring of her phone jarred her. It was Anna. Blindly, she pressed the button. 'Not now.'

'But I have Tony on the line.'

Jennifer could sense the girl's frown, could see

her turn to look at her through the glass from her desk outside.

'He says it's urgent.'

She wasn't listening—not properly. 'Tell him I'll call him back. I have a visitor.'

'A visitor?' Anna's eyes left her to zone in on the man now only a few desks away. 'Right—a visitor. No problem.'

She was sure if she bothered to look Anna would be as transfixed by him as she was. Hell, everyone would be. He demanded attention.

But the only attention you're giving him is the been-nice-knowing-you kind.

Her tummy sank and she took a breath.

She could do this...

If someone had been riding his bollocks right now, Marcus didn't think he could have been any more uncomfortable.

Her eyes were on him. He could feel it. And, God help him, he couldn't even look in her direction. Andrews had been clear enough in his instructions. Out of the lift, across the foyer, through the rows of desks to the office straight ahead. That was where he'd find her.

And then the guy had pleaded. *'Let me speak to her first.'*

Like hell he was going to agree to that. The man had missed his chance. There was no way Marcus was going to let anyone but him deliver this news. He needed to do it, needed to make sure she gave him a chance to explain.

He paused at the desk positioned just outside her

office door and looked to the petite blonde sitting on the other side of it. She was currently doing something of a fish impression, a phone receiver hanging limp in her hold.

'Hi,' he said. 'I'm here to see Jennifer Hayes.'

'Uh-huh,' she said, making no effort to say any more or deal with whoever was on the other end of the line.

'Soooo…' he drawled, raising his brows and waving in the direction of the door. 'Can I go in?'

She didn't respond, but her eyes shifted to the office as the faint sound of the door opening reached him and sent every hair rising with the knowledge that she was approaching.

And then she spoke. 'Mr Wright?'

Take a breath…

'I think we can drop the "Mr", don't you?' he said, turning on his heel and feeling the hit of her beauty like a slug to the stomach.

He righted himself against it, adopting his faithful mask. The one that had got him through deal after deal. Only this time he questioned its success. The power of his reaction was so strong he was sure even her PA, who was still in full-on fish mode, was picking up on it.

'It's Marcus,' he said, putting one foot in front of the other and extending a hand, fixing his eyes on her face, not daring to lower his gaze, not wanting to see, but acknowledging all the same, the way the fabric of her green blouse clung distractingly close to her upper body. Or how the delicate length of her neck was accentuated by her hair being smoothed back and twisted into a severe knot high on her head.

Desire burned in his throat and he cleared it as her hand slipped inside his own.

She looked up at him, her crystal green eyes widening on a flicker of something—lust, nerves, fear... And then her hand closed around his and his blood rushed towards the contact, the softness of her palm doing things below the belt that he didn't want to permit.

He searched her face. *Did she feel it too?*

Her eyes glittered, streaks of colour shone through the make-up on her cheeks, and then her lips parted on a breath, the tip of her tongue flicking briefly across her lower lip. It was still there, the chemistry, he was sure of it. And the very idea that he could work with her and keep it platonic was fast becoming laughable.

But he would.

His no-mixing-business-with-pleasure rule existed for a reason. If only he'd been able to remember that last night, when he'd realised who she was, rather than letting her...

A flashback of racing images sent heat ripping through him and he coughed abruptly.

She started at the sound, her eyes narrowing on him. 'It's nice of you to come by,' she said, and then her eyes flitted about the room and saw their steadily growing audience. 'Do you want to go on in?' She gestured to her open doorway. 'I just need a brief word with my PA.'

'Of course.' He nodded and she stepped around him. He stared after her, teasing himself with the swaying curve of her hips, snug within a black pencil skirt.

For fuck's sake.

He snapped his eyes away and headed for her office. The sooner they could clear the air, the sooner he could focus on their relationship—their purely platonic, *business* relationship.

Entering her room, he was drawn to the bookcase running the length of one wall. Books were good. Books were calming. Books would get him in check.

He explored the titles, fingering the bindings—business, psychology, law... And then he paused, as a small collection tucked in the corner closest to the window drew his eye. He crouched and pulled one of the books out. He knew from the binding what he would find, and the entwined couple on the front only served to confirm it. He looked from the front to the back, scanning the blurb with a smile.

So the formidable Miss Hayes was a romantic at heart.

A throat was cleared directly behind him. *Shit.*

He looked at her over his shoulder. Her arms were crossed over her middle, her breasts bulging distractingly above them, and he tore his eyes away, slipping the book back into place and slowly getting to his feet to face her, his eyes carefully pinned above neckline.

'Sorry, it's an occupational hazard,' he explained. 'I like to understand people, and their books can give quite the insight.'

He smiled and watched her colour slightly, her eyes flicking over her little collection before returning.

She cocked a brow. 'Nosy, much?'

'What can I say? It pays to understand people.'

She surprised him with a laugh and, shaking her head, strode to her desk—just as her PA walked in, a roll of paper towel in her hand.

'Here you go,' the girl said, passing it to her. 'You sure you don't want me to do it?'

'Don't be silly—it's my mess.' She wrapped a fistful around her palm and tore it off. 'Thank you.'

'I'll let you get on, then.'

Her eyes flicked briefly in his direction before returning to Jennifer in a widened state. *Was this girl all together there?*

'Let me know if you need anything else.'

'Will do,' Jennifer said, her attention now fixed on the desk.

He followed her gaze to an upturned mug and a dripping mess. *How had he missed that?*

She righted the cup and started to mop at the liquid.

'Want some help?'

She gave him a brief look. 'You've done enough.'

Surprise made him chuckle. 'I'm not quite sure how to take that.'

She straightened, smoothing her free hand over her hair, and then she looked to him again, for longer this time—long enough for him to make out the pulse twitching in her neck and the re-emerging colour in her cheeks.

'Truth is, you gave me a shock when you came in and the coffee took the hit.'

'Ah.' He looked from her to the puddle. 'In that case, I'm definitely helping.'

He strode towards her, ignoring the flash of panic in her eyes, and held out his hand.

Reluctantly, she separated out some sheets and thrust them into his palm. 'You can do the floor.'

He smiled. Relegated to floor work? He could cope with that.

He could think again.

No sooner had he crouched down than he found himself face-to-face with her stiletto-clad feet.

Cope?

He'd be lucky to get back on his feet and keep his surging erection hidden.

Christ, but her ankles were hot, their delicate curves raising elegantly from shoes whose heels evoked desires so carnal and fierce they brought him to his knees.

And there he was, dropping forward, knees pressing into the hard floor as he began wiping at the puddle. It would be funny if he wasn't doing his damnedest to stay on task, trying not to get distracted by the shimmer coming off her legs, or the memory rampaging through his mind of how their stockinged lengths had felt beneath his palm. How it had felt to hook them over his hip and have her ride against his...

'Are you trying to polish a hole in my floor?'

He looked up to find her looming over him, her eyes burning into his own.

Christ, he wanted to bury himself between her legs.

Hell, if they weren't in her office perhaps delivering the news while driving her to climax would somehow take the edge off.

Yeah, real businesslike, that.

She was still looking at him, her eyes alive with some hidden thought, and he heard himself say, 'I like to be thorough.'

She gave a delectable little hum and nodded, muttering something that sounded very much like, 'Don't I know it?'

'What was that?' he said, rocking onto his feet

and tossing the dirty towels in the nearby wastebasket. His body was teetering dangerously close to the edge of reason.

'Nothing,' she blurted, her mood shifting so swiftly he wondered if he'd imagined her words.

It doesn't matter. Tell her. Now.

'Look, I—'

They both said it in unison.

'Jinx.' She gave him a smile that screamed regret. 'I'm flattered, I really am, that you've tracked me down and gone to all this trouble—it's lovely, it really is, and last night… Well, last night was probably the best—'

She was rambling. He knew it and she knew it, judging by the flush creeping up the exposed skin of her chest.

He tore his eyes upwards, forcing himself to look into her eyes as he cut her off. 'I'm not here because of that.'

She frowned. 'You're not?'

'Not entirely.'

Hell, just get it out. You've dealt with hostile takeovers better than this.

'I mean, I'm not here for what you think.'

Her brow furrowed further. Her genuine confusion was breaking him.

'Okay…' She threw her dirty paper towelling away, then returned her arms to her middle. 'So why *are* you here?'

He thrust his hand through his hair. The guilt, the alien sense of unease, the fear of hurting her—all made it impossible to think straight. He'd planned it out on the journey over, prepared his words, perfected his apology, but it all evaded him now that she was standing before him, waiting...

'Right.' The word was more for himself than her, as his hands came up in a definitive gesture that said *Let's do this.* 'There's no easy way to tell you what I need to, so I'm just going to come out and say it. But before I do you have to understand that when we met I had no idea who you were.'

Her eyes narrowed. 'Well, why would you?'

'Because the business I told you I was in town for...'

She nodded and he lowered his hands, shoving them into his pockets.

'It was Tony Andrews I was supposed to be meeting.'

Her lips parted in surprise. 'Tony?'

'Yes.'

Her head gave a little shake. 'But why?'

'We were discussing this business...*your* business.' He watched the confusion rain down over her face and pushed himself onwards, ignoring the sinking feeling in his gut, the sheer shittiness of what he was about to tell her.

'My business?' She shook her head more fervently, a lock of hair falling distractingly across her paling cheek.

Stick with it, Marcus.

'But that makes no sense,' she said softly. 'Tony hasn't mentioned any potential work with Tech-Incorp.'

She coloured slightly at the name, realising she had revealed too much in that sentence. So she'd looked him up? He would have been flattered if not for the fucked-upness of it all.

'That's because it's not a simple joint venture.'

She brought one hand up to her mouth, her expression changing as he could see her putting it together, piece by piece.

'He was supposed to have spoken to you,' he continued, very much on the defence. 'In fact, he was supposed to bring you to meet me last night so we could discuss the future in a more relaxed environment.' He withdrew one hand from his pocket to rake it through his hair again, his prepared words coming back to him. 'He wanted the opportunity to explain his reasoning and make you understand why he was doing it. All before the paperwork was signed.'

'The paperwork?'

'He kept saying he wanted to tell you himself, and I've been pushing him for weeks to speak to you, but there's no telling that guy.' He shook his head with genuine frustration. 'Last night was his final opportunity and he couldn't even get *that* right.'

'His final opportunity?'

She looked lost now, as if she couldn't believe what she was hearing.

'Yes.' He pushed on. 'Time was of the essence. He needed the deal done this morning and it worked for me too.'

She came alive on a harsh laugh. 'It worked for *you*?'

Shit...

'Just to be clear,' she bit out, the hand in front of her mouth moving to slice the air between them. 'What *exactly* has he signed?'

He looked at her head-on. The woman who had driven this company to the fore was very much pres-

ent now. Jennifer from last night was long gone. There
was no carnal promise to her gaze, no flirtatious tilt
to her mouth. Her countenance was like steel, cold
and hard.

And that suited him just fine.

This Jennifer he could work with.

'He's sold his half of the business.' He rolled his
shoulders and jutted his chin. 'To me.'

CHAPTER SEVEN

'You?'

Before her, Marcus nodded, the movement sending hair across his forehead with appealing charm.

He had no right to be appealing or charming. Not when she wanted to scream, to vent her anger and get to the bottom of what the hell had happened.

She'd been made a fool of. By the pair of them.

Betrayal clawed its way into her stomach, and nausea was instant and dizzying.

She'd been all out for anonymous sex—no names, no future, no nothing. And yet he—he had known. From the moment his driver had secured her name he had known who she was.

'I tried to stop things,' he said, as though reading her rampant thoughts.

'Yeah, you tried *really* hard,' she said, barely acknowledging the truth of his words, her fingers sweeping over her tingling cheeks.

'I tried to take you home to your place.'

She nodded. 'I remember.'

She remembered all too well. He'd tried and she'd pushed, seducing him until he'd bent to her will.

But she hadn't known. He had.

'I need you to go.'

'I think we should talk this through.'

She looked at him, her enlightened gaze seeing him clearly for the first time, and the fool inside her shrivelled and died. 'What? So you can lie to me some more?'

His eyes flashed. 'That's not fair. I didn't lie.'

'You lied by omission.'

She could see him struggling for an apt response, and his silence spoke volumes. Part of her wished he could smooth it over, make it all better, because the burn of humiliation was crippling her brain. She couldn't process any of it—his deceit, the dogged attraction to him she still shamefully felt, Tony's effing bail-out...

Christ—Tony!

The guy had truly surpassed himself this time. How could she have been so blind to his plans? And so trusting as to have delayed that sodding Shareholders' Agreement.

Such an idiot. That would have prevented it all, for heaven's sake.

But then, she'd never expected this. That he would actually jump ship and bring this potent heap of man trouble to her door.

It was a disaster.

An absolute fucking disaster.

'You need to leave.'

'Look, I understand that you're angry, and you have every right to be.'

'How big of you.' Inwardly she winced. She sounded like a disgruntled teen and she hated it.

'But the sooner we can put this behind us,' he

said, ignoring her little outburst, 'the sooner we can concentrate on the future and get our working relationship on the right footing. It's what's best for the business, after all.'

Words failed her. The more he spoke, the calmer he became, and all she wanted was to mirror that control. The fact that she couldn't made the situation a hundred times worse. And now he was using *her* business as a tool to reign her in.

Well, fuck that.

'What's best for the business is for me to understand Tony's motivation for leaving and get my head around your arrival. Then we can talk.'

He nodded, his expression one of annoying understanding. 'This afternoon, then? Or tonight? Over dinner, maybe?'

Afternoon...tonight...dinner...

She gave a manic laugh. 'Are you for real? You expect me to just roll over, take this news and pick up where we left off?'

'Hell, no!' he said, his eyes widening with what she could only read as horror. 'I want to talk business and strategy. Where and when doesn't matter to me. I wasn't suggesting a *date* of any sort.'

'Why?' she sniped. 'Does the idea suddenly seem repulsive to you?'

'Sorry, that came out wrong.'

He actually had the decency to look sheepish, and the change made him almost boyish. God help her if she didn't want to jump his bones as much as she wanted to kill him.

'I just mean it's not something I endorse. I have a rule never to mix business with pleasure.'

She stared at him incredulously. 'I repeat—are you for real?'

'Last night was different,' he stressed. 'Things had already gone way too far before I knew who you were.'

She clamped her jaw shut. *What the hell could she say to that?* By the time he'd discovered who she was she'd been like a dog on heat, and as for him... He'd been right there with her.

But still it didn't make it right.

She took a slow breath, smoothing a hand over her hair as she raised her chin and straightened her spine. This was happening, whether she liked it or not. The sooner she buried the emotional wreckage, the sooner she could deal with the professional fallout.

And that was all that mattered.

It had to be.

'Fine,' she said, purposefully shifting her attention to rifle through the papers on her desk. 'I'll have Anna clear my diary for tomorrow. We can meet then.'

She didn't look up, hoping everything in her tone and demeanour had delivered the dismissal he deserved. And yet he hesitated. She could feel his eyes still on her, the tension in the air still tight.

'What?' she suddenly blurted, her composure cracking as the need to goad him burst free. 'You can't wait until then to see me?'

Her gibe hit its mark, his eyes flaring. 'Very funny, Jennifer.'

'If you find this *funny*, I have serious concerns about your sense of humour.'

He looked as if he would say something else but stopped, his shoulders rolling on a heavy sigh. 'Look,

I know I've not done a great job of explaining myself, or the situation, but you must know that the sooner we get talking strategy, the sooner we can move forward and put this inconvenient start behind us.'

He studied her for a moment, probably waiting for a response, and when none came he turned and left, leaving her staring after him, the word *inconvenient* bouncing provokingly around her head.

Inconvenient?

Incon-bloody-venient?

The man was an arse!

She'd show him what *inconvenient* truly looked like.

Beneath her, her legs trembled against her bravado and her tummy turned. She was grateful she hadn't eaten breakfast that morning, because surely it would be making a return right now.

She could handle this. She just needed to break the problem down into two parts, or rather two men, and deal with each in turn.

First up—Tony.

Collapsing back into her chair, she reached out and pressed her index finger to the phone to dial Anna. She would know where Tony had been calling from. Anna wasn't just her PA, she was good friends with Tony's wife. And Jennifer would be damned if she was having this conversation with him over the phone.

She rapped on the door and fought the urge to test the handle. What she really wanted to do was rip the damn thing open and confront Tony wherever he stood.

She knew Lucy wasn't home. His wife had apparently given him a kick up the arse, taken the baby and moved out. For how long would be up to him.

Things were worse than Jennifer had realised. Worse than even Anna had understood.

Guilt cajoled her anger. *She should have realised.* If not for everything else on her plate, she probably would have. But bailing out of their company without a single word to her, bringing a total stranger into their midst—it felt like the ultimate betrayal.

Through the bevelled glass of the heavy black door she could make out his approach and she stepped back. Her eyes scanned the traditional London townhouse as she waited.

She heard the latch shift and looked to the door as it opened, Tony's head appearing at its edge. She swallowed back a gasp. He looked like hell. His blond hair flopped around his face, his eyes were glassy and sunken in their shadowed sockets.

'Jenny,' he rasped, eyes squinting, one hand holding a half-empty bottle of Jack Daniels and swinging it upwards to rest against the frame.

'You going to let me in?'

'You sure you *want* to come in?' His words were slurred and he looked towards the street, eyeing it up and down as though someone might be following.

'I don't think you want this particular conversation out here.'

He snorted and swung back, the door moving with him. 'Suit yourself.'

Jennifer stepped inside. Holding her breath against his alcohol-tainted air, she bypassed him and headed straight down the Edwardian-style hallway for the lounge.

He couldn't have been home alone for long—the house was too clean, too orderly. The high-ceilinged lounge barely looked lived in. All a marked contrast to his haggard state.

Tugging off her coat, she tossed it on one of the beige sofas but didn't sit. She wasn't ready to make herself at home. Instead she strode to the window, and waited until she heard him shuffle in behind her.

She tried to muster up the anger, the hurt, but as she turned to face him all she felt was sadness. He was pale and clammy, his white shirt hanging half open, his dark trousers out of place and a dramatic contrast to the pasty white feet sticking out beneath.

She took a steadying breath. 'I'm going to put the kettle on.'

'Suit yourself.' He swung the bottle and took a swig, wincing as he swallowed it down.

For fuck's sake!

She strode across the room and reached for the bottle. 'Let me get you a cuppa.'

His gaze dropped to her hand, his eyes wavering with the effort to focus. 'I'm good.'

'You'll be better with tea.' She closed her hand around the bottle and pulled.

He resisted, but only for a second, then his hand dropped away. 'Ah, Jennifer, you always know best.'

'And don't you forget it.'

She'd managed to inject a jovial confidence into her tone, but inside she was trembling, tears biting at the backs of her eyes. She needed to get away from him before she broke down.

'Go and sit down. I'll be back in a second.'

He slumped off to fall onto the nearest sofa and

Jennifer hurried into the kitchen, her shaky hands tapping on the kettle and reaching for mugs. She placed them on the worktop and pressed her fingers to her cheeks, breathing back the tears.

How long had he been this bad? Why hadn't she seen it?

She wanted the truth out of him—all of it—and she wanted it yesterday. But right now she'd settle for having the old Tony back. The one who had given her a career break and the backing that had got her where she was today. She'd forgive him everything and deal with whatever the future held for the company, for her, for Marcus...

The kettle bubbled with its impending boil, but its sound was broken by the shattering of glass.

What the hell?

She sped back through the house, her pulse racing. She entered the lounge just in time to see Tony hunching forward, reaching for the pieces of a broken photo frame at his feet.

'*Wait.*' She hurried over and squatted down before him. 'I'll take care of it.'

He didn't even acknowledge her as his fingers slipped the family photo from beneath the shards.

'What have I done?'

'Shh.' She rested her palm against his knee. 'It's going to be okay—you'll see.'

'How can it be?' he said on a shuddering sob, his distraught gaze crushing her. 'I've ruined everything. My work, my family...everything.'

'We can fix it... *I promise,*' she said, desperate to calm him. 'Here—put your feet up so I can clean this up.'

Silently he did as she asked and she fled to the kitchen, telling herself it *would* be okay. She would get him the help he needed, whether he was willing to accept it or not. Lucy would certainly support her.

And as for Marcus—what the hell did he think he was playing at? Entering into a deal with a man who clearly wasn't of sound mind?

Screw his charity work and his exemplary public profile—that son of a bitch had a lot to answer for.

And she would see to it that he did.

CHAPTER EIGHT

MARCUS PRESSED THE speed button, increasing the already punishing pace of the treadmill. Around him music blared, his breath was coming in hard grunts, sweat trickled down his body and still she was there, filling his mind, teasing his body.

He tore his T-shirt over his head, swiping it over his face and across his torso before tossing it aside. He wasn't stopping until he was free of her.

He'd tried telling himself it was business that was getting him worked up, that they needed to be talking strategy ASAP and ensuring they were on the same page.

But like hell was it business.

He'd tried to work, to concentrate on anything other than her, and yet she persisted. Her appeal still resonated through him long after he'd left her standing there.

It didn't matter that she was mad at him, that he'd screwed up and jeopardised their business relationship. His body simply didn't care.

And that was unacceptable.

He hammered the speed button once more, his frustration burning through him. He would exhaust her out of him if he had to. Whatever it took to get himself back under control.

His mobile's screen flashing in its rest caught his eye and he cursed. He didn't want to be interrupted. He wasn't ready to finish.

He checked the ID and saw it was his doorman. He wouldn't ring unless it was important…

Easing off the speed, he muted the music and put the phone on speaker. 'Yes?'

'Sir, I have Miss Hayes here to see you.'

'Miss Hayes?' He stopped the treadmill entirely.

'Yes, sir, would you like me to send her up?'

He felt his pulse kick rebelliously and thrust his fingers through his hair.

So what if she'd changed her mind? So what if she couldn't wait until tomorrow? So what if she'd tracked him down?

'Sir?'

'Yes.' He pulled sweat-slickened strands of hair off his forehead and met his own determined gaze in the mirror ahead. *Business. It's all about business.* 'Bring her up.'

He grabbed the towel slung over the machine and cut the call, launching his contacts list next. He scrolled through them, drying off his face as he headed into the foyer, his mind made up. He would deal with Jennifer and then he would go out on a date. He had options. Even if a suitable companion wasn't leaping out of his contacts just yet, he would find one.

He came to a stop before the mirror-finish lift doors, his semi-naked body reflecting back at him. *Should he chuck some clothes on?* He was hardly dressed for a business discussion, not on any level, but to hell with it—what did she expect, coming to his home uninvited? If the sight made her suffer half as much as he had already, then it would be worth it.

Grinning, he slipped his mobile into the back pocket of his shorts and took hold of each towel-end, casually leaning back against the wall as he waited.

The lift slid into place, its doors opening and presenting him with the doorman, who stepped back to allow Jennifer to pass. She froze mid-step, her mouth parting in that appealing way he had become fascinated with.

'Marcus?'

'In the flesh,' he said, spreading the towel-ends and straightening up, his eyes leaving hers to dismiss the doorman. 'Thank you.'

The guy nodded and pressed the button to close the doors behind her.

She wore the same clothes she'd been in earlier that day, overlaid by a long beige trench coat—the kind she could wear with nothing beneath when the need arose.

His cock twitched. *Just get through this. Fun can come later. And not with her.*

'So, to what do I owe this pleasure?'

She scanned him from top to toe, her cheeks heating, her eyes alive. And then she swallowed, a shutter falling over her expression as she stepped forward, closing the distance between them.

'Can you do something for me?' she asked softly, pausing an arm's reach away.

The word *anything* rushed to the tip of his tongue and he buried the crazy retort. 'What is it?'

She raised a hand to his chest, and the unexpected

touch sucked air into his lungs, holding it there as her fingers trailed down, spread out over his naked torso.

'Can't you guess?' she purred, her eyes following her fingers and her delicate touch sending ripples of pleasure straight to his defiant groin.

What the fuck?

He fought to keep his head clear, to remember his plan of action—*the sensible one.* 'Considering you couldn't wait to be rid of me a few hours ago—'

He broke off as her fingers met with the waistband of his shorts and he dropped his gaze, saw his cock swelling at her touch mere millimetres from where he desired it. His mouth dried up, and his well-exercised muscles turned rigid with anticipation.

'No,' he continued tightly.

Business. It needs to be about business. But, God, the desire to push her, to see how far she was going to go...

'You're going to have to enlighten me.'

She stepped closer, her eyes lifting to his mouth. 'It's you that needs to enlighten *me*,' she said, raising her hands to twine them through the ends of his towel and pulling him down.

He told himself to stop, to end it before things went too far, but his head still bowed. Her smell was invading his senses, her mouth beckoning.

God, he wanted her.

She was a hair's breadth away when the mood suddenly shifted, her eyes snapping to his as she shoved at him. 'You can start by telling me what the *hell* you're playing at.'

He stumbled back against the wall, surprise knocking him off-kilter. She was beyond angry—he could see that now. Her eyes were shooting daggers, her skin flaring like her hair.

'Hell, Jennifer.' He righted himself, fingers raking over his face, desire still burning through him, intensifying his confusion. 'Seems I should be asking you the same question—coming here, throwing yourself at me and—'

'No,' she cut in. 'That little scene was about making myself feel better for what you did to me. Make no mistake. I had no intention of following through.'

'Is that so?' He shook his head.

So it was payback?

It was about getting him back for the wrong she felt he'd done her. Hell, he could understand that, even respect her for it. But the rest...?

'You came all the way here just to tease me?'

'Absolutely not,' she said. 'There's plenty I wish to discuss with you.'

Plenty to berate him for, if her whole demeanour was anything to go by. And, hell, he deserved it. He knew he did.

'In that case, you'd best take a seat in the living room.' There was no way he was having this conversation half-clothed, or without a cold shower first. 'I'll join you in ten.'

'In ten?' She frowned. 'Where are you going?'

'To take a shower,' he said, adding, for his own devil-like amusement, 'unless you want to join me?'

Her cheeks flooded anew.

'No, I didn't think so.' He spoke for her. 'Look, I need a shower. You can either wait or you can leave and we'll do this tomorrow? It's up to you.'

With that he turned and walked away. His intent was to show her that he didn't care. In reality he needed to put distance between her and the erection still pressing painfully against his shorts. It was clearly slow at getting the message that he'd been played.

Jennifer stared after him, hands fisted at her sides, her head a mess as she struggled to rise above her warring emotions.

She'd been fuelled by anger. On the taxi ride over she'd plotted her attack, determined to tease him, catch him on the back foot, make herself feel better over his deceptive behaviour and then, when she was happy she had him, to pull him apart over his dealings with both her and Tony.

It had been a great plan.

She just hadn't factored in a semi-naked Marcus, all pumped and slick, so ripped and mouthwatering she'd hardly believed her eyes. But the reality had been there, and the sight had been enough to send her best-laid plans departing with the lift and her knickers wet through.

It was disgraceful. Add to that his ability to dismiss her so readily off the back of their little exchange and she was hopping mad.

She'd had him right where she'd wanted him. It had been visibly evident. His hardness had been pleading for more. And she'd take heart in that, if it wasn't for the fact that it had taken every ounce of her strength to thrust him away.

In spite of her anger, and her hatred for what he'd done to her, to Tony, she still wanted him. It was unforgivable, intolerable and totally undeniable.

She wanted to scream her frustration, but sense won out. There was no way in hell she would risk him hearing how much he got to her.

Tearing her eyes off his distracting rear, she headed for the living area, her heels clicking against the rich wooden floor.

She didn't dwell on the last time she'd been there. Then, she'd navigated it in the dark, her hands feeling their way, hot from their recent exploration of his body. A body she'd felt completely within her rights to explore, to enjoy, to devour.

What a fool!

She scrunched up her face, forcing out the memory. *It hadn't been her fault—she had nothing to be ashamed of.* And, striding forward, she entered the vast living space that ran off the foyer.

It was impressive, to say the least, its glass walls making the London skyline and its setting sun the perfect backdrop. A large cream L-shaped sofa dominated the room, its clean lines made inviting by various oversized cushions. Plush rugs adorned the floor, softening the hard wood throughout.

And in the corner, halting her appraisal of all else, stood an exquisite grand piano, gleaming in the accented lighting. It called to her, and she felt a bittersweet warmth pulling her back to another time and place.

She headed for it automatically, slipping her coat from her shoulders and dropping it over the sofa as she went. She reached out, her fingertips gliding over the sleek black top, following its curve with pleasing familiarity and pausing when she reached the key lid.

She itched to lift it. *Could she still play? Would she remember anything her father had taught her?*

She nibbled at her lower lip and raised the lid, her fingers dropping to toy with the keys. The notes resonated through the air and she glanced anxiously in the direction of the foyer.

Ah, hell, what did she care?

She needed *something* to do while she waited— anything to keep busy...

Slipping onto the bench, she tested out a melody, surprising herself with what she could remember, and a soothing calm seemed to be taking over as her fingers ran away with it.

She missed this. Maybe it was time she got a piano for her apartment. Inwardly, she laughed. It would never fit. She'd have to move. And even then it wouldn't be as beautiful as this one. Or the one that sat untouched in her Yorkshire home. She'd never transport that down here either. It wouldn't feel right. Even though it would never be played—not while her mum was still with them—it belonged there.

Her tune changed with her mood, and melancholy consumed her as she let it flow through her fingers.

She played and played, relaxing into the rhythm, losing sight of where she was—until the air became tight and an awareness rippled through her. Her fingers froze, her eyes shooting to the foyer.

How long he'd been there she had no idea, but there he was. Freshly showered, his damp hair curling around his face, he wore a grey sweatshirt that clung indecently to his upper body, and faded jeans. His bare feet were super-casual. All very laid-back and chilled, save for the man himself.

She swallowed.

His face was hard, set like stone, but his eyes—
they blazed, and an emotion she couldn't read seared
her across the room. Heat consumed her, swirling
through her core as guilt swelled.

She slipped her fingers from the keys, folding them
onto her lap. 'I'm sorry.'

There was a flicker of something—anger, pain, she
didn't know—and then it was gone, his face turned
away as he crossed the room, heading for a drinks
cabinet that looked fit for an exclusive bar.

'Don't be—you play well,' he remarked.

There was no edge to his voice, no emotion. As if
she'd imagined the whole thing. Except she hadn't.

'Can I get you a drink?'

'I really am sorry.'

*Christ, why was she still apologising? He'd said it
was fine. Only she didn't believe him...*

'It's been a while, and when I saw the piano I
couldn't resist.'

'It's fine.' He extracted a bottle and glanced over
his shoulder. 'I was just surprised. I don't know many
people who play.'

She rose and stepped out from behind the piano,
her mind scrambling to get back to her purpose, to
the reason she'd come. But her brain felt clouded with
the memories, the pleasure of playing, and then him
in all his appealing and confusing glory.

He turned and walked towards her, two glasses
of red wine in his hands. He offered one out. It was
presumptuous, but it was what she needed, and she
took it.

'Thank you.'

He watched her lift it to her lips, then lowered his eyes briefly before returning them to lock with hers. It was fleeting, but she felt the trail of his eyes over her skin like the warmth of the alcohol gliding down her throat and her pulse skittered.

She looked away, needing to protect herself, to hide his effect on her, and she sensed him smile—*did he know what he was doing to her?*

'Why don't you take a seat?'

She bit back the ridiculous retort *I'd rather stand.* This wasn't going to be quick and easy—sitting made more sense. Even if it did appear too comfortable, too relaxed.

Feeling his eyes on her, she walked to the sofa with deliberate grace and perched at its edge, her glass cradled between her hands.

He followed, his fresh, clean scent washing over her as he passed by, dropping onto the sofa alongside her. He was far enough away that they didn't touch, but not so far that his scent didn't continue to tease her, its heady quality drying her mouth with a multitude of wants and desires.

None of which tallied with the reason she was here.

She took another sip, using the wine's soothing influence to urge her back on course.

Think of Tony.

Think of Marcus's deceit.

Think of all that is bad, for Christ's sake.

'So, are you going to tell me why you're here?' he said. 'Or am I going to have to tease it out of you?'

That did it, and his implication sparked an indignant fire that had her eyes spearing his. 'I'm surprised you can't guess.'

'I'd like to think you couldn't stay away from me,' he said, and she ignored the flutter in her tummy. 'But after that display it's clearly not the case.'

'At least you're not deluded.'

He cocked a brow, his smile soul-corrupting. *'Touché.'*

She considered him, all laid-back charm and charisma, and her internal warning sign flared. He was dangerous to her on so many levels. Either he was an utter bastard, or he was a man she could like... really like—

Like? Was she crazy? He'd near enough lied to her.

'How could you do it?'

He tensed, all trace of humour evaporating. 'Do what?'

'Sleep with me when you knew we'd have to work together? Let me do all manner of...' Her voice trailed away. Memories now tainted in shame burned her through and she looked away, taking another drink before she could speak again. 'How could you?'

'I really am sorry.'

'Sorry isn't enough,' she blurted, looking back to him with rising anger. It didn't matter that his apology sounded sincere—she needed more than a simple sorry. 'Did you not think about how it would make me feel? How mortifying it is to know you kept it from me? That you let me do all that, knowing we would have to sit in a *fucking boardroom together* and deliver a professional front?'

The knuckles of the hand holding his glass flared white—he was going to snap the stem if he wasn't careful. She almost wished he would. Red wine all over his pale furnishings was the least he deserved.

'I wasn't thinking,' he said quietly. 'The truth is, there's no excuse I can give for my behaviour.'

'So, you're not even going to try?'

'I don't think it'll help.'

'Let me be the judge of that.'

He studied her, long and hard, his eyes wavering. 'Okay, I'll give you my excuse,' he said eventually. 'So long as you assure me it won't affect us going forward.'

'*Affect* us?' She gave a small snort. 'It's a bit late to worry about that.'

Silently, he studied her, his inner battle written in his face, and then he hunched forward, his eyes flicking away, to return dark and brooding. 'The truth is, the moment you walked into that bar I was hooked.'

Her eyelids fluttered, along with her heart, but she kept herself steady, refusing to look away.

'When you returned my interest I would have moved heaven and earth to have you.'

She swallowed, and the warmth spreading through her belly now was nothing like shame as her defences took a direct hit.

'And, as I've already told you,' he continued, 'when I found out your identity I tried to stop things. But you can be very…*persuasive*…when you want to be.'

Her cheeks coloured. 'You still should have told me.'

'I know,' he admitted. 'And under any normal circumstances, with any other woman, I would have— could have. But with you…' His eyes trailed over her, a subtle crease breaking his brow. 'For some reason I couldn't. I couldn't even think straight. I couldn't think past what you were doing to me.'

'You expect me to believe a man like you is ruled by his penis?'

He flinched, his own cheeks streaking with colour.

Fuck his boyish charm, she thought. *Why did he have to do that?*

'Last night, with you, for the first time in my life I'm ashamed to admit I was.'

Fuck—what was he saying? That the attraction between them had been too strong to deny? That he'd never felt that way before?

Panic bubbled in her throat. *Wasn't that how she felt too?*

Or—her stomach twisted—*was he hoping that flattery would see him free of her wrath? Well, screw that.*

'Are you trying to flatter your way out of this?'

'No, I can assure you I'm not,' he said strongly. 'I'm not proud of my actions, and I'm angry for not keeping myself in check, but I can assure you I'll do my damnedest to keep myself in check from now on.'

She pressed her lips together, a confusing mix of emotions was raging within, disappointment hitting the crescendo.

Hell, she shouldn't be disappointed, she should be grateful.

She needed it gone—this attraction, the desire, the distraction...

But where was the off switch?

Even his questionable behaviour regarding Tony wasn't enough to rid her of it. Or maybe it was if his justification on that score was full of shit.

She grabbed at it like a lifeline. 'Fair enough, but what about Tony?'

His eyes widened, her change in topic clearly surprising him. 'What about him?'

'Well, from all I've read you're a man to be admired,' she said evenly, 'not one to be despised for taking advantage of a man not in his right mind.'

He frowned, and she could see her words had stung. 'Is that what you think I did?'

'I don't know what to think,' she admitted with a sigh. 'I only know that the broken man I saw today had no business signing your agreement.'

'He needed that deal.'

'Is that what you told yourself to make it all better?'

'Look, Andrews came to me with a sound offer and I took it,' he said. 'Whatever his personal situation, it didn't come into it.'

'But you must've known something wasn't right— that *he* wasn't right?' she flung at him, her desperation to paint him bad ringing through her words. Working with a man she disliked would be hard, but it would be doable. The alternative—she raised her drink and took a long, slow sip—didn't bear thinking on.

'I had my suspicions at the time,' he said truthfully. 'But I'm a businessman, Jennifer. I didn't get to this point in life by being all soft and understanding.'

'So you just took advantage?'

'No, I did not,' he snapped. 'Surely you can see that ultimately my involvement has given him a getout? A chance to fix his mess?'

Her fingers trembled around the glass. She didn't want to accept his argument but felt it register all the same. 'It's not right. He should've come to me, not you.'

'What?' he said incredulously. 'Why do you think *you're* the one to help him out of this? Do you know how much money we're talking? How much it's taken just to keep a roof over his head and see off his creditors?'

'I would've been able to do something.' Even as she said it she realised it was nonsense, that Tony was in too deep for her alone to have given him enough. 'Now he has nothing.'

'Only if he chooses it to be that way,' he said softly, his anger disappearing as quickly as it had come. 'I've given him ample money to start afresh and get himself sorted out. Yes, I know he's not in a good place, but I've given him the best possible chance. What he does with that is up to him.'

His words silenced her, his logic doing away with every rebuke, rational or otherwise, save for the desperate. 'He still should have come to *me*.'

'Why?' He shook his head and placed his glass on the table, turning in his seat to give her his full attention. 'I just don't understand it. You've done enough for him already. From all the digging I've done, it's clear you're the brains behind this operation—you're the reason the company has done so well. What is it that Andrews has over you to make you care so much?'

Her head swam with his admiration of her even as her need to defend Tony was roused. 'You don't understand.'

'Then *make* me understand.'

'Tony's a good man—a *really* good man,' she stressed when she saw he would refute her. 'He's not just a business partner to me.'

His jaw clenched and he looked away. 'I see.'

'No, I don't mean it that way,' she rushed out, feeling her mutinous body getting high on the tension in his. 'Seriously, there's never been anything like that between us.'

Her impulsive need to reassure him riled her. Yes, it helped Tony's case, but she wasn't blind to the infuriating fact that she cared for Marcus's opinion.

Raising her chin defiantly, she said, 'Not that it's any of your business.'

His eyes locked with hers, their depths so fierce she had the wretched impulse to take her words back.

'You're probably right,' he said, 'but it pays to know exactly what I'm walking into.'

She fidgeted beneath his probing gaze, not liking the direction of their conversation. It was too private. Too personal. She wanted an out and it came swiftly, loaded with heat.

'Like you knew what you were walking into when you slept with me?'

He stilled, and his intensity was all the more severe for it. 'And I told you I couldn't think straight with you seducing me.'

Her lower belly contracted, cutting off her breath. The ache was instant and dizzying as the memory of those moments in the car flooded her. She tried to push it out, not to dwell, but she knew he was reliving it too, could read it in the flecks lighting up his gaze.

'We're digressing,' she said, her voice annoyingly elevated, and she looked away, staring at the calming piano in desperation, hoping he would get the message.

She heard him shift and her pulse skipped. *Was he reaching for her?*

'You're right,' came his level response. 'Let's get back to Tony.'

Surprise, disappointment—all manner of things she shouldn't feel washed through her and she chanced a glance his way. He'd settled back, drink in hand, one arm draped casually over the sofa-back.

Bastard—how did he do that?

She lifted her glass to her lips, using the drink for cover. Her voice wasn't ready—hell, her brain wasn't…

'What I was trying to say,' she said eventually, 'is that I've known Tony a long time and he's done a lot for me.'

He nodded his acceptance of that much and she continued on. 'We met at a university recruitment fair in my final year and I impressed him enough that he offered me a job before I'd even graduated. I guess he saw the potential in me, and the drive to make it big.'

'I'm sure he did. I imagine you were a force to be reckoned with even back then.'

She smiled slightly. *Was that how people saw her? How* he *saw her?*

'Perhaps,' she said, 'but I had my reasons and he understood them.'

'Reasons?'

She hesitated. Not many people knew her true motivation, but Tony did—and that was what it really boiled down to. 'It was more than just a desire to make something of myself. I *had* to be successful and Tony did everything he could to help me.'

'*Had* to?'

She took a breath and let it out with her next words. 'My father died when I left for university.' There—she'd said it. It always killed her a little when she voiced it. But she needed him to know, to understand. 'He left behind me, my mother and my younger sister.'

'I'm sorry,' he said, his gaze softening. 'I take it you were close?'

She frowned. It was a strange question. He had been her father—of course they'd been close. But then... *Did he not have a father he was close to?*

'Very,' she said, burying the thought—*she didn't need to know that about him*. 'No matter how busy he was, he always made time for us—in fact, he was the one who taught me to play.'

She gestured to the piano, a brief memory of being sat down with her father the Christmas he'd had it delivered filling her mind, and she gave a small smile, the gesture falling as the emptiness of him no longer existing returned.

'What happened?'

She met his eyes and something inside her cracked, his interest blindsiding her with the urge to cry.

'A heart attack.' She swept a hand across her dry cheek, smoothing away phantom tears. 'It was a long time ago, but it was unexpected. I guess the shock has never quite left me.'

He nodded with understanding. 'And so you do it all for him?'

'In some ways,' she acknowledged. 'He effectively ran himself into an early grave, making sure we had everything we could possibly want. And when he went… Let's just say things weren't too straightforward financially. My family home costs a small fortune to run and my mother isn't well. She needs a lot of support and living at home helps keep her settled…'

Thoughts of her mum had sadness welling up inside her, and she broke off as the helplessness of their situation sucked at her resolve and she felt exposed, too vulnerable, the tears too close to the surface.

'Your sister and mother both depend on you?'

She shrugged. 'I'm the breadwinner. My sister's due to start university next year, so there is only me, but I want to do it. I love my career, and I want to keep my father's promise of a good life for us all. I want to do him proud.'

'I think you've done that in spades.'

She smiled. 'You'll understand why I'm so indebted to Tony, then?'

'I wouldn't go that far.'

'*I* would,' she said, tears now forgotten with the acute need to make him understand. 'Seriously, it never would have happened without him. You didn't know Tony back then—how amazing he was, how he could read a situation or an opportunity so well and make the perfect call. He could handle people and business deals with such skill that it left us all in awe, and he taught me so much.'

Marcus nodded, decent enough not to argue, but she could tell he wasn't convinced.

'It's only in recent years that he's started to be so—' She broke off, unable to label it.

'Unreliable?' he provided for her.

She nodded ruefully. 'But after seeing him today

I'm beginning to understand it all. The gambling, the poor investments… I just had no idea he'd got himself into this bad a state.'

The shock of seeing him hit her anew and she shuddered. Her wine sloshed in her glass but she was too lost in the memory to care.

'It was soul-destroying to see him so out of it. So *drunk*. I mean, he looked *ill*. Properly ill.'

He reached out and took the glass from her shaky hold. 'He's an alcoholic, Jennifer. What would you expect him to look like?'

She froze. 'Don't be ridiculous.'

'I'm not.'

'I don't think getting off your face on the day you sell your share of your own business to cover a multitude of gambling debts and keep a roof over your family's head labels you an alcoholic.'

He studied her, his eyes searching.

Did he think she was lying? Covering up on Tony's behalf? Or in some strange denial?

'I'm serious. I know he has a gambling addiction and needs help—but an *alcoholic*?'

He leant forward to set his drink down and angled his body towards her. 'If it was a one-off I'd completely agree with you, but it's not.'

'What makes you say that?'

'From what I've seen, and heard on the grapevine, I believe he's been hitting the bottle for quite some time.' He rested his elbows on his knees and linked his hands together. 'The gambling is just another of his vices.'

'But I would *know* if he had a drink problem,' she said. 'He wouldn't have been able to hide it from me.'

'It's amazing how well it can be hidden.'

'But he didn't *say* he had a problem—not in that regard. He spilled his all to me today, but…'

'He probably doesn't even realise it himself. High-functioning alcoholics like Andrews often don't.'

Jennifer racked her brain, thinking over the times she had seen Tony of late. Had he ever been without a drink nearby, even at the office? His mood swings, his irrational behaviour, his forgetfulness… And then there were the cold sweats, when he'd told her he'd simply been unwell. Had that been something else entirely?

'Have I really been so preoccupied that I've totally missed the signs?' she asked, her voice distant, the truth of the situation and the magnitude of her failure as a friend setting in. 'I mean, Christ, he's given me so much and I've repaid him by—what? Not even *noticing*? Neglecting him when he needed me the most—not giving him the time—'

'Stop it, Jennifer.' He reached out and cupped her hands in his, the warmth of his touch contending with the chill running through her. 'Look at me.'

She did as he asked, her eyes meeting the fervent heat of his own.

'None of this is your fault,' he said. 'He has done this to himself. *He* is the one to blame—*he* is the one who has hurt those around him and let them all down. Not you.'

The bitterness in his voice cut through her. He made it sound so detestable, so personal…

'You talk like you're speaking from experience.'

His hands flexed around hers, his eyes flashing with a pain so raw that her heart clenched and her own problems—Tony's problems—temporarily faded.

'Are you?'

He blinked, his gaze falling away. 'Am I what?'

'Speaking from experience?'

A warning bell rang, but the question was out anyway, and the need to know rose from a part of her she couldn't ignore.

CHAPTER NINE

HE'D ASKED FOR THAT—her question.

He should have been more prepared, more composed. But seeing her break down, listening to her talk about her family, her responsibilities, and then having the whole Tony situation piled on top had thrown him off guard.

And then there was his guilt. *Christ*—now that he knew how much rode on her career... and along he'd come, shaking it up with his out-of-control cock. *What an arsehole.*

And now he'd made another blunder—giving her a glimpse of the demons that no one had any business knowing about. No one saw that side of him. Not ever. He'd learned the hard way that emotions were for the weak, and that wearing them on your sleeve earned you a fist or worse.

But he looked to her now, and suddenly his philosophy no longer applied.

Her emotional tirade hadn't made her weak. It had made her beautiful—admirable, even—and the need to pull her towards him was killing him. He wanted to take away her pain and his past with the passion that flared so readily between them.

'You don't have to tell me,' she assured him softly. 'Not if you don't want to.'

Over her hands, his thumbs caressed her skin and for a split-second he considered doing it—silencing her with his mouth, making her forget it all.

And what would that make him?

An even bigger fucking arsehole.

He released her hands and dropped back into the sofa, arching his neck over the back of it as he looked to the ceiling.

If sex was out, what was left? More of the truth? Didn't he owe her a little after all she'd told him?

'My father was a drunk.'

The words resounded around the room, out before he'd even mentally agreed to them, the spoken confession so strange and alien.

'Your father?'

He flicked his eyes over her, taking in her sympathetic beauty and wishing he'd buried his decency and gone for sex. It would be easier now that she knew who he was. Less complicated.

And that in itself was ridiculous. He had his rules for a reason: business and sex didn't mix. And yet letting this personal exchange continue felt far more threatening.

'You don't need to listen to this.'

'I want to,' she said, leaning towards him, her palm coming to rest on the sofa between them, her compassion filling the air.

Christ, she was good.

And he didn't have to tell her everything—just enough to make her feel he'd shared...

Resigned, he glued his gaze to the perfectly

smooth white ceiling and linked his hands together behind his head. 'My father wasn't like Andrews,' he began, matter-of-fact. 'He was what you'd call a chronic severe alcoholic—one who liked to take his anger with the world out on me and then use alcohol as an excuse.'

'My goodness—that's awful,' she rushed out, her obvious horror making it impossible for him to overlook the brutal truth of his confession, of his past.

But he wanted to. He wanted to forget it all save for the lessons it had taught him.

The hairs prickled on the backs of his arms and he clasped his hands tighter. 'It is what it is.'

'Was he always that way?'

'No,' he acknowledged, his stomach drawing tight as the chill continued to spread under his skin. 'He was a Welsh miner. Life was tough, but he did all he could. He worked hard and he was well liked.'

Memories he didn't want pushed to the surface, telling him of happier times—of Christmases, birthdays, *eisteddfods*, picnics in the park; all three of them happy and content. And then...

'Everything changed when I was eight. My mother got sick, and by the time they detected the cancer it was too late. She was gone within a year.'

He felt Jennifer's touch before he sensed her move—felt her hand curving over his thigh and soothing the chill directly beneath.

'Oh, Marcus, I'm so sorry.'

He gave a forced shrug. 'Dad never recovered. He hit the bottle hard and never came back from it.'

'And he beat you?'

She sounded dazed, and her fingers were starting

to move over him in a gentle caress. He looked to her hand and then to her face. *Was she even aware she was doing it?*

'He was angry,' he said simply.

'But still…'

Her eyes watered and he snapped his own away, fixating on the ceiling.

'It was hell for a while,' he admitted after a pause. 'But when I turned twelve my grandparents took me in. I was a scrawny misfit who'd borne enough bruises to make people aware of what was happening and they couldn't sit by any longer.'

'Did you live with them for a while?'

'A few years,' he said. 'Long enough for my gran to teach me how to play the piano.'

His head rocked to one side, his eyes resting on the piano and bringing to him the evocative memory of Jennifer playing. She had been so beautiful, lost in the music—and, *fuck*, it had hurt like hell. Memories of his mother doing the same were thrusting his past in his face, pulling him apart with love and loss.

This was why he didn't let people in. This was why he shouldn't be letting her in now.

'How sweet.'

'*Sweet?*' Christ, he actually smiled, her choice of words sucking him out of the darkness descending. 'I'm not sure Gran would agree. Teaching a grumpy teen something as uncool as the piano came with its own challenges.'

She gave a small laugh, and her amusement lifted him further.

'I bet!'

'But what can I say? She knew what she was doing.

I was so full of angst and in need of an outlet for it.
When sport simply ended in fist fights she opted to
give me a more solitary hobby—even if I wasn't so
keen in the beginning.'

'She sounds like a brave woman.'

'Or simply stubborn,' he said. 'When she puts her
mind to something there's no stopping her, and she
was determined that I should have something of my
mother in me.'

'And so you should.' The emotion caught in her
voice as she squeezed his leg. 'It's a lovely thing she
did. I'm sure your mum would have been very proud.'

Lovely. Proud. He needed to get a grip on the situation. There was so much sentiment flying around he
was starting to wonder where the real him had gone.

'Are your grandparents still around?'

He nodded, his gut knotting as thoughts of them
in the present brought a new kind of pain.

'Do they still live in your home town?'

'Not the same house,' he said distractedly. 'I helped
them secure a little cottage a few years back—close
enough to the amenities but away from the hustle
and bustle.'

'Do you see them often?'

'As often as work permits.' *Liar.* The knot in his
gut twisted and turned with rising guilt. *But going
back—it was so fucking hard.* 'Not as much as I
should, I guess.'

'And your father—where's he?'

Dad. Christ!

His nails pierced the backs of his hands and his
breath left him on a rush.

Her fingers above his leg froze. 'Sorry. I shouldn't—'

'He's dead,' he cut in over her. 'He died not long after I left home.'

'I'm sorry.'

'I'm not,' he said, sending her a look and seeing nothing but shock reflected back at him.

Hell, what did she expect? But then, what could she know about it? She'd been lucky enough to grow up safely ensconced in the love of her family, whilst he...

He quit the thought. His sudden anger was irrational—especially when it was directed at her, and especially when she'd been through her own kind of hell, losing her father and now her mother's sickness.

Fuck, he was a mess. In a pent-up state of hurt and need. And that *was* her fault.

He needed this over with now—before he did something stupid...desperate, even. His earlier battle came back to haunt him as his eyes flitted to those parted lips and he thought about what he'd threatened do. Before she'd coaxed the tale of his past out.

Don't do it. Sex is sex. You can get it anywhere. You can't get another her.

As much as the last thought came as a warning—*keep the business safe*—it also rang true for his bed. He wanted no one else.

'It's getting late,' he said tightly, aware of her fingers still upon his thigh and no longer finding her touch soothing or comforting. Far from it. They were urging on the part of him that still felt cheated and aroused by her earlier ploy.

But she deserves better than you... She pushed you away... Take the not-so-subtle hint.

Leaning forward, he reached inside his pocket for his phone. 'I'll give Colin a call and get him to take you home.'

'Home?'

It wasn't the first time she'd said that to him in that almost indignant tone, but what was she after this time? Did she want more misery out of him? Or was she after something else far more appealing, far more on his wavelength?

Don't be an idiot. Only fools make the same mistake twice.

'I think it's time we called it a night.'

He stood and took their wine glasses to the drinks cabinet while his mind refused to play ball. It was teasing him with a multitude of possibilities, all of which heated up as he heard her move, closing the distance between them.

His back prickled with rising awareness but he refused to turn. He set the glasses down, purpose-fully avoiding her as he looked at his phone and un-locked it.

Just a few minutes. He just had to hold out long enough to get Colin.

'Wait,' she said, her voice so close, so coaxing.

Don't wait. Just do it.

'I'll just—' He broke off as she reached around him, his body coming alive as her hand smoothed over his, and then he felt the phone shift, slipping out of his hold as she took it from him and set it down next to the glasses.

'Don't, Jennifer.' He tried to step away but there

was nowhere to go. Between her and the cabinet he was locked in.

'I'm really sorry.'

Sorry? She was sorry?

He twisted his head in surprise, getting her in his peripheral vision but not daring to focus. 'You have nothing to apologise for.'

'I do if I've upset you.'

'Don't be crazy.'

He turned to her with the ardent need to reassure and realised his mistake too late, the brush of her body against his front sending all hell breaking loose inside.

He breathed through it, thrusting his hands into his pockets. 'I'm the arse in all of this.'

'As much as I want to agree…' Her smile was small and wavering, and her eyes lit on his mouth a moment too long before returning to his. 'I can see I've upset you enough to want me gone, and I'm sorry for that.'

'Christ, Jennifer, this isn't about you upsetting me.'

Her eyes searched his. 'It isn't?'

She was so close. It would be so easy.

He let go of a ragged breath, his eyes lost in the intense green of hers, and he spied the moment it dawned on her, her breath catching, her teeth dragging in her bottom lip. The gesture was nervous and endearing and sexier than it had a right to be.

'Do I really need to spell it out for you?' he asked as she stayed quiet, and she nodded, all innocent and curious and purposely teasing.

He shoved his hands in deeper, imprisoning them.

'Don't do this, Jennifer. Don't let me go back on my word.'

'Your word…?' she pressed softly, releasing her bottom lip and leaving it distractingly slick.

He forced his eyes away. 'I told you I'd keep myself in check.'

'You told me you'd try your hardest.'

Fuck, show some mercy.

'I did, and that's why you should go.'

'I know what I *should* do…but…' She looked at him, eyes wide with desire, and his body reacted in kind.

Shit.

He took hold of her hips, intending to turn her away, but the delicious heat permeating through her skirt killed his intent. 'Please, Jennifer, you need to help me.'

'I can't,' she said, and for a second he saw her own uncertainty, her own confusion. 'I don't know what it is… Maybe it's the fact I've shared more with you tonight than I ever would normally.' She shrugged. Her eyes, bright with honesty, flitted to his lips and back again as her hand closed around the base of her throat. 'I just feel so open, exposed…raw, almost…'

'You and me both,' he said, realising the truth of it, knowing it should bother him and not caring all the same.

'Maybe it's that you're forbidden territory now…' She cocked her head to the side and studied him, a kind of confidence coming over her as she seemed to shift gear. 'Or maybe it's simply the fact I feel cheated—that you fucked me knowing exactly who I was, whilst I…'

Her words trailed off, her eyes burning into his and sucking him in completely.

Do it. You know you want to. Screw sense.

'And if we do this,' he said, 'then what? We just act like it never happened afterwards?'

Her hands slid up his chest, brushing over his pecs, curving over his shoulders. A trail of crazed sensitivity erupted in their wake as she nodded.

'Exactly.'

His fingers flexed against her hips. The desire to lift her, carry her to the sofa and do all manner of things raged through his brain. But he needed to hear her say it. He wanted there to be no risk of misunderstanding, no risk to their business relationship.

'So, what are you saying?'

'That I need a chance to get you out of my system,' she said, holding his eyes, 'to have sex with no lies. You can see it as an IOU, if you like.'

An IOU? Christ, had she really just said that?

'One night?' he pressed, bowing his head.

She hooked her fingers around his neck, loving how his heat permeated her fingers, how the scent of his recent shower engulfed her.

Yes, an IOU—a night to burn him out of her. But would it work?

Doubt nagged, but she didn't care—not with this crazy need building that only he could slake.

She raised herself on tiptoes and felt his breath catch as she paused, lips hovering a hair's breadth from his.

'Just…' she tugged on his lower lip '…one…' she flicked her tongue out to tease his upper lip '…more…'

she pressed her bottom lip against his parted mouth
'…night.'

'Fuck, Jennifer,' he growled, thrusting his hands
into her hair and crushing her mouth with his, his pos-
session wild and feverish and everything she craved.

'Yes…' she moaned into his mouth, her fingers biting into his neck as she sought to keep them together,
fearing he would back away, would change his mind,
return to his earlier plan and get Colin.

*Fuck Colin—there was no way she was leaving.
Not yet.*

Desperately she dropped her hands to the hem of
his sweatshirt, wanting it gone, needing him bare to
her touch. She scrabbled it up his chest, felt his hands
manoeuvre to do the same to her blouse, to pull it out
of her skirt. She heard the faintest sound of tearing—
his top, her blouse? She had no idea. She didn't care.

'That was Armani, you know.' He chuckled against
her, breaking his mouth free only long enough to deliver the words.

She ripped her own mouth away. 'I couldn't give
a fuck.'

'You will soon.'

He claimed her mouth again, his fingers working
at the buttons of her blouse, and a frustrated sound
gave way at the back of his throat.

He pressed her away, glaring down her front. 'I
hate buttons.'

And then his hands were on the parted fabric
and he yanked at it hard, the buttons flying free as
she gasped, his impatience flooding her belly with
an excited rush as the fabric fell loosely around her
shoulders.

His eyes burned into her exposed body. 'I'll buy you another.'

She shook her head. 'I think it makes us even.'

She tugged his sweatshirt over his head and he took advantage of the move, bowing his head to her upper body as she pulled the sleeves from his arms, administering kisses, nips and sucks. His hands kneaded her above her bra, his attention urgent and driving her crazy. She tossed his top aside and forked her fingers through his hair, holding him against her.

'Yes—God, yes!' she cried, and he spun her, twisting away from the cabinet and bringing her up hard against the wall. She threw her head back into the hardness, her eyes closed as tension built like wildfire.

His fingers slipped around her back, finding the fastening to her skirt and doing away with it, shoving it down her legs. His head lowered with the move, down to the valley between her breasts, to her undulating belly, until his heated breath was sweeping her panties.

She felt his fingers flick open each suspender, his touch gently coaxing as he circled her thighs with each move. Her legs quivered with the thrill. And then his mouth was back, tracing a path down one leg as he slipped off one shoe and stocking and repeated the move with the other.

He was sending her clit into a frenzied state of need. Her wetness was slipping between her thighs, her whimpers heedless, her words nonsensical as she heard herself pleading with him to do something… *anything*.

And then his mouth answered, his tongue probing above her knickers, and she bucked into it, shamelessly riding his face in desperation. His hands slid up her hips, hooking beneath the lace of her thong and tugging it down.

It dropped to her ankles and he cupped one thigh, coaxing it over his shoulder, forcing her to use him and the wall for balance and part before him. And then his mouth was upon her, his tongue hitting the nested nerve-endings that were so desperate for him, and she lost sight of everything except the tension coiling through her limbs.

'You taste so good,' he rumbled against her, his fingers slipping up to tease against her opening. 'So wet.' He sucked on her clit and she bucked wildly. 'So ready for me.'

He slid his fingers inside and the need to have him fill her, to have him inside her when she came, had her fingers clawing into his shoulders.

'Marcus, fuck me.'

'We have the whole night for that.'

'But I want you in me,' she rushed out. 'Please, Marcus, *now.*'

He groaned, unhooking her leg as he shot to his feet, his hands moving roughly to her hair as he pulled her head back and locked their gazes together.

'You have no idea what those words do to me, coming from your lips.'

She hooked her leg around him and pressed herself against his hardness. 'I can feel what it does.'

He gave a jagged breath and she felt the rough seam of his jeans biting into her sensitive clit as she wriggled into him, finding her spot, finding a rhythm that soothed and built.

He released her head, his hands falling to curve

around her hips, his eyes lowering to watch as she rode against him, and then he rasped, *'Condom.'*

She gestured to the sofa. 'My coat, my purse…'

It took a moment for her meaning to hit and then he swept away, back in seconds, her coat in his hand. She took it from him, shaking with pent-up need as she forced her hands to do her bidding, locating her purse, extracting the packet and tossing the rest away.

He was back with her, his body pressing her against the wall, his hands lifting her thighs around him, his mouth hot and urgent as he devoured her lips, her neck, the heated flesh above her bra. She didn't need more teasing…she needed him filling her—now.

'Marcus,' she pleaded, pressing against his chest, feeling his skin burn into her fingers. *'Now.'*

He raised his head, eyes ablaze as he straightened and lowered her legs. He moved to take the condom and she lifted it, holding his eyes as she locked her teeth around the perforated edge, freeing her hands to undo the button fly of his jeans.

His cock sprang free against her, and his bareness was both surprising and exhilarating as she slipped her hands around him. 'Commando?'

'I was in a hu—'

His words died on a hiss as she pumped him, the slickness over his tip telling her he was close, and she smiled up at him.

'Don't,' he groaned, his hands flying to the wall either side of her, muscles flexing, jaw clamping shut, the pulse working furiously in his neck.

So close.

Her thighs clenched, the ache painfully acute as she tore the packet open and took out the condom, one hand holding him tight at his base, the other rolling it down, taking her time, enjoying the way his jeans hugged tight over his hips, his cock protruding above, so big, so hard for her.

Her eyes shot to his face in fascination. His hands weren't even on her and the tension still built. Her body was getting off on his visible fight to keep contained, his eyes glazed with need, every muscle rippling with tension. Fuck, he was beautiful, in every which way, and she wanted him with every ounce of her being.

It should scare her.

It would scare her.

But not now.

Reaching his base, she squeezed, and he reacted instantly, his hands flying to her wrists, drawing them up and away, pinning them above her head as he pressed her back against the wall.

'You enjoy torturing me.'

She bit into her lip, the desire raging through her system making it impossible for her to respond.

He imprisoned her wrists in one hand, his other coming down to take hold of his cock, lowering it down her belly. Instinctively she raised herself on tiptoes, desperate to get him where she wanted him.

'My turn,' he said, bending his knees, sliding his hardness between her legs, rocking teasingly against her clit, across her opening but not inside.

His gaze burned down to where their bodies met, and hers did the same, watching as he moved back and forth, back and forth, the condom slickening with her need.

'Please…' She sounded pained, the desperation too much to bear, and she writhed over him. *'Fuck me.'*

He cursed, the noise primal as he released her wrists, shifting both hands to grab her thighs up and around him, getting her steady before freeing one hand to position himself at her entrance. And then he thrust, so hard, so deep, he filled her instantly.

'You feel so damn good,' he said, withdrawing before plunging once more, the move slow and sure.

Her blouse was tangled up in his fist, pulling tight over her arms, restricting her, pushing her onwards and upwards. She worked with his thrusts, sparking off a frenzied rocking fuck that had her tension spiralling out of control, the position offering up the perfect friction, the perfect everything.

It was so good.

So right.

She was flying, her entire being swamped by pleasurable heat, and then she shattered over him, head thrown back, lids clamped shut. She wanted to ride the wave for ever, to draw it out…

And then her ears were filled with his guttural groan, and the buck of his lower body was telling her that he was gone, his head falling forward to press into her shoulder, his arms around her bulging taut. She clenched him inside her, wanting to hold him, keep him there, loving how he pulsed inside her, how his entire body trembled its release. It was so sexy, so beautiful, and pain ripped her apart.

She didn't want to give this up. She didn't want to give him *up.*

She shut her eyes and pressed a kiss into his shoulder, pushing it all out. It didn't matter what she wanted. It wasn't possible. It wasn't sensible. It wasn't right.

And yet as she listened to their elevated breaths, felt their bodies relax with sated need, something shifted deep inside her.

The tight hold she'd always had over her life, that kept everything heading in the right direction, no longer felt so tight.

CHAPTER TEN

MARCUS HIT THE shower, its spray veering on cold.

She'd gone again. Left before morning. But no note—no handwritten *thank-you*. This time he'd got an email, asking that he review the attachments enclosed before they got together later that day.

Her message was clear: all work from here on in.

Hell, it was your message too, remember.

So where was the sense of relief? The clear head that was supposed to accompany the morning after?

The moment he'd realised she was gone a punching great weight had settled in his stomach. It had to be disappointment. The realisation that he'd had his last of her, that there would be no morning goodbye. If he'd known he would have kept her awake for longer, savoured that last session all the more—the way her face had flushed, her body had glistened, her breasts had bobbed as she rode above him...

Heat seared him through, his cock stiffening with maddening intent.

He raised his head to the cold jets, fingers thrusting through his hair. He did not—*he would not*—get himself off. He hadn't needed to in years, and he wasn't about to start now. Christ, he'd come enough times already, so what was his fucking problem?

Looking for distraction, he forced his mind to the email she'd left him with and the attachments that detailed her vision for the company's future, as it had been before he'd come along.

It included a presentation she'd delivered to the workforce the previous day. Notably, Tony Andrews had appeared alongside her own name in the slides, suggesting it was supposed to have been a joint delivery. He'd obviously left her in the lurch with that too.

His fingers ground into his scalp. Why did he care so much? And what did it matter now? Andrews had gone, and things would be very different from here on in.

She had him.

Snatching the soap, he lathered himself up and ignored the peculiar way those words played with his mind. He had far more important things to think on—like the morning ahead.

He'd called a meeting for ten-thirty, bringing together the UK-based heads of product development from both companies. He hoped Jennifer would join them, but either way it was going ahead. They had no time to waste.

His Stateside head of marketing had emailed the previous evening, calling multiple times thereafter because he wanted to deliver some critical news.

Had he noticed? *Had he fuck!*

He'd been far too busy wrapped up in what he'd felt to be far more pressing at the time—*her*.

This *never* happened. He answered his phone, checked his email, did whatever work demanded. He was on call twenty-four-seven, as befitted his multi-national corporation and its time zone stretch.

Always available. Always at hand.

Until now.

Until... *Jennifer*.

He slammed the shower off and stepped out, grabbing his towel and drying himself off. It was time to move on.

Now they had a potential product launch in jeopardy because a competitor was about to pip them to the post. And, yes, he might be confident that their product would be better, but being the market leader didn't ring true when you were second out of the sodding gate.

He should have been holding a conference call while he and Jennifer had been *getting-to-know-one-other*. His lapse in focus meant he now had to wait for sun-up in the US to discuss the issue with his marketing expert.

Needless to say, he wasn't going to hang around.

He had a plan brewing.

He'd picked through Jennifer's business strategy, studied the organisational structure, current projects and existing priorities. There was an opportunity to save the situation if they moved quickly enough.

But still the feeling of chasing his tail persisted, and it bugged the hell out of him.

He tossed the towel aside and strode into his bedroom, dressing in a dark suit, a white shirt but no tie. His throat was already constricted enough.

He raked his hand through his hair, absentmindedly scanned his reflection and headed for the door.

It was time to get down to business.

Pure. Business.

* * *

Jennifer checked her mobile for the umpteenth time,
one foot tapping impatiently as she waited for the lift
to reach her office floor.

He had to be shitting her.

It was unsettling enough having him join the company unannounced, but to call a meeting like this
without waiting for her, to take such an impudent step
on his first real day, was taking the piss.

And she was later returning than she had intended.

Lucy's need to talk had been evident in her honesty that morning. Jennifer had managed to give her
some reassurance, promising to get her husband the
help he needed, and seeing the strain in the woman's
face ease, even just a little, had been worth every delayed second.

Or so she'd thought.

It was pushing lunchtime now, which meant the
meeting was in full swing.

And without her...

Frustration bubbled up her throat and she forced it
down. She needed a level head to deal with the situation appropriately—*professionally.*

Finally the lift doors opened and she stepped out,
faltering mid-stride as she spied Tony's office—in
use. Its new owner leaned back against the glass wall,
his arms folded, one leg crossed over the other, totally relaxed as he gave Maxine—her head of product development—his full attention.

Her petite, feminine charm shone across the distance as she stood at a flip chart and spoke to the
room. There were two other attendees, both men she

didn't recognise—likely part of his product development team judging by the invitation he'd sent her.

Jennifer was starting to draw looks from the staff and, forcing a smile, she put her legs in motion and headed over to Anna. 'How long have they been in there?'

'A couple of hours,' she admitted. 'Can I get you a coffee?'

'Please.'

She speared Marcus through the glass. Seeing him so at home, straight off the back of her morning's dealings with Tony's wife, only compounded her anger. Yes, he'd cleared himself of any wrong-doing in the business deal, but it didn't make seeing him in his predecessor's shoes any easier.

And then he turned his head, his eyes meeting hers, and defiant sparks of delight shot through her.

She looked away and strode straight into her own office, closing the blinds to shut him out as her anger swelled.

You're not angry at him for Tony's sake. You're angry because you can't control how you feel about him and you're angry because he's called a meeting that's pissed you off and still you want him.

She threw her coat over the stand and headed to her desk, extracting her mobile from her bag to check the meeting invitation. Double-checking, triple-checking that she'd declined it.

Sure enough, she had, and her response had made clear that it should be rearranged. A meeting entitled Product Prioritisation made her presence mandatory.

He should have re-bloody-scheduled.

Behind her, Anna walked in, mug in hand. 'Here you go.'

'Thanks.' She took it and breathed it in, waiting for the usual comforting magic to hit.

Yeah, right, like coffee's going to do it.

Only one thing was going to make her feel better...

'Can I get you anything else?'

The man's head on a plate?

'Could you ask Mr Wright to join me?'

'Sure.' Anna turned to leave and paused to look back over her shoulder. 'Would you like me to do it right now?'

She set her coffee down and nodded with a smile.

Her PA returned it, a mirroring spark in her eye. 'No problem.'

She waited for Anna to close the door and then lowered herself into her chair, smoothing her hands over her black pencil skirt. She took out her laptop and placed it on the desk, interlacing her fingers and resting them on top as she waited.

It didn't take long. There was a short rap on the door and she forced her shoulders to relax. 'Come in.'

'Jennifer,' he greeted, entering the room and closing the door behind him.

The thrill of his proximity mixed with her wrath and it was a wonder she could raise her eyes to his, avoiding the open collar of his shirt, the appealing frame within the designer suit, the hint of his cologne crossing the distance between them.

She swallowed subtly, praying he wouldn't spy it, and forced words out in a level voice. 'Marcus, please take a seat.'

His eyes flickered. 'You know I'm in the middle of a meeting, right?'

'One that I was supposed to attend—yes.'

He wavered. 'We're just about to wrap it up with a vote—why don't you come and join us?'

'A vote?' She raised her brows with a wry smile. 'On something I have yet to be brought up to speed with?'

He tucked his jacket behind his arms and slipped his hands into his pockets. She didn't want to think about how the move pulled his shirt taut against his firm expanse of chest.

'Well, I would hope that you'd have enough faith in Maxine to trust her opinion—she's quite impressive.'

Something smarted but she ignored it. 'Please take a seat, Marcus.'

She needed him sitting, with at least some of him concealed by furnishings.

He cleared his throat and walked towards the chair across from her, his eyes flicking over her, their chocolate depths assessing.

'I don't have long,' he said, placing his hands on the arms of the chair and resting back into it.

He gave the impression of being relaxed but his eyes were sharp, doing their damnedest to read her.

She'd save him the trouble.

Turning in her seat, she got to her feet and stepped around her desk, feeling his eyes follow her. She didn't stop until she came alongside him, resting back against the desk-edge so that she towered over him.

Much better.

He looked up, his gaze sweeping her front, and for

a split second she saw it, the unguarded fierce hunger, and it almost broke through her anger. *Almost*.

'I trust Maxine implicitly,' she began, 'but that's not the issue here.'

'Mind telling me what is?'

His deep husky voice reverberated through her belly. His nearness was taking over that part of her she wanted to ignore.

'The fact you need me to explain worries me.'

'If this is about me holding a meeting without you, then I'm afraid there was no choice in that.'

'There's *always* a choice.'

She crossed her arms over her middle and saw his eyes fall briefly as the air-conditioned draught swept through the expanding V of her blue silk blouse. He might not believe in mixing business and pleasure, but his body certainly did.

Power rushed through her, upping her resolve as she asked, 'How can you hold a meeting to discuss the future of our product development without me?'

He shifted in his seat, his hands coming up to clasp one another upon his lap, over his... She smiled inwardly.

'It's complicated, and I need to get back in there to get this wrapped up,' he said. 'I have a conference call shortly with the States.'

'Okay, then, give me a high-level summary.'

He rolled his head on his shoulders, his tension evident. 'It's been brought to my attention that one of our competitors is about to go live with a product Tech-Incorp should have delivered first. We need to throw everything at it so we beat them to it.'

'And you couldn't wait until this afternoon to have your meeting?'

'No. I want this dealt with before my call with the States and I want a press release drafted ASAP.'

'My question remains—could it not have waited?'

'Look, my head of marketing over there has been trying to reach me since seven last night—that's how urgent this is. And had we not been—'

He broke off and a rising tide of anger within her had the word *'fucking'* bursting from her lips.

His eyes flashed, a muscle moving in his jaw. 'Yes.'

'Then you wouldn't have missed it?'

'No.'

The atmosphere shifted. Memories of them entwined, of the passion that had seemed impossible to sate, were making the air practically crackle between them.

'I need to get back in there.'

The raw edge to his voice, his obvious discomfort, made her want to push him that little bit more, and so, outwardly casual, she crossed one stocking-clad thigh over the other. His eyes traced the movement, just as she'd known they would.

'Fair enough,' she said, 'but let this be a warning. If you treat me like a subordinate again, then this "relationship"...' she gestured between them, the nail of one finger trailing down his front before returning to her own '...you and me, will get a whole lot more inconvenient than you first pitched it to be.'

His eyes blazed, his tongue brushing across his lower lip, and suddenly her own tongue felt too thick for her throat.

'I know what I said, Jennifer.'

He shifted, one hand curving around her hip, and her skin buzzed uncontrollably beneath his touch. *Don't react, don't react...*

'And I stand by it. It wasn't the best start to our working relationship.'

She raised her chin and looked down at him, doing her damnedest to maintain her composure. But words weren't forthcoming—not through the drunken haze of his touch.

'What I should have added is that I don't regret it one bit.'

Her breath caught at his honesty.

Did she *regret it? If she was honest, did she wish they'd never gone there?*

His thumb started to circle over her, the skin beneath treated to a whirlpool of sensation, and her body answered with a resounding *no.*

'And what I should also like to make very clear to you,' he said darkly, rising to his feet and side-stepping to stand before her, his proximity keeping her pressed into the desk, 'is that you should never tease me—not unless you're willing to deal with the consequences.'

She sensed his other hand come up, felt his fingers brushing against her jaw, sending a traitorous shiver down her spine.

'You assured me you would behave,' she blurted suddenly.

Christ, did she have to sound so breathless? So desperate?

He didn't budge, didn't even blink, and she tried again. 'You have your rules too.'

'That's the funny thing about rules.' He smiled

mercilessly, his eyes fixed on her parted lips. 'They're all the more fun when they get broken.'

He dipped his head slowly. Alarm bells rang through her head. *Knee him in the balls, push him away—anything!*

Instead she whimpered, the sound erupting from nowhere. And watched with self-loathing as his smile became one of victory and he stepped back. An immediate chill swept down her front.

'Like I said, you're welcome to join us,' he said, his palms turned outwards in an overly innocent gesture, 'but it's time I got back in there.'

And then he turned and went, opening and closing the door behind him, his message clear. He didn't expect her to follow.

Well, fuck that.

She breathed through the daze—the desire, the frustration, the anger...

What the hell had possessed her?

She knew, all right. She'd been playing with fire; wanting to replace the shitty feeling of being undermined by overpowering him, and she'd used her sexuality to do it. It had been a low move. It was beneath her.

But the rush—the way it had made her feel—beat any boardroom conquest. That was until he'd turned the tables on her.

She took a far more controlled breath, pushing herself up off the desk. It was time to show him that she didn't need her sexuality to do that. It was time to show him that, professionally, she was someone he didn't want to screw over.

Screw with, on the other hand...

Quit it!

She drowned the thought in some coffee and focused on her laptop.

She'd show him.

'Apologies.'

His eyes shot to the doorway, to the exquisite redhead holding her laptop over her chest, coffee in hand.

Fuck.

Marcus wasn't ready to have her in the same room again—not yet. He'd expected her to stay away, prayed that she would.

She was stronger than he'd given her credit for. He shouldn't really be surprised. Not when she had surprised him on every other score.

'I had some urgent business that needed attending to,' she continued, addressing the room, her smooth, honeyed tone washing over him, hinting at the husky resonance it gained when she came apart under his hand, his mouth...

She walked towards them, her expression pointed as she looked at him.

Introductions, you idiot!

He cleared his throat. 'Jennifer, this is Gary, my Head of Product Development, and his close second, Dan.'

The two men stood as she placed her coffee at the table they occupied and her hand reached out to shake each of theirs in turn. Her smile was that soul-crushingly gorgeous one that had his brain departing. And probably his team's now too.

For fuck's sake, stick to work. Not a day in and

you've almost thrown your assurances out of the window. So much for keeping yourself in bloody check...

But then, she'd been the one to push first, the one to put—

'Marcus?'

They all looked at him expectantly, especially Jennifer, who'd been the one to say his name, her brow raised as she said it.

'Care to fill me in on where you're at?'

The spark to her eyes said she knew *exactly* where his head was at, and it wasn't at work.

This just kept getting better and better.

He gave a brisk nod, forcing himself to get with it. 'Maxine was just summing up the impact of my proposal on your product stream.'

Her eyes narrowed. 'I assume we're talking about using some of our resources to get Tech-Incorp's product out of the door ahead of schedule?'

She'd hit the nail on the head and, to her credit, there had been no emotion in her supposition.

'That's right,' Maxine said, stepping forward to give Jennifer a copy of the project plans she'd scribbled her amendments on. 'The impact shouldn't be too great, but it will mean pushing back on Projects Azure and Topaz.'

Jennifer nodded, placing her laptop and the papers upon the table, her eyes scanning the pages. 'Do you have time to give me a brief breakdown of this Tech-Incorp product?'

She looked to Marcus and he immediately looked to Gary. 'Do the honours?'

'Sure.'

That was him out of her sight for a spell. He settled back into the chair behind his desk, letting Jennifer join the others at the table while Gary sold the product to the room.

He could see Jennifer liked it. But if he'd thought her eyes being off him would reduce her hold over him, he'd been wrong. Watching her unhindered had just given him an added opportunity to appreciate her further—the professional Jennifer, asking the right questions, listening carefully and offering her own insightful input. And all in a beautifully captivating package.

Could she be any more perfect?

'I assume Maxine has told you we have something similar in development?' She directed the question to them all, pulling Marcus back to the conversation at hand.

Maxine nodded. 'I have.'

'And I assume you have debated which product should get the weight of the combined team behind it?'

'We have.'

It was Gary who gave the confirmation, but Jennifer looked to Maxine, wanting her affirmation.

'We have,' she said tentatively, her gaze flitting over the other attendees as a hint of colour crept into her cheeks. 'And I did suggest we incorporate some of our features.'

'But we decided that would take too long,' Dan argued.

Jennifer pinned him with a look. 'What kind of timescales are we talking?'

'A few weeks,' Marcus confirmed over Dan's reply. 'At least I'm hoping so. My conference call this afternoon will confirm it.'

'Then I think we should put time into ensuring the product is the best it can be, in the timescale permitted, and if that means merging specifications then so be it.'

'But we're practically at the finish line,' Gary pitched in.

'I understand that.' She gave him a killer smile, but her eyes were hard. 'Nonetheless, my team has worked hard on this product to date, and for you to sweep in now so soon after your arrival in this firm and have it canned would be unwise.'

The room fell silent as the impact of her words hit home.

'Not only will this ensure our employees don't feel shafted by your presence,' she continued, 'we can also ensure we put the best product out there.'

Marcus felt both men look to him, sensed Maxine's smile of approval, but his eyes were locked with hers and he was lost in them, his admiration swelling with irritating vigour.

'Very well,' he heard himself say. 'Get the teams together. They have until the end of the week to get it mapped out and underway.'

Her lips quirked with triumph and, *fuck*, did he want to obliterate it with his own.

'Seems to me you have a lot to get done.' He glanced over them all, settling on Jennifer last. 'Why don't you get to it?'

They all stood, save for her.

'I assume you'd like to stay for this conference call?' he said.

She gave him a brisk nod, the movement drawing his eye to the crystal droplets swinging from each ear and to the soft, expanse of skin just behind. His mouth dried. The desire to taste her was instinctive—to drive out the whimper he so loved to hear, to trail a path from there all the way to her collarbone and further still…

The room had emptied before he came to, and he did so with force. 'Are you doing battle with *me*? Or are you truly fighting the corner for your product and your team?'

She gave him a coy smile, crossing her legs as she brushed a distracting hand across her thigh.

'I *want* to say I'm being entirely noble…'

She cocked her head serenely, her eyes dancing with mischief, and God help him the rush beneath his waist was instant.

'But doing battle with you is kind of fun.'

'Did you not listen to my warning?'

'Oh, I listened,' she said smoothly.

His mouth opened to respond but nothing came—nothing that would make sense.

What did he want to propose? Did he really want to act on his threat? And where would that leave him? Leave them?

He was rescued by the phone ringing, signalling his incoming US call.

She rose from her seat to join him at his desk and he answered the call.

He'd have liked to say his attention moved fully to the call. He'd have also liked to say that for the remainder of that week his focus revolved fully around work.

But he hadn't been born a liar.

He wasn't about to start being one now.

As for his assurance that he would keep himself in check—it was crippling him. Her constant presence was a permanent tease that no one could see off. Or rather, no woman.

And his mood suffered with it.

Celibacy, it turned out, was *not* good for him—on any level.

CHAPTER ELEVEN

SHE'D BEEN READING the same article for the last hour and still it wouldn't compute.

What an utter waste of an early start.

'You can't go on like this,' she muttered under her breath, taking up her coffee mug and rising out of her swivel chair to head to the window.

She looked down at the street below, at the early-morning commuters going about their business.

Were any of them suffering the same way? Their thoughts stuck where they shouldn't be, on something else, on someone else?

There'd been a closeness between them that night, when they'd opened up about their pasts. A closeness she'd never shared with anyone outside of her family. She doubted he had either. She'd sensed his disclosure had come from him feeling he owed it to her, that he'd had to force back his unease at doing so. And all that he'd told her of what he'd been through. Her heart swelled anew. To have pushed through it when many others might have let it ruin them...

But then wasn't he ruined in some way? Broken, almost? She'd seen the hurt he harboured, the bitterness, the discomfort when he'd talked of his grandparents. All of that she had so badly wanted to heal, to take away. It had swallowed her whole that night, when she'd given way to the need that had ravaged them both.

The morning after she'd been able to throw herself into Tony and his problems, but in reality she'd just been trying to shut Marcus out, to stop the seed of caring for him from flourishing.

But it had taken root—good and proper.

She clenched both hands around her mug and rested her forehead against the cool glass window.

It was useless.

No matter how hard she tried to push him out he always came back with a vengeance—especially at night, in dreams she was helpless to prevent, in which they could do everything they wanted, and it would feel so real, so right. Then she would wake up, needy and breathless, and have to come to work, pretending none of it had ever happened. Knowing it would never happen again.

It had been less than a week, yet it felt like several. Having him in the same building was driving her crazy. Always on high alert for her next glimpse of him, hanging on for their next encounter. None of it was conducive to work.

She'd tried to gain some breathing space, had worked off site, even at the coffee shop down the road, but her head would soon wander, and no sooner had she returned than he was calling on her for some matter or other, going overboard on the inclusion front.

She only had herself to blame for that. She'd told him what would happen if he didn't keep her in the loop.

Well done, Jennifer.

She brushed her fingers over her lips, remembering how he'd goaded her, how close he'd come when he'd pressed her up against her desk…

But, to his credit, he'd been nothing but businesslike since, and she'd been careful not to give him cause to be otherwise. It didn't make her happy, though. More…dissatisfied, antsy—like a cola bottle about to explode with the need fizzing up inside her.

'Knock-knock.'

Anna's chirrupy greeting sounded from the doorway and she turned to see her leaning in. 'Morning.'

'Eww!' said Anna, pulling a face and crossing the room to study her. 'Are you feeling okay? You don't sound great.'

'Long week.'

Anna gave a flourish of a nod. 'Just be thankful you don't work for Mr Wright. I heard his PA in the kitchen yesterday, saying she's never known him to be so difficult—a week from hell, she deemed it.'

'Oh,' she said, feigning uninterest, ignoring the flurry of excitement that just his name evoked. But she had to ask. 'In what way?'

'Apparently he's impossible to please—coffee's too hot, too cold, too sweet, too milky.' She waved her hands about dramatically, eyes rolling. 'Documents flying back and forth, stuck in draft stage, meetings and agendas up in the air, yada-yada-yada.'

Jennifer felt her insides smile. 'And this isn't usual?'

Anna laughed. 'I don't think his PA would work for him if it was. From what I overheard, she's about ready to give notice. And she's worked for him for five years.'

'Maybe he's finding it hard to get his feet under the table here.'

'If that's the case, maybe you could help him?'

Anna's smile was innocent, unlike Jennifer's brain, which was delighting in the many ways she could help settle him. None of which were acceptable.

'If he carries on like this he's going to become a thorn in your side too—albeit a good-looking thorn. But still, you don't need the stress.'

Anna was right. She didn't. And maybe she should be more concerned. If the two of them were struggling to function, how on earth was the business supposed to?

'I'll speak to him when he gets in.' She glanced at her watch. It was late for him, and the worry Anna had triggered started to spread.

'Speak of the devil,' her PA said, looking to the outer office beyond the glass and the man now striding through it.

No fucking way.

'It should be forbidden for any man to come in looking like that.'

Jennifer barely registered her PA's words, her mouth parting, the hand holding her coffee lowering as her eyes followed him across the office. He'd been for a run—likely a long and punishing one, judging by his slick body, his clothing clinging to every honed muscle, making her fingers tingle with their first-hand knowledge of it.

She swallowed and moved to tear her eyes away before he could catch her gawping—but too late.

His energised gaze swept to hers, his smile not quite reaching his eyes as he acknowledged her.

She tried for a smile too. *Hell, hers was probably just as off.*

'Well, there's no time like the present,' Anna said, seemingly oblivious as she made for the door. 'I'll tell him you need a word, shall I?'

'No.'

Anna looked back at her, eyes narrowed, and, taking a breath, she expanded with reasoned logic. 'I mean, yes, but I'm sure he'd like a shower first.'

'I guess,' said Anna, glancing back at him wistfully. 'Still, I'll just let him know you'll be needing him when he's ready.'

And with that she was gone, returning not a minute later, face aglow. 'He says to call by in ten.'

'Okay.'

Did he say he'd be appropriately attired by then? she wanted to ask, but didn't dare. It wouldn't do to give Anna the impression she was overly bothered.

But it was bad enough that she already knew firsthand the consequences of catching him post-workout— or mid-workout, or whatever he'd been that day in his apartment. She didn't need a repeat.

Ten minutes—she'd give him fifteen, just to be sure.

He checked his watch. She should be here by now. He glanced to the doorway, across the quiet office through the glass. No sign. Should he just go to her?

But maybe she'd got caught up in something. He didn't want to appear eager. Hell, his biggest challenge in the role to date had been to strike the right balance in his dealings with her, to dampen his relentless need to see her. Hunting her down didn't fit with that.

But she'd asked to see him—she'd given him a reason…

Christ, stop overthinking everything!

His run to work that morning had been about trying to clear his mind, to get himself focused, back to how he'd been before she'd come into his life. What it had really proved was that it couldn't be done. Not easily. The only way he could foresee being able to think straight by day was having her in his bed by night. And surely that was madness.

But, madness or not, he was fast running out of options.

Maybe she was too. Maybe that was why she wanted to see him. *Hell, he could hope.*

Grabbing his mobile, he made for the door just as the device started ringing in his palm. He checked the screen and halted in his tracks—*Gran.*

He cut the call instinctively. He'd text her back… tell her he was busy and that he'd—

It started to ring again and he thrust his fingers through his hair. The early hour, the repeated ringing—it had to be urgent. In spite of his recent run, ice ran through his veins and he glanced up, spying movement across the office. Jennifer was approaching and still his phone rang.

He looked from it, to her, and back again, knowing what he had to do and fearing it all the same.

Just tell her you'll call her back.

Jennifer rapped on his door and he gestured for her to enter as he swiped the screen to answer the call, raising the phone to his ear. 'Hey, Gran—can I call you back in just a minute?'

'It's me, son.'

The familiar voice of his grandfather rasped down the line and he frowned in confusion. 'Pops?'

'Sorry to call you so early, but it's your grandmother. She's in hospital.'

The world around him closed in. His lungs sucked in air. 'Hospital?'

'They suspect she's suffered a stroke.' His grandfather cleared his throat, the sound clearly a cover for the crack in his voice, and Marcus's own chest tightened further, his grip around the phone tightening with it.

'How bad is it?'

'She's stable,' his grandfather said. 'They say she's doing well. She's resting now, but… Well, I just thought you'd like to know.'

Guilt wrapped around him, suffocating him. He looked to Jennifer. Her concern was shining bright in her furrowed gaze, her arms wrapped defensively around her middle.

'Of course,' he heard himself say. 'Will you keep me posted?'

'Absolutely, son. I'll let you get back to it.'

He felt lost. He didn't know how to react, what to say. All he knew was that he hated the feeling working its way through his gut.

'Marcus, are you still there?

'Sorry, Pops. I'll call you later?'

'Sure.'

He sensed his grandfather hanging up and the one thing he knew he had to say sprang forward. 'Pops?'

'Yes, son?'

'Give her my love.'

He heard him sigh down the line. 'Of course.'

And then he was gone.

'What's happened?' Jennifer asked, stepping forward, one hand reaching out to rest on his arm.

He stepped back instantly, breaking the contact, something like panic hitting him. The concern in her voice, the softness in her touch, was a soothing balm to the raging torrent within.

How could she do that so effortlessly?

His skin prickled, the chill intensifying as worry for his Gran heightened.

'Marcus?' She frowned up at him, arms returning to hug her middle. 'What is it?'

'It's my grandmother.' He walked away from her, eyes averted as he headed to his desk. 'She's in hospital. They suspect she's suffered a stroke.'

She made a small sound, but he refused to look her way, speaking before she had the chance to. 'What did you need to see me for?'

'Marcus,' she said softly, 'look at me.'

Christ, couldn't she take the hint?

He didn't want to talk about it. Not with her. Not with anyone.

He shut his face down and forced his eyes to do her bidding. 'I don't want to talk about it.'

She studied him, the bright office lights glinting in her compassion-filled gaze. 'Okay, but don't you think you should be leaving?'

'Leaving?' He frowned at her. 'Are you mad? We have a product meeting in under an hour.'

She mimicked his frown. 'And the woman who practically raised you is lying in a hospital bed!'

'Apparently she's stable…she's doing well.' He threw his grandfather's reassurances at her, purposefully ignoring the tug of her words. 'She doesn't need me there.'

'Of course she needs you there.' She stepped towards him, stopping as he backed up again. 'You should go.'

Go. Go back. To Wales.

His stomach clenched and he shook his head at her, turning away once more. *What could she know of it? She'd never understand.*

'Did you need me urgently, or can it wait until later?' he asked.

'Marcus, for what it's worth, time is precious,' she said. 'I'd give anything to have had more with my father. Like I'm sure you would with your mum.'

He clamped his eyes shut, grateful she couldn't see the effect her words were having.

'Don't let this…whatever it is…get in the way of the time you have left with your grandparents.'

She went quiet, the room with it. And he refused to turn, to move, any response impossible.

Eventually she sighed, and the sound of her heels clipping against the tiled floor told him she was leaving. Relief mingled with an irrational surge of disappointment.

'Please,' he heard her say as the door swung open, 'just think about it. I can hold the fort here.'

And then she was gone, the door clicking shut, her heels receding on the other side.

Above the churning a warmth started to spread—

admiration, respect, something more…? *Damned if he knew.* Her concern for him, for his situation, flummoxed him. The sensation swelled with freakish intent and confusion paralysed him to the spot.

What the hell did he do with any of it?

CHAPTER TWELVE

CONCENTRATE, JENNIFER. It's none of your business. It's not your concern...

The document on the screen before her swirled grey over white, not making sense. It had been the same for most of the day—as if she was in some weird state of limbo, swinging from the need to go to him and demand that he leave to wanting to maintain her professional distance and keeping well out of it.

She'd already overstepped. She knew it. But she hadn't been able to help herself. Not when she'd seen the distress in every line of his beautiful face. And her worry had only mounted when he had not left. Not only that, he'd barely spoken to her—barely even looked at her since.

She felt crushed. The terrifying realisation had hit home that she cared far too much—that against her better judgement and her best-laid plans for the future he'd got under her skin. When she'd looked into his eyes and seen the desolation, the fear and the confusion, she'd wanted desperately to go to him, to soothe it away. But he'd made it clear he wanted none of that from her. In fact, he couldn't have moved away faster or dismissed her any more decisively.

She should be grateful for the reminder of where their professional line lay. But it wasn't gratitude making her gut ache and her mind wander...

She pressed a hand to her tummy, closing her eyes slowly and opening them on the computer screen, refocusing her efforts.

There were things she had to get done...things that were her responsibility.

A sharp rap on the door had her jumping and she looked up to the glass as Anna swung it open. 'Sorry, I didn't mean to startle you, but have you seen the time?'

She stilled, her eyes snapping to the clock on her screen. *Shit*—she had forty-five minutes until her train to Leeds departed.

How could she have lost sight of that?

She shot up.

What a damn stupid question.

She started shoving things into her bag, her mind racing with what she needed to take.

'Sorry—I would've come sooner, only I've been wrestling with that bloody photocopier again.'

'It's not your fault. I might just—'

'What's the hurry?'

In her panic she hadn't seen Marcus approach, hadn't even sensed it, and now he was in the same room with no forewarning and she struggled to breathe.

'Jennifer's late for her train to Leeds,' Anna supplied.

She plucked her loaded bag off the desk and headed straight for them, eyes averted and grabbing her coat off the stand as she went. 'I have to get home to my family.'

They parted for her to pass, but she could feel him move, hot on her tail.

'Colin will get you to the station.'

She paused, turning to argue.

Don't be an idiot—not when he's the best chance you have.

'Thank you.'

He was already activating his mobile and she looked to Anna—anything to ease his pull and the painful ache that now accompanied it.

'Do you have those info packs for me?'

'Sure.'

She headed to her desk and gathered them up while Marcus issued his driver with instructions and hung up.

'I'll join you in the car,' he said to her. 'There's something we need to discuss.'

Her lips parted with another impulsive refusal but Anna's return silenced her.

'Here you go.' She passed her the documentation. 'They have Lucy's approval.'

'Thank you.' She slotted them into her bag and managed a farewell smile. 'Have a good weekend.'

'You too.'

She watched her PA turn and walk away, her nerves rocketing as she was left with Marcus. Pretty much just the two of them in the open office, most of the staff having escaped for after-work drinks to ring in the weekend. But they might as well have been in a broom cupboard for the effect his nearness was having on her.

'He's ready for us,' he said, urging her to the lift.

She took in his black shirt, sleeves rolled back, collar open, and self-preservation took charge. 'Do you want to get a jacket first?'

'I'm good.'

She met his darkened gaze and tripped out.

This is madness. Make your own way...miss the train...get another—anything but... Christ, did he want to talk privately to tell her she'd overstepped?

Heat flooded her cheeks.

God, no, she knew that well enough already. She didn't—

His hand curved around her elbow and her head emptied, her body being propelled forth under his encouragement.

Outside, Colin stood, rear door of the car open and at the ready. He'd got his instructions well enough, and no sooner were they inside than he was in the front and pulling out into traffic.

'You didn't need to do this,' she said, her sights fixed on the outside world speeding past, her hands gripped together on her lap.

'I wanted the opportunity to apologise.'

Surprise had her eyes sweeping to his. 'What for?'

'This morning. I was short with you.'

He shook his head, the movement sending a lock of hair across his forehead and drawing her eye to the crazy state of the remainder. A sign of much hand-thrusting that day, she was sure.

Sadness consumed her. *He should've gone.*

She looked away before he could read her. 'It wasn't my place to get involved. I shouldn't have interfered.'

'Be that as it may, you were right.'

Her chest tightened, her throat with it, and she straightened her spine. 'I was?'

'Yes.'

He reached out to brush some escaped hair behind her ear and her breath caught. A red-hot shiver ran to her core, a warmth taking up camp there that she was powerless to prevent.

'I didn't like hearing it but, yes, you were right. I need to go.'

'Then why are you still here?' she asked, relief at his decision drowned out by the over-familiarity of his touch.

Don't soften. It's good that he's going but it doesn't change who he is to you. Who you are to him. Business partners. No more.

'Why delay by taking me to the station?'

'Because you need to make your train and I needed to apologise. Don't worry—I'm leaving straight after. My grandparents already know I'm coming.' His eyes turned inward momentarily as a smile played about his lips. 'It felt good to tell them. And I have you to thank for that.'

He studied her, eyes unwavering. The air was charged with an unidentifiable emotion and she struggled to say, 'I'm glad.'

'Me too,' he said softly. 'I would have left earlier but there were things I needed to take care of—and then there was you. I couldn't go without apologising. And, though I hate to admit it, building up the nerve has taken some doing.'

'Chicken?' The realisation ripped through the heavy mood, making her feel strangely light-headed.

He grinned *that* grin. 'Something like that. I'm not one for admitting I was wrong.'

She returned his smile, his honesty making it impossible not to. 'Fair enough.'

'But there's something else I need to discuss before I disappear off.'

Her skin prickled, her smile becoming forced, 'Something else?'

He nodded, and the deepening sincerity in his gaze held her captive as he reached out.

'The truth is, I've not been myself all week because of you.'

His fingers brushed the nape of her neck and the red-hot shiver sparked anew, multiplying fiercely.

'Trying to act like nothing happened between us has been torture. Knowing you're there, just down the corridor, and I can't have you—it's all I can think about.'

She clutched her hands in her lap, unable to look away, unable to move, the fear of what she might do holding her still as the warmth in the pit of her belly became a rolling ache.

'I can't work,' he continued. 'I can't sleep. I can't go home without the memory of you being there plaguing me, teasing me…'

His honesty pushed through her defences, toying with her heartstrings, teasing her with a multitude of possibilities that no amount of trepidation could quell.

'The truth is…' he repeated, and her every sense waited for what he would confess next, a spark of hope flaring that had no right to exist. 'I don't think I can function properly without having you, without letting this thing between us take its course.'

She frowned, a real chill working its way in.

Take its course? Did he think it was finite? That he would wake up one morning and it would be gone—the want, the need, the persistent ache?

Isn't that what you thought? When you asked for that extra night, didn't you hope it would do the same?

Hell, she knew better now.

It wasn't that simple.

Not for her.

She took hold of his fingers, forcing herself to stop his heady caress. 'Please don't, Marcus.'

She sounded weak, but her hand lifted his away and she returned her own to her lap, her eyes to the window.

'Don't tell me you don't feel it too,' he pushed. 'Don't tell me you haven't struggled all week. I know you've tried to avoid me. I've seen how you escape the office. I've seen how you look my way when you think people aren't looking.'

She swallowed, shaking her head in denial.

'And these,' he said, gently flicking the crystal droplet hanging from the ear that was closest to him, 'are killing me.'

What?

She looked to him, brow furrowed. 'Why?'

'The way they swing when you move your head, like they did just then… You do it in meetings and I'm sucked right in, drawn to the skin just *here*.' He swirled the pad of his thumb over the exact spot. 'Remembering how it feels, how it tastes, how it makes you whimper…'

Christ, she wanted to whimper right now—could feel the need bursting through her.

Don't do it.

'You know what else it makes me want to do?'

She felt her head shake and he leant in, his breath sweeping over her sensitised neck and making her tremble with want even as her brain screamed *Stop him!*

'It makes me want to drive that sound out of you... that small, tiny noise that starts just here,' he whispered, his mouth devouring the space his fingers had just occupied.

Her body exploded in a rush, that whimper breaking free, the impulsive sound jarring out as a feeble, 'Don't...'

'Why?' he rasped with need, cajoling her along despite everything else telling her otherwise. 'Why deny something that feels so right?'

'Because it's bad for business.'

'Denying it is bad for business.'

His tongue did a crazy dance over her skin, prickling over the area with dizzying effect.

'Or are you telling me your week has been particularly fruitful?'

As he said the words he curved his hand around her neck on the other side, coaxing her to arch her neck and grant him greater access.

'Christ, Marcus, I'm trying to save us from potential disaster.'

She was trying to save herself from a broken heart.

'I admire your diligence,' he whispered against her dampened skin, 'but you're worth the risk.'

Why did that feel so special? Why had her tummy gone to goo?

Something broke inside her—something that drove

her hands into his hair and turned her body to liquid beneath him. It was the need to have him fill her, complete her, take away the painful ache, the worrying thoughts…

'You taste like honey and vanilla,' he breathed against her, his fingers following the arch of her neck, stroking across the curve of her collarbone and dipping to meet with the fastened buttons of her blouse.

And then his fingers were undoing, and she couldn't stop him—didn't want to. The throb between her legs was desperate, her breathing erratic, her nails biting into his scalp.

He parted the fabric, letting the cool air of the car sweep across her front, and he cursed under his breath. 'I can't get enough of this.'

She looked to him through the haze, saw his gaze burning into her skin and she hit insanity, the lust curling through her obliterating all reason.

'I need to taste you.'

His voice was raw, his face asking for permission and, Christ, she couldn't speak, could only nod.

'We don't have long.'

It seemed he was making excuses, but for what she couldn't understand—until he dropped to his knees and pushed her skirt to her thighs.

'I'd devour every last bit of you if we had the time, but as it is…'

Cupping her behind, he pulled her forward and shoved her legs apart, pressing her knees back against the cold leather. Somewhere in the rational part of her brain she knew she wanted to fight him, and knew why, but the painful reasoning, the painful ache—she wanted it all gone.

Obliterated by him.

'Hold yourself open for me.' He drew her hands in to replace his own, coaxing her to obey. 'That's it...'

He rested back, his eyes drinking her in, his burning desire choking the very air from her lungs, and then he reached out, hooking his fingers into her lace panties and pulling them aside, his free hand coming up to spread her open before him.

'So wet...so fucking beautiful,' he murmured, his head dropping forward, his mouth honing in on its target.

Fuck!

She threw her head back into the leather, a spasm shooting through her as he took her clit in his teeth. Pleasure ripped through her, and her nails bit into the skin of her inner thighs as she held herself open.

He worked her, his mouth sucking, tongue flicking, teeth nipping. And then his fingers thrust into her, invading her like his cock would. One, two— *yes, fuck, yes*—three, four—*Christ, yes.* She ground herself against him wildly. She couldn't fit more... she couldn't—and then he curved in his thumb, his whole hand fucking her deep as his tongue lashed over her clit.

'Come for me, baby,' he urged.

And the heat in his voice, the endearment rumbling over her, his fist completing her—she was gone. Shattering over him, screaming his name as her whole world fell apart around her.

He sipped at her, withdrawing his fingers slowly and holding her hooded gaze as he licked them clean. 'I don't think I could ever tire of tasting you.'

If only that were true, came her internal voice,

louder now in the aftermath, and she felt chilled, snapping her eyes away.

'We shouldn't have done that.'

The bitterness, the self-loathing was back. It bit into her tone and he shifted into the seat alongside her, his confusion penetrating the air.

'Are you telling me you didn't like it?'

He smoothed his hand over her thigh and she pulled her skirt back into position, brushing him away. Moving to fasten her blouse next, she felt the need to cry, sudden and chilling.

'We can't work together and do this.'

'I beg to differ,' he said confidently. 'I think this is essential if we are going to get our heads back in the game once more.'

She shook her head.

Back in the game? Was that all this was to him?

'Hear me out,' he said. 'We both work too hard to support any decent relationship outside of work.'

She didn't respond, her fingers shaking as they fastened up the last button.

'So why not get this fix on the doorstep?'

She could feel the heat of his gaze on her as her brain struggled with the very idea he was putting forward, as her body impulsively demanded her agreement.

'We're both grown-ups,' he pressed. 'We can sate this need, free our brains to concentrate on work and not worry about the usual relationship baggage.'

No baggage. No feelings. Just sex.

Jennifer felt her heart shrivel and hated it for being so pathetic. Why couldn't she simply say yes? No one had ever driven her as wild as he could. She'd never desired anyone the way she desired him.

But you've never been as crazy about someone either.

'Take the weekend,' he said into her continued silence. 'Think about it and you can give me your answer on Monday.'

How did he remain so focused when her entire world was shattering?

Because he wants this, wants you... But he doesn't want more.

That was the real issue. He could take the sex and leave the rest.

She only wished she was capable of the same.

'I'll think about it,' she said, grateful that the car was pulling up at the station and she'd soon be free.

Shrugging on her jacket, she didn't wait for Colin. As soon as the car stopped she opened the door and stepped out, closing it behind her. She didn't say goodbye, she didn't thank his driver—she needed space, *now*.

It turned out space wasn't enough.

He hounded her the entire journey home.

She threw herself into her to-do list: co-ordinating Tony's rehab, paying the bills, managing her inbox and so on. But he was always there...at the back of her mind.

By the time the taxi pulled up outside her home her head was swimming and the tension knotting at the base of her neck signalled the onset of a full-blown migraine. She rubbed at it as she stepped out of the car and followed the driver to the boot.

'Jenny!'

She turned to see Kate bounding down the stone-stepped entrance towards her. 'Hey, sis!' she called, turning back to the driver as he handed over her weekend bag. 'Thank you.'

'You're welcome, miss.'

Kate's arms came around her from behind, squeezing her tight. 'It's so good to see you.'

'You too.' She turned, easing her sister's embrace enough to give her a kiss on the cheek and hook her arm through hers. 'How's Mum?'

'She's good—really good,' Kate said emphatically as they headed towards the house. 'She's reading in the library—we've found it helps settle her with the nights drawing in.'

Jennifer nodded. It was good that they'd found something to help with the evenings.

'Tell you what—give me your stuff and I'll dump it in your room. You go and see Mum.'

'Great,' she said, even as she felt the familiar pull of anxiety bed in.

Kate took her bags and bounded back into the house. Jennifer followed slowly, her belly twisting with nerves as she crossed over the threshold and headed down the hall that led to the library. The smell of food reached her. Marie, their housekeeper, was likely making her favourite—lasagne. But hunger was the last thing on her mind.

She paused at the library door, her hand resting on the handle, and took a breath, her shoulders rolling back as she braced herself for whatever was to come.

She opened the door and stepped inside. The room was well lit, the fire notably out. Her mother sat reading in her favourite chair overlooking the grounds, although the curtains were now drawn against the darkening outdoors.

'Mum?' she said tentatively.

Her mother looked up, lowering the book into her lap as she dipped her reading glasses to look at her.

A smile of recognition spread across her face. 'Jennifer, darling, you're home.'

The air left her lungs in a whoosh. Her mum knew who she was today. *Fuck you, Alzheimer's!*

She swept across the room to draw her into a bear hug, emotion welling as she held her mum close.

'Why, Jennifer, you're going to suffocate me if you keep this up.'

'Sorry, Mum.' She backed off a little, her eyes raking over her mother's face, taking in her glowing complexion and bright green eyes with glee. 'I've missed you.'

Marcus had made the decision to drive himself to Wales, keen to have the distraction of the roads to occupy him. And the solitude. He didn't like the way he'd been all week and he certainly didn't like the way he was now.

He'd watched her enter the station with the feeling that he'd just made an epic mistake swelling uncomfortably in his gut.

But it didn't make sense. She wanted him. He wanted her. It was win-win. Only her face, the way her post-orgasm glow had drained so swiftly, had twisted him up inside.

Had he gone too far? Did she truly think he was endangering their business? Was that what it all came down to?

He couldn't believe it. It didn't sit right.

The sign for his home town lit up in his headlights, blurred through the rain, and his heart skipped, his stomach lurched and his thoughts quit, drowned out by the memories that came pouring in uninvited.

He shifted in his seat, squinting through the windscreen to take in the surroundings that never seemed to change: the stone-built terraced houses lining the road, the corner shop that wasn't on a corner, his primary school—the gates of which he'd stood at many a night, waiting for his father to collect him and eventually setting off alone, scared witless in the dark.

His grip over the steering wheel tightened and he diverted his gaze straight ahead. He'd left that life behind long ago…and neglected his grandparents in doing so.

His throat closed over and he swallowed through it.

He was back now. That was what mattered.

He stopped at a set of lights, the only sound that of his windscreen wipers beating away the rain, and then a laugh reached him—the high-pitched ripple of a teen. He turned his head towards it. A young couple were just leaving a house, a lad with his arm hooked around his girl, his grin happy, her laugh even more so.

The scene reached inside the car, engulfing him with its warmth, coaxing out a smile as his hold over the wheel eased.

Just because it had been bad for him, it didn't make it bad for everyone. It had never been the place that had been the problem…

And yet he'd kept fleeing it, when all he'd ever

wanted was to flee *him*. But he wasn't his father, and his father was long gone.

His eyes pricked at the sudden lightness inside him.

Before him, the lights turned green, but he didn't move. He was caught up in a conversation with her—with Jennifer. Remembering her words, her compassion.

'Don't let this get in the way of what time you have left.'

The strange warmth from that morning spread like wildfire. *How had she done it?* Gone through the death of her father and ploughed it into something so wonderful—a successful business, a stable future for her family.

She didn't run from the darkness or live in fear of the *what if*.

Not like him. Fear and darkness had been his driving force since for ever.

A horn honked behind him and he flashed his lights apologetically, setting the car in motion.

Could he change? And what did change even mean? Would it make him happy? Was happiness even possible for him?

Contentment, yes...

But happiness...?

CHAPTER THIRTEEN

JENNIFER RACED BACK through the grounds, her breath sending puffs of white into the crisp morning air.

She loved it here. The fields, the open spaces, the wildlife. Even in autumn, with the leaves disappearing from the trees and the flowers dying back, there was still a serenity to it all, especially when the sky was as blue as it was today.

It was the perfect day for a run, the perfect opportunity to forget everything for a while and just enjoy the peace and fresh air. Only her thoughts had been far from peaceful, wrapped up as they were in a certain male and his far too appealing proposition.

Not even the fear of falling too deep could stop her thinking on it.

It had kept her up until the early hours and sent her out running at the crack of dawn. Anything to kill the restlessness it instilled.

But the run hadn't worked. She was back, slightly less agitated but no less distracted. Frustrated, she yanked at the laces of her trainers and slipped them off. Picking them up to pad through the old tradesman's entrance and into the kitchen, she felt the cold stone floor biting through her socks, the sensation soothing her with its familiarity.

She entered the kitchen and set a fresh pot of coffee going before grabbing some cold water from the fridge. She had drunk most of it when Kate walked in.

'I hope you've put enough on for me.'

Jennifer glanced at her watch. It wasn't even eight yet—her sister never saw this part of the day unless she was at school.

'Are you feeling all right?' she teased her, replacing the water bottle with a mug and pouring herself a coffee.

She frowned. 'Yeah—why?'

'You *do* know it's still your beauty sleep time?'

'Ha-ha, very funny, sis. You going to carry on taking the Mickey or be kind and pour me one of those?'

Jennifer laughed and poured her sister a coffee. 'Well, it's not like it's a school day.' She leant back against the counter-top and considered her over the cup. 'What has you up so early?'

Her sister looked away swiftly, her attention fixed on the fridge as she took out the milk. 'Want some?'

She offered it to her without meeting her eye and Jennifer shook her head, dread creeping up her spine. 'Kate…answer me.'

'Look, don't get mad, okay?'

She frowned, the dread becoming a full-blown chill. 'Tell me.'

'Mum has been caught wandering recently,' she said, slopping some milk into her mug, her nonchalance clearly forced.

'Wandering?' A lump wedged in her throat and she forced it down. 'How long has this been happening?'

'A couple of weeks—it tends to happen early in the morning, and when I ask her where she's going she says she's going to the office, to help Dad.'

'Kate, why haven't you said anything?'

'Because you have a lot going on and we've been managing okay.' Her sister slotted the milk back into the fridge and took up her mug, mimicking Jennifer's stance against the worktop.

'*We?*'

'Me and Mum's support workers.'

'But what about your studies? You have university coming up next year.'

'That's not a problem.' Kate gave an easy shrug. 'I'm going to study from home.'

Jennifer almost dropped her coffee. 'You're *what*?'

'Chill out, Jen. I can do what I want.'

'You *can't* want to study from home! Your grades are exceptional—you're Oxbridge material. You...you should be going off, living the student dream, studying hard, playing harder...' Her desperation to have her sister see sense had her words tripping over one another. 'You should be doing what *I* did.'

'It was different for you. *Mum* was different.' Her sister looked away, her determination giving way to sadness. 'I can't leave her now—who will look after her?'

Jennifer had known this day would come and she should have pre-empted Kate's decision, stopped her from making it in the first place. Time had crept up on her. Her sister was suddenly all grown up.

'It's not your responsibility,' she assured her. 'I will get more help in.'

'You know it's not that simple. Each new face only

unsettles Mum further, and it's good for her to have family around.'

There was no other family save her and her sister. There was no one else…

'Then I will be here more often.'

Kate looked to her in disbelief. 'How?'

'I should never have left you as much as I have.'

Guilt was her new default position, it seemed—if it wasn't Tony, it was her own family she was neglecting.

'I'm sorry—it wasn't fair. You've had to sacrifice your childhood to care for Mum while I've swanned off to London and lived out my dream.'

'*Shut it!*' snapped Kate, her coffee hitting the side and sloshing over the rim, her index finger wagging. 'Don't you *ever* apologise to me. You've done *everything* for us. If not for your career we would have nothing now. We wouldn't be able to stay in the house that Mum knows and loves. I wouldn't have university to look forward to, a car on the drive—a licence, even. Christ, you even pay the food bill.'

'I get all that, love, but seriously—if you don't go away to university I'll never forgive myself.'

'And I'll never forgive myself if you sacrifice your career for *me*.'

'I'm not talking about sacrificing my career.'

And she wasn't. Now that Marcus was on board anything was possible. It not only felt feasible from a business perspective for her to leave London more often, it also felt like a sound personal decision too. More space between them, more frequently. Then maybe her body would cease its crazy hedonistic craving for him and she could rein her heart back in.

Kate didn't look convinced. 'How would you make it work?'

'I have a new business partner now.'

Her sister's eyes narrowed on her. 'That wasn't expected, was it?'

'Hardly.'

'How come you didn't mention it last night?'

'It's complicated.'

'Complicated?' Kate nodded with interest. 'What's his name?'

'Who says it's a he?'

'Your secrecy, the way your voice has gone all funny and the way you've gone bright red... Need I go on?'

Damn it. 'Am I that obvious?'

''Fraid so,' she said, her eyes dancing. 'So come on—spill.'

'His name's Marcus.'

'Ooh, *Marcus*—nice name.'

She shot her sister a look and Kate immediately straightened, her fingers moving to her pursed lips and making a zip-like motion.

Jennifer rolled her eyes and continued. 'He already heads up several successful ventures, so I have complete faith that he will keep things ticking over if I were to split my time fifty-fifty between here and London. More if need—'

Her sister gave a dramatic yawn. '*Dull, dull, dull!* I meant, what's *he* like? There must be *something* about him if he's managed to get my unflappable sister's knickers in a twist.'

'He isn't doing anything with my knickers.' Her cheeks flushed over the outright lie and at her desire to have him play with them a hundred times over. 'And you're missing the point. Having Marcus means I can be at home more without jeopardising work.'

'But won't that mean time away from your hunky partner?'

'I didn't say he was hunky.'

'You didn't have to.'

'If you think teasing me about my new business partner is going to take the focus off you, missy, you're very much mistaken. University—you're going.'

Kate floundered before her.

'Look, you have to make your choices now, and you need to get it right. And, since I'm paying, I get a parental vote.' Her sister bristled a little at the last, but she continued. 'Besides, you won't leave for another year or so—plenty of time for me to take care of things operationally.'

Perhaps even move up north for good...

With a sigh, Kate picked up a cloth from the side and started to wipe up the coffee she had spilled.

Jennifer sipped her drink and said nothing, hoping the next words out of her sister's mouth would be the right ones.

'I'm not saying it's a definite yes,' she said eventually, 'but I'll think about it.'

Jennifer smiled. 'You'd better make it a definite yes, or I'm taking back that Mini Cooper you love so much.'

Kate visibly recoiled. 'You wouldn't?'

Her smile became a grin. She was happy to rib her sister a little. 'Wouldn't I…?'

'Just you try.' Kate waved the dirty cloth in the air

and stepped towards her. 'You want some coffee to mix in with that sweat, sis?'

Kate lunged for her and she squealed, making a break for it and doing her utmost not to spill her coffee in the process. 'Put that rag anywhere near me and the Cooper goes today.'

'Yeah, yeah—whatever you say.'

'I mean it.'

'Whatever,' her sister said, flouncing off to the sink and leaving Jennifer to head for her shower unscathed, her plan to put some much-needed distance between her and Marcus occupying her mind.

The question was, would he agree to it?

And would it be enough?

It turned out that the longest week had nothing on the weekend. Two days without her and Marcus had the oddest feeling of what it was like to actually miss someone.

He owed her. He'd spent two days playing the perfect grandson, making up for lost time, being ribbed by his grandmother and led astray by his grandfather down at the local pub. It had felt good. *Really* good. And some strange cloud had lifted over his past.

Still, none of it truly explained why he was currently standing outside King's Cross Station waiting for her train to come in. Not when he should be sitting at his desk getting some much-needed work done.

When Anna had told him Jennifer's train had been delayed, that she'd been stuck stationary for over an hour and was going out of her mind, he'd offered to collect her out of the goodness of his heart.

Whatever.

Yes, there'd been an element of that, but the truth came down to a multitude of reasons—some he barely understood. He wanted to thank her, he wanted to see her—badly—and he wanted her answer. He craved that above all else.

He prayed he'd imagined the weird mood she'd left in, but when Anna had told him she didn't want to be collected it had stirred up his worry and made him all the more determined to go.

And he'd not come empty-handed. She'd grumbled to Anna about the coffee on board and he'd already learnt how much she liked her caffeine fix. Cue him, two coffees in hand, his eyes skimming the crowd for her unmistakable red mane in the flurry of people.

He spotted her as soon as she emerged, her hair once more pinned up, her face distracted as she towered above the majority of those around her. And then she spotted him, her eyes narrowing, her face becoming set.

Ah, hell, she looked pissed off.

She wove through the masses towards him, her beige trench coat tied snugly to her waist, her jaw-dropping walk unhindered by the trolley suitcase she towed or the hefty handbag hooked over her shoulder.

'I told Anna to tell you not to come,' she said, as soon as she was within earshot.

He grinned. He couldn't help it. The fighter in her just got him every time. 'And *I* told Anna that it made sense for me to collect you—and you can't tell me you're not happy to see this.'

He held out the coffee and his keen eye detected

the minute semblance of a smile as she took it from him. 'On that you're right.'

She sounded weary, and now she was close he could see the shadows under her eyes, the stress lines he hadn't noticed before creasing her brow.

His grin became a frown. 'Are you okay?'

'I'm good,' she said, taking another sip. 'Or I will be when this caffeine takes effect.'

He didn't believe her. But standing outside a busy station trying to get to the bottom of it wasn't going to work.

'Here—let me take that.'

He moved to take her suitcase but she twisted to block him. 'I can manage just fine.'

'Ah, yes—sorry, I forgot.' He backed away, palms raised. 'Modern world and all that.'

She gave an unexpected laugh, the melodic sound warming him through—it felt good that he could still coax a laugh from her when she was clearly suffering in some way.

'Colin's not far away,' he said. 'Shall we go?'

'If you don't mind, I'd rather take a short walk first,' she said, her lids lowering as she faced the wind, one hand smoothing over her hair. 'After being stuck on that train I'd like to get some fresh air and stretch my legs.'

'Of course. We'll drop your bags with Colin on the way.'

'You don't need to come wi—'

He silenced her with a look. 'I could do with a walk too.'

'Fair enough,' she said, and her resigned expression worried him all the more.

'He's just over here.'

He looked away and started moving, trying to ignore the anxiety creeping its way in.

Colin straightened as they approached, a smile Marcus hadn't seen from him before breaking across his face.

'Good to see you, Miss Hayes, shall I take that?'

He reached out and she gave him a warm smile, passing him her bag. 'Thank you.'

'We're just going to take a walk,' Marcus said as Colin placed her bag in the boot. 'If you park up locally I'll call when we're done.'

'Very well, sir.'

He turned to offer her his arm, just as he'd done that first night, but her eyes darted away. It was a damn stupid move, really—they weren't on a date... they weren't even together. He morphed it into a gesture for her to precede him, and together they wove through the pedestrians, neither saying anything for a while.

'It's actually good that you've come,' she said eventually, giving him a sidelong glance.

'You've changed your tune,' he remarked, pulling his gaze up.

'It means we can discuss your proposition.'

It wasn't what he'd expected, but it worked for him. 'Sounds good to me.'

'Don't get too excited,' she said. 'It's a no.'

'A no?' He nodded thoughtfully, doing his best not to acknowledge the weird sensation pulling at his gut. 'Might I ask why?'

She looked at him, for longer this time, and then

she was off once more, picking up her pace. 'It's not easy to explain.'

'Okay,' he said, walking after her. 'Can you at least try?'

Again her eyes flicked back to his, but this time he could see wariness—fear, even—and she made no effort to elaborate.

'I'm going to get a complex if you keep this up.'

'*You* with a complex?' She rolled her eyes at him but her humour didn't reach her voice. 'If you say so.'

'Okay, it's true that I know from the way you climax when you're with me that it's not because you hate the sex.'

She let go of a breath, her eyes flickering, that knowing hint of colour hitting her cheeks. He'd done it on purpose—throwing her back into another time, another place.

'No, it's not that.'

Her husky intonation rippled through to his groin.

'Then you really *are* confusing me, because all I'm asking for is more of the same.'

She nodded. 'You're honest—I'll say that.'

'That's something you can always be certain of. Now, if you'll only do the same and put me out of my misery...'

'I don't have time for this between us.'

'What—sex? We've made a fair amount of time for it to date. Granted, not enough, but we can work on that.'

'No, not for sex.'

'Then I'm officially lost.'

She halted to look at him properly now, an unidentifiable emotion flaring in her eyes. 'It's everything else,' she said. 'We're meant to be *business* partners, doing what's best for the *business*. Not ourselves. But you dominate my every thought, whether we're together or not, and I can't give work the best of me when I'm so wrapped up in you. I can't sit in a business meeting, my entire focus on the job, when you are sitting right there with me, tempting my brain away.'

'Hey, it's been the same for me,' he said. 'It's precisely what I was saying in the car. Denying this between us only makes us distracted. I see us humouring this attraction as a way of keeping a lid on it, getting our heads back in the game...'

She studied him, and the pulse working in her throat, her clenched hold around her cup spoke volumes. 'This isn't some game.'

'Okay, sorry—I don't mean it flippantly,' he backpedalled. 'I just mean that it'll help us to concentrate, to focus again.'

'And then what?'

'What do you mean?'

'When you've had your fill? What happens then?'

He shrugged, confusion reigning. 'We'll deal with that when we get to it.'

She shook her head at him, a strange smile quirking her lips. 'If only life was as simple as you make it out to be.'

'It *can* be that simple.'

'Not for me,' she said, pressing on once more without giving him a backward glance. 'It's too risky—*you're* too risky—and I have enough to worry about with my sister leaving for university soon and my mother's health declining.'

'I'm sorry to hear that.'

She ignored the way his concern warmed her, the way it urged her to look at him. She knew it would break her resolve and she spun on her heel, eyes averted. 'Look, let's get back to the office—we've lost enough of the day as it is.'

'But we haven't finished our talk.'

'Yes, we have,' she said, starting to retrace their steps without waiting for him. 'I don't have time for a relationship.'

He fell into step beside her. 'And I'm not asking for a relationship.'

'No, sorry—I forgot.' She shot him a look. 'You're just asking for some *mutual fun*.'

The way she said it messed with his head, and something inside him turned desperate. *Was she looking for more? Was that where he'd gone wrong?*

But what did it matter if she was? It sure as hell wasn't what *he* wanted, was it?

She was still charging ahead, and the sudden need to have her undivided attention had him tossing his coffee into a nearby bin and cutting off her stride. He pulled her into a deserted side-street and spun her to face him.

'Tell me this isn't fun for you,' he said. 'Tell me you don't *want* me and I'll drop this.'

'Marcus.' The way she said it—breathless, almost fearful—made his body ache.

She looked up at him, her green eyes wide, and he stepped forward, forcing her back.

'Tell me this isn't explosive.'

She shook her head, pressing her free hand feebly against him. *'Marcus.'*

'Tell me it doesn't make your heart beat uncontrollably, your blood ring in your ears and your sanity leave you.'

He continued walking her backwards as he raised his hand to cup her chin. 'Tell me it doesn't take it all away—the stress, the pain, the worry.'

He could feel her wavering, feel her trembling beneath his touch. 'Please let me be your escape.'

It was what *he* wanted—so much it scared him—and he dropped his head, pulling at her lower lip with his teeth, taking it back to the sexual, back to the comfortable.

'Let me drive you wild…let me make you wet.'

She gasped, her back hitting the shielded recess of a fire escape. 'Marcus, we're *outside*. There are *people*.'

'No one can see us here,' he whispered against her parted lips, getting off on knowing the busy bustle of the street was within earshot and feeling her imminent surrender. 'And I can't wait any longer. I need to know—are you wet for me?'

She shook her head, clamping her eyes shut.

'Liar.'

'Please,' she whispered, her eyes lifting to his, and he paused.

She wanted him—he could see it burning in her gaze, in the hand that grasped his chest, pulling him closer. *Damn it, she probably didn't even know she was doing it.*

'Tell me, you don't want me right now and I will stop.'

His cock pressed painfully against his fly, against

her, but he *would* back away—it would kill him, but he'd do it.

'I... I—'

She broke off, shaking her head as though she couldn't believe her own mind, her tongue brushing nervously across her lower lip. 'I can't.'

'Can't?' he pressed, hope surging.

'I want you.'

It was hushed, it was uncertain, but it was there. A groan ripped through his restraint, and his lips crushed hers with every possessive ounce of his being.

Coffee and lip gloss invaded his tastebuds, its effect like a drug. Her mouth relented to the force of his, her blissful whimper singing through him as heat coursed through his blood.

He heard the sound of her cup hitting the ground, felt heat against his leg as the liquid seeped into his trousers but he didn't care.

'Marcus...' she moaned, raking a hand through his hair as her other hand clawed at him through his jacket.

'This kind of fun is worth fighting for,' he rasped.

Their mouths collided, their kiss spiralling out of control, their tongues exploring one another with invasive delight; twisting, probing, desperate for more. His cock was practically bursting on that alone, and then she buried her head in his neck.

'I'm losing it.'

'Not yet, you're not.'

His hands dropped to her waist and he yanked the tie of her trench coat undone. He reached for her thighs, coaxing her skirt up, desperate to seek her out.

He slipped a hand between her legs, felt the wet fabric of her knickers greeting him. '*Fuck*, Jennifer.'

She clung to his shoulders, her body arching to grant him access, and he slid inside. She was so warm, so inviting, and he buried his fingers in her, pulling back to slide them over her clit. She bucked against him, her teeth biting into his skin as she suppressed a cry, their public location clearly not lost on her.

He circled over her, gently at first, loving the way she undulated against his touch, and then faster, harder, in time with her breathing. Her tension mounted—he could feel it in every rigid line of her body as he pressed against her. And as she rocked against him forcefully, her climax claiming her, he covered her mouth with his own, drowning out her cry, swallowing it as her entire body shattered against him.

It was swift, it was brief, it was soul-crushing. And the shift in the atmosphere from mind-obliterating lust to heavy regret was sudden and disorientating.

Quietly she buried her head in his shoulder, normalising her breathing, and he extracted his hand, careful not to leave a trace on the fabric of her suit.

He planted his hands either side of her as she straightened, her eyes downcast, her fingers trembling as she smoothed her clothing back into place and re-tied her coat.

He wanted to say something—anything. He just didn't know what.

'We shouldn't have done that,' she said quietly.

Her words from the car played back to him. 'Not this again.'

She sent him a look and his frustration died, guilt

crushing him. 'I'm sorry. I just needed you to remember what it's like—what it could still be like.'

She held his eyes, her expression one of such misery it pulled him apart. 'Please, Marcus, if you care for me in any way, promise me this will stop.'

He took hold of her upper arms, his thumbs stroking her coat, his caress aimed to soothe and reassure. 'I'm not asking for a relationship.'

'Don't you *get* it?' she blurted, her eyes glistening. 'I can't keep having sex with you without *wanting* one.'

The tightness twisted him up inside. *She wants more.*

'I can see you understand,' she said, her eyes skimming his face, turning hard. 'So promise me?'

He released her, raking an unsteady hand through his hair as he struggled to take it in.

'Promise?' she pressed.

'Okay, okay—I promise.' He was barely aware of the words coming out of his mouth, so lost was he in her revelation.

'Good.'

She stepped out of his hold, and through the haze he could see her composure falling into place.

'I think some space will do us good,' she said, looking over to where the alley met the main street. 'With Mum's health on the decline, I'm going to be needed at home more.'

He frowned at her. 'In Yorkshire?'

'Yes.' She nodded calmly, without looking back. 'I need to take the pressure off my sister and make sure she gets her education.'

Slowly he nodded, but the twisted feeling in his

gut was getting worse. He'd called it fun, just sex, so why did her refusal disturb him so much? Was it because she wanted more? Or because she was intending to be away more?

Christ, he had no clue.

'How often do you need to go back?' he asked tonelessly.

'I don't know.'

She shrugged, and her poise was starting to grate against the loss of his own.

'Fifty-fifty split, I think.'

He nodded, the impact of her words sinking in. 'Of course you must go if they need you.'

He suddenly felt like an utter shit. Here he was, pursuing her, when she clearly had bigger things to worry about.

He should be grateful he was avoiding that future complication too.

So why did it feel as if his worst nightmare was coming true?

He thrust a shaky hand through his hair. The rollercoaster inside his head was scaring him.

'Let's go.' He forced himself to move forward, to head for the high street, and she stepped into line beside him. 'We can discuss a strategy to make the split work on the return journey.'

'Thank you.'

He sent her a sidelong glance, looking for the emotion he'd witnessed not five minutes before. But there was nothing.

He had to admire her for that.

And it was time he did the same. He'd do what he should've done ages ago and sort out a date elsewhere, hope the distraction would help him live up to his promise and leave her the hell alone.

It was time to stop behaving like a love-sick puppy.

Love?

Where the fuck had that *come from?*

CHAPTER FOURTEEN

A FULL TWO weeks had passed since the alley incident—since Marcus had promised he would leave her alone, and she'd confessed her desire for more and scared him off entirely.

And the greater the distance he put between them, the greater was her need to have him back, to accept what little he was able to give—because the current situation was unbearable.

The change in him drove her crazy. He communicated via email, even when a simple conversation would have been quicker and easier. When she forced him to talk he rarely looked her way. In the few meetings they attended together his attention was on everyone else.

It wasn't that he was rude. Not at all. He was businesslike, platonic—everything she'd asked for.

And she hated it.

Then there was her goal to split her time fifty-fifty. It was feasible, but her worry over letting go had had her upping her efforts to the point of exhaustion, convinced that putting in the extra time would ensure her handle on the company didn't slip. Not for anything. Or anyone.

As for her feelings—they would go with time. They had to.

Planting her elbows on the desk, she massaged her temples and pushed through the mind fog, the emotional turmoil. She had work to get done. It was long past home-time and she was poring over financial projections that she should have finished reviewing hours ago. She squinted at the figures. The computer screen and her desk lamp offered the only light since the main office was dark and deserted.

Half an hour later she was reviewing her feedback when her office was lit up, by light leaking in from the main office outside.

Heart in her mouth, she glanced up.

Who'd be here at this hour?

Marcus.

Her pulse took charge and did its thing, and her body tripped out at the mere sight of him. As much as she tried to force it down, it just kept on coming. The feeling of being ignored for the best part of a fortnight only served to intensify it all.

Would he ignore her now, when he realised that she was still here? That she was the only one here?

To her surprise, he didn't head to his office—he strode straight for hers.

Definitely not ignoring her, then...

Slowly she got to her feet, readying herself for his proximity, searching for what to say and the numerous reasons he might be here.

She walked to her door, reaching it at the same time as he did.

His eyes raked over her, something close to anger sparking in their depths. *What was wrong now?*

Cautious, she swung it open. 'Hey.'

'Hey, yourself,' he said, his mouth returning to form a grim line.

'What are you doing here?'

'I was about to ask you the same thing.'

She brushed her hand over her hair. 'I've yet to leave.'

'Yeah, I got that much.' He looked to the empty office and then to her desk, covered in various papers and several coffee cups. 'You know, it's not good to work this late.'

'What can I say? I'm a workaholic.'

'Tell me something I don't know.' He sounded beat, and his eyes returned to her with a frown. 'It's been every night for the last two weeks, though. It's not sustainable.'

'I have things to get done.'

'Those *"things"* can wait until tomorrow.'

'Not these.'

'*Christ*, Jennifer.' He thrust his hand through his hair. 'What is this about? You can't always work like this.'

He was concerned for her wellbeing. It was obvious now. And it warmed her through, its effect as powerful as the desire she so missed. She liked it that he cared, regardless of whether it was wise or not.

She gave a small smile. 'I'm more used to it than you know.'

'But you've done your father proud already. You don't need to keep on pushing—'

'This is not about my father,' she interjected without thinking. A strange softening sensation curled its way in—he'd listened to her, really *listened*.

'Then what is it?'

He leant against the doorframe, his frown deepening, his presence dominating her vision and the scent of freshly applied aftershave filling the air. Suddenly she felt inadequate. Her hair was falling out of its bun, and her dress was crumpled from her sitting down for the best part of a day. God knew what she smelt like. And now he was asking why she was like this. *Why?*

She bit into her bottom lip. *Because of you!* she wanted to scream. *Because you can't offer me more.*

'Tell me,' he said, pushing off the doorframe and closing the gap between them. 'I'm worried it's because you think you're somehow giving up by leaving—'

'I'm *not* leaving,' she cut in. 'I'll be just as present from my desk up north.'

'Okay.' His eyes widened, his palms raised outwards. 'I meant splitting your time between Yorkshire and here.'

She crossed her arms around her middle, not liking the unease creeping in. 'It's doable.'

'I agree—it is.' He nodded. 'But I worry you're having trouble believing it.'

'I believe it just fine,' she said, shaking her head and feeling her hair falling across her face. She saw him move to touch it and backed away.

'Sorry.' He bowed his head, raising his hand to rub at the bridge of his nose instead, his stress permeating the air.

Should she say something? Anything? Like, It's okay?

But it wasn't.

He took a long, drawn-out breath, lowering his hand as he lifted his gaze to her. 'Then is it me?'

She froze, her cheeks chilling, his accurate conclusion startling her. 'I've always worked hard.'

'I know.' His eyes pierced her, their depths earnest, deep with concern. 'But I feel like this is different, like I'm somehow to blame.'

'Marcus, don't flatter yourself,' she blustered, raising her chin. 'I'm working because I want to.'

He looked as if he would argue further, and she spoke over him.

'And the sooner you leave, the sooner I can finish and get off home.'

'Have you at least eaten?'

She blushed. She knew she didn't look after herself, and him pointing out the obvious made her feel doubly foolish. 'I'll get something shortly. What about you? You look like you're off out.'

His eyes wavered. 'I'm meeting up with an old friend.'

'Old friend' sounded like code for old flame.

She itched to ask, and hated herself for it, turning away instead. 'Well, don't let me keep you.'

He reached out for her arm, the warmth of his fingers permeating the thin fabric of her dress and she caught her breath, her eyes flicking questioningly to his.

'Promise me, you'll leave soon.'

She'd had the ridiculous notion he was going to pull her into him, kiss her, anything but his concerned plea. Disappointment clogged up her throat, clipping at her words, 'I'll leave when I'm ready.'

She pulled away and headed to the desk. The lack

of movement behind her telling of his hesitation and
she lifted a document, any document, throwing her
focus into it.

'Fair enough,' he said eventually, his voice disturbingly raw. 'I guess I'll see you in the morning.'

'Uh-huh,' she murmured, her eyes fixed on the
page of swimming grey, her ears attuned to his every
sound.

She listened to him walk away, not daring to turn,
not wanting to watch him go, scared that the tears she
didn't want to shed would start to fall.

What the hell was he doing?

Opposite him, his ex Zara was discussing food with
the waiter, her pregnancy making her extra-cautious
with her choices, and he was using the time to berate
his idiotic move.

He should never have gone into the office—never
asked that Colin drive by the building on the way to
the restaurant. He just hadn't been able to leave well
alone.

And yet he'd done everything she'd asked of him,
fought every urge to see her to ensure he stood by
his promise. His conscience should be clear. Even if
it hurt…even if it felt wrong.

But tonight he'd had the urge to check that she'd
gone home. She was losing weight, the worry lines
and dark shadows on her face ever-present, and it was
pulling him apart inside. When he'd seen her light on
he'd been determined to get her to leave.

Only the main office had been deserted, just the
two of them in the entire space, and his restraint had
hung dangerously in the balance. And instead of doing

what he'd intended he'd annoyed the hell out of her. *Idiot.*

'Sir, what can I get you?'

The waiter looked at him and he stared unseeingly at the menu, ordering his usual dish and passing the menu back. The idea of eating when Jennifer so clearly wouldn't plagued him. He should send Colin with something. At least then he would know she'd eaten.

Zara smiled at him, her cheeks glowing. Pregnancy clearly suited her. 'So, to what do I owe this unexpected pleasure?'

Hell, he didn't know. He could hardly say he'd needed to get out but he didn't do lads' drinks and he couldn't do dates. Not any more.

'I had some time on my hands.'

She laughed, her blonde hair bobbing, blue eyes twinkling. 'You with time on your hands? Impossible.'

He smiled. She was right there.

'You look well.'

'Is that you changing the subject?'

'Maybe.'

Her smile grew, one hand dropping to stroke over her bump. 'I am well,' she said. 'I never thought I was the maternal type. It's funny what love can do to you.'

Love. There was that word again.

'I'm glad. You were always too good for me.'

Her eyes narrowed. 'I don't think that was ever the case.'

'No?'

He didn't believe her—not in the slightest. But he wasn't the same man he'd been then. He could feel it. His concern for Jennifer told him as much.

Bloody Jennifer—she needed to eat.

'Hold that thought.'

He took up his mobile and issued Colin with a text.

Check she's still at work. If she is, take her food. She won't say no to you.

She'd kill him. But he didn't care.

He placed his mobile back down and looked at Zara with fresh eyes. She was beautiful, she was clever, and they'd got along well. So how come she'd never got under his skin in the same way?

'Why didn't we work out?'

Her eyes widened, and he couldn't blame her. He'd never indulged in the personal—not when it came to conversation—not until Jennifer.

'What? You mean besides the fact you always told me you didn't want anything serious?'

'Besides that.'

She took a sip of water, her eyes assessing him. 'You want the truth?'

He nodded. 'The whole ugly lot.'

'I never felt like you were fully *with* me,' she said softly, her gaze reminiscent. 'Your mind was always on the next big project, your next acquisition, your next whatever. You couldn't live in the moment and I couldn't compete with it.'

He let her words sink in, comparing them to how he felt when he was with Jennifer, how he wanted to draw out each and every moment, how she filled his mind whether he was with her or not...

'It's far easier to cope with you being distracted when we're just friends.'

His phone buzzed with a reply from Colin. He was on it.

'Take now, for example.' She gestured to his phone. 'Another big project, by any chance?'

He met her eyes, the answer sticking in his throat, and her brow furrowed with his hesitation. 'It's not, is it?'

He shook his head.

'Well, I'll be...' she said, a grin breaking across her face with dawning realisation. 'Someone's managed to crack the great Marcus Wright.'

Crack?

It wasn't a bad way to put it. He certainly felt as if someone had ripped him apart and put him back together all wrong. 'It seems that way.'

'Now, *this* I have to hear.' Zara settled back into her seat, making herself nice and comfortable.

'Why do I get the feeling you're going to take some weird twisted delight in this?'

'Not at all, Marcus,' she said softly. 'It's high time you realised everyone deserves a piece of happiness—including you.'

As the outer office lit up again Jennifer's heart leapt. When she saw Colin striding towards her, takeaway bag in hand, her tummy did a weird dance of disappointment and pleasure.

Marcus had sent her food. He cared enough to make sure she ate.

She beckoned Colin in and he opened the door.

'From Mr Wright,' he said, walking in and depositing the bag on the desk before her.

'You shouldn't have gone to so much trouble,'

she said, but she opened the bag with glee, glancing inside. The smell of Chinese food wafted up to her and her tummy rumbled in excited protest. 'It smells lovely.'

'There's a mixture—hopefully something you like.' He shifted awkwardly on his feet. 'I would have asked you first, but...'

'But you knew I'd refuse?'

'Something like that.'

She gave him a reassuring smile. 'Well, it's just what I need. Thank you.'

She expected him to turn and leave but he still stood there, doing that weird uncomfortable dance. 'Is there something else?'

'Aye, I'm to wait and give you a chance to eat,' he said, moving to clasp his hands in front of him as he stilled. 'Then I'm to take you home.'

She coloured. *Really? A bloody chaperone?*

But there was no use arguing. Not with Colin, at any rate.

And, hell, the truth was Marcus was right. She did need to eat, and she did need to go home.

It would just be easier to accept if she knew her unoccupied mind wouldn't be filled with *him*.

It was late when he bade Zara goodnight. The evening had been good for him. In a way it had been good for her too. It had been like some weird closure for her to see him so wrapped up in someone.

And he truly was wrapped up—in deep, over his head. Whatever way he looked at it he was falling for her. *Hell, he already had.*

But what did he do with that? It was one thing to

realise he was capable of love, to accept it was too late to shield himself. It was another to know what to do with it.

Right from the outset he'd never stood a chance. The moment she'd come into his life his world had changed. And so had he. She'd opened his eyes to how his life could be if he let go of his past.

But he was still scared. Scared of what would happen if he let those feelings take hold, risked it all to tell her and ask her to take a chance on him.

The question plagued him. *What if he lost her?*

The very idea winded him. Yes, he'd parked his past, but it had still moulded him, left ingrained in him the life lesson of love ripped away.

How did he unlearn that?

CHAPTER FIFTEEN

No, no, no, no, no!

Jennifer stared at her mobile news feed, her coffee and toast forgotten, her freshly showered hair dripping over the reports she'd brought home after her impromptu Chinese takeaway the previous night. She ignored them now, the news taking all her attention.

Despite their best efforts, their US competitor had beaten them to their product launch.

Marcus was going to be pissed off. Hell, she *was pissed off. Had she made the right call? Fuck, would he blame her?*

Leaving her breakfast untouched, she raced upstairs, pulled on a pair of trousers and a polo neck, plaited her hair and applied some gloss to her lips.

That would have to do.

Grabbing her mobile, she hit the stairs and issued a hurried text to Marcus.

Work emergency. Need to talk asap.

It was six a.m. *He had to be up, right?*
If he didn't reply by the time she got to the office

then she'd ring him until he did. The situation was still salvageable. She knew it. She just needed him to know it too.

When she arrived the foyer was deserted, save for the security guard. She greeted him and took the lift to her floor. She knew someone was in because she'd seen the lights of the main office from outside.

It had to be him. Who else would be in at this time?

The usual rush had her pulse skipping and she breathed through it.

It wouldn't always be this hard—it couldn't be...

Exiting the lift, she looked towards his office. The lights were on behind his blinds.

Definitely him, then.

Her tummy somersaulted and she ignored it, shrugging off her coat and heading straight to her office. She dumped her belongings and immediately left for his.

The noise of him moving around reached her. Her tummy was taking on the feats of an Olympic gymnast but she fought it.

She rapped on his door and, swinging it open, strode straight in. 'Marc—'

The remainder of his name died on a gasp and her legs halted mid-stride, an instant fire making further somersaults in her stomach impossible. He was standing in the open doorway to his bathroom, his virtually naked rear glistening with an indecent strip of towel slung low about his waist...

He started to turn towards her and she twirled on her heel, cheeks burning. '*So* sorry.'

'Hey, easy,' he said, his husky intonation teasing

every rigid stretch of her body. 'I think you've seen enough of me before not to get bashful all of a sudden.'

'Sorry, I should've knocked properly—should've waited. I shouldn't... I just didn't expect... Well, I didn't think you'd be so...*naked*,' she babbled, standing at the doorway to his office, needing to move through it yet finding herself rooted.

'I wasn't expecting anyone to be in yet.'

She bit into her bottom lip. She could hear him moving behind her, and the urge to look was driving her crazy. *Just one glance...*

'Granted, having seen the news this morning, I should've expected you to be.'

'Uh-huh.' It was all that could come out, and was high-pitched as it was. She should leave him to get dressed. Their conversation could wait that long, at least. She moved away from the door. 'I'll just—'

'Did you see what the press are saying about it?' He talked over her, and his tone and topic drew her in.

'Not yet.'

'Take a look at this.'

Her eyes wavered between the doorway and him, without truly focusing on either. She needed to get past this. *She* was the one who had said no more sex, but, Christ, she'd hardly expected to find him half naked...*again*.

Forcing herself, she turned and headed to where he was bent over his desk, one hand hovering over his trackpad, one finger pointing at the screen.

She fixed her gaze on where his finger rested, doing her damnedest to ignore the steamy male scent and the inviting warmth radiating off him.

She planted her hands on the cold glass desktop and read. And then she read some more. But the words weren't going in. She couldn't set her focus, her head going dizzy with his appeal.

He straightened on a sigh, and she caught sight of his chest flexing as he did so, which sent desire climbing up her throat.

He was less than an arm's reach away. *Why couldn't she just give in?*

And then came the painful retort—*He can't love you back*—and she almost choked with it.

Love? Was that where she was at?

'What do you think?' he asked.

'Think…?' *Get with it, Jennifer.*

She swallowed and he coughed. She glanced at him and caught a brief sweep of his tensed muscles, his heated gaze, and knew he wanted her.

But he doesn't want more.

It served to up her resolve. 'I have some ideas.'

'Ideas?'

'Yes.' Pulling her plait over her shoulder, she righted herself and turned to face him fully. 'Why don't you get dressed and join me in my office?'

He brushed a hand over his hair, sweeping the damp curls away from his face and she almost snapped, almost reached up to repeat his exact move.

She fisted her hands at her sides. 'Unless you want to do this half-naked?'

He gave her a lop-sided grin. 'I will if you will!'

'Marcus.' She whirled away and threw her hands in the air, her sexual frustration and teetering resolve sending her storming for the door. 'My office—when you've bothered to put some clothes on.'

* * *

He would have laughed if he hadn't been working so damn hard to appear normal.

Seeing her, knowing now how he felt, had intensified every sensation. When he'd heard her say his name his heart had ballooned, cutting off his ability to breathe. And then he'd seen her, his eyes devouring every last inch of her, and his towel had been lucky to stay steady.

It was fortunate that he hadn't just kissed the look of shock right off her face. The hint of lip gloss glistening on her otherwise innocently bare features had pleaded with him to do as much. Her woven hair, still wet, told of a recent shower, and the thought of her in it, naked and slick, had teased him senseless.

And if someone had told him he'd find a polo neck and trousers sexy he would've laughed them out of the room.

In the bathroom he hit the cold tap, turning it on full, and doused his face, trying to send a message to the searing burn making camp in his gut.

The thing was, if it was *just* that—desire—then he would be able to cope. He knew he would. It was the fact it was so much more than desire now. Seeing her and knowing that left him all kinds of vulnerable, and it was chewing him up inside.

He'd barely slept the night before, battling with it all, the risk weighing heavy on him. But he couldn't carry on like this. He knew that now. He just had to work out how to broach the subject and not send her running for the hills with his turnaround.

He raked the towel over himself and got dressed, prepping his mind for the topic at hand—the competitor's product launch. They would deal with that and then he would make sense of the rest.

He found her at her desk, scribbling furiously on her notepad. The professional Jennifer he had come to know so well was in full swing. She was every bit the businesswoman he had come to respect above all others, her brain working like no one else's he knew, piecing things together even quicker than him—and that, frankly, was saying something.

'I see you really *do* have some ideas.'

She glanced up, her eyes bright with excitement.

'I do—check this out.'

She beckoned him over, moving so she could stand directly behind her and could read what she was working on.

'I think our product is better,' she said. 'I've taken a look at what they're offering and ours outstrips it by far.'

'Okay…' he said, his hands sinking forcibly into his pockets.

'I told you it was a good idea to merge product specifications!'

She was ribbing him, but all he felt was pride blooming. He had the crazy urge to pull her into his arms and tell her as much.

'So, I reckon the best solution,' she continued, 'is to have a red carpet affair for our launch and do it now.'

'Now?'

'Well, not literally—but certainly within the next week or two, hot on the back of this. I think I can pull a few strings, get some big names in the business to attend, bring in the press, and it'll bury this morning's news.'

He chuckled. 'Remind me never to get on your bad side.'

She smiled up at him, her expression unreadable. 'Our product *is* better,' she stressed. 'It deserves to be treated as such.'

'No arguments here.'

Her eyes went back to the page and she traced her index finger down the list she'd created. 'These are my first thoughts on guests, location, theme, catering and—'

The trill of his phone interrupted, but it was a while before he even registered it because he was so lost in her and what she was saying.

'Do you want to get that?'

Her question brought with it his senses. Of course he should get it. Someone ringing at this hour had to be important. He slid his phone out of his pocket and checked the ID. *Gran.*

He stared at it, a thread of unease coiling steadily up his spine.

'Who is it?'

He could hear the concern in her voice. *She was so astute.*

'It's my grandmother.' *Or would it be Pops again?*

He knew he needed to answer but his fingers were frozen around the phone. If he didn't answer, whatever news was coming wouldn't be real…

Christ, don't be ridiculous!

Next to him, Jennifer stood and placed a hand on his arm. 'Would you like me to step out?'

The comfort of her touch radiated through the ice and his fingers came alive. 'No.'

She nodded and he answered the call, lifting the phone to his ear. 'Gran?'

'Marcus.'

'Pops?' It came out gruff, unrecognisable even to his own ears.

'She's been rushed in—'

His grandfather broke off and Marcus felt as if someone had a noose around his neck, was pulling it tight, his very life being squeezed out of him.

He needed to speak, but the words weren't coming. He shut his eyes, then opened them to seek out Jennifer, and she was there, her own eyes shining with an emotion that he knew mirrored his own.

He burned to reach for her but didn't dare. And then she was doing it—slipping her arms around him, tucking her head beneath his chin, and his breath was freed up, leaving him in a rush.

Thank you, he wanted to say. But his free arm closed around her instead, taking the strength she offered, the comfort, the love… *If only*.

His grandfather coughed. 'Sorry, son.'

'It's okay, Pops, tell me what's happened?'

He heard him take a shaky breath and then he was rambling—something about another stroke, her being in critical care, the doctor's current assessment…

It was all coming at him in a blur, but he knew he needed to get moving—he needed to be there *now*.

'Okay, Pops, listen.' The words came out controlled, and for that he was grateful. He wanted to reassure him, no matter what was going on inside himself. His grandfather needed his strength. 'I can be with you in a few hours. I'll check flights or I'll drive. Either way I'll be with you by lunchtime.'

His grandfather let go of another shaky breath, 'Thank you, son.'

'I'll see you soon.'

Marcus cut the call and sucked in some much-needed air, feeling Jennifer tighten her arms around him as he let it out.

'How bad is it?' she asked softly.

'She's in critical care,' he said, his skin prickling as his gut rolled. 'Another stroke.'

'I'm so sorry, Marcus.'

She lifted her head off his chest to look up at him, and there was so much compassion in her gaze that he could almost—*almost*—believe she loved him too. That there was already so much more between them.

He searched her face, wanting to ask, wanting to confess.

'Go now,' she said. 'I'll get the launch finalised, and if you can't make it, it doesn't matter.'

He nodded, knowing she spoke sense but feeling rooted to the spot, rooted to *her*.

'And if you can make it, all you need to do is turn up and do what you do best—schmooze.'

'Schmooze?' He gave her a wry smile. 'Is that all I'm good for?'

'Maybe...' she teased gently.

God, he wanted to keep hold of her, take her with him. The weirdest feeling took hold—that nothing could hurt too deeply if she was near.

'Go on, Marcus, be there for your family.' She stepped back and paused, her eyes flickering, and then she swept her arms around him once more, raising herself up to say against his ear, 'Know that I am here for you if you need me.'

She turned into him, her lips pressing softly into his cheek, and the world stopped, warmth flooding him as his love for her swelled.

And then she was gone, dropping back as a shutter fell over her expression, wrapping her arms around her middle. 'Let me know when you get there safely?'

'I will.'

He had to fight not to pull her back, to make her kiss much more than a peck, but the moment was so special, so right, he didn't want to break it.

Slipping his phone into his pocket, he headed for the door, pausing on the threshold to give her one last look. 'Thank you.'

And then he left, with the chill resurfacing, increasing with every step he took away from her.

Jennifer watched him go, her insides trembling as she fought the desire to follow.

He'd needed her—she'd seen it in him. She didn't know what it meant but it had called to her. It still did. It had been emotional rather than physical, and had he said *Come with me* she knew beyond a doubt that she would have gone.

But he hadn't, and she hadn't expected him to—not really. So she would help in the one way she knew how: she would keep on top of work and make sure he wasn't disturbed. She would field his calls, organise the best product launch he'd ever seen, and work every waking moment.

She knew she wasn't being entirely selfless, that it would help her too—because being awake and busy meant not thinking about the mess her heart had become. And, no matter what she'd seen in him today, it didn't negate what he had said to her previously.

She'd come so close to blurting *I love you*—had felt it on the tip of her tongue as she'd drowned in his agonised gaze. The only thing to stop it had been the memory of his obvious horror when she'd hinted at wanting more in the alley.

But for the briefest moment she'd believed he felt it too, that something had changed between them.

Was it too much to hope for?

The fear-filled flutter in her belly kick-started and she pushed her mind to work.

Concentrate on something you're good at—something you can control...something that doesn't ache as if it's never going to stop...

CHAPTER SIXTEEN

WHEN HE CLIMBED into bed that night, absolutely wiped out, he expected sleep to come quickly. He should've known better. As soon as his head hit the pillow his thoughts turned to Jennifer.

He smiled as he remembered his grandmother's face when he'd told her about Jennifer. His intention had been to distract her from the tubes and the machines beeping around them; what he'd got had been a lecture.

'Don't let this woman slip through your fingers,' she'd told him. 'If you don't try you'll wonder forever, and life's far too short for that.'

Having those words uttered in a hospital, in a building so full of loss, his own deep-rooted argument had collided with hers. Yes, you could have a long and happy life together, just as his grandparents had proved, or by some mean twist of fate it could be taken away from you far too early, like his parents.

But the idea of not trying for the former, of letting Jennifer go, was agony in itself.

He rolled over and picked up his mobile from the bedside table. Propping himself up on his elbow, he scanned his messages. He'd had several from her throughout the day. They'd all contained work updates, but he'd sensed her intention had really been to check on him. The fact that she cared was obvious and it gave him hope.

Another message came through.

How's your gran?

Doing well, all things considered.

Thank goodness. And you?

Missing you. He wanted to type it so badly, but not yet. It wasn't right.

I'm okay. You should get some sleep.

Yes, boss.

His smile grew.

Night.

Night. x

The 'x' heated him through, and without thinking he sent a simple 'x' back.

He stared at it, at the harmless letter glowing and pulsing at him from her message to him.

Hope swelled.

He stayed just over a week—until the day of the launch…until he was certain his grandmother was going to be okay.

He stopped by the hospital on his way home. The beeping machines were thankfully long gone, and his grandmother's new private room was cosy, with splashes of yellow, and the flowers he'd brought her lit up the window ledge.

'You're stubborn, my boy—remember that.' She positively beamed up at him. 'Don't you be taking no for an answer.'

He chuckled and bent to press a kiss to her brow. 'I'll try not to. But she can be rather stubborn too.'

'Good—I like a girl with a bit of backbone.'

'Oh, I have no doubt you'll like her.'

'Well, make sure you bring her home soon, so we can see for ourselves.' Sadness swept across her features. 'I often worried that you would never settle... that somehow your past had seen to that.'

'Hey, easy, Gran.' He placed a hand over hers. 'It just took me a while, that's all.'

She nodded, her eyes glittering with a smile, and his throat tightened.

'We understood why you didn't come home much. We knew how hard it was for you to keep coming back here.'

'Don't make excuses for me.' He squeezed her palm. 'I should've come back more. I was being selfish— foolish, even.'

'It's not foolish to want to avoid those memories.' She took a shaky breath. 'Nonetheless, the past is the past, darling. You can't change it, but you shouldn't let it taint your future either.'

'I know,' he said softly. 'I get that now.'

'Aren't you done lecturing the boy yet, Angie?'

His grandfather's booming Welsh lilt invaded the room as he joined them, a fresh bouquet in his arms.

'I don't *lecture*,' his grandmother bristled.

'Whatever you say, dear.' He smiled and bowed down to plant a kiss upon her forehead, adding with a wink, 'The important thing is, did it work?'

She returned his smile, happiness filling her cheeks with colour. 'How could you ever doubt me?'

His grandfather chuckled and looked to Marcus, his gaze warm and hopeful. 'You finally ready to stop running and start living?'

Marcus grinned, loving their interchange, and loving the whole promise life suddenly held. 'You'd better believe it, Pops.'

'Diolch i'r Arglwydd.'

His grandfather pounded him jovially on the back, back to his best now that Gran was on the mend.

'So what are you waiting for? Be off with you and bring us back a granddaughter-in-law.'

'I'll do my damnedest.'

'Language!' came his grandmother's warning.

He exchanged a look with his grandfather and they both erupted with laughter.

'He has you to thank for that, Angie.'

She gave an exaggerated huff. 'I have no idea what you're talking about.'

'Whatever, Gran,' he teased. 'I'll see you both soon—*very soon*.'

And he would. He could say it and mean it now.

Over a week had gone by in a crazy, manic blur. During the week Jennifer had thrown herself into work, and at the weekend she'd thrown herself into her family. But in between she'd thought of *him*.

They'd exchanged messages regarding work and she'd asked after his grandmother. And as time had gone on she'd started to doubt what she thought she'd seen in his face, what she thought she'd felt change between them, and her hope had slowly died. Even the 'x' had become a distant memory.

It was now launch night and here she was, supposed to be getting ready, but her tummy was in knots. She knew that he would be here soon, that she would see him again, but she didn't know how to react, how to feel.

She frowned into her bathroom mirror, her unmade-up face staring back at her. She was going to have to do something. The shadows beneath her eyes spoke of sleep deprivation, and her pale and hollow cheeks were the result of her non-existent appetite.

'It's not going to make itself look good, you know,' came Anna's softly spoken remark through the open doorway, and her smile was one of concern. 'You want me to help?'

Jennifer ignored her question and tightened the belt on her dressing gown. 'How long do we have?'

Anna glanced at the mobile in her hand. 'Taxi's due in an hour.'

'Have you heard from Marcus?'

'Not recently, but he—' She broke off as her mobile started to ring. 'Ah—one sec… Hello?' she said wandering off, phone to her ear.

Jennifer looked back to the mirror and took up her foundation as if on autopilot. She made a start, trying not to think and wondering all the same how things could have changed so much. It was launch night, and it was a huge deal, but she no longer cared enough. Somewhere between falling in love and fearing her love could never be returned, work had lost its shine.

She gritted her teeth against the pang that had become oh, so familiar and forced her hand to do its work, finishing off her make-up with meticulous care. She pulled her hair over her shoulder, threading it into a loose braid that would work well with the black dress she had chosen to wear.

Shrugging off her dressing gown, she hooked it on the back of the bathroom door and took the dress off the hanger alongside it. Dropping it to the floor, she stepped inside the pool of fabric and shimmied it up over her hips, pulling the sleeves up her arms before reaching behind her for the zip.

'Need a hand?'

Her fingers froze over the clasp, her heart hammering in her chest, her eyes hitting the doorway as she turned to face—

'Marcus?'

He leant against the doorframe, dressed in his dinner suit, his bow tie hanging limp in a sexy, *I-don't-give-a-fuck* kind of way as his rich, dark gaze raked over her and her stomach drew tight, her legs weakening beneath her.

'Jennifer?' he said thickly, and the emotive ring to his voice teased the walls around her heart.

The pulse working in his jaw told her he wasn't as relaxed as his poise suggested.

She searched his face, his eyes, their rich chocolate depths almost wild, and asked, 'Is everything okay?'

He nodded slowly. 'Or at least I hope it soon will be.'

She swallowed. *What did that mean?*

'The launch is going to be perfect,' she said, remembering her fingers were still poised over her zip and attempting to fasten it.

'Let me.'

He closed the distance between them and she started, her already insane pulse tripping out. She had to reach for the sink to stop herself tumbling as she turned around.

'Steady,' he said, concern deepening his voice and the heat of his body radiating down her bare back.

He curved his hands around her hips, the heat of his palms forcing a small sound from the base of her throat— *Please don't notice that.*

'Jennifer...' It was a warning, and instead of taking up the zip he turned her into him, pressing her body against the hardness of his own. 'You need to start taking better care of yourself.'

His forceful command disturbed the hair atop her head. 'Yes, Mum!'

'Look at me.'

She couldn't raise her eyes from the pulse beating in his neck. She felt his comforting, heady scent wrapping around her. He hooked his fingers beneath her chin and gently coaxed her to obey. She felt her lashes fluttering until she had no choice but to meet his eyes.

'What?' she said, defiance bursting from her. 'I've been *busy.*'

'I know, and I'm sorry for leaving you in the lurch like that.'

She softened instantly, regretting her crabby retort. 'Please don't apologise. *I'm* sorry. I've just...'

What? Missed you? Fallen in love with you? Lost my mind? All of the above...?

'What am I going to do with you?'

He gave a small shake of his head, his voice husky, and his thumb started to brush over her chin. His eyes lowered to her lips and instinctively she drew her bottom lip between her teeth, the provocation both impulsive and purposeful. *Please kiss me*, it said.

Her lids lowered, her breathing hitched, her head was dizzy with hope... But there was no kiss.

Reality speared her and she opened her eyes to delve into his. 'What's wrong?'

'Christ, this is hard.' He squeezed his eyes shut, and when he opened them again they looked ravaged, lost, unsure.

She slipped her hands over his shoulders, partly to reassure him and partly to hold herself steady against the mounting trepidation. 'What is it?'

He shuddered on a breath. 'I'm here to ask you for *more.*'

She frowned, their past conversations coming back to haunt her.

Did he mean...? Or was it still sex? More sex?

'I know I don't deserve it, and I know what I've said, how I've behaved...' He shook his head again, his tortured gaze beating down into hers. 'But I was confused. I had no idea what I wanted—not truly.'

She was struggling, her sleep-deprived brain trying to make sense of what he was saying.

Was he this desperate to keep her in his bed?

A spark of anger flared. 'Are you asking for a *fuck buddy*?'

He flinched. 'Hell, no! I'm doing such a shit job of this. I'm sorry.'

She let go of a relieved breath and he moved to cup her face, his thumbs caressing her jawline, his impassioned sincerity holding her captive.

'I'm asking you to take a chance on me—to be with me.'

Her ears started to ring, hope flaring.

'I've lived my life ruled by my past—running from it, living in fear of my father, fear of becoming him, fear of falling in love and losing it.'

Tears pricked at her eyes. *Did he mean...? Was he saying...?*

'Meeting you made me question it all. You opened my eyes to how foolish I've been.' He brushed an escaped tear from her cheek. 'I don't want to waste another second without you.'

'What are you saying?'

'That I love you, Jennifer. Christ, I should have just led with that.'

He gave her a half-smile that made her tummy dance.

'I loved you long before I even realised it myself.'

He dropped his head, his forehead coming to rest against her own, his eyes intense.

'I know I've made a complete cock-up of our beginning, but if you'll just take a chance, let me show you how things can be, I'll do everything—'

'Marcus,' she interrupted him, feeling as if her heart was going to explode if she didn't put an end to his misery this second.

He stopped, raising his head, his expression open and vulnerable.

'Shut up.'

She reached up on tiptoes and softened her words with a kiss—one so filled with her love for him that when she broke away they both had to fight for air.

'Does this mean…?' His voice trailed off, his hands still as they cupped her face, his eyes searching her own, daring to hope.

'I love you, too,' she said, tears falling freely now. 'And, for my sins, I've known it for a while.'

'You *have*?' he said in disbelief. 'But everything I said about relationships, about it just being sex…'

'Yes, in spite of all that you couldn't hide the good man you are, Marcus. It follows you around with annoying presence.' She poked him playfully in the chest. 'Believe me, I *tried* not to love you—*especially* after all you said—but you captured my heart and the damn thing wouldn't let you go.'

He grinned, that delicious dimple appearing in his cheek, and she pressed a kiss to it.

'Thank fuck your heart is as stubborn as you,' he said.

She dropped back and raised her brow in mock hurt. 'Stubborn?'

'Yes.' He reached around, resting his hands against her lower back, holding her to him. 'Just like an ass.'

'An *ass*?'

'Only better-looking.'

She laughed, her happiness spilling over as she prodded him in the chest some more. 'Tread carefully, Marcus. You have a lot of making up to do.'

'Making up?' His grin turned mischievous, his eyes flashing with wicked intent. 'I like the sound of that.'

'I bet you do.'

'And I know just where to start,' he drawled, taking hold of the zip fastening at her back and toying with it. 'Shame we have a product launch to get to first…'

'Well, you have Colin driving us, right?'

'Yes…' He looked at her, bewildered, and she simply smiled, turning in his hold.

'Then zip me up and let's go celebrate in style.'

She didn't need to look at him to know he'd got her meaning this time…

* * * * *

LET'S TALK
Romance

For exclusive extracts, competitions
and special offers, find us online:

 facebook.com/millsandboon

 @MillsandBoon

 @MillsandBoonUK

Get in touch on 01413 063232

For all the latest titles coming soon, visit
millsandboon.co.uk/nextmonth

Want even more
ROMANCE?

Join our bookclub today!

'Mills & Boon books, the perfect way to escape for an hour or so.'

Miss W. Dyer

'Excellent service, promptly delivered and very good subscription choices.'

Miss A. Pearson

'You get fantastic special offers and the chance to get books before they hit the shops'

Mrs V. Hall

**Visit millsandbook.co.uk/Bookclub
and save on brand new books.**

MILLS & BOON

COMING SOON!

We really hope you enjoyed reading this book. If you're looking for more romance, be sure to head to the shops when new books are available on

Thursday 21st March

To see which titles are coming soon, please visit

millsandboon.co.uk/nextmonth

out turn?' he answered with